GLISSER
THE IRONSIDE SERIES
BOOK FIVE

JANE WASHINGTON

CONTENTS

Also by Jane Washington

Seraph Black

Book 1: Charcoal Tears

Book 2: Watercolour Smile

Book 3: Lead Heart

Book 4: A Portrait of Pain

Beatrice Harrow

Book 1: Hereditary

Book 2: The Soulstoy Inheritance

Oh, the horror of this gold, ornate and cold,
Framing stars plucked and clipped and sold.
The painting cracks and fades, bleeding glitter,
While little men ask, "Why isn't it any fitter?"

TRIGGER WARNINGS

sexual harrassment
references and instances of child sex trafficking
sexual assault
gore and death

Please take these warnings seriously and look after your
own mental health.
If you or anyone you know needs support, please visit
lifeline.org.au.

IRONSIDE ACADEMY MAP

To view the map of Ironside, please scan the QR code below.

IRONSIDE ACADEMY PLAYLIST

To listen to the playlist for the Ironside series, please scan the QR code below.

IRONSIDE ACADEMY CHEAT SHEET

To view the character cheat sheet for the Ironside series, please scan the QR code below.

I
TOO SOON

"Isobel."

Her name was a gentle croon of sound in a voice she was intimately familiar with. It was a voice as soft and silky as the glide of fingertips against her thigh, as light and teasing as the touch that skirted where the seam of her panties hugged the curve of her ass. Her leg had crept out of the sheets to hook around a soft, plump pillow while she slept, but there was now a body on the other side of the pillow. Whoever it was, they must have only just joined her, otherwise her leg would have been hooked around him instead. Her sleep-heavy mind stalled, forgetting everything except the heat of a big male hand pushing up her shirt and cupping her hip, fingers digging into her spine, thumb pressing into her stomach. She arched into the touch, waiting for him to yank away the pillow and hook her leg over his hip.

Sweet, tangy bergamot coated her throat, spraying her tongue with the slightest burn of citrus. She loved it when their scents were strong enough for her to taste. She arched forward, pushing her suddenly aching, cotton-covered breasts to a hard chest. A low, distinctly male chuckle fell against her cheek, and the grip on her hip flexed.

Kilian.

"Time for a ..." He trailed off, his nose brushing across her cheek, her jaw, before burrowing into her warm neck. "Hmm," he groaned, his voice muffled, "a group meeting." He pushed her suddenly to her back, his beautiful face appearing above hers in the dark as her eyes flew open.

His eyes were a stunning, soft meld of pale green and yellow. Sometimes, they reminded her of a snake—not a real one, but the sly, cartoon snakes with narrowed, glowing pale eyes. Those beautiful eyes were currently heavy-lidded, pupils dilated, brows lowered in concentration. His tongue ran along his lush lower lip, making the light pink flesh shimmer, and his chest began to rumble.

"Huh?" she slurred sleepily, her nails running lightly over the soft T-shirt covering his chest.

That was what she wanted to wear today.

"Meeting," he murmured, his perfect, symmetrical features barely illuminated by the light sneaking into her room through the open bedroom door, a glazed, distracted look falling over his face.

Wait ... open door?

His pale eyes crawled slowly down over her flushed neck to her rumpled shirt—well, Theodore's rumpled shirt that she had stolen—to the stretch of toned stomach he had bared by pushing up the faded blue cotton, and then to her matching blue panties.

"Can we dye these green?" he asked, pinching the elastic waist of her panties and snapping them back against her skin.

She grinned at him. "I'm always green for you."

It was true. They hadn't had time for any moments like these in a few weeks, and she missed him. She missed the way he took her gently but firmly, thrusting into her with ownership while kissing her with such tender care.

He groaned, his thoughts likely travelling in a similar direction, his forehead falling to hers. His erection dug insistently into the soft skin of her thigh as he lowered his weight over her, forcing her legs to part as he pressed her deliciously down into the mattress. Taking his full weight made it hard to breathe, and she *loved* it.

"I swear I came in here for a reason," he whispered, his soft lips lowering to hers, his sweet breath fanning her mouth.

For a brief, beautiful moment, it was easy to believe this

was her life. This beautiful room, with the giant, carved bed and the fluttering silken canopy, moonlight slanting over the shadowed edges of a velvet chaise and gleaming softly from the marble floors. This warm body, so sweet-smelling, so heavy and hard and comforting, so safe and familiar.

This could be her life.

This bliss, this sweetness.

"Group meeting," Elijah snapped loudly, passing by the doorway, a tight edge of annoyance to his voice.

Kilian's growled sound of frustration was so fierce, it had her body flushing with heat. He dropped a quick kiss to her lips, making her skin tingle, before he rolled off the bed and held out his hand to help her up.

It took her a few moments to regain her composure and clear away the hazy remnants of sleep before she allowed him to pull her out of bed and back to reality.

Her life was *not* bliss and sweetness. It was forced smiles and aching muscles, with stolen moments snatched from closets and bathrooms. There was a type of sweetness and softness in those secret, hidden moments, but they could also be as painful as they were pleasant and, as soon as they were over, she felt the sting of wondering when she would be able to snatch another.

They congregated in the lounge room, where most of the other Alphas were already waiting. Elijah, Gabriel, and Niko wore dark workout clothes; it had been their turn to guard the dorm. They always took turns in groups of three so that one person could watch the

Ironside feeds Elijah had hacked into while the other two were stationed in blind spots along the outside of Dorm A. During the day, Mikel and Kalen kept an eye on the cameras. Nobody would be getting near the dorm without one of them witnessing it.

The two weeks since receiving Teak's message had been chaos. The bond specialist had warned them that the officials planned to kill them, urging them to announce their bonded status, and it had derailed everything. It felt like they were all stretched too thin, hanging off the edge of a cliff with their stiff fingers slipping one by one. Ironside trying to control them was one thing. Ironside trying to *kill* them was a whole other matter. It was a wrinkle in their plan they hadn't prepared for.

They spent every night paranoid and hyper-vigilant. They survived on very little sleep while acting carefree and unbothered by the cameras during the day. The situation was growing rapidly unsustainable, but they had to be sure that the tip Teak had sent them was real.

Mikel and Kalen had debated the best course of action for a week, pulling in favours with their contacts to determine if there was a credible threat. It was a painfully slow process, especially since they were adamant they shouldn't expose Teak with their probing. After confirming the threat as best they could, they spent another few sleepless nights exploring every available course of action before finally devising a plan.

The lingering vestiges of Isobel's lust cooled as the reality of their situation settled back into her restless mind like a fog slowly creeping through her thoughts, but it didn't cool completely. She was surrounded by partially undressed and rumpled Alphas with adorable pillow marks on their stern faces, their hair so silky and dishevelled it made her fingers itch to reach up and touch the strands. She was sure she had never seen Kalen so disordered.

Gabriel looked like he slept standing upright, with a comb in his hand just in case a strand of hair fell out of place. He looked like wrinkles apologised to him, like night terrors were careful to respect his boundaries. She was convinced that if she checked behind his door right now, she would find a photo studio instead of a bedroom, outfitted with a camera crew and bedroom props that were never actually used. She desperately wanted to peek in there, just to see if he had made his bed even though he would be returning to it in an hour. Maybe he had done a little light dusting as well.

Cian was only wearing black sweatpants, though he had decided to pair them with teal slippers and a matching teal headband to keep the tousle of his golden hair from his face. The outfit was at complete odds with his inked chest, arms, hands, and neck—not to mention the nipple piercing, the brow piercing, or the lip piercing. Or the cock piercing—not that she could currently see it, but her imagination was never *not* seeing it. That was

Cian. A beautiful contradiction of dangerous hard edges and lazy, flirty softness.

Theodore was in boxers, stretching his neck from side to side, a hazy look in his stormy eyes. He was struggling to wake up. His frown was etched deep, making his square jaw flex as he swallowed. Mikel was also in boxers, and she felt like she had to avert her attention from him completely, her cheeks pinking when their eyes caught for a moment.

Kilian, Kalen, and Moses all wore actual pyjama pants, though Kalen's looked suspiciously like he pressed them after he washed them, and Kilian's looked just perfect enough for her to want to steal, even though they would slide right off her.

"Absolutely not," Kilian said, a smile in his voice, his gaze on her face, reading whatever expression was there. "The day you start wearing pants to bed is the day I stop letting you borrow my clothes."

She bit her lip to hold back her laugh because he was *obviously* joking.

"She can wear whatever she wants," Niko snapped, his face twisted with annoyance.

The rest of her soul pieces still hadn't been located despite Oscar going back to the Stone Dahlia every night in search of them. Niko's aggression problem had grown steadily worse. The sickness that had taken up residence in his mind fed off chaos and discord wherever he could find it. He had begun sleepwalking, the restless belligerence inside him persisting even while he slept. Both Moses and Theodore had gotten into violent fights with him as he tried to escape the dorm while they were on guard duty.

"Oscar isn't back yet?" Isobel asked, peering around the room.

"He got back a few minutes ago," Mikel answered. "He needed to stop by his room."

"He was bleeding all over the foyer," Niko added carelessly.

Isobel stiffened and tried to flee the room, but Elijah gripped her shoulder, gently turning her back to the group. "He'll be out in a minute. It wasn't that bad." He gestured to one of the plush armchairs. "You're going to want to sit down for this."

"For what?" she asked, frowning at their closed-off expressions. She couldn't feel them—either through the bond or with her Sigma ability.

She had learned to become immediately suspicious when they all unanimously shielded themselves from her.

She glanced at the watch she wore even when she was sleeping so that any security alerts would wake her up. It was their scheduled meeting time. Their video was about to go live, and they were supposed to be watching it together. There was nothing else on the agenda, but the guys were acting like something else had happened.

She dropped into the chair just as Oscar strode into

the room. He had a bandage strapped low on his torso and a fresh slew of cuts—both old and new—scattered about his bare chest, arms, and face. She was too busy tracing every inch of his skin with her eyes in an attempt to make sure he wasn't seriously injured to notice what he was holding. When she did, she froze.

His fist was clenched around a handful of braided necklaces.

"You found them," she croaked, suddenly faint.

She understood why the others were shielding now. So much time had passed. Reassimilating the pieces of her stolen bond had worked the first two times, but even though they hadn't discussed it, they were all unsure if it would work the third time.

Maybe it was too late.

"Actually, it was Gabriel," Oscar answered, stopping a few paces from her, his knuckles turning white as his grip around the necklaces tightened. "He made a trade with a well-connected client and found out which room they kept them in. I purposely lost my fight because it was right by their emergency medical room."

She frowned, upset that Oscar had intentionally hurt himself, but then his words registered.

"What kind of trade?" she asked, her attention snapping straight to Gabriel.

"Private dance. No big deal." He didn't even *try* to look nonchalant. He was as blank as a brick wall.

"That's a very big fucking deal," she shot back,

jumping out of the armchair, bile spilling across the back of her tongue. "I can't believe you did that without talking to me." She felt nauseous and horrified, the note Gabriel had left on the back of his door at the previous dorm swimming back to her with dizzying clarity. He hadn't invited her into his room in this dorm, and since he was so particular about his space and his things, she had stayed out ... but now she wondered if the notes had been put back up on the door.

I am not for sale.

Because of her, he had sold himself.

"It's not just your bond, Isobel," he responded calmly.

"It's n-not just yours either." She stumbled over the words, her eyes growing blurry.

His face collapsed just a little. "Please don't cry." He took two steps toward her before Niko suddenly jumped in front of him, shoving him back hard enough to almost send him tumbling over a marble side table. Elijah managed to catch him, and they both straightened, eyeing Niko.

"Don't touch her," Niko snarled. "Don't even look at her. You made her cry."

Isobel quickly scrubbed her cheeks with the sleeves of Theodore's stolen T-shirt, desperately bidding her tears to dry.

Nobody tried to talk any reason into Niko.

They knew better than to try at this point.

Gabriel gave her a look that said *we'll talk about this later*, and the tears welled up again, spilling free from the net of her lashes. Luckily, Niko had his back to her—*guarding her*—so he didn't see the fresh outpouring of emotion.

She nodded at Gabriel because fighting around Niko was just a bad idea—his particular brand of madness grew infinitely worse in environments of conflict.

"Niko," she said gently.

He tensed but refused to turn and look at her.

"The pieces of our bond," she prompted him, hovering her hand over the middle of his tense, broad back, not quite daring to touch him. "Can I try to fix them?"

He glanced at her over his shoulder and then followed her gaze to Oscar, frowning at the braids of her hair in his grip. Either he had already forgotten, or he simply never noticed in the first place because it was shock that finally replaced the rage twisting his features.

He seemed frozen.

Oscar strode past him, motioning to the chair Isobel had sprung out of. She fell back down. Oscar considered the back of his hand for a few moments, his brows low and pinched together, before he lifted the necklaces, offering them to Niko. He stared at his own hand as though it had somehow betrayed him, and a grimace chased across his pinched features.

Niko snatched up the braids—though he did it with

11

slightly less ferocity than they had all come to expect from him. He was fidgety and distracted, his features tight as he dropped to his knees before Isobel and stretched her arms out across her thighs, exposing her forearms.

He glanced down into her eyes, the fingers of his right hand trembling slightly as he lifted it to his face, combing back some of the hair that had fallen over his eyes. He had always preferred to bleach his hair lighter colours—at least as long as she had known him, but the cream, pastel, platinum, and silver tones apparently didn't appeal to him anymore. He had dyed his hair dark, closer to the natural colour of his roots, and the strands were now a deep, burnt chestnut, longer on top with soft, tousled layers and tapered shorter along the sides. Sometimes—like now—he gathered the longer sections of his hair into a small knot, leaving stray, naturally wavy locks to frame his face, accentuating his strong jawline and sharp features. He used to have a look that screamed bold, self-assured charm, but he was more withdrawn now. There was an edge that hadn't been there before. He still had a certain magnetism, but instead of making people flock to his charming personality, they whispered about him from a distance.

She could feel his fear, though he tried to hide it. It shivered over her skin and raised goosebumps along her arms. It wasn't something she sensed through any ability —it was just there in his eyes, in how he held himself.

"It'll work," she told him quietly.

He just knelt there, frozen, the faint tremor still in his hands.

"You don't know that." His attention narrowed, fixing her with a cold stare—even though he leaned into her legs, his free hand wrapping around her thigh, seeking the comfort and warmth of her body.

He *wanted* to believe her.

She wanted to believe it too.

But ... time had passed.

Possibly too much time.

She wanted to offer him some kind of platitude— that if it didn't work, nothing between them would change, but the sentiment would be closer to an insult. Everything had already changed. His mind, his personality, his self-control, his emotions—all of it had been severely altered. His smile. His laugh. His carefree, good-natured approach to everything.

Niko was already changed.

"The video is about to go live," Mikel prompted them quietly, patient but firm. This was a scary, vulnerable moment for them, but there wasn't any time in their schedule to indulge in scary, vulnerable moments.

Niko sucked in a deep breath and unravelled the first thin braid of hair, settling it over the skin of her forearm.

They all waited, not so much as a breath disturbing the suddenly still, thick air, but nothing happened.

Nothing at all.

The hair didn't glow and smoulder and burn through the remainder of her scars. It didn't even twitch. It just *sat* there.

Fuck.

"Blood." Elijah spoke so suddenly that she jumped. "The soul artefacts are activated by blood, maybe—"

Niko picked up her other arm, tugging her wrist to his mouth.

Theodore and Kilian jumped forward, low sounds of alarm and warning bursting out of them.

Cian swore, tunnelling his hands through his hair, his eyes wide, his body tense like he was about to jump into action and tear Niko away from her.

Oscar laughed, but the sound wasn't quite *right*. It was utterly devoid of humour. Oscar hadn't been quite *right* for a little while. "What the fuck do you think you're doing, Niko?"

Niko ignored them all, his eyes on Isobel's face, measuring something in her expression. She realised the others didn't even exist for him right now. It was just her and him, this limp, broken thing between them and the faintest threat of how far he was willing to go to revive it.

"You're insane," she told him quietly.

He smiled against her skin—thin and hard, and pressed his lips to her pulse. It wasn't quite a kiss. More of a taste, a test. She tried to recall if it was the most intimacy they had shared since *that* night. The night they had crashed together in a whirl of fear and rage, finding part of their bond again and losing her virginity in the process.

"Niko—" Kalen jerked forward, a sharp command in his voice, but it was too late.

Niko had waited for her to stop him, and she hadn't. He sank his teeth into her wrist, biting down hard enough to break the skin as she yelped, and then he lifted his head, his beautiful hazel eyes blazing as he wrapped the braids of hair around her wrist, covering the wound and holding them there, his forehead falling on top of them like he was praying.

She didn't even realise that she had stopped breathing until she felt the hair begin to burn her skin, and then the air rushed out of her in a shaky, disbelieving rush.

She hadn't really believed.

She hadn't, but he had.

Niko lifted his head and quickly flattened her arms out on her thighs again, wincing as he pulled the burning, glowing strands of hair across her forearms. They were singeing his fingertips, but he still laboured to cover the remainder of the scars Eve had created on her arms.

Kalen pulled a stone out of his pocket, examining it as he stepped closer. She recognised the soul artefact that monitored the health of their bond. A sharp, multi-faceted gem small enough to nestle in the palm of the hand. It was washed with soft gold, but the longer her arms burned, the lighter the gold became, glowing brighter until it almost dispersed a glow across Kalen's fingers ... and then it faded again, back to a soft, almost rosy gold.

"No more scars," Niko murmured, drawing her eyes back to her lap. The glowing strands had fully reassimilated, leaving her skin reddened and smooth, slowly sinking back to a pale, pearlescent colour.

She *thought* she had felt something—a kind of disorganised confusion, a little moment of chaos, but then there was nothing.

She felt no different whatsoever.

There was no magical sensation of a bond clicking back into place, no wash of warmth and wonder travelling through the bond from Niko. He was still closed off, still locked firmly away from her. The other Alphas drew closer, waiting for Niko or her to say something.

"Three minutes until the video starts." Mikel's mismatched eyes flicked between Niko and Isobel. She hadn't realised before—likely distracted by their dishevelled clothing and bared chests—but he wasn't wearing his contact. She could see the multihued iris with the little flecks of gold and silver spattered like stars across a dark sky streaked with an aurora of all their colours.

For a moment, it stole her breath, but then she forced her attention back to the Alpha on his knees before her, his hands on her thighs, his head lowered, hair falling forward to hide his eyes.

"It's gone," he finally said, looking up at her through his hair. "The void."

"But?" There was more. There was a sinking sensation in the pit of her stomach at the barely guarded devastation in his expression.

"But the damage it did ... was permanent."

Elijah let out a sharp breath. "Okay. Fuck. Dammit. Okay. We'll deal with that later. We'll figure something out, all right?"

He set a hand on Niko's shoulder, and everyone in the room tensed, waiting for Niko to snarl and shove him off or start a fight. Instead, he nodded and stood, glancing down at Isobel's wrist, ensuring his bite had healed along with the rest of the skin on her arms.

The scars from what Eve had done were gone. Like it never happened.

"We'll figure it out," Gabriel promised.

"Yeah, if we survive another month," Niko muttered, moving to the couch and flopping down to face the TV, which Mikel had turned on. The professor was tapping at his phone, ready to cast to the bigger screen.

They all fell around the couches, Cian tugging her onto his lap in the corner of the largest couch, Moses beside him, and Niko at the other end. Theodore perched on the arm of the couch beside her, bending down to catch her eyes.

All right? He spoke the word in her mind through their bond.

She nodded slightly.

Now that Niko was allowing people to touch him, Elijah seemed reluctant to leave him alone, standing behind him and leaning over the couch to anchor his hands to Niko's broad shoulders.

The screen filled with the image they had deliberated over for several days, with a countdown to the video. The comment section was full of people waiting and speculating on what the video would be about, the comments moving too fast to read properly.

The image was of Isobel, Theodore, and Elijah. Isobel sat on a stool between the two towering Alphas, her arms and legs crossed, the seat raising her to their height —not naturally, but thanks to the blocks placed beneath the legs of the stool, not that they were visible in the photo. Her body language was powerful and bold, belying her small stature—something that had taken several dozen takes and concepts to achieve.

Apparently, "powerful and bold" wasn't an instinctual look for her.

She wore her outfit from their first official group performance: combat boots, high-waisted, dark camouflage parachute pants, a tight white tank, and a black chest harness. Her hair was in long, thick braids over her shoulders, and her chin was raised, a vague challenge in her eyes despite the slightest curve to her mouth.

Cian had directed the photoshoot. He planned the concept, dressed them, arranged them, and drew out their expressions as he drifted around with a camera and a focused frown. She couldn't deny the effect of the image. The subtle subtext.

The hint of power.

The whisper of challenge.

The glaring *fuck you* and the coy, *but only if you want to*.

Without Cian's direction, it would have just looked like … a Sigma sitting on a stool. He had a unique talent for drawing out the best in people.

Elijah and Theodore were also in their costumes from the performance—tight black jeans, black combat boots, dark shirts, and puffy camouflage jackets. They looked so stern and imposing. Theodore had a dark eyebrow cocked, eyes a cloudy, stormy grey. Elijah wore a cold, dead stare, his arms folded across his broad chest. Theodore had an arm wrapped around the back of her stool.

The lead singer, the lead dancer, and the lead rapper. She caught that word—*leader*—popping up in most of the comments.

ELEVEN flickered in giant neon letters behind them —an effect Gabriel had created while editing the image, though it looked like a real sign. Thanks to Cian's photography and Gabriel's editing, they made a striking trio, the glow from the fake sign cast over their complexions and etched into their provocative but formidable expressions.

As the seconds ticked by in the silent common room and they stared at the screen, waiting, Theodore grabbed her hand, tugging it up to his lap, his large fingers pushing between hers. "Here goes nothing," he said as the countdown reached zero.

Ironside had cornered them and said, *Checkmate*, and this was their calculated countermove. This plan *needed* to work.

She sucked in a deep breath, hugging her other arm around her stomach, feeling Cian's torso tighten against her back as he leaned forward, his breath stirring against the top of her head.

"This better work," Moses muttered, so low she almost didn't catch it.

And then the video started.

Eleven bodies gathered before a camera in a practice room. Isobel, Theodore, and Moses were at the front— the guys cross-legged, her sitting on her folded legs. Elijah, Gabriel, Niko, and Cian sat in chairs behind them. Kilian, Oscar, Mikel, and Kalen stood behind the chairs.

"You all watched us come together," Isobel spoke first. "You watched as this group adopted me, protected me, and kept me alive at Ironside without a mate."

"You watched as our friendships formed," Moses

continued. "As we grew closer and supported each other through every challenge we faced."

Theodore spoke next. "You watched as Mikel Easton and Kalen West tested and assessed us. As we fought for positions in this group."

"You've been here with us every step of the way," Elijah added. "Supporting us the same way we supported each other."

"That's what Ironside means to us." Gabriel's firm lips gentled into an uncharacteristic half-smile, softening his stern expression and sending the comments flickering by even faster. "It means teamwork. Community. Connection. Support. Family."

"We wanted to thank you." Niko's voice emanating from the speakers was a deep roll of comfort, the madness in his eyes expertly masked. "For helping us see what's most important."

Isobel barely covered a wince as she watched the video, remembering that Niko had failed the first four takes, accidentally sworn during the fifth, and had forced everyone to take a twenty-minute break while he stared at the wall and spoke furiously to himself beneath his breath.

But in the end, he had nailed it.

"For teaching us the value of valuing each other." Cian quickly drew the attention from Niko, not wanting to push their luck. "For championing us until we championed each other."

"We don't make this decision lightly." Kilian's angelic features twisted into a gentle plea. "But we feel it's the only way forward for us, and we hope you'll support us."

Oscar's hands curled around the back of Elijah's chair in the video as he leaned forward. "We're prepared for the consequences. But this is what we want to do."

On the screen, the eleven of them fell into silence as the comment section scrolled and scrolled. People began to scream in capital letters, question marks littered all over the place, the words still moving too fast for Isobel to read them, though she tried a little harder to focus during the brief silence.

Despite it being the middle of the night in Paris, in other parts of the world, it was daytime or evening time, so there were plenty of people online.

She saw Kalen and Mikel's names pop up in most of the comments. That made sense—the viewers saw them more as professors and tutors than actual members of the group. There seemed to be a lot of people saying that they were about to quit Ironside.

The Mikel on the screen pulled in a short, measured breath before he spoke. "From this moment on, we are a unit. The nine performers you see here, plus me and Kalen West. We will be managing and producing the group. That makes eleven—*we* make Eleven. We aren't asking Ironside to change the rules. Nobody has ever tried to win as a group before, so there is no legislation against it."

He didn't mention out loud that students' management contracts could only be broken if they didn't win—another oversight, as students typically don't ask for other Gifted to represent them. Thanks to Elijah, that little piece of information now conveniently popped up after a quick Google search on Ironside policy. These fans were about to run to Google and discover that if their group won, Ironside couldn't break them apart even though Mikel and Kalen weren't students.

It would be too obvious now if the officials tried to change the rules after their announcement.

"We believe this is for the best," Kalen spoke up. "Because nobody knows the Gifted better than other Gifted. And nobody knows these brilliant performers better than we do."

"That's why we have decided to win together or fail together." Elijah folded muscled arms and levelled the camera with his signature blank, icy expression, his pale grey-blue eyes serious. "And if that means we're—" He paused deliberately like he was choosing his words, hard lips pinching. "—*disqualified*, then so be it."

It was borderline anti-loyalist speech.

From the looks on their faces, none of them cared. But Isobel had been sitting on her hands for a reason.

"Please support us," Kilian said softly. "Support us,

and we will dedicate our lives to you. This is up to you now."

The video ended, and Moses dug his hands through his hair, letting out a wobbly breath. "Someone in the comments section definitely fainted."

"The support is there," Elijah noted, scrolling through his phone. "Kalen is a meme."

Gabriel scoffed, also staring at his phone. "The only repercussions I want are from Professor West," he read aloud. "Dorm Daddy has my vote. For this, for president, whatever."

Kilian also had his phone out and was frowning at the screen as he read a comment, "'For a hot minute there, I really thought they were going to announce that Carter's mate was one of the Alphas, and I was this close to denouncing her and ripping out her hair. I should have known our precious, perfect princess would never betray us like that.'"

Isobel schooled her expression. "Too soon. I am precious and perfect, though."

Kilian shook his head at her attempt at humour, flicking through the comments with a small frown. "There are more along that vein."

"That's exactly why we chose this plan," Elijah reassured him, tone calm, expression a little drawn. His exhaustion was seeping through. It seemed that more than any of the others, he had serious trouble sleeping when he was stressed. "If we announced that we were mates, we would lose their support—but this way, we call attention to the fact that we're going against the academy without dividing the fandom. The officials can't kill us now. It would be far too obvious. They can't even cut us from the show. Right now, we *are* Ironside— the viewers don't even care about the graduating year. We just need to keep it this way."

"Doesn't mean the officials won't find some other method of retaliation." Kalen's deep voice was sombre. "And they will. We're not escaping this situation unscathed. We'll be punished no matter what we do."

Isobel glanced between Oscar and Niko—the two more volatile members of their group. Everyone was attempting to shield their emotions from her, but it must have been harder to close themselves off from her Sigma power because she could feel the muted distress and fear trickling through from so many different directions that she couldn't possibly differentiate and assign the feelings to any of the Alphas.

They must all be reaching the limits of their exhaustion to be suddenly letting their walls slip.

She had barely tensed to rise from Cian's lap before he stood, anticipating the subtle shift in her body and lifting her to her feet.

"We'll stay up," Kalen said, tipping his chin toward Mikel, who nodded in agreement. "The rest of you, get some sleep. We've got an early start tomorrow to deal with the chaos this video will cause."

Isobel took the time to carefully sip away at their worry and fatigue as they all dispersed into the hallway and headed toward the large marble staircase in the foyer. The stolen emotion sat heavily in the pit of her stomach, weighing down her eyelids as she pushed into her room and fell onto her bed, sleep claiming her far quicker than it usually did.

ANNALISE TEAK WASN'T A LIGHT SLEEPER, BUT IN THE PAST FEW weeks, she had developed a strange habit of jolting herself awake whenever she drifted too deep. Her brain and her body were in agreement: there was no time to relax, no space to let her guard down.

And her brain and body were right.

"Is that ...?" Charlie stirred, sounding groggy, her head lifting from the pillow. Poe pounced from the edge of the bed, his hair on end, his tail stiff and alert. He gave a single *meow* of warning before the crash sounded in the living room of their apartment.

"Stay here," Charlie ordered, rolling out of bed and grabbing her phone before looking around helplessly.

They were at Ironside, for fuck's sake. In a highly secure, off-limits residential building. They hadn't prepared for a *break-in*. A mass shooting, maybe, but not a break-in, and not in the officials' residence. Annalise ignored her wife's order, rolling to the other side of the bed and springing to her feet beside Poe, her entire body trembling.

She couldn't feel anything in the other room, no matter how hard she searched with her Sigma ability. No fear whatsoever. "Maybe it's just a ..." she started, but the bedroom door flew open before she could finish the sentence.

Five armed men filled their bedroom, and her blood turned to ice.

"Charlie Teak," the first man stepped forward. "We need you to come with us."

2

IRONSIDE SPEAKS

THE FOLLOWING DAY, THEY GATHERED IN THEIR USUAL GYM room at six in the morning. It was a Saturday, and they were all wary and sluggish after a turbulent night of interrupted sleep, but that was their normal now. They fell into their routines without thinking or waiting for direction from Mikel or Kalen, the latter of whom attended most of their training sessions now.

Isobel joined Oscar, Moses, and Cian for half an hour of warming up on the treadmill, but her exhaustion quickly threatened to catch up with her, so she moved to the mats and started up a yoga routine on the tablet Mikel had prepared for when they needed a break from the high-intensity training. Kilian soon joined her, and she spent the next hour trying not to get distracted by his shirt always slipping up to reveal stacked rows of streamlined, porcelain muscle or the flexing of his firm thighs when he shifted positions.

Before they finished up, Mikel cycled through each of them, checking over their tired and strained muscles, briefly working out the kinks in their necks and shoulders, or stretching out muscles that were prone to cramping. She only had ten minutes with him, but she already knew they would be the best ten minutes of her day. They were often so tired during these sessions that the others didn't bother to shield her from the bond, so she was aware that Mikel's hands on them felt purely medicinal—*magical*, sure, but medicinal.

That was why she always slammed her barrier down when he motioned her over to the bench, patting the leather for her to sit. They felt a little less medicinal to her. When she sat this time, she immediately grappled with her walls only to find them non-responsive. She chalked it up to how little sleep she had gotten and did her best not to moan until Mikel finished, but she still drew a few surprised looks, and even Mikel's fingers paused when a sharp bolt of pleasure tingled through her body as he worked the tension from one of her muscles. She was too tired to care, and they were nice enough to pretend they didn't notice.

Sweaty and bleary-eyed, they dragged themselves back to the dorm to shower. Isobel almost fell asleep with her head anchored against the tiles and the spray doing a terrible imitation of Mikel's capable, strong fingers kneading into her shoulders. Her phone timer had her head jerking up in confusion as she sluggishly fought her way back to alertness. Most of their minutes were timed these days. There was too much to do and too little time to accomplish everything.

She dressed in tights and a sleeveless black crop top with a flowy, cutoff shirt thrown over the top. She was too tired to consult her schedule for the day without at least one cup of coffee, but there wasn't a single day in her schedule that didn't involve something active.

They were mostly silent on the way to the dining hall, with Elijah, Gabriel, and Niko leading the group, Oscar and Moses a few steps behind, Theodore and Kilian behind them, and Cian keeping step with Isobel at a slower pace than everyone else.

She had noticed that even though the entire Alpha group was close, everyone seemed to have at least one person they were even closer with than the others. Elijah, Gabriel, and Niko made sense since they had grown up together before Elijah and Gabriel were separated and sent to a different settlement. Theodore and Kilian seemed to gravitate toward each other naturally. Possibly attracted by their shared positive attitude, energetic nature, and unfailing optimism. Or maybe it was just because they were everyone's favourites.

Must be nice at the top.

Even though Theodore and Moses were brothers, they seemed to be attracted to the opposite type of person, with Oscar and Moses usually pairing up. They were more introverted than the others, needing more time alone in their rooms or the library. They seemed perfectly content to be in each other's company without uttering a single word or trying to force a conversation.

Of course, being the oldest, Kalen and Mikel spent more time with each other than anyone else, especially since they organised the entire group, discussing their plans while they worked out in the gym several hours before the rest of Dorm A had even woken up.

It seemed like Cian was the only one who didn't have a best friend within the group, despite being one of the most affectionate people she had ever met. He was always sensitive to everyone else's feelings and was usually one of the first to notice something wrong and jump into action to cheer someone up.

Isobel might have felt bad for him, but since the start of their third year, she and Cian had naturally fallen in beside each other, almost like the dynamics of their group had been incomplete without her. It was nice to have someone to walk beside and confide in while all the others were paired up in their close friendships.

They were too tired and grumpy to talk about anything that morning, but she felt a little bubble of gratitude welling up inside her as they walked together, just as in tune with each other as Theodore and Killian appeared to be, silently striding together a few paces ahead.

The students they passed on the way to the dining hall stopped to whisper to each other, but it was nothing compared to the sudden weight of silence that fell over the hall after they were several paces into the room and the rest of the room registered their presence.

Isobel wasn't sure what she expected, but it wasn't the Gifted students to tumble from their seats ... and start clapping. It wasn't quite a celebration—there was no whistling or cheering, but there were stiff smiles and nods and several calls of "Big call, guys!" or "We've got your back!"

I don't understand. She spoke to the eight Alphas through their bond, opening all those doors in her mind and inviting them into the conversation.

They think it's a ploy, Elijah answered. *No Gifted in their right mind on the Icon track with a clear road to the end would risk it all for the sake of "friendship."*

What the hell kind of ploy could it be? Moses' voice grumbled back, though he didn't really sound surprised.

Look at all the attention it's gotten us, Gabriel responded. *It could have been something we cooked up to pull us ahead of the human students. For all they know, we're planning to disband in our final year and fight to the death.*

They'll look like assholes if they don't support this, even if they think it's a stunt. Cian sounded like he agreed with the others. *They'll try to sabotage us privately instead.*

Isobel puffed out a short sigh, glancing over the food bar. The theme was clearly cereal because there was a whole wall of glass containers with antique bronze scoops stuck into too many different kinds of cereal to count. Isobel was too tired to make a decision, and she didn't even recognise half of the brands on show. Gabriel must have noticed because he took her tray out of her hands and began to fill a few different bowls.

Isobel drifted away in search of coffee, Oscar shoving his tray off onto Moses before trailing after her. He didn't speak to her and kept a few steps back, so he wasn't there for the pleasure of her company. He was there for safety.

Mikel and Kalen reminded them almost daily not to go anywhere alone, but in her exhaustion, she hadn't thought that walking across the dining hall was really "going" somewhere.

"Sorry," she muttered just before they reached the drinks station.

Oscar brushed his knuckles down part of her spine, right between her shoulder blades, in a wordless acknowledgment. They mostly communicated wordlessly, these days. Neither of them were handling the stress and lack of sleep well.

"Quite the announcement, Carter." Bellamy was already at the drinks station. A few third years hovered around him, but they scattered at the sight of Oscar, whose sleep-deprived expression made him even less approachable than usual.

"You think so?" she asked mildly.

"Mhmm." Bellamy arched a brow at her, turning and leaning his hip against the table.

Who wants coffee? she asked through the bond, testing whether she could speak to them from her current distance.

A chorus of grumbled responses tumbled back to her.

Everyone, then, she replied, amused.

Make it a triple, Cian pleaded.

"You sure you want to give up the crown just like that?" Bellamy asked, brow still cocked, green eyes surveying her. He shot a brief look to Oscar but averted his attention just as quickly.

Isobel scoffed, lining up the coffee cups. "I was never going to win, Bellamy."

"You had a pretty damn good chance."

She hugged her torso, tilting her head as she returned her friend's stare, wondering at the thoughts she could see shadowed behind his eyes. "Every single one of those Alphas had a better chance at winning. They're *Alphas*."

"Sure, they're Alphas, but you're *the* Sigma." Bellamy waved his hand down over her front, though it wasn't a very impressive front at that moment, with her arms wrapped around her torso and her slightly hunched posture. "The Princess of Ironside. Cinderella without a

prince. The little darling of dance. The pride and joy of
Dorm A."

A choking laugh bubbled up in the back of her
throat, almost bursting out. "The pride and joy of
Dorm A?"

He grinned like he was preening that he had almost
made her laugh. "That's right, and speaking of pride and
joy, you remember you have a boyfriend, right?
Because—"

"Quit flirting," Oscar snarled, hooking a finger into
the back of her shirt and pulling her back.

He twisted to the side, depositing her behind him
and stepping up to Bellamy, who immediately backed up
several steps, his palms displayed, his head shaking back
and forth.

"No way," he said. "That was *talking*. When I flirt, it
works."

"Fuck off," Oscar snarled. "While you still have shit
that works."

"Nice chatting." Bellamy peered around Oscar,
pretending to be unfazed, even though he was still
backing away. "Let's try this again sometime."

"I hate that fucking guy," Oscar grumbled, turning
back to the table to help her prepare the coffees. Nobody
else dared to approach the drinks station.

"You hate everyone," Isobel said, too tired to care
that Oscar was being a big, snarling bully.

"I like you." The words were a scrape of gravel,

utterly without warmth. They still made her stomach burn, her skin tingling with pleasure.

"You also like Moses," she noted mildly.

He made a sound that might have been an agreement.

"And you like Elijah and Gabriel when they're arguing."

This time, his mouth hooked up at the corner into a small, dark smile. It seemed to be another agreement.

"And Kilian," she continued. "Everyone likes him."

Oscar shrugged. It was as good as a resounding *yes*.

"And—"

"Okay, we get the point," he snapped.

"That you're basically the Taylor Swift of Ironside?" Isobel wasn't deterred. "Got a whole squad and everything."

He gave her a droll look. "I'm not responsible for you lot. Don't put that on me. Make Elijah the leader."

"Elijah *is* more fabulous," she mused, hiding a yawn behind the back of her hand.

"Don't tell him that. He'll think you're making fun of him."

She glanced back to the table, noting Elijah's perfectly styled hair, the silvery blond strands cut to an exact length as they drifted across his forehead, his reading glasses tucked into the pocket of one of the loose, oversized shirts he liked to dance in, his aristocratic features arranged into a sigh as he stared at the likely-not-nutritious-enough cereal in the bowl before him.

"You're right." She felt her lips twitch, but she bit back the smile.

Oscar frowned down at her before shooting a murderous glance across the room—in the direction Bellamy had backed away. "You'll smile for *him*."

"Cut it out," she grumbled, swatting at his arm.

He cut his eyes to her, dark and fierce, and said nothing.

Sometimes, she forgot how terrifying Oscar was. He had been very careful with her in the past month, always keeping his distance and biting his tongue, swallowing whatever it was he wanted to say.

He was doing it again now: being careful and swallowing his retort.

She nervously cleared her throat, feeling heat creep up the back of her neck as *possession* began to pound away at her. It wasn't the bond telling her about his feelings—it was simply the overwhelming weight of it, so vast and terrible that even though she wasn't trying to suck in his emotions with her Sigma ability, she was being assaulted anyway.

He still wouldn't speak, even when her breath picked up and the cardboard takeaway cup he had been holding collapsed in on itself, spilling scorching coffee all over his arm. She felt no pain from him, no awareness of it whatsoever. Only that raging, insistent, terrible possessiveness.

She swore, snatching up a bunch of napkins and trying to mop up the mess. Once she was done with the table, she grabbed his arm and gently wiped it down, ignoring how his dark eyes tracked her every movement, ignoring the muscles that twitched beneath her touch, ignoring the way his fist loosely formed, ignoring the way he shifted closer.

He suddenly turned away from her, snatching up a fresh cup. "My bad."

Isobel chewed on her lip, searching for a light-hearted response. She felt him reining in his emotion and bringing himself back under careful control for the cameras.

"You just wanted me to look after you," she teased, playing the *little sister of Dorm A* game. "You don't have to hurt yourself to get my attention."

As soon as he turned to glare at her again, she reached up and bopped him on the nose and then quickly grabbed one of the drink trays that was ready to go, hurrying away. She would have liked to think she walked calmly, but she was almost jogging by the time she got to the table.

She deposited the tray onto the table and had barely slid into her seat before the lights were cut, the electricity flickering out.

Oscar was there in a second despite the sudden

darkness. She could smell his burning oleander right beside her. The doors to the kitchen burst open, briefly filling the room with light again. A group of people spilled into the hall. They wore full face coverings pulled up over their noses and dark caps with *EDGC* printed in white lettering across the top of them. There were twelve of them, dressed in fitted black combat gear, with long guns in hand and fierce, blank eyes above their face coverings.

The European Division of Gifted Control, Elijah spoke through the bond. *There's been some chatter online about a special task division since they moved Ironside to France. I wasn't sure if it was real or not.*

This isn't good, she answered quietly, even though nobody else could hear them.

"Grab your stuff, everyone," Elijah said as two officials—one male and one female—followed the special division group through the kitchen doors.

Isobel's eyes were already adjusting to the lights being cut, so she could easily make out the group as the kitchen doors fell shut again—there was just enough morning sunlight from the few windows around the hall to illuminate their hard, focussed eyes—eyes that were fixed to Isobel and the Alphas.

Oscar's hand fell onto her shoulder, and she slipped out, standing beside him, the rest of the Alphas following suit, grabbing their gym bags or computer bags. They stood as a group, waiting as the officials strode toward their booth, the female official pulling ahead. All Isobel could think about was why they had cut the electricity. They could have just stopped the camera feed—if their goal had been to keep the encounter from being filmed.

It seemed like they were trying to scare everybody. Judging by the looks on the silent faces scattered around the hall, they had succeeded. The ashen faces of the other students tugged at a fearful memory inside her, and she briefly thought about how cruel it was to march an armed task force into a hall of Gifted still recovering from a mass shooting. They didn't talk about the tragedy of their last Consolidation Day, but it wasn't because they had forgotten. It was because the officials wanted to wipe it from the history of Ironside. No footage of people discussing Crowe or the shooting had aired, and Isobel had heard a few people gossiping about receiving emails from officials to stop spreading *misinformation* about the event, with vague threats of punishment.

"Please follow us," the female official requested as soon as she reached the booth.

She spun just as quickly, marching back the way she had come. The male official followed. The special forces group remained, fingers on triggers, faces impassive. Students were slowly inching into the booths, crowding and huddling together for protection.

Isobel found herself glancing toward Elijah. His jaw was set, his eyes hard as he assessed the display of force on show before he stepped forward, speaking from between his teeth.

"Let's go."

They were led through the kitchens and into the human-only grounds at the front of the academy, pausing in what appeared to be an office or official production building. It spanned only four or five levels but had a sprawling, glamorous reception area and suited officials bustling about in an important, hurried sort of way. At least it wasn't a secretive room in the Stone Dahlia. Surely, they wouldn't kill them in bright daylight in the middle of a busy office building.

Surely.

They were separated into three groups and ushered into elevators, which took them to the fourth floor. Then, they were led to a glass-walled meeting room and told to take seats at the massive table. The EDGC forces lined the sides of the room, just as watchful and wary as when they had stormed into the dining hall.

As soon as they were situated, the two officials disappeared, leaving them to wait. A few minutes later, Kalen and Mikel were also led in, and four more armoured men joined the other men and women lining the walls.

Well, this is about to get interesting. Mikel's voice drifted through her mind, that slight echoing quality telling her that he was speaking to them all. *Looks like we've finally been invited to the big kid table*.

41

Oscar's mouth twitched, and Moses glanced up to the ceiling like he wanted to roll his eyes but didn't want to chance the punishing workout Mikel would put him through tomorrow if he did. The others remained stoney-faced.

"Should have brought my coffee," Isobel grumbled, just in case they were being monitored. It was best if nobody guessed they could actually communicate in their heads. "I can't do this un-caffeinated."

"Any chance for coffee?" Cian asked casually, leaning back in his chair and eyeing one of the guards along the wall. His handsome face was utterly unbothered, his gaze a muted sapphire, his muscled arms casually stretched out to anchor against the table as he leaned away.

To Isobel's surprise, the guard nodded and exited the room.

"How about some bagels?" Moses added, glancing behind him, expression dark and challenging, mouth tipping into a smirk. "Breakfast muffins? Croissants? Macarons? Champagne? No?" Nobody answered him, but two of the guards exchanged a questioning look.

Oscar scoffed quietly, fierce gaze fixed on the table. He raised it when he felt Isobel's attention, the dark pools of his eyes swimming with amusement as he looked her over.

They were deliberately acting unaffected.

She tried to force a smile, but her lips trembled, and

she bit down on her bottom lip to hide her fear. She slipped her shaking hands beneath her thighs and tucked her head down, trying to calm her mind.

A large man burst into the room, followed by three women—all of them impeccably dressed, though there was something just *slightly* off about the man's appearance. His suit was too big—like he was trying to hide his protruding stomach—and his skin was a little pasty and patchy. On the other hand, the women were in form-fitting designer outfits without a single hair out of place with their make-up done so well they might as well have been walking into a televised interview.

Isobel only recognised one of the officials: a brunette with a sharp fringe wearing fitted, high-waisted cream pants and a navy blue silk shirt with a simple golden chain peeking out from the open collar. Olivia Frisk. Assistant to the Director of Ironside. She somehow managed to look tired and alert all at once. She seemed like a woman who excelled under pressure.

Isobel's hands began to sweat, and something intangible *snapped* in the air around her body before sensations were crashing over her from all directions.

Fear, anger, violence, anxiety. There was also a fierce, dark protectiveness that had goosebumps popping up along her arms, too large to belong to just one of them.

The Alphas had lost control. They were no longer able to shield against her Sigma ability, though they were still managing to separate their emotions within the bond.

"I'm going to cut right to the point," the man spoke, dumping a box onto the middle of the large conference table before rounding it to sit at the head of the table, right between Mikel and Kalen. The box was filled with microphones, straps, and battery packs.

She realised the Alphas had placed themselves around the table very carefully. Kalen and Mikel framed the head of the table, where they apparently assumed an important official would sit, while Theodore and Moses were framing Isobel, Kilian and Niko directly across from her, with Oscar and Cian on either side of them. Gabriel and Elijah were at the other end of the table, where they could clearly see everyone.

Callum Rowe, Kalen said through the bond. *The Director of Ironside. He likes to stay out of the spotlight.*

"I'm here to offer you a deal," Rowe continued, without introducing himself, as he waved toward the box he had dumped onto the table. "The eleven of you walk out of here fully mic'd up, your every fucking action recorded from sunup to sundown, while you're sleeping, while you're hiding away in bathrooms and closets ..."

He paused, leaning forward, gripping the table's edge, misting up the shiny wood around his thick fingers. "Or you agree to play this game *our* way, by *our* rules."

His eyes were shiny and dark, like wet marbles, as

they rolled from face to face, pausing when he reached Isobel. He sat back, releasing the table and slowly taking her in.

"You're pretty for a Sigma," he admitted. "Even prettier in person. But not pretty enough to be the main character of this show. We'll have to fix that." He let out a low laugh, short and cruel enough to turn her stomach.

"I have a few suggestions." The tallest of the women spoke, her words slightly accented. She had long, sleek blonde hair and bright, icy blue eyes with a full set of thick, fake eyelashes that looked like they were perfectly designed to flatter her angular features, and she spoke with a slight accent.

"Who are you?" Kalen asked calmly, levelling her with a blank stare.

Does he know the others? Isobel whispered through the bond to Mikel. The scarred Alpha glanced over at her, his mottled, blue-black eyes considering.

"You can call me Yulia," the woman responded, arching a perfectly winged brow.

She's the only one we don't know, Mikel's deep voice rolled through her mind. *The other woman is Tilda, my ex. She's the creative director.*

Isobel tried to keep the shock off her face, and it took all of her self-control not to turn and stare at Tilda immediately.

"Yulia, who?" Kalen pressed, still the embodiment of

45

calm. His expression didn't so much as twitch as Yulia stepped toward him, her eyes crawling down his chest.

Something hot and ugly rose up inside Isobel, making her hands tingle.

"Novikov," Yulia replied, her lips curving into a tight smile. "COO of the Stone Dahlia. I don't really have much to do with the show, so our paths haven't crossed before. But I've monitored a few of your performances in the Dahlia."

Kalen dismissed Yulia as soon as the words were out of her mouth, glancing at the other two women by the door before turning his attention back to Rowe. "What are you asking us to do? Be specific."

"You're *not* the one who gives orders in this room," Callum snarled, smashing his fist onto the table for emphasis before he seemed to regain control, running his hand through his rich-brown hair—hair that didn't seem to match his complexion at all. It seemed far too thick and lustrous.

Isobel cautiously reached out with her power, attempting, and mostly failing, to resist the draw of the heightened Alphas all around her.

It was illegal to use a Gifted power on a human.

A death sentence if the power could be used to inflict harm.

But she had been stealthily sipping away at the anxiety and exhaustion of her mates for weeks now, with none of them the wiser. She had learned how hard to push and exactly when to back off to remain undetected.

Callum Rowe was humiliated and furious. It was boiling and bubbling up within him, threatening to spill over and scald them all.

Tread carefully, she addressed the bond. *He's on edge, about to snap. He's angry and humiliated that we ruined their plans.*

None of them answered, but Mikel cut his mismatched eyes to her in a stern warning, softened slightly by the bolt of fear she felt from all of them. They were just worried she would be detected, but she had already withdrawn, quiet and light as a ghost, the taste of burning fury still on the tip of her tongue.

Isobel, Elijah's steady, deep voice captured her attention, so clear that she knew he was talking only to her. *Can you keep Moses and Theo calm without them noticing?*

Done, she responded, curbing her curiosity. They hadn't seemed to be concerned about Moses and Theodore going feral in a while, despite the stress they had been dealing with. She was sure that of all the Alphas, Elijah was the one who might have clued onto her subtle siphoning tricks. She often found him studying her when the others deescalated conflicts instead of surging, tearing into each other, or losing control. Something seemed different, now, but she wasn't sure what.

Everyone at the table remained silent, locked in a battle of wills. Rowe was waiting for Kalen to speak, and finally, the large Alpha crossed his arms and relaxed back into his chair, regarding the Director with a calm that seemed to be a physical blanket over the entire room.

"We're at your disposal, naturally," Kalen drawled.

Rowe's thick nose twitched, his brows inching together like thick caterpillars crawling across his forehead. He had a very elastic, expressive face.

"You've put us in an incredibly difficult situation," he said. "Ironside isn't just a silly little talent show. It's an *industry*. Ironside is the Stone Dahlia; with the Dahlia, we can make or break the economy of more than one country. We could hand-pick the next American president if we were so inclined. The last four French presidents were chosen by us, just so that we could influence their foreign policies and conservation laws while we developed the new Ironside. We could start a fucking war just for the sake of it. While you're frolicking around in this little playground we built you, we're out there in the real world making real moves. So if you want us to change the rules for you, you must make it worth our while."

Isobel stared at Rowe with a sinking feeling, realising the magnitude of what he was saying. He gestured to Tilda, who stepped away from the wall, pulled out the chair beside Gabriel, and sat down. Her blonde hair was pulled back into a sleek knot, sharpening her features.

She had a slender nose and a cool, blue stare. She was very beautiful, very composed—but there was a sliver of steel to it all. Even her sensuality seemed to have a knife's edge, as she levelled them each with a searing, heavy-lidded stare.

Isobel felt a few of the Alphas' eyes flicker her way as she gawked at Tilda. She rechecked her walls, realising she had been so focused on her Sigma power that she had accidentally opened herself to the bond. It was happening so much that she was starting to wonder if she had lost the ability to close herself off at all. They could feel everything she was feeling, including her stab of jealousy. She could too-easily picture this stunning, terrifying woman with Mikel. Challenging him. Pushing him. Teasing out that dominant side of him.

Isobel swallowed, fighting back a slow roll of nausea. This was too much. Rowe, Tilda, Yulia, and Frisk. These powerful, bloodthirsty, cunning people. At least Rowe wasn't as intimidatingly beautiful as the women, but Isobel wished they would *show* how rotten they were on the inside. She hated their cruel perfection.

Tilda opened a folder and extracted a piece of paper, looking down the table at Kalen. "We will allow performance groups to compete and win the *Ironside Show*—"

Wait, what?

"But they will be managed by Orion—Ironside's new recording label."

Tilda paused, allowing that to sink in.

They want money, Elijah muttered through the bond. *Money is the only thing that will make this right.*

Seeing that nobody was going to interrupt her, Tilda continued. "All groups will be required to declare themselves and their specialisations in their third year, where they will sign provisional contracts with Orion. If they win, their provisional contract turns into a fifteen-year permanent management contract. While at Ironside, your stipends will remain the same, but after you graduate, Orion will take 90 per cent of your earnings for the entire fifteen-year term. The remaining 10 per cent will be split between the members of the group."

Isobel blinked at the table. She was shocked that the officials still had the ability to shock her. She quickly did the math, realising they were offering less than 1 per cent to each person.

They have to discourage large groups from forming, Moses scoffed through the bond. He didn't sound surprised.

We've officially made it too inconvenient for them to arrange our deaths, Mikel added, *so they're pivoting to the extreme alternative. They're making* use *of us.*

"There will be rules," Tilda added, unaware of their internal discussions, "and that's where I come in. As the Creative Director of Ironside, it's my job to make sure we put on a good show no matter what's going on behind the scenes. Eleven against one isn't fair or entertaining odds, so we'll do our best on the show to challenge your group dynamics to make groups look more difficult and annoying than convenient, and we expect you to play along. For the privilege of having a group application approved in the third year, all groups will be tested and provoked to our fullest ability to prove to the viewers that we aren't playing favourites or giving you a leg up."

Tilda swept her eyes over them in a bored sort of way. "Furthermore," she said, this time not waiting to see if they had any objections, "there will be a blanket no-fraternisation rule for all groups. Orion expects 100 per cent of your focus, effort, and determination. No dating within the group and no dating outside of the group. If you want it easy, you can compete in this game the way it was intended. If you want it your way, you'll have to *prove* you want it; you'll have to give us your all. Your time, your talents, your damn souls."

A no-fraternisation rule? They were pretending not to know about the bond, and Isobel couldn't fathom why.

"The group already has a management contract," Kalen said, though his tone wasn't challenging. He tilted his head at Tilda before shifting his gaze back to Rowe, waiting for one of them to explain.

"If groups would like to recruit other Gifted as producers, choreographers, or songwriters, they will be permitted to make that choice, as long as those Gifted are already at Ironside," Tilda answered. Her cool blue eyes settled on Mikel for the briefest moment, her expression utterly neutral, before she returned her attention to Kalen. She ignored everyone else. "Since you and Mikel Easton have proven to be such valuable talent-makers, we have decided to utilise those special skills with our other groups. Each group is being assigned an Orion manager, and you will make yourselves available to the managers to consult as needed on all groups."

"And when *our* group graduates?" Kalen asked plainly.

"If you can make them that famous despite everything we throw at you," Rowe answered, eyes hard, "you can leave with them. You'll be permitted to sign roles as producers or assistant managers under the management of your Orion-appointed representative. You will be subject to the same fifteen-year term and share in the same 10 per cent of earnings."

Isobel would be nearing forty by the time their permanent management contract with Orion ran out. Ironside was *offering* to rob them of their earnings for the highest earning years of their lives.

"Additionally," Yulia added, immediately putting Isobel even further on edge, "your Stone Dahlia contracts have been amended. Since you have proven yourselves to be so *beloved* by the public, we would like to capitalise on that interest. Miss Carter," she was the first of the women to meet Isobel's eyes, "you will be moved to the main stage in the Dahlia Room, which only our most important VIPs have access to. Your performances must be provocative and entertaining, sensual but tasteful— you will be marketed as an untouchable prize. The Princess of Ironside. Everyone's darling, alluring little sister—"

That's not messed up at all, Moses grumbled through the bond.

Yulia finished, "We can hire a professional to plan and direct your performances—"

"That won't be necessary," Isobel interrupted, trying to mimic Elijah's cool, unbothered expression. She already knew she didn't have a choice, so there wasn't any point in putting up a fight. If she wanted to keep some control, she needed to step up now, before they assumed she couldn't think and speak for herself.

"Very well." Yulia arched a brow at her, and Isobel tested the other woman with her Sigma power, tasting the spike of frustration from Yulia as she seemed to fail to read anything in Isobel's expression. "You will need to run your ideas by Cesar Cooper—he will either approve or reject your concepts and better guide you on our performance expectations."

"What's Cooper's role in all of this?" Kalen asked, a slightly darker note in his voice. He seemed to be the only one speaking, the others sitting back and allowing him to take the lead.

"Cesar Cooper will be your Orion-appointed manager and liaison," Rowe answered. "He will manage your group and your performances and negotiate with the record label on your behalf."

"You mentioned that all of our contracts had been adjusted." Kalen switched his attention to Yulia, showing no reaction to what Rowe had said.

"You've all been transferred to floater contracts." Yulia shifted behind the table, watching Kalen. "But only for two hours a week while Carter is dancing."

"And the rest of the time?" Kalen pressed, thick arms folding tightly across his broad chest.

"All eleven of you will serve in our Icon Cafe. We want you there every Saturday morning until midday. It's a room for the wealthiest people in the country—and abroad, naturally—to book time with their favourite Icons. You'll be required to pour their drinks, serve them food, compliment them, ask them polite questions that don't broach their privacy, and pay them special romantic attention. Your clients will be international, so there's no need to learn French."

"It's illegal to—" Kalen, began, but Rowe cut across him.

"We aren't asking you to fuck them, West." He rolled his eyes like Kalen's almost-objection was beyond ridiculous. "At most, you'll be asked for a hug or to put your arm around them for a photo. It's within our interest to keep you all shining, pure, and untouchable. It makes the clientele want you even more. The Icon Cafe is the gold standard of Icon interaction, and you'll be expected to represent the grace and humility of our Ironside Gifted during your shift. Nothing less will be tolerated."

We can't pull Oscar from fights, Elijah's voice echoed into her mind.

He needs the outlet, Mikel agreed. *I was hoping to train Niko, Theo, and Moses to get them in there too.*

"Oscar Sato and Mikel Easton earn a significant amount of money from their fights," Kalen addressed Rowe, subtly grinding his teeth together, his jaw flexing. "Far more than they can get from a floater contract."

"Very well." Rowe waved a large hand. "Whoever wants to fight can apply, but they must perform at the same time as Carter. Everything you do from now on, you do as a group, that includes time spent in the Dahlia."

Kalen's jaw looked like it was about to crack, but after a moment, he rubbed a hand over his mouth and nodded, forcing his pretend calm to roll over the table again. "While we're negotiating—"

"This is not—" Rowe started, but Kalen didn't break stride.

"—we want the cameras out of the Dorm A bedrooms."

Rowe scoffed but didn't immediately object, and Kalen only waited a moment to continue.

"Historically, Dorm A bedrooms have been camera-free, and my Alphas are uneasy with the change. You want them to train harder and give more than any other student, so in return, I'd like you to give them back a modicum of privacy while they're sleeping. You have cameras in all the hallways and all around the dorm so it's not like they'll be sneaking other people into their beds. I just want them to be able to relax for the few hours they have every night to themselves. If you give them that, they'll work harder for you. Isobel will, as well. It was unfair to make her work her ass off for a private room in Dorm A only to make it public the day she finally moved in."

Rowe actually seemed to be considering it as he leaned back in his chair and regarded Kalen. He glanced over at Tilda, who gave a short nod, and then sighed. "Fine. If you sign the contracts, all recording devices will be removed from inside the bedrooms only."

Kalen's expression wasn't victorious. "How long do we have to think about this?"

Rowe smiled unkindly. "As you know, your Stone Dahlia contracts can be amended at any time. That's already done. But if you're referring to—"

"I am," Kalen said.

"Then we'll give you an hour." Rowe stood, straightening out his jacket. "Olivia, leave them the contracts."

Frisk nodded, dropping a pile of booklets beside the box of microphones, before opening the door for Rowe, who paused in the doorway, glancing back at the Alphas and Isobel.

"As I said," Rowe's features tightened, "you accept this deal, or you'll be wired up at all times, in all areas of the academy. It's your choice."

He left the room, Frisk following him. Tilda and Yulia exited without a second glance, and then the two EDGC men returned carrying trays of coffee and several brown takeout bags. As soon as the scent of pastry filled the room, Isobel's stomach grumbled loudly. She was shocked and scared, devastated by the options set out before them, but apparently, her stomach didn't care.

The men set everything onto the table as Elijah and Gabriel reached for the stack of notebooks, grabbing one each and sliding two copies down the table to Kalen and Mikel. The rest of them were silent as Isobel and Cian began dividing up the coffees and croissants.

"Thank you," she said quietly, catching the eye of the armed man who had brought in the food.

He paused, not expecting her to try to talk to him. He dipped his head in a short nod before averting his attention to the wall.

Isobel devoured her croissant and downed half her coffee, eyeing Niko, who was only pushing his pastry around on a paper plate while he stared at Gabriel and Elijah, flicking through the pages of the unbelievably thick contract as fast as they could, while wincing at the scalding coffee they kept sipping without tearing their eyes from the pages.

After a few minutes, Niko seemed to register the food in front of him and somehow stuffed it into his mouth in three bites, inhaling it the way he used to eat food. It made Isobel want to cry, and several eyes flicked to her face. She quickly reached for one of the contracts to distract herself, but the language was far too technical for her to understand, and she eventually closed the pages, feeling defeated.

"Do we really have a choice here?" she asked, lifting her eyes to Kilian sitting directly opposite her.

He shook his head, answering with the perfect amount of defeat and hope to colour his voice, putting on a performance for however the officials had chosen to monitor them during their hour of "decision making." Better to be safe than sorry.

"Not really." He shrugged delicately, pale eyes dropping back to the table. "They're right—the investors in this show aren't going to allow something like this unless it benefits them. They can't only allow us to form a group without offering the same recourse for others, but they also need to consider measures to control the group sizes to keep the show competitive and entertaining. Students may consider forming a group now, but they might decide against it for the sake of the money. If they win as a single Icon, they have the freedom of their own career and get to keep all their earnings. If they win as a group, they only get their share of 10 per cent and are still owned by Ironside for another fifteen years. The fans and other students will probably consider this a fair trade-off since it would be easier for a group to win due to the combined popularity of all the members."

"You're right," Theodore muttered, tipping his head back to sigh at the ceiling. "And it's in our Ironside contracts that the level of surveillance can be increased or decreased at any time without notice. They're even technically allowed to put cameras in the bathrooms. They could realistically make it very unappealing for us to not sign these contracts. We could lose all privacy."

And, he added, through the bond, *if we take this option away from them, they will probably try to kill us again. They don't have many avenues here. Turning ourselves into a money-making machine for them might be the only way to ensure our safety.*

Isobel nodded at the table, and they fell back into silence, finishing their coffees and food as they waited. Mikel absently nudged his croissant over to Niko, who inhaled it without thought.

Isobel was going to grow obsessed with watching him eat.

"It's comprehensive," Elijah finally said, after their hour was almost up. He closed the booklet and tossed it back into the middle of the table, pinching the bridge of his nose after pulling off his glasses. "They will own us, but they're at least giving us a modicum of creative freedom. They're entitled to suggest changes in our performances and songs and to impose deadlines and mandatory practice time on us, but we can come up with our own songs and choreography."

The others set down their booklets, waiting for what else Elijah had to say, since he seemed to be pausing only to consider his next words.

"The ... lifestyle restrictions might be more of a challenge," he allowed, making eye contact with Kalen and Mikel, passing them some sort of unspoken message. "No fraternisation between members or outside of the group. No marriages or engagements until the end of the fifteen-year contract period. No pregnancies for the contract term—if anyone comes forward saying that one of us got them pregnant, or if Isobel gets pregnant by someone, then the entire group will be dropped by the label, and each member will be sent back to their respective settlements until the end of the contract term. After that time, we will be free to live as citizens of the United States, but we won't have any money and our careers will be dead."

Isobel blinked at his impassive, handsome face. "Why?" she blurted.

"I assume they want us in peak performance condition, untethered and unburdened by family commitments until the end of our contract term," Elijah answered. "They want us to make as much money as possible while we're tied to their label—they want our full commitment, attention, and energy."

"Is that all?" Moses asked, brows drawn low, lips pressed tightly together, his long eyelashes lowered to conceal what Isobel was sure would be a stormy expression.

"No," Elijah sighed out. "There's more. There are weight and body fat ratio requirements. We have to record our data and send it to Cooper, who is allowed to tell us to lose weight, change our diet, or change our exercise regimes to reach specific goals. And," he continued before any of them could respond properly, "there's a zero-tolerance drug policy, a two-drink alcohol policy, and you must apply to Cooper for permission for any body modifications such as piercings, tattoos, or significant hairstyle changes."

"Jesus—" Cian cut himself off on a heavy breath, shoving his hands through his hair, pulling the golden strands out of the loose bun they had been swept into. "Okay. What else?" He tugged out a silk hair tie that looked like Isobel's and retied his hair.

"We have to produce a demo album before the end of year three—"

"*Before* we graduate?" Kilian interrupted, frowning.

"Year *three*," Elijah emphasised. "*This* year. If they don't like your demo album, they can disband your group. At the end of the day, they only want groups who will earn them money."

"How the fuck are we going to produce an entire demo album before the end of the year?" Moses growled, thumping his palm onto the table. "Between practice and classes during the week, Friday evenings at Ironside Row, Friday nights in the Stone Dahlia, and Saturdays at the Icon Cafe, we aren't even going to have time to sleep."

The others grumbled their agreement.

"It's doable," Kalen mused. "We can make it happen. They're making this all seem impossible for a reason—to dissuade people from choosing this option and to filter out anyone who thinks this might be an easy road to the finish line."

"Why are we even discussing this if we don't have a choice?" Niko grumbled, crossing his muscled arms tightly over his chest, hazel eyes scanning the armed men and women silently lining the edges of the conference room, acting like they couldn't even hear the discussion happening before them.

Technically, they *did* have a choice. *On paper*, they could compete as individuals and give up the remaining vestiges of their privacy for a shot at ultimate freedom and earning potential, or they could give up their earnings and freedom for fifteen years after they graduate for a shot at staying together as a group in the outside world.

But that was only on paper.

The officials were well aware that Isobel and the

Alphas were bonded despite everyone pretending it was still a secret. In reality, this truly was their only safe option.

If they walked out of the room with microphones strapped to their bodies, it would only be a matter of time before the officials added cameras to their closets and bathrooms. They would find a way to expose the bond and destabilise their fanbase until the group lost the support of the public and, by extension, their untouchable status.

Or they would just organise another accident and make a martyr out of their golden boy, Theodore Kane.

There was no option.

Elijah sighed, reaching for a pen.

3
NOT FUNNY, MOSES

Isobel wanted to kick something.

Callum Rowe had made her—had made *all of them*—feel two inches tall. She was accustomed to feeling unimportant, to being condescended to, to being put in her place, but this was on another level: this feeling of being a product on a shelf, wrapped in plastic, stapled with tags, and confined to the fine print on her packaging. The *only* thing that mattered was whether they would make money. That was *it*. It was more important than their hidden bond, than the fact they had lied, than the reputation of the academy.

The only thing that mattered ... was money.

As soon as they got back to the dorm, she dove into the shower, stripping off her clothes and sinking onto the bench, her legs pulled up to her chest. The water wasn't even touching her, but the steam and the sound were soothing, and she desperately needed a moment away from the cameras. Her face felt tight from controlling her expression, and a headache threatened to bloom behind her eyes.

She sighed, dropping her forehead to her knees, breathing in the scent of the dried flowers perfuming the bathroom. She was going to indulge in ten minutes of feeling sorry for herself, and then she would pull up her socks and woman up, like the guys seemed to have done.

It would be great if the world was different, but it wasn't, and it wouldn't change in a day. In their world, influence meant power, and power meant freedom. They were balancing blindfolded on a tightwire of popularity, the floor dropping further away with every tentative step, widening their stakes. Now wasn't the time to declare war against the system, even if that was something they could safely do. They were only one misstep away from a fall they wouldn't survive.

CIAN STARED AT HIS PHONE, FROWNING SLIGHTLY AS HE LEANED against the wrought iron balcony railing.

Isobel: We don't need to go everywhere as a group anymore, right?

Isobel: Coming after us would be a huge waste of time, resources, and planning now that we've signed the contracts.

Isobel: Right?

It was probably the most she had ever said all at once

without anyone replying. He frowned harder, picking at the side of the phone with his nail. He didn't need to text her to know how she was feeling. It had taken her two hours squirrelled away in the shower to get her emotions back under control, though she still wasn't closed off from the bond despite what he assumed to be her best efforts.

He also knew she was about to flee the building before she sent the messages—that's why he was on the balcony, staring out toward the front of Dorm A. His gift wasn't always straightforward, but every now and then, he would just *know* when things were about to happen— usually useless things.

"Come on, Kalen," he grumbled, glaring at the screen. His grip relaxed slightly when Kalen began typing.

Kalen: The officials aren't the only ones you need protection from.

"She knows that," Cian sighed out.

Niko: She knows that.

"This guy is honestly begging someone to punch him." Cian poked at his lip piercing with his tongue, a restless, fidgety energy prickling through him.

He trusted his friends. The Alphas were his second family—closer than his real family, in some ways, but they were volatile. Volatile, possessive, and jealous.

It was hard enough to come to terms with the fact

that their mate wasn't *theirs*, alone, without taking into account all the people who wanted to hurt her.

Who *had* hurt her.

Isobel: Eve is dead. Crowe is dead.

Moses: Oscar is still alive.

Kalen: Not funny, Moses.

Oscar: Agree to disagree.

Kilian: That it was funny, or that you're alive?

Oscar: Am I alive or is this hell?

Oscar: Daily conundrum.

Theodore: Why are you so emo?

Isobel: Back to the point?

"She needs space," Cian muttered, agitatedly tapping his free hand against the railing.

Mikel: I highly doubt the officials will organise another attack on you, not when they want you focussed and producing music that will make them money.

Elijah: I think the students are more likely to sabotage you in other ways, now. Targeted, underhanded attacks on your reputation and image are now far more vital than bullying, threats, and intimidation.

Still, they didn't give her permission.

This decision was up to Kalen.

Cian shifted from foot to foot until Kalen began typing again.

Kalen: The buddy system and the surveillance shifts through the night are no longer necessary. The danger has passed, for now. Still, I want everyone to continue sharing their locations with the group at all times.

A flood of relief poured out of him, and he bent at the waist, resting his forehead against the cool iron railing. "Thank fuck for that," he groaned out, realising his agitation hadn't entirely been on behalf of Isobel.

He was going stir-crazy. Privacy was already a luxury at Ironside, but never getting a full night's sleep and always having to be attached to half or all of the group during every waking hour was slowly driving him insane, as much as he loved them.

"I'm trying not to be insulted," a droll voice commented from the neighbouring balcony.

He picked up his head, glancing over at Gabriel. "No, you're not—you're impossible to insult," he said, rolling his eyes. Gabriel was hard to ruffle, except for the million tiny things that ruffled him. Hurting his *feelings* was nearly impossible, but lord help whoever put a fork into the cutlery drawer facing the wrong way.

"Fine," Gabriel agreed, leaning over the railing and staring out across the seemingly endless miles of manicured gardens from their elevated vantage point atop Alpha Hill. "Do you feel the rattle?"

"The what now?" Cian blinked, momentarily thrown.

"The rattle," Gabriel repeated, still staring off into the distance. "Like when you're driving one of those golf carts and there's something rattling around in the back but no matter how hard you look, you can't find it. Something in the bond is unhinged. I can feel it."

"Oh. That."

The rattle.

That was a good way to put it. The more Cian tried to ignore it, the louder it persisted.

"Well?" Gabriel prompted.

"Yeah." Cian dragged his hands down over his face, checking to make sure the door to Gabriel's room was closed. "It happened when Niko repaired the bond." He spoke lowly—there were no cameras out on the balcony because the space was too small to get a good angle, but he didn't want to risk speaking at a normal volume.

"Is it better if you glue it back together?" Gabriel asked just as quietly. "Does it matter if the cracks are still there? Isobel hasn't noticed."

"I was wondering that," Cian admitted. "I didn't want her to feel it."

"None of us wanted her to feel it," Gabriel said. "And so she hasn't felt it."

"Is it really that easy?" Cian frowned.

"No idea."

"You know everything," he shot back.

"I know my limits," Gabriel smirked, pushing away from the balcony and spinning to the doors. He paused before walking back inside, turning to face Cian. "Be on the lookout. This restless feeling ... this rattle ... it reeks of side effects."

"Oh joy," Cian drawled.

Gabriel smiled, but there was no humour in the slight twist of his lips. "I'll warn the others. We'll come up with a plan."

Cian nodded, pulling up his phone again. There was a new message waiting for him.

Isobel: What are you doing later?

His nights were free again.

Her nights were free again.

His cock filled with blood so suddenly it was almost painful, and he stormed inside, pushing into his dressing room, eyes wide, heart pounding.

Holy shit calm down, she didn't mean it like that.

Cian: Bringing my camera to the studio?

Isobel: I love it when you read my mind.

He didn't text back. He didn't trust his fingers. He should have been exhausted enough to sleep for a week, but instead, he had to stand there and think about Gabriel rearranging his clothes by colour and style until his swelling erection died a slow death by organised boredom.

OSCAR PULLED HIS GLOVES OFF, TOSSING THEM TO THE ground as he stalked away from the boxing bag. He had suspected that the bond might have been blanketing the volatile, violent urges he was used to, but now he was sure of it because as soon as Niko returned the bond pieces to Isobel, Oscar felt that blanket lift.

He was no longer leashed and repressed. The bond had settled into something imperfect, contained by glue and pure, stubborn will. It had settled into something unnatural. It could no longer keep him contained, which meant it wouldn't keep the others contained either. They had suspected that the bond had been playing a part in preventing Moses and Theodore from going feral all the time, but now they were at risk again. Which was just fucking *great*. Exactly what they needed.

He fell to one of the weight benches, dragging a towel across his face as he fished his phone out of his pocket.

Oscar: You know what you've done, don't you?

The reply came immediately.

Kalen: Elijah warned me you might text.

"Fucking Elijah," Oscar muttered, his thumbs flying across the screen.

Oscar: You've just cleared up all our nights.

Kalen: I know.

Oscar: They're going to start fucking her again.

Kalen: I know.

Oscar: Her room is next to mine.

Kalen: I know.

Oscar: You know how long it'll take me to murder one of them?

Kalen: You won't touch any of them.

Kalen: Including Isobel.

His head fell back, a laugh bursting from his throat—rough and unhinged.

Oscar: So much for the lecture on how it's her body and her choice.

Kalen: As long as it doesn't put her in danger.

Oscar: It's her body to damage.

Kalen: If it's her body to damage, then it's her body to give to someone else.

Oscar: Not if I kill them first.

Kalen: You're not even going to wait for them to fuck? Who are you going to kill first?

Oscar: Probably Theodore, that smug fuck.

Kalen: He's our lead singer, you idiot.

Oscar: Then Kilian, that fake gay smug fuck.

Kalen: What happens if you surge when you're with her? What if you hurt her?

Oscar: What does that have to do with me killing my friends?

Kalen: Just think about it.

Oscar: IT'S ALL I THINK ABOUT.

Kalen: I'm sure she's flattered that you admire her heart and personality so much.

Oscar: You know what I mean. Stop antagonising me.

Kalen: I could order you not to touch her.

Oscar: Then I'll kill you first.

Oscar shoved his phone back into his pocket, done with the conversation. His hands shook, his vision blurry with a rage that he worked to quieten. After pacing for a few moments, he snatched his phone back out and dialled his little sister, but after only one ring, he quickly hung up. It was early morning, and she needed her sleep. He texted the old woman who was living in the hut next door, checking in. He split all his earnings between Lily, the neighbour who checked on her, the woman from the schoolhouse who spent some afternoons with her, and the settlement medical centre, and still, it wasn't enough.

Would it be enough if he could only take home less than 1 per cent of their earnings?

They might have secured their safety, but they sure as fuck hadn't solved any of their problems.

CIAN OPENED THE DOOR TO THE DANCE STUDIO AS QUIETLY AS he could, slipping into the room. He shouldn't have bothered. Isobel wouldn't have noticed if he had run inside, screaming, on fire. She was lost in her dance, the music loud enough to shake the floor.

He placed his camera on the bench where she had left her shirt and bag and leaned over to check the song playing on her phone. "Burn," by Tom Walker. It was on repeat, and she seemed to be nailing down the choreography. Trust the Sigma to deal with the upheaval of their plans and their future with a frantic, angry, rebellious dance.

He loved that about her.

73

Liked.

He *liked* that about her.

What the fuck?

Jesus fuck.

Fuck fuck fuck.

He pulled the camera into his lap, and Isobel seemed to notice him. She stopped dancing, her chest heaving, her skin shimmering with a dusting of sweat. She was wearing tights, sneakers, and a crop top. She kicked her sneakers to the side of the room and ran her hands through her hair, taming the riotous waves away from her face.

"Ready?" she panted, calling across the long practice room as she jogged toward him. She tapped her watch to stop the song.

"Ready if you are," he confirmed.

"Thanks for helping out." She flashed him a haunting smile, her pretty lips pushing at her cheeks—she always smiled like that, like her mouth was too narrow for it, creating multiple little dimples in her skin. With lips like hers, it was a smile that drew the eye. It wasn't cute like she could sometimes be, or cold like she could sometimes be. It was plush and soft and inviting—like she almost never was.

Isobel was only soft and inviting when his dick was inside her, distracting her from the guard she always had up and the fear she always swam in. Or when she was in those rare moments halfway between sleep and sanity. It should track that alcohol would soften that cool mask of hers, but alcohol only managed to make her sassy.

"You're welcome," he finally said after fiddling with his camera, pretending he hadn't just glitched out thinking about her smile.

What the fuck was wrong with him? He was making himself sick. He wasn't the *type* to know all the ways to tease out every facet of a woman's personality. He loved women, but this wasn't a casual appreciation for her gender. This was an obsession.

"Are we doing this video for anything in particular?" he asked, trying to get his head in the game. Stress was making him scattered.

"I need to work harder," she muttered, stretching her overworked muscles. "It's not enough for me to keep up with you guys. I just ... need to work harder."

"You're not keeping up, doll." Cian raised his brows at her. "You're a better dancer than any of us. You have more natural talent *and* you're more experienced. That's not keeping up. That's leaving us behind."

She rolled her eyes. "Then I want to be further ahead."

"Savage little thing, aren't you? I thought we were in a group now. Where's the team mindset?"

A small chuckle tumbled from her lips, and some of the darkness lifted from his chest.

"I already emailed Cooper and asked if I could release this as a personal project, so I don't have to wait a week."

She padded back to the centre of the room, glancing at her watch. "I'll upload it tonight."

What's the rush? he asked through the bond.

People might think we're taking the easy way out. I'm going to flood them with content, so they don't have time to even consider it.

"Sounds like a plan." He palmed his camera and waited for her to get into position. She tapped her watch to start the song, and they ran through the choreography a few times to fix up the invisible mistakes she claimed she was making.

He tried to move with her, drawing close for the slower moments of her dance and smoothly retreating as she began to speed up, widening her movements, beginning to leap and extend. It was exactly her style—lyrical, expressive, and highly technical. She didn't dance to music; she *showed* the music. She dove into the emotion of a song and somehow expressed it vividly, cleanly, painfully.

It was hard not to believe in fate when he watched her like this. Nobody else at the academy had worked as hard as her to get as far as she had come.

Nobody except him and the other Alphas.

It was clear now that he knew her better and had seen how her father had treated her—her whole life was *training*. Nothing had existed for her except constant and relentless betterment. It was how Kalen and Mikel had trained them, after recruiting each of them. None of them really had a choice, but for different reasons.

"One more time," she panted, watching back the video he had just taken. She was shaking her head. "I messed up my extension."

He thought it was perfect, but she was the lead dancer, not him. So he nodded, and they did it again.

And again.

And again.

ISOBEL WAS ASTOUNDED AT HOW THE OFFICIALS HAD successfully managed to frame the narrative of their group forming as something they had *allowed* her and the Alphas to announce. Like it was Ironside's plan, not theirs—and it was hardly a privilege. The new rules effectively scared off most people from trying to register as a group.

Most people, but not all people.

On Wednesday, the humans shocked the entire academy by registering as a group. Each of them had a good shot at winning the game and were willing to throw that away to share the spotlight... but perhaps the contracts they had been offered were different, since they weren't Gifted. They had no training in singing or dancing, but they had Kalen and Mikel, who weren't allowed to play favourites, so Isobel was worried that the professors might just be able to make something spectacular out of them. The human group was announced on social media first thing in the morning, and when Isobel walked into Icon Matters, everyone was on their phones, whispering excitedly.

She sank down into a seat, dropping her bag by her legs. She tried to wipe away the worry from her features as the Kozlov twins walked into the room, grinning at everyone and taking their seats at the front of the auditorium. Alissa James and Irene Ellis—Gabriel and Elijah's fake girlfriends—slipped into the seats on either side of the two muscled blond men, cosying up to them with coy smiles, light touches, and feminine laughter. Isobel blinked in shock, and then pulled her phone out and snapped a quick picture, sending it to the group chat.

Isobel: Um, so ...
Elijah: Oops.
Gabriel: What am I looking at?
Theodore: Your fake girlfriend.
Gabriel: Which one is mine again?
Moses: The one who had Slavic sausage for breakfast.
Isobel: Gross.
Cian: The one on the left?
Isobel: Actually, it's the one on the right.
Moses: No wonder they dumped you guys.
Isobel: Did they dump you guys?
Gabriel: No idea. I blocked her number.

Isobel: When?

Gabriel: The day we started fake dating. She texted me good morning. I needed space.

Kilian: Are you going to storm in there and demand to know how long she's been Behind Enemy Lines?

Elijah: You're thinking of Bosnia. The Kozlov twins are from Russia.

Kilian: Oh, so you do remember things.

Elijah: War movies? Yes. Girlfriends? No.

Isobel: Will you remember me?

Theodore: I've never actually seen Eli panic before. Where you at, E? Send us a picture.

Elijah: If you want to be my girlfriend, there are better ways of asking.

Theodore: Who, me?

Elijah: I violently resent the pep in your step this morning.

Theodore: Keep that up and I won't want to be your girlfriend much longer.

Isobel glanced over her phone to the centre row of the auditorium, where Jordan Kostas and Naina Kahn had joined the other humans. Kostas did actually have some experience singing and dancing, now that Isobel thought about it. Not much, but she often put out short videos on social media, singing or participating in dance trends. Plus, she was a model. As far as lumps of clay came, she would be an easy one for Kalen and Mikel to mould. Kahn, on the other hand … made chocolate

79

sculptures. That had nothing to do with being in a performance group.

Isobel surveyed the rest of the auditorium, wondering where the Alphas were, before switching her attention back to her phone.

Isobel: You guys are going to be late to class.

Niko: I'm not coming. Training with Kalen.

She nibbled on her lip, concern spiking inside her chest. Kalen and Mikel had both been spending more private time with Niko lately. Not just him, but also Moses, Theodore, and Oscar. Something had shifted in the dynamics of the group ever since their bond was repaired, but she couldn't put her finger on exactly what it was. The bond itself felt fine, but there was an invisible fissure of tension in the air whenever there was more than one Alpha in the room. Unless it was Gabriel and Elijah together—they seemed fine. Even Theodore and Kilian together seemed a little tense around her. She wanted to ask, but she wasn't sure *what* to ask. She couldn't even adequately describe the feeling.

With a sigh, she flicked through everyone's answers to her question.

Elijah: We're busy this period.

Gabriel: He means he and I are busy.

Elijah: Who else would I mean?

Moses: It's hard to see anyone else when you're in love.

Elijah: Shut up.

Theodore: On my way. Had to stick around while they

were taking the cameras out of my room. I didn't want them
snooping.

Oscar: Afraid they'll find your dirty magazines?

Moses: Sigma Penthouse.

Kilian: Sigma Hustler.

Cian: Sigma Playboy.

Cian: Also, I'm on my way.

Theodore: My tastes go beyond Sigmas.

Isobel: Do they?

Elijah: I've never seen Theo panic before. Send me a
pic, T.

Theodore: Shut up.

Theodore: And yes.

Isobel: What are these tastes?

Kilian: Are you jealous, baby?

Elijah: No, she's fucking with him.

Isobel grinned, tapping away at her phone faster.

Isobel: I'm hurt.

Isobel: The bond stone is probably pure blood red
right now.

Kalen (admin): Can confirm. It is.

Theodore: I know you're fucking with me but the
adrenaline I have right now.

Theodore: Stop it.

Isobel: Make me.

Oscar: Stop flirting in the group chat.

Isobel: That was fighting.

Oscar: As I said.

She rolled her eyes, tucking her phone away and returning her attention to the middle of the auditorium again. Mei Ito and Luca Santoro had joined the rest of the humans. Santoro was another social media performer, she realised. While dancing for a trend wasn't the same as dancing for a career, it did give them some basics, and Mei and Santoro were powerhouses of popularity. They were both already wealthy and could probably bring in outside help to level up their performance skills. If Isobel and the Alphas wanted to stay out of danger and prove to the officials that they were a good investment, they would have to do more than their new contracts stipulated. Their impossible new standard was truly just the bare minimum—it put them on an even playing field with the humans, who already had the support of the outside world, the funds, and the previously established fan bases.

Isobel and the Alphas would have to work twice as hard and be twice as good.

A body dropped into the seat beside her, and she turned to slowly eye her own fake boyfriend. He grinned at her, flicking his head to get a dark curl out of his eyes.

"Hey, babe." His arm fell over the back of her chair. "Was beginning to think you were avoiding me."

She blurted the words without thinking. "Let's break up."

He reared back, staring at her in shock. "Can you do that?" he asked, also without thinking.

She was only just realising why Elijah and Gabriel had shown no reaction to James and Ellis suddenly attaching themselves to other guys. They weren't *allowed* to date anymore.

"I—I mean, what?" Silva started backtracking, realising what he had said. "Why?"

"I signed a contract," she told him. "It's part of the new group rules. We aren't allowed to date anyone."

He looked pissed. His face was turning red, his eyes flashing with a hint of something that had her stomach turning. He had only ever been jovial and good-natured with her, but he *was* still the person who had delivered her a package full of razor blades and attempted some sort of Gifted voodoo magic to bond her.

"Is this a joke?" he asked, leaning closer to her. "Let's go talk in private." He stood and grabbed her arm, trying to pull her out of the chair.

She quickly planted her feet against the back of the chair in front of her, locking up her body. "Let's not?" She laughed awkwardly, trying to keep it casual.

He tugged harder. "Seriously, Sigma—"

Silva was suddenly jerked to the side and tossed into the chair beside her. Moses sat on his other side, holding him to the chair by the neck. Theodore was pulling his arm, trying to pull him out of the chair while Moses held him down.

"*Seriously, Beta,*" Theodore mocked. "Let's just go talk. Somewhere. Private." Each word was accompanied by a yank of Silva's arm until the Beta screamed.

It all happened so quickly that Isobel barely had time to react, and what frightened her the most was that she felt *nothing* from Theodore and Moses. She couldn't even sense a *drop* of the absolute rage that vibrated through their bodies or flashed in their eyes.

She was too shocked to move, or to react, as Moses leaned in close to Silva—as close as Silva had leaned into her. "Why aren't you moving, Beta?" he whispered dangerously. "Just get up."

Theodore pulled harder, and there was an audible *crack*, accompanied by another scream from Silva, who was now trembling in his seat, tears in his eyes.

"S-shit." Her brain finally overrode her shock, and she jumped out of her seat, shoving at Theodore. "Let's go."

He dropped Silva's arm, and she pushed him harder, forcing him back a few steps toward Moses.

"You too," she ordered, glaring at Moses, who scowled and released Silva.

She managed to drag them both out of the auditorium, which had fallen into shocked silence, most of the students too stunned to even pull out their phones.

"What were you *thinking*?" she managed, glaring at both of them. A year ago, she would have been cowering, cracking open her walls to take all their anguish. But she wasn't that person anymore, and they didn't scare her anymore. Well, maybe a little, but not in the same way. She was scared *for* them now.

Theodore and Moses looked at each other, both still sullen and furious but a little sheepish now that Silva was out of their sight. She could also feel them, little sparks of trepidation pattering against her chest.

"He had his hands on y—"

She interrupted Theodore. "Are you okay?"

He winced in answer.

"What's going on here?" Professor Dubois, their teacher for Icon Matters, asked, causing her to spin around and take a swift step away from Theodore and Moses, as though they had been doing something illegal.

It was hard not to be on edge when Processor Dubois was human, one of the few officials who taught at the academy.

"Nothing," Isobel quickly said, but unfortunately, Moses had spoken at the same time.

"Just teaching Mateus Silva that it's not okay to grab people just because he's stronger than them."

"If you're going to attend my class, you'll do it without violence," Professor Dubois lectured snippily, yanking open the auditorium door and disappearing inside a little too fast for the steady threat he had summoned to his voice.

Isobel puffed out a sigh, glancing between Theodore and Moses. "What's going on with you two?"

"We stick together, Illy-stone." Theodore gave her a devastating smile, packing away all his rage in the blink of an eye. "You come for one of us; you come for all of us."

"He wasn't coming for me," she said, though her tone lacked conviction. She felt guilty admitting it, but it was nice to know that someone had put his hands on her and was immediately punished. It felt better than nice. She only wished she had the strength to dish out those kinds of punishments herself.

"Mhm." Moses rolled his eyes, reading something in her expression or perhaps feeling her quiet satisfaction through the bond. "Let's get back inside."

4
REMNANTS

AFTER ICON MATTERS, ISOBEL CAUGHT UP WITH GABRIEL AND
Elijah outside the hall where their Acro Duo class was
usually held. Since the three of them had formed a group
and Professor Lye didn't want to "mess with anyone's
chemistry," they weren't forced into any other pairings
and were allowed to retreat to their corner of the hall to
work on the last choreography assignment they had
been given.

Usually, Gabriel and Elijah could hyper-focus during
tasks like this, no matter how much was going on, but
even they seemed to be a little unsteady. It was once
again so subtle that she couldn't even put it into words,
but she could feel *something*. Something small,
something off. Like a high-pitched ringing or a faint
rattle. She thought she knew it was there, but it was so
faint that she couldn't help second-guessing herself.

Kostas and Santoro, who were also in her Acro Duo class, had paired up and moved to their corner of the hall, putting Isobel on edge. She worked to block them out, as well as Silva, who had partnered with Wallis and positioned himself as far away from Isobel as possible.

She wouldn't allow herself to feel bad for Silva.

He had been blackmailed into posing as her fake boyfriend. He knew exactly what the deal was, and he had no right to be upset that she ended it because "it" wasn't real.

Still, she was a little worried about how he stared at her ... and the sudden, piercing, heated look in his eyes. It reeked of hatred, and it didn't feel stable.

"Did you guys break up with James and Ellis?" she asked as they paused at the end of the choreography to take a quick break, Elijah reaching for his water bottle while Gabriel scrubbed a towel over his face before hanging it on the hook that nobody else was allowed to use.

She deliberately turned her back to Silva.

"This morning," Elijah confirmed. "They were good about it. It wasn't a serious thing with them anyway. We were just having fun."

"They moved on quick." Isobel could still feel Silva's eyes heavy on her back. "They were all over the Kozlov twins in first period—don't the humans have the same no-dating rules as we do?"

"Flirting isn't dating." Gabriel shrugged.

"So, will you keep flirting with them?" she asked ... for the audience's sake.

Not at all for herself.

Elijah arched an elegant brow at her, dropping his water bottle back into his bag and pulling at the neckline of his shirt, trying to get it to stop sticking to his skin. "Do I look like I flirt, Sigma?"

"I could see you flirting," she hedged. "Maybe with a scientific manual of some kind? I could see you stroking its spine by the fireplace, fingering its pages."

He looked amused, so she continued. "I could see you flirting with a documentary on binary code—snuggled in with some wine and fondue."

His firm lips twitched, giving her a flash of the reaction she craved.

"Do I look like I eat fondue?" he asked blandly.

"Did you really just say fingering?" Gabriel interrupted.

Isobel, whose cheeks began to burn, ignored him, keeping her attention on Elijah. "Not fondue. Souls, maybe."

"Souls," he repeated dryly.

"And tears," she added. "And dreams. And hopes."

"Tears and dreams and hopes," he parroted. "Right."

"You look like you'd eat me alive."

When his expression suddenly went blank, she let her smile break free, battering her lashes at him. "That, Mr Reed, is how you flirt."

"How was that flirting?" Gabriel asked, looking unimpressed.

"It's tailored to the person." Isobel looked between a frozen Elijah and a frowning Gabriel. "You *should* be great at it, in theory. Because of your little perception thing."

Gabriel rolled his eyes, but he hadn't made any move to end their break—and that was how Isobel knew she was entertaining him.

"How'd you keep James around, anyway?" she asked him, lifting a brow and planting her hand on her hip. "You don't flirt, you don't fondue."

"*He* doesn't fondue." Gabriel jerked his chin at Elijah.

Isobel scoffed. "You won't even share a hook, and you expect me to believe you'll share a fondue?"

She felt a jolt of adrenaline when Gabriel's lip tipped up slightly at the corner. It was almost as addictive as watching Niko stuff his handsome face with food.

"My personality," Gabriel answered, the tilt to his lip evening out, his expression as frighteningly blank as ever. "That's what kept her around."

"Oh?" Both of Isobel's brows shot up this time. "Can I see it?"

He chuckled, rising suddenly. "Come here, puppy."

She squeaked and tried to run away, but Elijah was there in a second, scooping her up with one arm and carrying her back to their spot like she was nothing more than a ragdoll. "Back to work, Sigma. You can stir up trouble later."

They were growing quite talented at dancing over that line of playfulness for the public. The spectacle of Isobel's close relationships with the Alphas was something the Ironside fans *loved* to debate. Some swore that they were flirting. Others swore it was more of a sibling-like chemistry. Some people claimed she was secretly in love with different Alphas and that different Alphas were secretly in love with her. Many people believed that she was in a secret relationship with one of them, and most of the internet was divided over who it could be.

They were getting more and more attention, clips of them regularly going viral. They needed to encourage the momentum and stoke the fire ... but never push it too far. It was their job to keep the fans guessing, to keep playing along that line, never resting in the middle for too long. They couldn't be *too* flirty or *too* platonic. It had to be both and neither at all times.

She ducked into the bathrooms to change after class because she was too sweaty after the acrobatic partner dance they had been rehearsing. She headed to the dining hall during the short morning break to grab another coffee, knowing she would find Cian there. He utilised most academy breaks to dose up on caffeine.

He picked up his head as soon as she entered the hall, glancing at the entrance before reaching for a second takeaway cup. She sidled up to him, looping her arm through his and leaning into his body.

"Tired?" he asked, ducking his head to catch sight of her expression. "You smell like you worked hard."

She stiffened slightly. "I smell bad?"

He chuckled. "I didn't say that." And then his voice dropped into her head. *I'm addicted to the scent of your sweat.*

Finally, someone who knows how to flirt, she responded.

He laughed out loud, almost spitting out the sip of coffee he had taken. After wiping his mouth, he extracted himself from her and gripped her chin, tilting her head up so that he could read her better. "You went to your acro class, right?"

For a moment, she was confused, and then she realised he was asking if she was sweaty from exercise or something else.

"What?" She nervously swatted his hand from her chin. "Of course. Is this mine?" She glanced at the second cup.

"Who else?" He smirked and handed it to her, and they made their way out of the hall. "Are you coming to class or going to see Teak?"

Isobel checked her phone. Teak had been sick and unable to attend their last few sessions. "She hasn't cancelled yet, so I guess she's finally better?"

"I'll walk you there." Cian dropped his arm over her

shoulders, steering her toward the family centre, which was just a small building attached to the restricted area of the academy. He left her at the row of hedges sectioning off the administration area, and she entered the room with semi-private booths inside, all of them with a computer to video call families back home.

The room was empty. It often was because, of course, the majority of settlement homes weren't set up with webcams and fast Wi-Fi, or smartphone plans. Past the row of booths was a door to a few private meeting rooms. She knocked at the one she was supposed to meet with Teak in, and the door opened to reveal the bond specialist.

She looked *terrible*. Her usual dusky-rose skin tone had a strange, sickly pallor, her eyes dull, and her lips pulled down.

"Isobel," she sounded numb, "please, come in."

"If you're still sick, we can—"

"Sit, sit." Teak waved her off, sinking into one of the armchairs, her posture loose and exhausted. There were a bunch of used tissues bundled onto the table beside her, and the light in the room was off. As soon as Teak sat down, the sunlight from the window spilled over her expression—pallid and red, splotched and swollen. Had she been ... crying?

Teak forced a wobbly smile, that dull, dead look still in her eyes. "Congratulations on signing with Orion," she said, the sincerity in her tone forced. "You and the Alphas have had quite an impact on Ironside—I don't think anyone has ever managed to persuade them to change the rules before. Certainly not in their favour."

"I'm not sure it's entirely in our favour," Isobel replied carefully, Teak's strange countenance making her nervous. The nerves slowly turned into fear, prickling along her skin. She didn't know what was happening, but she didn't like it. "We'll be forfeiting most of our earnings."

"Better than your lives." Teak's emotionless smile was ... frightening.

"Where's Charlie?" Isobel asked hesitantly. Usually, Teak's partner sat in on their sessions.

Teak's expression spasmed slightly. "She caught what I had. She's sick. Why don't we speak freely, Isobel? Have you fully formed the bond with all the Alphas?"

"Don't tell her anything," a voice whispered, making Isobel's eyes widen, her head turning slowly to the side, fear and dread swamping her. It was suddenly hard for her to breathe.

Charlie.

Charlie?

The Beta woman was suddenly leaning up against the wall behind Teak. She was dressed in cotton pyjamas, her silver-ringed, dark eyes sad. Her darkly tanned skin still appeared to have the flush of life, her short, dark hair still bouncing and shining. Her silver piercings, scattered along her lobes, her nose and her eyebrow, should have been glinting in the sun that shone through the window, slanting over her expression. But they weren't. Isobel had no idea why that detail stuck in her head.

Charlie was ...

"Isobel?" Teak prompted, her eyes narrowing slightly. She couldn't see Charlie.

She couldn't hear Charlie.

She would never see or hear Charlie again ... because Charlie ... was dead.

"Don't tell her anything," Charlie reiterated quietly.

Isobel took one deep breath, and then another, carefully packing away her grief and panic, treating it so delicately it could have been a bomb she was attempting to diffuse. She stared at her knees and spoke slowly, her voice sounding garbled to her own ears, like she was trying to listen to the sound from underwater. "Why?"

Charlie and Teak spoke at the same time.

"Because your session is being recorded," Charlie whispered.

"Because I can't do my job if you aren't honest with me," Teak said.

"She's completely under their control," Charlie rushed out. "They've been sending her pieces of ..." She wavered, her face contorting, and then suddenly she was gone.

Isobel's hands were numb as she clasped them in her lap, still unable to lift her eyes. *Holy shit.*

Her mother took Charlie's place, standing there with a quiet, empathetic look on her face.

"You're okay, Illy," she whispered.

"I don't want to talk about it," Isobel choked out, overwhelmed.

"I'll stay with you," her mother promised. "You can do this."

"You have to," Teak snapped, pulling in a sharp, wobbly breath, her tone suddenly changing. Suddenly desperate. "Please, Isobel, just—" She cut herself off, suddenly laughing. "What am I doing?"

Isobel looked up, seeing the hysteria, the devastation, the madness in the other woman's eyes. She reached out to Teak with her ability, but the hungry, awful void that loomed at her from the other side of the room was too vast, too horrific, too monstrous. Even if she only took a little, it would make no difference, so she built her wall back up again, more solidly than was really necessary, twisting her shaking fingers together. The feeling was too familiar, too triggering.

She could almost feel Niko on the other end of that void, being ruthlessly sawed from her soul as pieces of her hair fell around her prone body, brushing against her skin with the softness of feathers, yet somehow feeling like razor blades.

"Pack it away," her mother whispered.

So she did.

"Are you on medication?" she managed to ask, her throat tight. "For your illness?"

She wasn't sure if Teak was the anchor or the tether in her bond, but if she was the tether, she would die without the surrogate pills. Even if she was the anchor, she would be forever changed. Isobel knew that look in her eyes. She had seen it in Niko. In her father.

Teak had lost her bond and was falling through the darkness with no end in sight. The fall would twist her and the darkness would taint her—and that was only if she lived.

Isobel almost lost control of her emotions, then, but managed to wrangle them back, shoving them down. Teak was staring at her like she *knew* there was a second meaning to her question.

She searched Isobel's face and then finally nodded. "I ... am. I have medication. Don't worry about me."

Teak was the tether. She was taking the surrogate pills.

The officials could be using them to control her and using Charlie's death to torture her. *What would happen if she proved useless in these sessions with Isobel?*

"We formed the bond," Isobel finally said, after considering the situation. It wasn't ideal that she couldn't discuss this with the Alphas first since it impacted all of them, but she couldn't just walk out of the meeting. She couldn't do anything to tip off the officials that she was aware she was being recorded, or that Teak was under their control. Teak would likely be punished—and there wasn't much more they could take from the bond specialist except her life.

Isobel couldn't let that happen.

She owed her *life* to Teak, and the lives of her mates. She had to do what she could to protect the other woman and what remained of her life, as painful an existence as it may be now.

Teak began to shake her head, almost like she was pleading with Isobel suddenly not to talk, but Isobel continued anyway.

"We didn't need to scar each other, so there are no bond marks," she lied carefully. She wasn't an expert on bond magic, but giving them a tangible target on her body to harm the bond seemed like a bad idea. They had already cut into her veins and cut off her hair. She didn't want them going for her tattoos next. "Eve Indie stole pieces of our bond before it was formed, and when those pieces were returned to me, the bond just magically completed without us having to do anything at all."

Teak knew she was lying.

"A-and what s-side effects are you getting?" Teak stumbled, reading something off her phone like she had a list of questions she had been given and she needed to remind herself.

"None," Isobel lied again.

"You can't hear each other's thoughts? Feel each other's emotions?"

"I guess we have a better sense of each other, but we can't read each other's minds or anything. I guess because the bond was damaged before it was formed, we didn't get many of the benefits."

"Have you been tampering with the cameras?" Teak asked suddenly. She was gaining back the smallest note of confidence in her voice, perhaps realising that Isobel was lying.

"No?" Isobel arched a brow. "What do you mean? Like turning them to face the other way or something?"

Teak didn't specify her question, moving on to a new one. "You don't seem to have much alone time with any of the Alphas, like Theodore Kane or Cian Ashford, even less since you moved in with them."

Isobel shrugged, her body stiff. "We have this bond, but we're not in relationships or anything. We're literally just a group of friends. The only difference is that we can't be away from each other, or I'll get sick. I haven't needed to sleep beside them or anything now that I live with them because I'm always around them."

"So you're not romantically involved with any of them? Not even Theodore? Or Cian? Or Oscar?"

Isobel forced her eyes to roll, a soft scoff leaving her lips. *Damn*, her acting skills really had improved. "No, we just flirt for the cameras sometimes to spice things up.

We're close friends, but nothing more than that. Our focus is winning the game. We can't afford to be distracted."

Tears were falling freely down Teak's cheeks, but she nodded, encouraging Isobel to continue. "And you haven't had any side effects since you came to France and formed the bond?"

"None at all." Isobel finally allowed her eyes to wander, crawling over the wall-mounted shelf behind Teak. It was the only place they would have been able to hide cameras, possibly tucked behind one of the ivy plants, and if one was placed up there, it would have a clear view of her, but it wouldn't be able to see Teak very well.

She flicked her attention back to the bond specialist, not daring to examine the shelf for too long. Teak was reading her phone again. "So you're really going to try and win as a group?" she asked. "This isn't a tactic of some kind?"

"Well, it can't be." Isobel forced a laugh. "We signed a contract. But no, there's no alternative plan. We're out of options," she said honestly. "Obviously, going home to separate settlements after graduation isn't possible with the bond. We have to win, and we have to do it as a group. We're all in on Orion. We *will* win. We'll be the biggest thing Ironside ever produced, and after all of this is over, they'll be thanking us. They'll never want to let us go."

Teak nodded, some of the tension leaking from her shoulders, though she was also still leaking tears. "You don't think you'll want to settle down at any point?" she asked. She looked so pale, even a little green, like she was about to be sick. "Choose one of your mates to marry? Have kids?"

"Not interested," Isobel said firmly. "It's not like that with any of them. We don't want romance; we want to be famous. We want to make money, not babies. Besides, our contract forbids all of that." She waved her hand, diminishing it to a non-issue.

She bluffed and acted her way through the rest of Teak's questions before saying her goodbyes and walking calmly all the way to Lyrical Dance, her second lesson with Professor Lye for the day. She joined Theodore and Kilian along the side of the room as Lye introduced their guest choreographer. Both Alphas immediately frowned at her, sensing her muted turmoil even though she had put in significant effort to push it down. She had finally come around to accepting the fact that ever since fixing the bond with Niko, she had lost the ability to block them from her emotions completely—and they had gained the ability to block her flawlessly. She subtly shook her head at them, indicating she didn't want to talk about it.

Not yet.

She couldn't even allow herself to think about it. All the lies she had told would be for nothing if she couldn't hold it together long enough to make herself appear unaffected for the rest of the day.

She repeated the same subtle shake of her head as they all took seats in the auditorium for Influencer Intensive. Professor Chen started his presentation without any sort of introduction—the man was another human official, and he didn't like to waste time.

Every one of the Alphas had turned up to class this time, and usually, she sat somewhere in the middle of the group, with them all guarding her from every angle. Now that they were being more relaxed about security, they had deliberately spread out. Elijah, Gabriel, and Niko were in the row of seats ahead of her, Kilian, Cian, and Theodore. Oscar and Moses were sitting behind them with an empty row in between, their feet up on the backs of the chairs. Their group reserved the entire left wing of the auditorium as though an invisible boundary had been drawn.

Theodore had been sticking to her like glue for over an hour now. He wasn't throwing her concerned glances or asking her questions, but he was always touching her in small, subtle ways. She had become drenched in his scent, warmed by the constant heat of his body hovering over her.

As usual, the human group sat centre stage in the middle section, spreading out along the front row with their chosen fan girls and boys for the period.

Should we have a meeting over lunch? Elijah's voice echoed through the bond.

She considered it before biting her lip and replying. *No, but tonight. We have to keep things casual. The officials can't see me doing anything out of the ordinary.*

What the hell happen— Moses began to question, but Elijah quickly cut him off, a subtle note of command carrying along his tone.

Don't ask.

Isobel flinched slightly, blinking her eyes. She was sure that if the words had been spoken out loud, they would have been in Alpha voice.

ELIJAH DIDN'T LIKE NOT KNOWING THINGS, BUT BEING ABLE TO feel the sickening mix of grief, fear, and nausea that poured through the bond from Isobel and not having the slightest idea what put it there was an unfamiliar brand of torture. He pulled up her location history and casually retraced her steps during lunch, slotting in headphones so that nobody would disturb him and he could pretend he was just going for a walk.

Slowly, the picture came together.

Teak had called in sick for weeks, but today she finally turned up.

The officials had gotten to her somehow—in a devastating way if Isobel's emotions were anything to go by. This could only mean that the officials knew about the text message Teak sent last month. They knew Teak had warned them and saved their lives.

And they had taken revenge.

They would use Teak now that she had earned Isobel's trust by saving her life. They would monitor Isobel's sessions, using Teak to get information about their bond.

He felt a little jolt of pride at the intelligence of his mate, who had obviously figured it out and was acting accordingly. There was a lot he liked about the Sigma, but he *respected* her ability to keep a cool head, and respect wasn't something he gave out easily.

Of course, there were also plenty of things he didn't like about her. Namely, the way she kept fucking Theodore, Kilian, and Cian.

He didn't like that at all.

He pulled out his headphones and headed to the music room for sixth period. Luckily, it was his private piano lesson with Isobel, so he didn't have to spend another hour guessing at her state of mind. They were all now splitting their sixth and seventh periods into private or small group sessions. Elijah usually tutored Isobel for an hour, and then Mikel took her and a few others for private vocal lessons. Now that Kalen and Mikel were both training the human group as well, their time had grown more scarce, but they were managing to balance things.

For now.

"Sorry, I'm late." Isobel shook the light spattering of rain from her coat before hanging it up by the door.

Elijah blinked, glancing at the window. *When had the weather changed?* It had been a perfectly clear day only ten minutes ago.

He pulled out his phone, sending a quick message to Mikel.

Elijah: Is this you?

"Let's get started." He gave her a short smile, trying to put her at ease.

It didn't work. She was deep into her own head.

He checked for a reply on his phone.

Mikel: Fucking Tilda won't stop texting me.

It was one thing for some of the more volatile Alphas to feel unbalanced from the damaged bond, but Mikel usually had better control. This didn't bode well.

Elijah: What does she want?

Isobel dropped onto the piano stool, glancing up at the sheet music he had set out for her—the same song they worked on last week.

His phone vibrated again, but this time, Mikel had sent through an image. A screenshot of the messages he had been ignoring for days, according to the timestamps.

Tilda: Were you fucking your student while you were fucking me?

Tilda: You're a disgusting pervert.

Tilda: I know you were fucking her.

Tilda: Did she dress up in a little schoolgirl costume for you?

Tilda: Did you spank her naughty, slutty little ass?

Tilda: You know you could never play with the Sigma like you played with me.

Elijah's brows jumped up. *Okay then.* He texted Mikel back.

Elijah: What the fuck is she trying to do?

Mikel: She's trying to restart our relationship.

Elijah: She's going a weird way about it.

Mikel: She's going the perfect way about it. Or at least she would be if I had any interest in her.

As Isobel lifted her hands to the keys, Elijah noticed her fingers shaking. He checked the Eleven app, making sure the cameras were deactivated the way they were supposed to be, before he set his hands on her shoulders, pulling her back against his thighs. Her head fell to rest against the hard planes of his stomach, momentarily arresting him as he watched the silky slide of her pretty golden hair brushing across the dark material of his pants.

He kept his grip deliberately light on her shoulders, even though he wanted to gather up her hair and tug her head further back. Far enough to bend her pretty spine.

If she was his, he could distract her from these awful emotions in a matter of minutes. She would still end the session in tears, though.

Unfortunately, she wasn't his—or at least not *just*

his, or at least not "his" outside of their souls being tied together—and she wasn't ready for that sort of thing. She needed softness and comfort, and not just as part of aftercare.

Softness and comfort weren't his forte. He wasn't even sure if they were in his repertoire.

Say something, dickhead.

"Close your eyes," he murmured.

He didn't check to see if she had obeyed. The sound of his voice had her body softening, her head turning slightly like she wanted to nuzzle up against him. Her scent was a cherry tree stripped bare, fruit turning sour, brittle branches stripped of their coat. It was peeled bark and bleeding sap, overpowering her usual sweetness. He smoothed his hands along the tight black cotton of her crop top to the edges of the sleeves that were capped right at the tipping point of her dainty shoulders.

Her sigh was devastated.

Kilian would have asked if there was any way to help her.

Theodore would have distracted her with his stupid smile.

Cian would have fucked her on top of the piano.

What could Elijah possibly give her that she wasn't already getting somewhere else?

He dug in his fingers, massaging away the tension lining her muscles. He knew she liked this, at least. Her blissful, torturous reactions to Mikel's ministrations every morning after their small group sessions had been taunting him for a while now. Her head rolled back against his stomach, threatening to distract him again with the brush of her hair over his thighs. He wasn't sure why that was such an erotic sight, but it filled him with fantasies of pushing her between his legs while he sat at his desk, and without warning, he was suddenly thinking about shoving into her throat and how she would gag and cry, and garble pleas for him to be kinder and gentler with her—like one of her other boyfriends would be.

His cock began to harden, and he dragged himself back to reality. That was the only comfort he could conceive of giving her, and it wasn't comforting at all, only a distraction. Probably an unwelcome one too. This was exactly why he hadn't pushed their relationship past the point of friendship, despite the kiss they had shared and the memory of her sweet little pussy clenching around his fingers.

He was too fucked up.

All he knew how to give was sex and dominance.

Here she was, broken and devastated, and he was thinking about fucking it out of her.

But the massage seemed to be helping, so he smoothed out every niggle of tension he could reach in the graceful line of her neck, the top of her spine, and the span of her shoulders, manipulating her into pliancy.

He wasn't sure when she began to cry, but it started

so softly, so silently. He waited for her to speak, but she didn't seem able, and when her cries turned into sobs, he quickly pulled her off the stool and into his arms. She wrapped her legs around his waist, climbing his body, her arms clinging tightly, her head burrowing into his neck, immediately soaking his shirt. She didn't seem to care that he wasn't soft and caring. She just took what she needed as he stood there stiffly, holding her up. She used his body for warmth, used his neck to soak her tears, and his scent to comfort herself.

His heart *hurt*, thumping with awkward, painful, audible *thuds* in his chest. Something about the fragile, vulnerable tremble in her limbs and the quiet, keening sorrow she tried to muffle against his skin had him almost unravelling.

"Did they hurt Teak?" he asked quietly, flattening her as tightly to his body as he could. Probably hurting her.

She nodded, barely.

"C-Charlie is d-dead. I s-saw her. They were recording the s-session."

Fuck.

Elijah fell to the piano stool. She clung tighter, hiking higher up his body, like she could somehow crawl inside him and live there, safe from the rest of the world. Like she thought he was the kind of person who could keep her safe.

"Shit," he said softly. "How is she—surrogate pills, of course. They must be using the supply to control her. You did so well, sweet girl. You probably saved her life today."

What life there was left to save. He couldn't say it out loud.

"This is all our fault," she wailed, slamming her fist against his back. She didn't even seem to realise she did it.

"Warning us was her choice," Elijah said calmly. "We didn't force her to do that. She did the brave thing. The right thing. We'll figure out how to help her."

"My father could help her," Isobel hiccupped, apparently delusional with grief. "I could make a deal with him."

"Absolutely not." Elijah tried to pull back to see her face, but she wouldn't let him.

"I don't need your permission," she huffed, voice muffled.

"What deal could you possibly offer him?" Elijah deliberately reeled in his influence, pulling it carefully back like a string, one handspan at a time, until he was sure he wasn't smothering her in Alpha dominance, and his tone sounded reasonable.

It wasn't easy.

"I don't know." She hit his back again, devolving into an immature fit. He liked that she felt safe enough with him to just give up on all pretence of control over her body and emotions, but a part of him also wondered if she was doing it deliberately because it made his cock

twitch and his hand itch to spank her in return for each
little blow.

No, she wasn't that devious.

Not yet, anyway.

"He always wants something," she said, still in a huff,
still annoyed that he had dared to try and talk sense into
her. "I've never had the upper hand before, but now I do.
He has an *illegal* ability. He was involved in a double
homicide back in his home settlement. He took away my
mother's memory of me so that she had nothing left to
live for, and she *died*—" She cut herself off with a
choking noise. "I know everything. His Alpha voice
doesn't work on me anymore. I have you guys. The bond
made me stronger, made it so that I can resist him now. I
have the upper hand," she insisted.

He loosened a breath, his lungs filling with her scent.
It wasn't any sweeter, but it had lost the damaged edge.
She was determined now. She wasn't going to wallow in
helplessness for long. That wasn't her. *Why did her
bullheadedness make her* so *fucking attractive?*

"I'm not sure I'd call that the upper hand," he said,
not even realising as his hand slipped through the silky
mess of her hair to cradle her skull. "But it definitely
changes the dynamic. And I don't think the bond has
made you resistant to his Alpha voice. I think half of your
mates could overpower him in Alpha dominance, and
since you're our mate, you can also resist him. You'll
probably be able to resist other Alphas weaker than us,

as well. But that's just my theory. He still hasn't tried to make contact with you?"

She pulled back, her hands slipping to his chest. "No ... I ..." Her eyes were unfocussed, her forehead crinkled in confusion. "I ..."

Isobel wasn't in the music room anymore, cuddled into Elijah's lap, his strong hand cupping her skull.

She was ... in a car ... and it was hurtling toward the edge of a cliff. There was a screaming boy in the passenger seat and a sobbing woman in the driver's seat.

"Mom! Please! Please stop!" the boy begged, pulling desperately at the door handle. It somehow snapped off in his hand, and his terror swelled like a physical thing, expanding inside the car until it shivered across the windows and rattled the back of Isobel's teeth.

"Mom!" he wailed.

She closed her eyes, trying to pull herself from the too-real vision.

It's not real. It's not real. It's not—

"What the fuck?" Cian's voice interrupted her internal chant.

She blinked her eyes open again and found herself standing beside the car as it teetered on the edge of the cliff.

All ten of the Alphas had been pulled into the vision

with her—almost like a punishment for her trying to escape.

"What kind of sadistic fucking side effect is this?" Gabriel spluttered, staring at the little boy desperately clawing at the car window. The car was about to go over. Theodore jolted forward, but Cian caught his arm, shaking his head.

"It's not real," Elijah said softly.

"It's my memory." Cian's eyes were wide with horror, fixed on the car as the woman finally turned and spoke to the boy, and he wound down the window, climbing out.

"Now you," he called back through the window, doing a small bounce on his feet that screamed of uncontainable panic. "Mom, hurry! Please!"

She didn't move. She just stared at him, her hands on the wheel, tears falling fresh, a strange sort of finality descending over her features.

Her mouth opened, and the car creaked, jolting violently forward before tipping over the edge. The boy chased it to the edge, falling onto his knees and screaming down into the valley below.

Cian's face was ashen, his breathing choppy as the little boy grabbed handfuls of grass and dirt, slamming his fists into the ground and screaming, "No!" over and over and over, until his body was depleted. And then he just sat there, aquamarine eyes full of water, golden skin smudged with dirt.

"I would have forgiven you," he cried. "It would have been okay, Mom. You didn't have to. You didn't have to."

Isobel didn't know what to do or say. It was too much, too sudden. They all seemed to be in complete shock. Not even Moses had a sarcastic comment about the sadism of the bond—or the gods, whoever was driving this. She tried to move to Cian's side—the real Cian—but with her first step, the vision wavered and faded, replaced by Elijah's cold eyes, now wide with shock and dismay.

"We've got a lot to talk about tonight," he rasped out.

5
DEAR PERVERT

THEY LOUNGED AROUND MIKEL'S OFFICE, SILENCE PERMEATING the room. They were all exhausted, talked out, and still a little shellshocked. Nobody had been expecting to hear that Charlie had died, and they were already on edge after the vision of Cian's childhood from that afternoon.

There was an immense relief hanging about the room that they finally had a modicum of privacy back and that their safety seemed secure for the time being, but that relief felt dirty—like something they had stolen, or like they had traded the horrible events of the afternoon for it. It was hard to shake the feeling that they were expected to live in the shadow of trauma and hardship and that anything else was wrong or forbidden.

"I really fucking hope the bond doesn't do me next," Gabriel muttered from behind the rim of his glass. The statement came out of nowhere.

They were all drinking. It had been that kind of day.

The others didn't laugh, and Isobel was pretty sure it wasn't a joke.

She also hoped she wasn't next.

"We were so careful," Mikel murmured, apparently still thinking about Charlie as he stared into his glass, swirling the dark-red liquid around. They were drinking wine out of fancy whiskey glasses because that was all he had in his office.

They fell into silence again, and Isobel took a deep swallow of the rich, fragrant wine, trying her best to numb her frayed nerves. She was halfway through her third glass—because to hell with that two-drink clause —when her phone vibrated, and she had to blink a few times to focus on the screen.

Cooper: Your first dance in the Dahlia Room is in two nights. Have you finished the choreography? I need to approve it.

She groaned, her head falling back against the seat of the couch behind her, right between Kilian's legs. She was stretched out along the floor, Theodore beside her, his arm thrown over his eyes. He could have been asleep for all she knew, but he moved his arm as they all glanced at her.

"I have to show Cooper my choreography," she whined. "For the performance on Friday."

"What have you got so far?" Mikel asked, still staring into his glass.

"I'll show you." She jumped up and stumbled over to the oak coffee table, stepping onto it and taking another sip of wine.

Moses, who was leaning against the wall beside the door, motioned to her glass. "You wanna put that down first?"

"Um." She thought about it. "No. So anyway, I'll start like this. No, like this. No ..." She laughed, clicking her fingers. "That's right. I don't have a dance yet. I don't *do* 'provocative and entertaining, sensual but tasteful,'" she mocked, imitating Yulia's accented voice. She flipped an imaginary, sleek ponytail over her shoulder for extra effect. Kalen smirked, and that was everything she needed because he was the one Yulia had been devouring with her thieving eyes.

Moses burst into laughter.

"Thieving eyes?" Theodore taunted from the floor, his teeth flashing in a brief show of humour.

"What?" She glanced around the room. "Did I say that out loud?"

"Didn't you?" Cian looked confused.

"I don't think so?" She froze, her hand gripping the whiskey glass even harder.

First Cian's memory, and now ... *they were hearing her thoughts again?*

"Oh boy," Oscar groaned. "Please don't think about Kalen's dick again."

"*Why would you bring that up right now?*" she

117

seethed, spinning rapidly to face the dark-eyed agent of chaos. He was sitting against Mikel's now-empty liquor cabinet with Niko, who was wincing as he stared at her feet, his entire body tensed like he thought she was about to topple off the table. "Why am I having side effects again?" she demanded. "We completed the bond."

They were suddenly all very interested in their glasses.

It was Kalen who finally spoke up.

"We think Eve permanently damaged the bond. With Niko separated from us, taking on all the pain and trauma, the bond was almost perfect, like cutting off a dying limb to preserve the body. When he was brought back into the fold, he brought the poison back with him. So to speak."

"H-how can you tell?" She frowned, glancing between Niko and Kalen.

"We can all feel it," Kalen told her, approaching the coffee table. He held his hand out.

She guessed she was making them all nervous.

She didn't take his hand, choosing to frown at him instead. "I can't feel anything."

"We didn't want you to, so we somehow cut you off from it, just like how Niko did when the bond was damaged."

"That's not fair." She folded her arms, glaring at him. Even standing on the coffee table, she still couldn't look down on him. The low table just made them *almost* the same height.

"Ten against one says it is." Moses sounded far too nonchalant.

"Can you all still hear my thoughts?" she asked.

Kalen nodded.

She imagined flicking Moses on the nose. In her imagination, she was standing on a bigger coffee table, so she was taller than him.

It was *very* emasculating.

Kilian spluttered out a laugh. Kalen's warm, amber eyes shone in amusement, but he was too mature to laugh. So she imagined flicking him on the nose as well, just to knock him down a peg or two.

He dropped his hand, arching a calm, challenging brow at her, some of his influence briefly brushing up against her like a tiny swell of power that he quickly worked to rein back in. "If you won't come down, then show us what you have so far. We can help."

She gave him the finger. "This is what I have so far."

"You're pushing it, princess."

She grinned, taking another swig of wine. It was *so much better* to be drunk than sad and afraid. They should do this every night. Or at least once a week. Wine party Wednesdays.

"We literally just signed a legal contract promising not to have more than two drinks at a time," Gabriel drawled, though he was watching her with a tinge of amusement—though a tinge of anything was an absolute outpouring of emotion for him.

"Hey," he protested. "I'm very expressive." This was said with a completely blank face.

"How long is this going to last?" She groaned, knocking her fist against her head. "I'll take requests," she decided. "We can decide the dance that way." She spun to face Cian, who was slumped back into the couch beside Kilian, his tattooed arms folded behind his head. "You first. Because trauma."

"Hey," Moses protested. "I have trauma."

She imagined flicking him in the forehead.

"Do it one more time," he threatened.

"Do what?" She played dumb, still facing Cian, who chuckled.

"Since you're taking requests," Cian drawled, his tone low.

Kilian shoved him before he could finish the sentence. "Don't even."

Cian hid his smile behind his hand as he rubbed along his mouth. "What, now you can hear my thoughts too?"

"We don't need powers for that." Kilian rolled his eyes.

"Fine." Cian bit his lip, folding his arms behind his head again. "How about I pick the song, will that help?"

"Yeah!" Isobel gave him a thumbs-up, trying to drain the rest of her glass. It was empty. Disappointing.

Kalen cooly snatched it from her hand before returning to lean against the desk beside Mikel.

"Provocative and entertaining," she muttered to herself as Cian scrolled through his playlist. "Sensual, but tasteful." *Like Kilian.*

"Why, thank you." Kilian smirked at her.

She waved him off, trying to focus. "Okay, I've got this."

Cian started a song. She had no idea what it was, and she decided to try a spin, just to test how drunk she was before she started dancing. She wasn't sure what went wrong, but she was suddenly tilting sideways, two strong arms catching her and smacking her against a broad, muscled chest hard enough to bruise.

"*Umph,*" she puffed out, clutching the shirt of the Alpha, who had apparently caught her mid-fall.

Niko.

"Damn, you're fast," she said, shocked.

"Damn, you're drunk." He set her on her feet, his hands anchored to her hips. His grip flexed before he released her, stumbling back to the cabinet and falling to the ground again.

He looked pretty drunk himself.

"Can confirm," he drawled, picking up his glass to salute her.

She tried to salute him back, but realised her hand was empty. She tucked her hand behind her back. They probably didn't see it.

"We saw," Theodore countered.

She stalked over to him and flicked him in the head. He grabbed her wrist, and she stared at his long fingers wrapping her pale skin.

"Why would I imagine you catching me?" she complained.

"How are you this drunk from three glasses?" He peered into her face, tugging her a step closer.

"This has happened before." Gabriel sounded like he was wincing, even though she couldn't see his face since he and Elijah sat on the couches behind her. "Last time we all drank, she seemed to take on our inebriation."

Theodore's eyes had trailed from her face, his grip on her wrist slackening, his attention fixing to the hem of her dress, which he probably had a straight view up from his position on the floor.

"Oops, sorry." She scooted back, smoothing down the material, which was a thick, ribbed cotton, so there was nothing to smooth. It was just a comfortable, lounge-around dress she had pulled on after her shower.

She returned to the coffee table and stepped back up, causing Niko to groan in frustration.

"It was so much easier to swing from some ropes." She toed the table's wooden surface with her socked feet, pouting and ignoring Niko. The slippery socks probably weren't helping their nerves.

"I would argue it was harder," Kalen murmured.

"Please don't bring up your dick while we're still in her head," Moses griped.

Isobel ignored them because her phone had vibrated again. Cooper had sent her a link to a video.

Cooper: How about something like this?

"Why is that fuck texting you at midnight?" Oscar demanded roughly.

"Because we're still in a 'meeting,'" Elijah returned, though he also sounded pissed off. "So he knows she's still awake."

The video was a pole dance. There was nothing "sensual but tasteful" about it, though it had the provocative part down. Oscar was making a scary sound in the back of his throat. Isobel ignored them and all their alpha-ness as she studied the video with a frown. *Physically*, she could do it, but it was a little too restrictive for her tastes. There were only so many moves you could do on a pole.

"Don't even think about it," Oscar snapped. "You're not grinding on a pole for that disgusting pervert."

"It would be easier to think with wine," she said, eyeing the bottle on Mikel's desk. He shifted his position, blocking it from view.

She imagined flicking his cheek.

His hand flexed around his drink, and she quickly looked away. Except now she was staring at Oscar, and he had murder screaming from the depths of his dark eyes.

She swallowed again. "Jeez, okay, I'll text him and tell him no."

She tapped out a quick message.

"You sent that to me," Cian stated dryly. "And you misspelled 'asshole.'"

"She called Cooper an asshole?" Kilian sat up straighter.

Cian lifted his phone and read the message out loud. "Dear Pervent, the ashholes said I'm not allowed, but even if I was, I'd rather you shove that pole somewhere not sensual or tasteful."

"Let's just ..." Kilian jumped up and plucked the phone out of her hand. "You can have this back later." He slipped it into his pocket and returned to the couch.

Isobel folded her arms, scrunching up her face. "Anything else you all want to confiscate?"

"I can think of something," Theodore rumbled, staring at the hem of her dress again, like he was still thinking about the peek he had gotten before.

She considered giving him another one.

He made a strangled sound in the back of his throat, his eyes dripping with heat.

"And you can stop *that* right the fuck now," Moses snapped, his eyes darkening with fury, his voice taking on a sharp, unsteady edge.

Whoa.

She held up her hands to him because even in her inebriated state, she knew that look. She hadn't seen it for a while, though, so it was confusing to have the hints of his ferality suddenly surging to the surface. She had thought he was gaining more control over it.

"I thought so too," he gravelled out. "But it turns out it was just the settled bond—which is no longer fucking settled."

"Shit." She jumped down from the table, shifting from foot to foot, unsure what to do. "Sorry."

"For what?" He dragged his hands down his face, forcing his chest to move with measured breaths. "You didn't drag us into your head. We all know you're fucking Theo. You guys aren't quiet *or* discreet."

"I thought we agreed it was my decision who I was intimate with," she snapped, feeling the heat of shame briefly brush her cheeks.

"I figured you'd have meek, quiet Sigma sex." He narrowed his eyes on her, seemingly regaining control of himself.

"Liar." She glared back at him and then deliberately recalled the time he and Cian had pulled her into a classroom supply closet, where Moses himself had almost fucked her, before driving into the back of her throat to come.

"Oh my god, my eyes," Theodore wailed, rolling onto his front and banging his head against the floor, punctuating each knock of his forehead with a muffled shout. "WHAT. THE. FUCK!"

Oscar strode over to the desk and snatched up the

wine bottle, his hands shaking as he tipped it to his mouth, drowning what was left.

"I'm going for a run," he announced, storming out of the room.

Mikel and Kalen were blank faced, but the rest of them looked like they wanted to tear out their own eyeballs.

Except for Moses and Cian. Cian's eyes were heavy-lidded, his tongue poking out to play with his lip piercing. All the fight had drained out of Moses and a new heat was flaring to life, his throat working, his jaw clenched. He looked like he was about to toss her over his shoulder and drag her off to his room where they could finish their battle of wills.

"I'm considering it," he rasped.

"Let's call it," Elijah suggested. "We've had too much to drink, and we have to be up in six hours."

Isobel blinked, swivelling her head from side to side like she needed to shake out of a trance. She looked woefully at the empty wine bottle on Mikel's desk before releasing a mournful, dramatic sigh. "I guess a wine party has to end when there's no wine left."

"Why don't you leave first, Carter?" Mikel was suddenly beside her, steering her to the door, his hand hot against the curve of her spine. "I need a quick word with the others."

"I thought I was the one stopping them from going feral," she whispered to him beneath her breath. "I thought I was controlling it all with my ability. I thought I was getting stronger. Now I feel dumb."

He paused at the door, and even though his fingers were light against her spine, the heat from his palm was spearing through her dress. "You help more than you know."

She thumped her forehead against the door. It was nice and cool. Maybe she should just rest there for a little while. Mikel suddenly flattened his hand properly to her spine, the pressure of it amazing. Because of their morning sessions, her muscles twitched, automatically expecting him to work out their kinks, and she pressed back a little, waiting for his magic fingers to go to work.

"Go to bed, pet." The words were whispered against her hairline. "Before you get yourself into trouble."

"I'll flick you," she threatened feebly.

His hand flashed up, gathering her hair into a ponytail and tugging her head from the door, and back, and back, until she could see the silent, stony command in his mismatched eyes. She swallowed hard, and then squeaked, "Goodnight."

He released her immediately and she raced off to her room.

OSCAR RAN UNTIL HE WAS SOAKED THROUGH WITH SWEAT, ignoring the barrage of notifications that began to blow up his phone until he was almost home. He pulled the device from his pocket, breathing hard, and swiped into the string of messages. It was the group chat without Isobel. He frowned, scrolling back to the start of the drama.

Kilian: Fuck.

Kilian: She doesn't know we're still in her head.

Kilian: And I still have her phone.

Kilian: Someone has to tell her.

Oscar frowned harder. He hadn't realised they were all still in her head—he had been freed from that torture after running some distance from the dorm, but now that he was climbing back up the hill, he could definitely feel *something* niggling at his brain, trying to get back inside.

Kilian: She's going to be so embarrassed.

Kilian: Guys?

Kilian: STOP WATCHING.

Oscar froze, the phone clattering out of his hand as image after image assaulted his mind. Pale, wet skin. Short, sharp breaths. Water droplets on pretty pink nipples, painted nails dragging over skin. Pleasure. Guilt. Sadness. Dizziness.

At some point, hearing her thoughts had turned into simply seeing what she was seeing, and now the little Sigma was touching herself in the shower, trying to distract herself from the hellish day she had endured.

He groaned, snatching his phone back up and trying

to read the rest of the messages, doing his best to block out the images.

Kalen (admin): *Just stop fucking watching.*

Moses: Can't tell her. She'll freak out.

Niko: Let's just pretend it never happened.

Kilian: I'm going to pull the fire alarm.

Oscar felt dizzy. He groaned, pressing the heels of his palms into his eyes before texting the group.

Oscar: Don't bother. I'll go knock on the door and say some asshole thing and put her right out of the mood.

He tucked his phone away, not waiting for a reply, and stormed into her room, knocking on the bathroom door. Now that he was there, he realised he didn't have a single thing to say, and it was too hard to think of anything while fighting back images of her touching herself, so he did the next best thing and barged inside.

ISOBEL SCREAMED, WHIPPING AROUND AND FALLING AGAINST the wall of the shower before creeping to the opening and peeking out, her heart pounding in her chest.

Oscar stood in the middle of her bathroom, releasing a loud groan of relief. "All you needed was the shit scared out of you," he said, looking right at her.

Her mouth was opening and closing, the edge of her orgasm ebbing away. This was exactly what she deserved for trying to distract herself from stress and misery for a single evening. A ruined orgasm, a heart attack, and a stubbed toe.

"W-what?" she stuttered.

"We were seeing everything you were seeing," Oscar told her, pulling out his phone and sending a text before tossing it to the counter. And then he kicked off his shoes. "It's over now." He dragged his shirt over his head.

She just stared.

Heart still pounding.

Toe still aching.

Body still screaming for the release he had ripped out of her grip.

"What are you doing?" she asked dumbly because she couldn't quite compute the truck-sized wall of embarrassment that had just slammed into her.

She was never leaving her room again.

"Saving time," he said roughly, dropping his shirt to the floor and ripping off his socks. "I would demand you undress me, but it'll take you too long with how badly you're shaking."

She was momentarily hypnotised by the ridges of sweat-slicked muscles he was revealing, so she still hadn't absorbed his words, even as he shoved his workout pants down his legs, revealing his cock, heavy and swollen. He was *beautiful*, and his penis was no less fascinating—long and thick, a darkly blushing head and thick, prominent veins, a drop of moisture already forming at the tip.

"Y-you must really like running," she squeaked, unable to tear her eyes away.

His erection twitched, and he gripped it, apparently enjoying the attention. He stalked toward her.

She backed away immediately, but he only followed, step by step, until her back was against the wet, tiled wall and he was stabbing into her stomach. He gripped her waist and dragged her up the wall like she weighed nothing.

From the moment he entered the bathroom, it felt like his stare hadn't dropped from hers, but it did now, dragging down over her wet skin, following the droplets of water that clung to her nipples. He leaned back slightly, his gaze dropping between her legs before he hiked her up higher, his head falling to hers.

"I need you," he groaned, the roughness of his voice gaining a desperate edge. "I'm going to claw out my skin if I don't have you."

There was something wrong.

She knew it, but just as it had been all day, the strange tension danced just out of the reach of her comprehension. It was like a ringing sound in the distance, the register so high she was constantly second-guessing it.

Oscar's lips crashed over hers, his tongue thrusting into her mouth. The sudden, forceful movement ripped a surprised groan from her throat. He tasted like wine and sweet, smoky nectar.

"You're so fucking *cute*, it makes me sick," he growled, palming her ass and squeezing, rocking his hardness against her until she was squirming and panting, trying to get more friction.

"You don't f—" She broke off on a moan as his lips latched onto her nipple, sucking roughly "—feel sick."

To reach her breast, he had pulled her up high enough that the tip of him was straining for the heat of her sex, notched into her warm, welcoming entrance like he had been fucking her for years, and their bodies knew exactly how to come together.

He didn't push forward, and he kneaded her ass, grinding her over his swollen head as she marvelled at their bodies moulding together like puzzle pieces despite their height and size difference. She felt like a magnet, her other half snapping into place, and when he paused for the barest second, pulling his head back to stare at her lips, she mouthed the word he needed to hear.

"*Green.*"

She mouthed it because her voice was lost. Her mind was lost.

He fed himself into her. She was already soaked from her earlier ministrations, but he still had to inch into her, his mouth falling over hers with every one of her hitched breaths or whimpers, like he needed to taste them. Halfway into her, he paused to breathe, like he needed a break. Like he was struggling for control.

"You're so tight." He groaned, voice low and rough. "I

just want to force my way in. I want you bent and b-broken ..." He trailed off when she clenched around him, sucking in a sharp breath. She wasn't used to hearing Oscar stutter.

"I want to be so deep inside you, you won't be able to *breathe* for days without thinking about how I filled you, fucked you, forced my way inside you."

He drove in another inch, pulling back, his dark eyes catching hers. She loved feeling him flexing inside her, trying to push all the way in. She loved the way he was holding her up against the wall like he didn't even notice how much she weighed. It felt like he could keep her up there for hours while he took everything he needed from her body.

But more than anything, she loved the tiniest glimmer of unsteadiness in his eyes. She liked that *she* had been the one to tip this powerful Alpha past the point of his own control. Even though Oscar wasn't typically a man she associated with good self-control, he had displayed it to her in spades when it came to the physical aspect of their relationship. She was a little scared of the ramifications, but if *these* were the only consequences of Oscar losing control, then she would welcome them again and again until she couldn't stand anymore, and then she would ask him to hold her up again just like he was doing now and force his way inside her one more time.

"You're mine," Oscar snarled, suddenly shoving all

the way into her and slapping her back against the wall. He paused as she hiccupped in shock, kissing her lips until they felt bruised, and she was desperately squirming for him to move.

"Mine," he repeated, nudging her head back. He licked her neck, pulling out and stabbing into her in another brutal movement. "Mine," he growled, gripping her thighs so tightly she felt a pinch of pain.

She *liked* it, but that ringing was getting louder.

She could hear it through a tunnel now. A tunnel that connected her and Oscar. She tried to say something, but he suddenly pulled out of her and carried her away from the wall, turning off the shower and snatching up a towel. He picked her up, wrapping her legs back around his waist as he stalked back into her room. He haphazardly flicked out the towel over her bed and fell back onto it, sitting her upright on his lap, his cock trapped between them.

"You feel worried." His eyes were pitch black, words clipped. "Now you're in control. This better?"

She nodded, chewing on her lip, her hands hesitantly resting against the twitching muscles of his abdomen as he pulled her hips up and angled himself to thrust back into her. Even after giving her control, he still managed to set the pace, guiding her into the speed and movement he wanted, while his thumb slipped to her clit, gliding over it in teasing, infuriating touches until she wanted to beg him for *more*.

He was driving her so crazy that she didn't even notice the ringing sound increase again. She didn't realise when it turned to a whine because *she* was already whining. Oscar was finally giving her what she needed and finally pushing her over the edge, his free hand flashing up to twist one of her nipples between strong fingers. It wasn't soft and sweet, but it wasn't fast and rough either. It was a steady, intentional wringing, a stern and deliberate manipulation of her body. It was gritty and sweat-slicked, quiet and heavy, like a silo of water filled with one drop too many, now breaking apart and flooding through the room.

He dragged her head back down to his, riding out the waves of her orgasm while he kissed her savagely, pressing so deep into her that she could feel every throb when he began to release, his lips parting from hers in a feral growl.

A feral, *animalistic* growl.

The ringing was now screaming, and the throbbing grew ... *more*. The base of his cock was getting bigger. His eyes turned impossibly darker, small black lines beginning to spider along his skin, reaching for his temples. Isobel felt another pinch of pain at her hips, where he had been gripping her.

Almost like he had cut her with his nails.

She didn't know what was happening.

All she could feel was fear.

Help, she called through the bond.

What happened next was a blur. Oscar had come inside her, but that part of his dick still seemed to swell until she felt locked onto him. She was sure that any attempts to climb off him would be impossible or impossibly painful, and she let out a whimper of pain and fear as the door crashed open.

They were surrounded.

Her Alphas had stormed the room—*all of them*.

There were growls and sharp words ripping all around the space. Oscar snarled, his hands yanked away from her hips and slammed down to the bed on either side of his head.

Someone grabbed her as though to lift her off, and she screamed at them to stop.

"I'm s-stuck," she stuttered, staring into a face she didn't recognise.

It was Oscar's face ... but it wasn't. Because Oscar didn't have ferality.

And yet there he was, with black eyes, black veins, sharp black talons, and a rattle emanating from his chest.

"What the fuck is going on?" Theodore yelled, sounding almost hysterical.

There was a scuffle behind her, and then Moses was talking low and fast. "No, look at me. Don't look at them. Focus on me. Count backward from ten—"

"Fuck that, fuck counting, fuck you, get the *fuck* off me—"

"Help," she whispered, still staring down at Oscar.

The scuffle stopped, and she finally managed to flick her eyes to Elijah and Niko, who had been the ones to secure Oscar's black-tipped hands. "What's happening?"

Mikel was beside her, his hand against her spine. He must have been the one to try and pull her off. "What do you mean you're stuck?"

Nobody was trying to talk to Oscar. They were all completely focussed on her. His stillness was terrifying. He wasn't fighting. The only movement of his body was the slow rise and fall of his chest and the slow throb of his swollen cock, and the only sound he made was that ominous rattle.

"I don't know," she whined, trying to shift her hips. She was barely able to move an inch. "H-he *grew*, he—"

"A mating tie," Elijah said. He looked horrified and confused.

"What?" Kalen demanded roughly.

"I don't know!" Elijah groaned, his eyes a little wild. "I only ... saw it mentioned once, but it's ... *none of this makes sense*. None of this." He shifted his position and slapped Oscar suddenly, causing the other Alpha to snap and snarl viciously, black eyes darting and fixing to Elijah.

"He really is feral." Moses sounded terrified. "What the hell is going on?"

"Can I have a shirt?" Isobel begged.

One was immediately tugged over her head. It smelled like Kilian.

"If he's feral, why isn't he moving?" she asked, her thighs aching with how tightly she was holding onto his hips, petrified that he would try to buck her off and tear up her insides. His dark eyes snapped back to her as soon as she spoke.

"It's common ferality behaviour." Kalen sounded like he was furiously pacing somewhere behind her. "He can see he's outnumbered. He's playing dead, in a way, waiting for them to loosen their grip on him."

It didn't make sense.

Nobody was holding his legs. He could have thrown her off, but he was keeping his body so still, almost like he was scared of hurting her.

"Can you hear me?" she asked him.

He nodded.

"W-what?" Theodore demanded, shaken.

She remembered when she had gone feral. She hadn't been surrounded by "people" in her mind. Only prey.

"Am I prey?" she asked, staring into those inky, dark depths.

He shook his head immediately, his cock throbbing again, heat coating her insides like he was still leaking semen.

"Ah—" She tried to fight the confusing reaction of

her body, which seemed torn between the reminder of her arousal and the terror of her current situation. "Are the others prey?"

His eyes narrowed. Even as black as they were, she could sense how calculating he had turned. He was thinking about lying to her.

Finally, he nodded.

"That's not how it works." Theodore sounded faint. "None of this makes sense."

"It might be because of the bond?" Gabriel spoke up. "You didn't attack Isobel the first day you saw her in the library, remember?"

"*But how the fuck did Oscar turn feral?*" Cian demanded, sounding like he was a second away from losing it.

"Elijah," Kalen snapped, "Explain." Alpha voice.

"I don't *know!*" Elijah shouted, tugging on his dishevelled hair, pale eyes wide. "I read something once in a book of dumb Gifted legends. It said Alphas had a way of forcefully breeding people through mating ties. It was just some stupid story about Alphas being monsters."

"*What?*" Isobel wailed, beginning to struggle. "No, no, nooo. This can*not* happen."

Mikel immediately caught her shoulders as a fissure of pain tore through her. He pressed her back down, and Oscar's cock pulsed inside her happily.

"You're on birth control," Mikel reminded her quietly, his tone strained. "It's okay. For the love of god, just try not to move."

"We need to talk to the Guardian." Kalen's voice was a deep, ferocious scrape. "But first we need to … make it go down."

"I never go down when I'm inside her," Cian spat out furiously. "We could be waiting hours. All fucking night, maybe. *That's* your fucking plan?"

"Calm down," Kalen rumbled, his influence like a heavy wave that rolled through the room, momentarily distracting her. "Isobel, can you *carefully* siphon away some of the ferality?"

"Do *not*—" Theodore started, but Mikel silenced him, muttering something too low for Isobel to hear before quickly returning to Isobel's side, his hands settling over her shoulders again, thumbs brushing along the seam of Kilian's shirt where it met her neck.

"I'll try," she said.

"Go slow," Kalen instructed. "I know you've been practising. Don't panic. Just test the waters. Don't try to do it all at once."

She nodded and carefully sipped at the dark mass of emotion clouding around Oscar. She was able to control the flow to a trickle, preventing it from flooding into her in a tidal wave. She watched as the black veins began to retreat, painfully slowly, from his hairline, sinking back into his eyes. The talons grew shorter, his black nails receding.

The lock his penis seemed to have on her lessened as he regained control of his mind. Her thighs were shaking violently as she eased her death grip on his hips. She knew she could pull off him without hurting herself, but she was suddenly weak.

The darkness sat inside her with a heavy, sickening heaviness, sloshing up against her insides and threatening to make her sick.

Oscar blinked several times, his panic spiking violently, but Mikel quickly released Isobel and punched the other Alpha hard enough that his body immediately went limp, his eyes rolling back.

Isobel jolted in shock, covering her mouth.

"Better than him freaking out and going feral again," Mikel explained, shaking out his hand.

Right.

Now she was just sitting on an unconscious Alpha's dick, with nine of his best friends gathered around her.

Awesome.

"Could I have a minute?" she asked, her voice strained.

None of them shifted so much as an inch.

"I'll stay," Kilian whispered. "You can all wait outside."

"We'll be in the hallway." Theodore's voice was tight with tension.

As soon as they filtered out, Kilian's hands were at her waist, lifting her away from Oscar. Her legs threatened to buckle beneath her, and he had to steady her as she tried to stand. As soon as she could, she stumbled into the bathroom for a towel, laying it over Oscar's hips. He was still half hard, glistening in their combined releases.

"He avoided sex because he didn't want to hurt you in any way," Kilian said, wincing, his hand scraping down his handsome face. "And look what happened."

"This isn't his fault." Isobel frowned, hugging herself and rocking back on her heels. "This is another fucked-up side effect."

"I can see the weird orgasm lock being a side effect," he allowed. "It's classic, unhinged bond behaviour. But ferality?"

"Why not?" She shrugged, but her shoulders barely shifted. They were too heavy. "It gave me ferality, remember?"

Before he could respond, the room was flooded with darkness, and when she blinked again, she was standing somewhere at the back of the academy. The *old* academy, back in Arizona.

Niko was a few steps in front of her, but he was blond again.

"Great," Niko sighed out ... from *beside* her. She turned, noticing all the Alphas standing with her.

Oscar looked torn between confusion and panic.

There was also a bright flash of self-hatred that had her biting her lip in worry.

"You're all right," she told him carefully. "In the real world, I mean. You're just ... uh ... resting."

"Who knocked me out?" he asked plainly.

"Me," Mikel responded.

"Thanks."

"You're welcome."

The blond Niko climbed up higher, scaling the mountain along the back of the academy, shifting a backpack on his shoulder.

"Where are you going?" Isobel asked, her steps slowing, her heart sinking.

"I was leaving." Niko stopped following, and the rest of the Alphas paused too. They watched as the blond Niko climbed higher, disappearing from sight. "I came back ... obviously."

He had tried to leave.

That thought sat heavily in her stomach.

"It was after our eyes changed colour?" she guessed.

He made a low sound of agreement. "The day after. I didn't want to share a mate. I didn't want to watch my nine best friends developing feelings for *my* mate. I didn't want to be here."

This was cruel.

She understood why he would want to leave, but it was cruel of the bond to show it to her all this time later ... after she had developed feelings.

"These gods are fucking assholes," she grumbled.

Cian snorted. "You're only just figuring that out?"

They stayed a little while longer, just watching the path, until Niko reappeared, swearing beneath his breath, and then Isobel was yanked from the vision and dropped heavily back into her body.

On the bed, Oscar groaned, opening his eyes and rolling to his side. "Motherfucking *fuck*," he swore, burying his head into the softness of her sheets, the towel around his hips threatening to slip and reveal everything. His eyes slitted, seeking her out.

"He always wakes up like that." Kilian attempted to diffuse some of the tension.

"You okay?" Oscar asked, his eyes tracing over her.

She nodded nervously. "You didn't hurt me. It's okay." She resisted the urge to defuse the tension with a joke about how he had gotten his wish, and she would *definitely* be feeling him inside her for a while.

"Mhm," he rumbled, eyes guarded.

She already knew he wouldn't want to touch her again anytime soon, but that was something she was going to have to tackle later. "We need to go and see Maya."

He nodded, stumbling from the bed, still holding the towel over his midsection, though only barely. "Cameras are looped?" he asked.

"For now," Kilian confirmed.

"I'll get changed, and then I'm ready." Oscar strode from the room.

ADAM BELLAMY WAS IN THE HEAVILY FORESTED AREA OF THE academy behind the chapel when he got the text.

Sophia: Can't meet you. Something came up.

He tried to call her, but she didn't answer.

He groaned in frustration. It had taken *weeks* for him to convince her to meet up with him. At first, she refused because of the cameras. So he suggested they meet in a blind spot. She refused because someone still might see them. So he suggested they meet in the middle of the night, in a fucking forest, like a total fucking creep.

To his surprise, she agreed.

And now she was backing out.

She didn't seem like the kind to go back on her word. He frowned, trying to call her again. *Was everything okay?*

The chapel was on his way back to the dorm anyway. He would just stop by and make sure she was fine. He picked through the trees back to the thin, overgrown walking path and returned to the chapel, pausing in the dark shadow of the treeline. The lights were on inside. Maybe there was some kind of ... religious emergency?

He didn't even believe in the Gifted religion, so he had no idea what that would entail. Before he could take another step, he caught movement from the path leading in the other direction. He squinted, making out four

145

bodies—three large, one small. He already knew who it was before they stepped into the soft glow of light emanating from the stained glass chapel windows.

Isobel bloody Carter. Always at the epicentre of the storm. Moses and Theodore Kane were with her, as well as Oscar Sato. He considered making himself known but decided to wait instead because it was the middle of the night, and Sato was a goddamn psycho.

Isobel pushed open the door to the chapel, breathing out a sigh of relief that Maya and Sophia were already waiting inside. She stumbled in with Theodore, Moses, and Oscar, pretending to be carefree and laugh at a joke Moses had made that wasn't even funny. Since it was now past midnight, they decided that they had to keep the group as small as possible to draw less attention to the fact that they had felt the sudden urge to pray at such an absurd hour of the night.

On their way there, Isobel had texted Sophia, warning her.

They sobered as soon as they were through the door, dropping the act. Isobel quickly moved to sit in one of the chairs lining the wall. She was starting to get dizzy and nauseous.

Sophia rushed forward, kneeling before her and grabbing her hands. "You're shaking. You look a little green. What the hell happened?"

"Just Sigma stuff," Isobel managed, waving her off with a smile. "I'm fine. It's ... um, actually, we're here about something else."

"Another soul artefact?" Maya asked, scanning them for objects.

"Yeah, that would have been nice." Moses scoffed. "It's something a little less ... of a gift."

Maya frowned at them. The Alphas all frowned back at her.

She knew their secret, and she had kept it ... but this was something different. The guys' ferality was the darkest, most heavily guarded secret they had. If Isobel hadn't been involved, they may have just found a way to deal with it amongst themselves, no matter how much Oscar's sudden transformation alarmed them.

"You knew they were my mates just from their auras," Isobel finally said.

Maya nodded, looking wary and confused.

"Can you tell anything else?" Isobel ventured. "Can you tell what their abilities are?"

"If I say yes, will I be in danger?" Maya demanded.

"Mama," Sophia hissed.

"Of course not," Isobel quickly rushed out, eyes widening. "W-we need your help. This isn't a test."

"Then yes." Maya shrugged, pointing to Oscar. "Chaos." She moved her finger to Moses. "Aggression." Then to Theodore. "Charm."

They stared at her, taking far too long to process what she had said.

"What?" Theodore finally asked.

Maya's brows pinched in, her finger retreating. "You didn't know?"

Moses and Theodore were eyeing each other like they had never even seen each other before.

"You do seem to make people more aggressive," Theodore said quietly. "You even rile up Isobel, and that's not easy to do."

"I've always wondered why everyone was in love with you," Moses returned.

"What the hell is going on?" Oscar demanded before whirling on Maya. "Have you heard of ferality?"

She jumped back a step, and Sophia rushed to her side, clutching her arm as they both eyed Oscar warily. Maya didn't respond right away, instead taking her time to survey Oscar.

"You have it," she finally whispered before turning her attention to Moses, a crestfallen look descending over her features. She examined Theodore just as carefully before taking another shaky step back. "You all have it, don't you? I didn't see it at first—I was wondering what that darkness was ... I've ... never seen it in person before."

"We're not going to hurt you." Theodore was frowning at her slow retreat.

She paused, Sophia stopping with her.

"We aren't going to hurt *anyone*," Theodore quickly added. "We've controlled it all this time. We'd never let it hurt anyone. We just want to know what *you* know about it."

He was lying through his teeth, but Maya either seemed to believe him, or else she believed his good intentions because some of the tension seeped out of her rigid posture.

Holy shit, Theodore exploded into Isobel's head. *She's right. I really can charm the pants off people, can't I?*

Shut up, you smug fuck, Oscar groaned back. *This really isn't the time.*

You're only saying that because Moses is here, Theodore responded sunnily. *I bet you're actually a really easy-going guy; you just* seem *unhinged because Moses is leaking aggression all over you all the time.*

"All Alphas are rumoured to have an animal side," Maya explained, interrupting their internal fight. "It's what makes them bigger and stronger, with enhanced senses. But the drawback is that some of us, with extreme stress or emotion, can find that animal side triggered. It's dormant until it's triggered, and then it can reappear in any moment of extreme stress. A little bit like a viral disease."

"All Alphas?" Isobel repeated, feeling numb.

Maya nodded. "The OGGB thinks it's an ability—and since it's illegal, people don't talk about it. Even just saying the name could get you into trouble in the settlements. Only a handful of Alphas know what ferality means. It's heavily guarded information."

"Is there a way to stop it?" Moses asked. "To make it ... dormant again?"

Maya shook her head. "I don't think so. Once you've switched, that's it. You have to live with it ... and hide it, and try to manage your stress so that you don't have outbreaks, because they'll be deadly to the people around you. And guard that secret with your life because your life absolutely depends on it. The OGGB are afraid of a lot of things when it comes to the Gifted ... but they're afraid of ferality most of all."

They nodded, even Isobel, and they all dropped into a slightly unsettled silence. It was Sophia who broke it, reading something on Isobel's face.

"There's something else."

Isobel braced herself, shoving down her embarrassment. "D-does anything else happen when an Alpha turns feral ... like ... when they're having sex?"

She winced as soon as the words were out of her mouth, because now that she was looking at Maya—a *female* Alpha—it was obvious that whatever had happened to Oscar wouldn't be able to happen to Maya, so it likely had nothing to do with ferality.

"Ah." Maya coughed awkwardly. "Not from anything I've heard. If something happened while you were being intimate, it must have been a bond side effect. Um ... would you like to discuss it?"

Isobel's face was flaming red now. "Actually, uh, maybe another time. I think you're right. It was a side effect. The bond has been ... less kind, lately."

"Have you done something to go against it?" Maya asked.

"We fixed the bond, returning the pieces that were stolen, but it seems like it didn't heal properly."

Maya made a sad humming sound, beginning to pace.

"That makes sense." Sophia was staring at the floor. "Most people don't survive a soul infraction like that at *all*, let alone without consequences."

"It probably won't ever heal completely," Maya advised them. "But I think ... time and consistency will help. You should imagine that the bond is a living, cognizant thing. Right now, it's punishing you. Lashing out because it's hurt. It might play games and experiment with you, trying to find ways to bridge whatever gaps it feels, but I think eventually, it will realise there's no healing those wounds, and it will settle. You might have side effects for the rest of your life, but if you are sure to tend your bond, they should become minimal and manageable. If you neglect the bond, it will punish you."

It was a lot to digest, and Isobel was getting weaker by the minute, so they decided to call it a night. She had only taken a single step toward the door, about to bid them goodnight, when Sophia suddenly put her finger to her lips, staring at the door with a confused expression. She tip-toed to the entrance, her brow furrowed, and pulled open the doors, revealing ...

Bellamy?

He looked like he had literally had his ear stuck to the door.

Sophia dragged him inside, slamming the door behind him.

"What the *hell*," she whisper-shouted, "do you *think* you're doing?"

"How did you know he was there?" Isobel was confused.

The Alphas, on the other hand, looked ready to tear his head from his shoulders. Maya included.

But they were Alphas and even they didn't know he had been there.

"I won't tell anyone!" Bellamy held both hands up in immediate surrender. "I was just curious when I saw you guys sneak into the chapel. I was *not* expecting to hear any of that."

"You are such a *weasel*," Sophia fumed, her mahogany stare flickering with bright fury.

"He won't tell anyone." Isobel felt the need to defend him, but she still cut him a sharp look. "*Right*, Bellamy?"

"Didn't I literally just say that?" he asked.

"He's being honest." Maya's shoulders inched down. "He was just worried about you." She frowned at Sophia. "How do you know him? Why is there so much concern for you in his aura? Who are you?" She shot that last question at Bellamy.

"Adam Bellamy." He shifted on his feet. "Sorry, Father. Uh—I mean, G-Guardian? That's what you people are called, right? I mean not *you people*, but like—"

"Shut up," Sophia said coldly.

He mimed zipping his lips and throwing away the key. Isobel wanted to laugh, even though everyone else looked like they were ready to kill him. He was just so ... Bellamy.

"You should ask for a bribe in exchange for your silence," she told him. "It's how we do things here at Ironside, remember?"

"Right." He clicked his fingers. "Of course. A date." He didn't even pause, his eyes on Sophia. "And you can't stand me up this time."

"Jesus." Oscar rolled his eyes. "This is just pathetic."

"We all saw your last attempt at romance." Moses glanced at Oscar. "You can't talk."

"Too soon," Isobel mumbled.

"I'm out of here," Oscar snapped, striding up to Bellamy and looming over him. "You breathe a single word of *any* of this to *anyone* and I will tear you the fuck apart, are we clear?"

"Crystal." Bellamy flashed the Alpha his teeth before turning back to Sophia. "As soon as she agrees to the date."

"One hour," Sophia bargained.

"Three," Bellamy countered. "And you have to wear something nice, and I get to give you at least five compliments."

"Two hours, three compliments, and I'll shower before."

"Sold. See you Saturday."

6

KISSES AND MISSES

ISOBEL MANAGED TO PUT OFF HER MEETING WITH COOPER BY filling her schedule with extra training sessions and private lessons with Elijah. For the next two days, she didn't even take lunch or dinner breaks, choosing to scarf down snacks between her classes instead. She made sure to return to the dorm around midnight each night, with just enough time to lock herself in her room, rush through a shower, and collapse into her bed.

On Friday night, Moses texted her to let her know Cooper was waiting at the dorm for her, so she went back to the library to work on choosing a song for her performance. She had several dances prepared; she just needed to pick one and then match her outfit accordingly. The song would do half the work for her, as far as setting the tone was concerned, and her clothes would do the rest.

She could perform the exact same dance in five different outfits under different lighting conditions and change the effect with each iteration. Toeing that delicate line between provocative and untouchable, entertaining and tasteful, was something she decided to relish as a new challenge. If she didn't get it right the first time, she would adjust. That was okay. She could do that.

She picked the song she would perform and then sent Cooper a link to it and to one of the rehearsals she had recorded.

He replied instantly, telling her he had to approve her outfit. It was too fast of a response for him to have listened to the song or watched the video, let alone both, so she assumed he wasn't actually interested in the technical aspects of her performance at all. She had to bite back her frustration before responding.

Isobel: I haven't chosen my outfit yet, but it will be appropriate.

Cooper: I need to approve it regardless. Your group is due at Ironside Row for the Friday games in an hour. I need to approve it before then.

Cooper: In person, Carter.

She cursed, packing up her stuff and shoving it all back into her bag. She ran into Gabriel on her way out of the library and he paused, looking her over. "You don't smell pleased."

"You're not supposed to greet people with how they smell." She grinned at him, unable to help herself. She found Gabriel's abruptness hilarious, though she would never admit that to him.

His eyes traced her smile as though he liked the shape of it. "Where are you off to?"

She kept her response camera-friendly. "The dorm manager needs to approve something for a performance."

"I'll accompany you." He immediately turned around, striding back toward the dorm.

"I'm sure you have better things to do." She half-heartedly resisted, running to catch up with him, though she was secretly happy that she wouldn't have to visit Cooper's office alone.

"I need to talk to him anyway."

They made their way back to the dorm in companionable silence, and Gabriel followed her into her dressing room as she sorted through her available outfits. She held up a dress against her chest.

"Is this provocative but tasteful?"

Gabriel frowned, pulling out his phone and aiming it at her, probably taking a video to ask someone who might actually know the answer to her question.

"Depends." He frowned. "What the fuck is provocative but tasteful supposed to look like?"

"You know—" She waved a hand in the air. "—rip my clothes off, but only after a sit-down at Olive Garden."

"What?" He looked like he was considering laughing one day.

"Like pull my hair but pretend it was someone else? Someone nicer?"

He laughed: the day had come. "I'm going to need another example."

"Like spank me but only with two fingers."

Gabriel's laugh grew louder, so she kept going because it was such a rare treat, and she needed to hear it again.

"Like spit *near* my mouth," she suggested. "Or I'll call you daddy but only if you complain about having to drive me around and offer to fix my squeaky door."

"Is the squeaky door a metaphor?"

"No, a literal squeaky door. The vibe we're looking for is: choke me, but only if you're an otolaryngologist ... or, like, call me a dirty whore, but *tasteful*, you know?"

He put a hand on his chest, his laugh dying to a chuckle as he ended his recording. "When do you want me to release that dance recording you did the other day, by the way?"

"How about tonight?" she suggested.

"Done."

"Are you uploading that?" She gestured his phone, indicating the video he had just taken.

"No. That's mine." He narrowed his eyes on her like she was threatening to take something away from him, so she bit back her response, tossing the dress aside.

She hunted through her drawers for a pair of high-waisted boyshorts and a bralette that had just enough support and coverage for her to dance in. She paired them with a silky coverall, which should ripple nicely as she danced. Since she hadn't yet seen the area she would be performing in, she didn't want to have to worry about a finicky costume. She tucked her clothes under her arm, and they went downstairs to meet Cooper, knocking on the wall partition that hid his office.

"Carter!" he bellowed with a little too much enthusiasm as soon as the door slid open. "You're a hard one to catch, aren't you? Come in, come in. Spade, if you'll give us a minute ..." He grabbed her arm and began pulling her into the room—in the process of putting his body between hers and Gabriel's—when the Alpha stepped forward, casually breaking Cooper's hold on her and pretending not to notice as he barged into the room.

"We should be quick," he said, planting himself in a chair and crossing his ankle over his knee. "We've got to be at Ironside Row in half an hour."

"You can wait outside, Spade," Cooper said cooly, some of his robust cheer dissipating. "I have private matters to discuss with Carter."

"I'm helping her plan her performance." Gabriel cast his eyes about the office, looking bored. There was nothing in his tone that invited discussion.

Cooper set his jaw. "We're going to have to establish some boundaries in regard to my office and my time," he gritted. "I'll be sure to talk to the board about it." He turned back to Isobel as she stepped away from the door sensor and it slid closed, cutting them off from the rest of the dorm. "What's the outfit you've chosen?"

She lifted the pieces one at a time, holding them away from her body. "This goes over it," she said, dangling the coverall. "It'll create an intimate and candid effect with the dance I sent for your review. The honesty is what makes it sexy."

Cooper snorted. "We have different ideas of sexy."

She shrugged. "No offence, but you aren't a dancer. I am. I know what will work with my body, with the music, and with the space I'm utilising, though I suppose I'll have to wing that part tonight."

Cooper's frown deepened. Gabriel's lips twitched. Isobel cracked open her wall for a moment, brushing up against Cooper's consciousness in a subtle, searching touch. *Disappointment. Frustration. Aggravation. Emasculation.*

"I know," she said, giving him a droll, commiserating look. "I was much easier to manipulate last year, wasn't I?"

"Get out," Cooper snapped, pointing at the door. "Both of you. And Carter?" He waited for her to turn back before continuing. "I don't know what's gotten into you, but you need to pull your head in. I'm your Orion manager *and* your dorm manager. You *need* me. If you don't make me happy, if you don't work with me, if you don't pull this attitude in line and show me some proper respect, I might just tell Orion that they shouldn't take a chance on you after all. I'll tell them they can't control you. I'll tell them you don't take orders or respond to authority. I promise that won't go well for you or your group."

Isobel's stomach turned to lead, and for just a moment, she stared at Cooper.

The man was like a cockroach.

He always walked away without a scratch, no matter what was happening around him. He only seemed to get more powerful and more important, and there was *nothing* special about him. From publicist to official, to dorm manager, to Orion-appointed liaison, his climb was terrifying, and it was a hard slap in the face to realise he was right.

He, more than anyone now, had her future cupped in the palm of his greedy little hand.

She gave him a stiff nod. "Understood."

"Sir," he corrected.

"Understood, sir."

She pulled Gabriel against the wall as soon as they left Cooper's office, because she knew that little corner wasn't covered by the cameras. His expression was tight, his red-brown eyes guarded as they snapped down to where she was gripping his sleeve. She quickly released him.

"Can we keep this between us?" she whispered lowly.

He stared at her mouth, mulling over her words before finally uttering, "For now."

He didn't need to ask why.

Cooper wasn't an issue she could fix or change right now, so there was no point in letting any of the others know. It would only test their tenuous self-control unnecessarily.

THEY GOT A TEXT ALERT FIVE MINUTES BEFORE THEIR scheduled start time at Ironside Row, assigning their group to the Pixel Play building. It was one they hadn't visited yet. The first building they went to was The Den, which had cinema rooms where they gathered to react to Ironside episodes, trending clips, or movies. After that, they were assigned to Reputation Race, which had several different indoor obstacle courses. Niko won that night, earning himself a small fortune in popularity points. The next week, they were assigned to the Trend or Die building, which housed over a dozen terrifying escape rooms or haunted rooms. Elijah had won that night. Apparently, it was impossible to scare him. Moses, Oscar, and Niko had all been immediately disqualified for hitting the actors who tried to jump out and scare them.

The rules for Ironside Row were extensive. They were limited to a certain amount of swear words—there were several officials in the recording centre whose sole job was to count such infractions. Nudity, accidental or otherwise, was prohibited. Any mention of the officials, the Ironside rules, or anything considered a "behind the scenes" topic was prohibited. They weren't allowed to specifically discuss any current drama from the show since the Friday nights on Ironside Row were recorded live, and footage for the *Ironside Show* was often delayed for up to a week.

The third years took up the Row on Friday nights, and then the fourth years appeared on Saturday, and the fifth-year students on Sunday. Sometimes, the viewers decided the winners each night with real-time voting, and sometimes—like when Niko was declared the winner—it was decided by whoever won whatever task they had been given or whoever completed it first.

Regardless, the public voted, and whoever got the most votes had a sizable sum of popularity points deposited into their account.

"Now that we're a group, I guess we win as a group?" Theodore wondered aloud as they walked toward the correct building.

The cobbled street was bustling with excited students. Isobel spotted Bellamy waiting beside one of the other buildings, checking his phone. He caught sight of the Alpha group and seemed to search through their bodies until he found her, giving her a grin and a wave.

She waved back, but Oscar pushed her hand back to her side. Her hand shot straight back up.

"Now he gets *two* waves," she grumbled.

Moses snorted. "Lord, give us strength."

"The only thing any lord is giving *you* is a pitchfork," Cian said. "And a brood of demons to rule over."

"Sounds like a cushy deal to me." Moses shifted his broad shoulders in a careless shrug. "If anyone deserves a brood of demon slaves, it's me."

"Can't say I've ever heard anyone claim to *deserve* a brood of demon slaves before," Kilian said.

"It's called the law of attraction, Kili," Moses crooned sweetly. "If you believe it, you can have it."

"I believe I'll be impaled by a clown before the night is through." Oscar held up his hands, fingers crossed, as they filed into the Pixel Play building. It seemed to be one gigantic arcade, with private rooms scattered along the sides of the hall.

Isobel spotted photo booths, popcorn machines, hot dog stands, cotton candy stalls, carnival rides, arcade machines, and karaoke rooms ... and the *Ironside Show* hosts standing a few feet from the entrance. Ed Jones and Jack Ransom had come equipped with an entire camera crew despite the building being armed to the teeth with lenses already.

"What's all this about?" Bellamy asked, sidling up to their group with some of his friends—third-year Betas Isobel didn't know the names of. He seemed to have ditched his friends from his first two years at the academy.

Moses, who stood between Isobel and Bellamy, turned his head slowly, his expression pinched. "I'm sorry, do I know you?"

"Don't be a dick," Isobel said beneath her breath.

"Don't ask the impossible." He flicked his hair out of his face, turning his back on Bellamy. "What's all this about, anyway?"

Behind him, Bellamy snorted.

"Now that we're all here," Ed Jones called out, "let the games begin!"

Isobel craned her neck to see the extent of the crowd. There only seemed to be around thirty to forty students. The entire human group was there, as well as Wallis, Ellis, and James … and Silva. All of their fake exes.

Ellis and James scowled when they caught sight of Elijah and Gabriel, but it was nothing on the glare Wallis gave *Isobel*.

"Keep me out of it," Isobel grumbled.

Theodore, who was standing on her other side, grinned down at her, somehow knowing exactly what she was talking about. The bond had probably given her away. "Not my fault I'm so hard to be mad at," he said, slinging his arm around her shoulders. "Take one for the team just this once, okay, Illy-stone?"

She punched his stomach.

He didn't seem to notice.

"I punched you," she informed him.

"Oh." He clutched his stomach. "Sorry. What was that for?"

She chuckled, and Wallis' glare turned murderous, so she quickly wiped the smile from her face. There wasn't much point in inciting the Beta to violence. She wasn't in the market for another psychotic enemy.

"Gather round, gather round!" Jack Ransom waved his arms enthusiastically, herding the students in closer, his expression painted in devious enthusiasm.

"Who's ready to play?" Ed called out, wearing a matching grin. "This is a little competition we like to call 'How well do you know your classmates?'"

"Don't you think the name is a bit too long?" Jack asked, stroking his chin.

Ed shrugged. "It's a new game. We're still working out the kinks."

"I see what you did there." Jack winked at him.

"Are they flirting?" Cian asked, confused. "Thought they have wives and shit."

"I think they're trying to hint that the game is sexual." Elijah sighed, examining his fingernails. "I think you were supposed to gasp and clutch the nearest attractive person for comfort. Like Ellis is doing." He pointed at his fake ex, who was gasping, giggling, and hanging off the arm of one of the Kozlov twins.

"We put out a poll to our viewers this week," Ed

announced as a digital sign was wheeled in behind him by one of the cameramen. It was ringed in bright lights, the letters on the screen displaying the long name of the game. "We announced the two groups that had registered with the change of the *Ironside* rules: Eleven, and Hero—"

"Hero?" Niko crossed his arms, his dark brows inching down. "Are they here to save us?"

"—And we had you vote on who you thought would have the best chemistry with each group member out of the rest of the students."

"What could go wrong?" Gabriel sounded as bored as Elijah.

"So ... you might be wondering how we'll test this chemistry?" Jack asked, rubbing his hands together. The man was practically giddy.

The human group looked equally giddy.

The Alphas looked like they were considering storming out of the building and punching a few giddy faces along the way.

"Whoever the public gave the most votes to will kiss our group member—who will be blindfolded. If any of the blindfolded group members can guess who just kissed them, they will get a point. At the end of the kiss, the group members will score whoever kissed them out of ten—any student who manages to score a ten out of ten will *also* get a point. They can choose to donate their point to either Eleven or to Hero. The members of Hero will score double points since they have fewer group members."

Most of the other students seemed torn between fear and excitement, with most of the females casting quick glances at the Alphas. She didn't blame them. When it came to boosting popularity and hitching your wagon to a possible winner, the humans were a good bet.

But when it came to *kissing*?

Please. The human men didn't stand a chance. Nobody at the academy stood a chance. Santoro was attractive in a boy-next-door way, and the Kozlov twins were attractive in a won't-stop-posting-videos-of-shirtless-wood-chopping way, but it just didn't compare to the Alphas. They were attractive in a life-destroying sort of way.

As much as she technically understood it, she wasn't happy about the situation. She was in a sexual relationship with Kilian, Theodore, and Cian. She had also had sex with Niko and Oscar ... although she wouldn't say she was in a sexual relationship with either of them. She wasn't sure if she would be having sex with *anyone* any time soon, for fear of their dick suddenly expanding and locking her in place like some kind of torture device.

She shuddered, torn between fear over her recollection of her last sexual encounter and fury at the possibility of anyone kissing any of her mates ... and maybe a little bit of lust, too, because she was *ill*.

Their new contracts made it clear that their active participation in the Ironside Row games was compulsory, and the officials had made it clear that they would be tested during these games, but she wasn't sure this test made sense when it came to "challenging their group dynamics."

They've reached the same conclusion we have, Elijah spoke through the bond. *They know that the fans will never accept us being bonded to Isobel. They'll lose all interest in us if they think none of us are available, and they'll hate Isobel.*

Gabriel's voice joined Elijah's in her head. *They want us to be available and accessible to the fans, and they're testing to see if our bond will prevent that.*

"The winning group for the night will get ..." Ed trailed off as everyone stilled, even the humans. It would either be a complete joke of a reward, or it would be something they would want to chew off their own arms for. He continued, "An exclusive, private, camera-free practice room branded with their group name. Any personal projects filmed within the room can be uploaded without the usual waiting times or approvals needed. It will be your group's room permanently until graduation."

Isobel stopped breathing. That was a *huge* advantage. Privacy, the absolute element of surprise with all of their performances, and the freedom to upload content whenever they wanted?

It was beyond what she thought Ironside would ever

offer. And … *dammit*, it was clever. It was the perfect bait to make sure the Alphas played along with what was obviously a very important game to the officials.

We have to win. Elijah's voice in her head was cold and determined. *Keep it minimal and respectful,* he continued. *A quick peck with someone we have no romantic connection with to win a game shouldn't cause any soul infractions—there's no emotional, romantic, or sexual connection behind it. They'll only pair us with people we've encountered before, so we can use their scents to name them and win the game that way. Isobel, we'll just tell you who is standing in front of you. Most likely, it'll be one of us, Silva, or Santoro—he's publicly said he has a crush on you. For us, they'll either pick you, one of the fake ex-girlfriends, or one of the humans.*

The idea of having to kiss Silva or Santoro made her want to vomit.

The idea of Wallis touching Theodore made her hand itch to grab the other girl's hair, drag her out of the hall, and shove her bold lips into the dirt—

Can everyone control themselves for one night? Elijah asked sternly.

It isn't us you should be worried about, Kilian returned stiffly. *The Sigma is contemplating murder.*

Actually, I was contemplating bodily harm, she sniped.

Grievous? Cian asked.

Provocative but tasteful, she returned.

How could I ever want to kiss anyone else. His voice was

a deep groan that echoed through her mind, soothing some of the ragged edges of her panic.

She could do this. She could—

"Moses Kane," Ed called, glancing at the sign behind him, which was now reading Moses' name.

She could *not* do this.

Moses stared at the sign for a moment, his expression twisting into something dark and stubborn, but there was no other option. They had been warned. Ironside would make them pay for the privilege of being allowed to exist every step of the way.

Moses approached the two hosts and allowed himself to be blindfolded and positioned where they wanted him. He didn't stop scowling, but he also didn't try to punch anybody, so he was probably utilising his self-control to the fullest extent.

"Who do the public think Moses Kane has the most chemistry with?" Ed asked, holding out his hand toward the sign, which was digitally flicking through letters as though searching for a name.

Moses was so tense he could have been made of stone, and the other Alphas were barely any better.

Can everyone control themselves? Elijah pressed through the bond.

Various grumbled affirmatives flowed back to him, and Isobel tacked on her own answer, packing away her panic and arranging her expression into mild amusement. If they succeeded in showing the officials that their bond would never get in the way, then maybe they would get bored of testing them.

Maybe—

Isobel Carter.

The sign had stopped flickering and was showing her name.

Everyone was staring at her, the other students laughing and gasping.

"We have the people's choice!" Jack exclaimed, motioning her over. "Come on up, come on, that's it, right here—do you need something to stand on?" he added in a stage whisper.

The swell of laugher grew louder, but Isobel seriously considered it before finally nodding. *Why make it harder than it had to be?* Jack and Ed looked beyond delighted as one of the camera crew fetched a small footstool and set it before Moses.

Of course, it was a *small* footstool.

Moses would know it was her as soon as she was in front of him. His nose was too good for anyone to trick him with a blindfold, though the crew obviously didn't realise that.

"Remember, no talking!" Ed warned, steering her toward the footstool. She stepped up onto it, and Moses automatically anchored his hands to her hips, steadying her.

She considered him for a moment, unsure how she was supposed to proceed. If she kissed him too quickly, people would think it was too natural, too *practised*, even though for them, that would be far from the truth. However, if she stared at his firm lips for too long, people would think she was secretly in love with him.

So she just stood there like an idiot.

Ed Jones chuckled. "You can start whenever you like."

Are you going to kiss me? Moses asked inside her head, so close and so clear that she knew he was speaking to her privately. *Or are we going to stand here until Ed Jones has a breakdown and decides to do it himself? That man is one forced chuckle away from snapping in the most spectacular way.*

Well, now she had to kiss him because if she didn't, she was going to accidentally laugh out loud. She tugged on his shirt and tried to pull him down to her because the stupid step stool wasn't tall enough. He resisted. She kicked his shin in punishment, and he laughed before grabbing her face and dragging her mouth to his. The kiss was short and sweet, his crushed-petal scent curling around her, sweet and intoxicating, his lips trembling as he seemed to pull away reluctantly. She had no idea what had been an act and what had been real. Maybe none of it. Maybe all of it.

"Ten out of ten," Moses declared before adding, "When do you think Ironside will get tired of forcing us to kiss, Carter?" His voice had a little hint of indulgence. It sounded like she was so precious to him that he wouldn't dare to rate her anything less than a ten, because he would never allow her to be hurt. But it didn't sound sexual, not at all.

His hands dropped back to her hips. The grip was protective but light. Familiar, but not too intimate. He was dancing along the line perfectly.

"Two points to Eleven!" Ed cried out as the crowd laughed and cheered, and Moses whipped off his blindfold, smirking confidently. He didn't look at her but lifted her carefully off the stool before winking at her and striding back to the Alpha group. He seemed to forget to act as moody and pissed as he had been on his way to get blindfolded.

Isobel trailed him, her expression fixed in slightly bored amusement once again.

"Next up, we have Theodore Kane—dare I say, a favourite Kane for some of you?"

It's you again. Cian's voice echoed into her mind before Theodore had even been blindfolded. *They're all you.*

Really? She was unable to help turning to look at him, brows raised.

He isn't usually wrong with hunches like these. Gabriel was the one to respond, sounding relieved. *Just make sure to keep it even with everyone.*

Okay. She watched as the sign formed her own name again and as the crowd's reaction grew even more boisterous. It almost felt *perverted*, like the officials had known what the people wanted to see and had known that Isobel and the Alphas would never give it to them, so here they were, forcing it. Just because they could.

And the people were eating it up—even the other students, who hadn't been involved in the voting. Everyone had wanted to see her kiss Moses, and now everyone wanted to see her kiss Theodore just as badly. It made sense, in a messed-up sort of way. She and the Alphas had ballooned in popularity ever since they began publicly forming their group, to the point where people didn't even seem to care about the two year groups ahead of them, who would all graduate before them. They just wanted Dorm A. Isobel and the Alphas were their current obsession.

When Ed waved her forward, she fetched the step stool herself. She slapped it down, climbed up, and tugged Theodore's shirt. He smirked and bent so that she could plant a quick peck on his lips. He didn't linger, but he also couldn't help his hands briefly gripping her waist, squeezing slightly.

He guessed her correctly and gave her a ten. Two more points.

Gabriel was next, and she was so nervous, knowing how pedantic he was about germs and people touching him. As she debated the best way to go about it, his hands slipped up her arms and cupped her face, gently lifting it to his. The kiss was so light and quick that she was left wondering if it had even happened, but when she returned to the line and licked her lips, she tasted him there. Clean and comforting, he tasted like ... skin. Like a body sprawled over cotton, kissed by sunlight pouring through the window. Like a lazy morning in bed. She wasn't sure how that could be a taste, but she was desperate for more. She wondered if the lazy bedroom scene would unfold the longer she kissed him.

Next was Elijah, and just like Gabriel, he didn't wait for her. His kiss was a hard, brief stamp that had her lips tingling and her thoughts scattering, though she was sure to school her features into exasperated amusement again. When her name flashed up for Kilian, the entire room erupted into whispers as though it was the most scandalous thing to happen all year.

She kissed his cheek, and he rated her ten out of ten for being respectful. All the girls in the audience seemed to melt over his sly, lush smile as he tapped her affectionately beneath the chin.

Oscar and Niko both made their bodies stiff so that she had to tug against their shirts, which had the crowd laughing at her, especially when she was forced to rise onto her toes to reach Niko's mouth. Cian considered giving her a five out of ten *out loud* while frowning and stroking his chin, saying that the kiss "lacked passion" before ultimately giving her a ten out of ten because he "pitied her."

It was so painfully apparent that they all knew it was her the second she stood before them, but she thought they played it off perfectly, teasing her and keeping their kisses chaste. The entire game showcased just how close and comfortable they were without making it seem like any of them were a couple.

Isobel was too busy silently congratulating herself for a job well done to worry about her own turn. It wasn't until she was standing there blindfolded that the nerves crept back in.

"So *this* is the person our viewers think is most suited to the Sigma?" Ed sounded smug and anticipatory.

Those fuckers rigged the poll, Elijah snarled into her mind.

Well ... that didn't sound good.

Who is it? she demanded.

Bellamy, Theodore spat back.

I can't let it happen. Oscar's voice was too cold, too matter-of-fact.

You don't have a choice, Elijah returned. *Contain yourself—that goes for everyone, and it's a fucking order.* Isobel wasn't sure she had ever heard him sound so stern.

Someone—presumably Bellamy—was standing in front of her. She cracked open her wall, almost laughing at the dread and discomfort emanating from him.

"I'm flattered," she said, unable to bite back her laugh. "You know I'm a Sigma, right? I can *feel* how much you don't want to do this."

She could hear a wave of whispering break out, likely

because she didn't talk about her Sigma power often, and many people still seemed to believe it wasn't real at all.

Bellamy grunted out an unhappy sound but couldn't answer her because of the rules.

He also wasn't kissing her.

"You're even more indecisive than the Sigma was!" Jack taunted. "We're going to be here all night at this rate."

She heard Bellamy take a step forward, but then he cursed and crashed into her, somehow tripping over his own feet. They fell into the sign, which cracked against the back of her head, and ended up on the ground in a tangle of limbs and cords. Luckily, she was in high-waisted jeans, or she probably would have flashed the world on live television.

"Ow?" she managed as she tugged off her blindfold.

Bellamy's face was flaming red, and he seemed confused, struggling to his feet and staring at the ground in accusation, though there was nothing lying there that he could have tripped over. He quickly helped her up, pulling her from a tangle of equipment as the camera crew scrambled to restore the set.

She glanced over at the Alphas, who wore carefully painted expressions of mild exasperation and amusement—all except Oscar. His firm lips were crooked into a small, smug smile, his onyx eyes glinting in devious pleasure.

"I think that was a zero out of ten," she said, deliberately dragging her attention back to the hosts before forcing a grin in Bellamy's direction. "Better luck next time."

"Sorry, Beta," Cian called out. "That was your one and only shot."

It was Santoro's turn next, and the public paired him with Mei Ito, which was unsurprising. They had the biggest fanbases of all the human students, with Kostas coming in close second. They decided to go with the same strategy of a chaste kiss, and Santoro managed to guess who it was, which was quite impressive, though the pool of likely candidates was admittedly small. Next was Alexi Kozlov, who was also paired with Santoro.

Isobel vaguely recalled reading somewhere that Alexi was bisexual but was fairly certain Santoro was straight. Santoro was a good sport about it, shaking his head with silent laughter as he planted a loud kiss on the other boy's lips. Alexi guessed him correctly, scoring him ten out of ten, and Isobel began to worry.

What would happen if they tied?

If the humans won the practice room, they would pull ahead drastically in the race. She couldn't let it happen. She shuffled nervously from foot to foot as Naina Kahn was paired with Santoro, guessing him correctly, and then Jordan Kostas was *also* paired with Santoro, and they scored again. Anatoly Kozlov was paired with Wallis, and some of the loud cheering and laughing died down, probably indicating to Anatoly that his partner was someone outside of his group. Wallis didn't kiss him chastely. She grabbed his face and held it there for a long, deep—and frankly, disgusting—make out that had the crowd *screaming*.

When she was finished, her expression was smug, and her hand trailed down his chest before she flounced back to Ellis and James.

"Nine out of ten," Anatoly announced. "Was that ... Carter? It felt desperate for some real action." He whipped off his blindfold, finding her across the room and winking at her.

"Zero points this round!" Ed exclaimed.

Isobel folded her arms, giving Anatoly a bored look, but Moses fired back before she could think of a response.

"Don't you know the rules?" he asked, shaking his head in disapproval. "Anyone wanting to kiss Carter, hug Carter, hold Carter's damned hand, or visit with Carter has to get permission from her group members first. You know damn well it wasn't her because you *don't* have permission."

"Is that true?" Jack immediately sidled up to Moses, holding out his microphone—which was entirely for show, because the building was already heavily rigged with microphones. "Do you screen her possible romantic partners? What do they have to do to get approval?"

"Actually," Elijah smoothly interrupted, "we're not

allowed to date anymore, so applications are closed for the time being."

Jack slumped a little, deflated by the lack of drama they were feeding him before he sprang back into action and called Mei to the stage. "Lucky last!" he announced as her blindfold was secured.

And then a name appeared on the sign, and Isobel's heart stopped.

Niko Hart.

He had been so stiff, so unsure, during her quick kiss, ending it so fast it almost didn't count. And now they were entirely relying on him. Both groups were sitting at sixteen points, thanks to the human team scoring double points. If Niko was scored a ten out of ten, he could choose to assign the points to his own team ... but if Mei guessed who he was and rated him less than that, the human team would win. If Oscar interfered with his chaos ability again, it would end in a tie. Nobody would get the practice room.

I don't know if my charm works this way, but I can try and hit her with it, Theodore spoke through the bond.

Does anyone have any other ideas? Niko sounded desperate for something else. *I don't think I can kiss her.*

Isobel pushed her voice into Elijah's head, trying to speak to him privately. *We shouldn't force him. We don't know exactly how much or what type of stress or emotion will trigger ferality until the bond has settled down.*

Agreed, he returned before his voice changed in

quality, seeming to address everyone at once. *Just kiss her cheek. Theo, try to hit her with your ability. Isobel, siphon off anything bad she's feeling. It's the best we can do.*

Niko strode up to the stage, and Isobel quickly opened her walls, trying to focus on Mei, gently removing the stress and feelings of pressure that built up inside the other girl.

Niko bent down and kissed her cheek. He didn't stick around but immediately returned to his group, his expression impassive. Mei's face was flushed, her hand at her chest.

"Um, ten out of ten?" She giggled. "He seemed tall, and he smelled really good. Was that ... I guess it was one of the Alphas. This is crazy. Was it ... Theodore Kane?"

Everyone burst into laughter, and Ed chuckled, announcing, "No points to Hero, but one point to Eleven, thanks to Niko Hart."

"And we have our winning team!" Jack exclaimed. "Congratulations, Eleven!"

7
THE IRON FIST OF NOVIKOV

THE DAHLIA ROOM WAS SMALLER THAN ISOBEL EXPECTED. AS soon as she stepped inside with Kalen, Cian, Kilian, Elijah, and Gabriel, the lighting shifted to a warm, low, ambient glow. The centrepiece of the room was a circular stage of polished black marble with shimmering gold and pearl threads mottled through the surface. It was illuminated by a halo of hazy golden light and surrounded by thick velvet curtains—currently pulled back to reveal the stage—giving it an intimate feel. The ambience would more than make up for the small space she had to work with for future performances, but there was no way of salvaging the dance she had prepared. Cooper hadn't thought to mention that her platform would be so small, even after she had sent him her dance recording.

There was no way she could make it work.

"What's wrong?" Kalen rumbled as she glared at the stage.

"Nothing." She realised they were all staring at her, and she gave them a tight smile.

Cooper was going to be a bigger problem than she realised. He had sabotaged her performance, either to punish her for not giving him a private show, or because he wanted the officials to think she was incompetent and *force* her to get his approval for every decision moving forward. Whatever the reason was, it wasn't good, and it was only going to make the Alphas angry about something they didn't have the power to change.

The entire group was already dangerously on edge. Theodore, Moses, Niko, Oscar, and Mikel had all received permission to participate in fights on Friday nights while she danced, so perhaps they would be able to work off some of their ragged edges without getting hurt.

That would be the best-case scenario.

They had yet to discuss the fights in front of her, so she wasn't sure what the worst-case scenario would be.

"Professor West, welcome." Yulia Novikov appeared out of nowhere. Her sleek ponytail was slicked back from her sharp, beautiful features. Her frame was wrapped in a gleaming silver dress with a slit all the way up to her hip bone. Her lips were painted a pretty rose, so glossy they almost looked like honey.

Isobel wanted to crawl into a hole and die.

If she could have pictured Kalen with anyone, it

would have been someone as glamorous as Yulia, dripping with sex, cool confidence, and opulence. Kalen nodded at her, and she briefly passed her eyes over Isobel, Elijah, Gabriel, Kilian, and Cian.

"Carter, Reed, Spade, Gray, Ashford. Welcome." She fired off their names and then immediately returned her attention to Kalen, giving him a slow, small smile. "I see you dressed for the occasion, Professor West. You didn't think to allow any of your Alphas access to your wardrobe for tonight?"

"I'm wearing my only good suit," he returned cooly, utterly unashamed. "It was my grandfather's. He wore it to my grandmother's graduation ceremony when she won the game here at Ironside. If you wanted the Alphas to dress a certain way, you should have provided them the means."

Yulia laughed, the sound a delicate tinkle, the diamonds dangling from her ears shimmering prettily. "So cold, so harsh." She faked a little shudder. "You've truly earned your reputation, Professor."

"Where would you like us?" Elijah interrupted.

"You four can report to the bar." She gave him a saccharine smile. "Cooper will be along in a minute to get Carter situated ... but I have a little surprise for our handsome professor."

None of them moved.

"The bar is over there," Yulia said, a hint of

something cold and hard descending over her features as she pointed a metallic nail.

None of them looked in the direction she indicated, but finally, Elijah stepped away from the group without a word. The others followed him silently. Isobel watched them go, her nerves increasing as Yulia waved someone over. It was another woman, probably around Kalen's age. She was dressed similarly to Yulia, though her dress dipped low in the front and the back, leaving most of her tanned skin on display. There was something oddly familiar about her, but Isobel couldn't quite put her finger on it. The woman had a cloud of shiny auburn hair floating around her face and was wearing minimal make-up to enhance her naturally beautiful features. She had a navy Omega rank ring, so she was Gifted. But ... *she was there as a client?*

It hit Isobel, then, where she had seen the woman. She had seen her through Kalen's eyes, bound and suspended. Kalen's *girlfriend*. She assumed they had some sort of non-monogamous relationship, especially since Kalen had spent his evenings in the Stone Dahlia playing with other women, but they were still together. The thought of him calling her every night to video chat —if that was what they did—had a sour feeling bubbling up in Isobel's stomach. She understood that he needed her as a connection in the settlements, but seeing her here, in the flesh, was doing something strange to Isobel.

Not that *she* was in a relationship with Kalen, but

they had grown closer. They had been intimate. They were friends, and she relied on him, had been vulnerable with him. The idea of his girlfriend had been such an abstract, a vague figment of Isobel's imagination.

Until now.

"Josette?" Kalen was thrown, his jaw tight, confusion radiating off him.

"Do you love it?" she asked in the prettiest, lilting French accent, spinning slightly to show off every angle of her body in the sparkly dress. "Ms Novikov just turned up with it and asked if I'd like to come and have dinner with you! I came on a *private plane*. Can you believe this? I'm not allowed to take pictures but without them, I don't know how I'll ever be able to convince anyone I was here!"

"You won't be able to," Yulia told her, a hint of condescension in her tone. "There's a nondisclosure agreement waiting for you at your table. Right this way?" She stalked off, and the other woman quickly sidled up to Kalen, looking excited and slipping her arm through his.

"I didn't think I'd see you again until you flew back to the settlement for summer break. Isn't this amazing?" she whispered rapidly. "You've been so busy, and with the time difference, I have to watch the show just to make sure you're still alive!"

So ... they hadn't been talking? If Kalen had been her partner, she wouldn't have been okay with that. *Oh god.*

If Kalen was her partner, would he want to fuck other people as well? He couldn't, of course, because of the bond. But would he *want* to?

Was she even in a position to care?

She was currently fucking three men. Or four? Or five? She wasn't sure if she was supposed to include Niko and Oscar.

She swallowed tightly and met Kalen's eyes over Josette's head. His jaw tightened further. She was surprised she couldn't hear his teeth grinding.

"He's in shock," Yulia laughed out, returning and slipping a manicured hand through Kalen's free arm. "Come on, Professor. We went to all this trouble for you; you don't want to look ungrateful now."

Isobel watched as they pulled him away, too shocked to move as both women just ignored her existence completely. Kalen pulled his phone out as he sat, and Yulia handed a pen to Josette, sliding a stack of papers her way. Isobel's phone vibrated, and she picked it out of her pocket, glancing at the screen.

Kalen (admin): We have a problem.

Elijah: No shit.

Gabriel: Is that Josette?

Kalen (admin): It's not the goddamn Easter bunny.

Theodore: What?

Moses: Josette is here? How?

Kalen (admin): They flew her in.

Niko: *Another test? Jesus Christ, how many times will they force us to prove it?*

Kalen (admin): Either it's another test, or they're letting me know that they know I've been using Josette's connections to bolster my reputation in the settlement, or they brought her here for me to break up with, to prove that their Orion program has my full attention.

Elijah: *If they wanted you to break up with her, they would have forced a no-fraternisation rule on you the way they did with us.*

Gabriel: *So they're either sending you a message or testing you.*

Kalen (admin): This could be bad.

Kalen (admin): Without Josette, my settlement reputation is dead. I won't be able to twist the rules. If anyone's families are in danger, I can't use my connections to help them, because my connections are her connections. Josette is the only thing stopping me from being profiled as an anti-loyalist.

Isobel: *How does she do that?*

Kalen (admin): She's on every settlement committee there is. She's turned in other anti-loyalists to the officials, spied for them, and spearheaded several of the campaigns they wanted to introduce to the Mojave settlement.

Kalen (admin): It makes her feel important to be with an Ironside professor, especially considering who

my family was, but if Yulia interferes and tells her I'm a person of interest, she won't choose me. She'll choose the officials. She won't even hesitate.

"You're up in ten minutes, Carter." The voice came out of nowhere. She jumped, glancing up from her phone as Cooper strode over to her, stopping too close, his hand shaping to her shoulder. She shrugged out of his hold, pretending that her bag had slipped from her arm and she needed to readjust it.

"I need to change," she said. "I sent you my song and my lighting preferences for you to pass to the stage manager. I'll be able to customise it better next week now that I've seen the space and capabilities—"

"Actually," he sighed out, a little dramatically, "the stage manager called in sick tonight, so you'll have to improvise as far as music and lighting."

She frowned, staring at the hand that landed on her shoulder again, much heavier this time.

"This is exactly why you can't spend a week ignoring me," he said in a commiserating tone. "We need to be on the same page, me and you, or you'll end up disorganised and thrown for a loop every Friday night, and Ms Novikov simply won't stand for that. She rules this place with an iron fist, I'm afraid."

"So I'm sure she has a backup stage manager," Isobel said, trying to remain calm. "For times like these."

"Well, yes," Cooper laughed, "of course ... but I

offered to handle things tonight since I was supposed to help organise this performance."

It was on the tip of her tongue to argue, to insist that she had been given the freedom to organise her own performances, but Cooper had proved to be sneakier and far more passive-aggressive in his control methods. If she argued now, she would be punished later.

"So, do you need me to send you my song again, sir?"

He slapped at his suit pockets in feigned exasperation. "I lost the damn key to the control room. You'll have to dance without music tonight. Anyway, bathrooms are just over there." He pointed over his shoulder, not even paying attention to where he indicated. "And like I said, you start in ten minutes, so better hurry up! I'll be sitting right by the stage. Do your best to impress me, hm?"

He stalked off, and she immediately walked in the direction he had pointed because the last thing she needed was for anyone in that room to catch her having a meltdown.

The stage was surrounded by dimly lit seating areas arranged in semi-circles, each round table outfitted with deep, emerald-green sofas and gold, velvety pillows. Each table had a chandelier set above it, dropping low to sparkle across the crystalware. Kalen was sitting on the opposite side of the stage, his amber eyes tracking her as he half listened to Josette, his long, thick fingers clutching a short crystal glass of liquor. He was squeezing it so hard, she winced, hoping it wouldn't shatter.

She ducked her head, finally spotting a hallway tucked behind the bar, which she assumed led to the bathrooms. As soon as she was hidden away safely in a stall, which was more of a private, marble-lined water closet, she dropped her bag and viciously kicked the heavy wooden door, swearing as loud as she could.

Guys? She tried to call for them through the bond, hoping one of them was close enough to hear her. She hadn't seen Elijah, Gabriel, Kilian, or Cian on her way to the bathroom, but her fingers were shaking too hard to text.

Are you okay? Kalen's voice sounded a little faded, but it came immediately.

There's been an issue with the sound. I don't have music.

He didn't immediately reply, and she quickly pulled off her dress and heels, switching them out for her dance costume, which felt suddenly odd now that she was ensconced within the luxury of the Stone Dahlia.

Are you confident singing? Kalen asked.

She scoffed quietly. *I've only danced and sung simultaneously for one performance, and it was with a crapload of practice.*

Could you sing if you weren't trying to dance at the same time? Elijah asked.

She quickly repacked her bag, stuffing it into one of the cupboards beneath the set of porcelain sinks against the marble wall in the bathroom corridor. There weren't even cleaning supplies stored in there, so she figured they were entirely for decoration.

She teased out the waves of her long hair in the mirror as she answered Elijah.

Without practising? I don't think so.

Right, Gabriel sounded sympathetic. *You're not that confident with your singing yet. What about one of the songs you and Mikel have workshopped? You've been singing some of those for a long time.*

She chewed on her lip, realising he was right. Those songs, she could probably sing in her sleep.

Yes, she responded.

Good. Elijah jumped in. *Because I asked the bar staff if they had any recording equipment lying around, and I found a microphone and a looper, so we can still make this work.* After a pause, he continued, *I just asked them to set it up for you. The microphone will be connected to a pedal on the stage —just tap on that, sing the song, and then tap it again and your recording will start playing back. So you can sing and then dance to it.*

Her hands immediately began to sweat.

Dancing was just ... an extension of her. It was her happy place, her safe space, her little bubble of the world that was all her own and felt completely like home. *Singing*, on the other hand, felt more like a cliff she had to dive off, with no idea how she would fall or land, or what she would encounter on the way down.

You can do this, Illy, Kilian whispered into her mind as she stood at the counter, paralysed.

There are curtains, Gabriel said. *The staff drew them to set up the equipment.*

He didn't need to elaborate. She knew exactly what he was thinking, and she hurried back into the Dahlia Room, ducking between the velvet curtains. There were two human men a few years older than her inside, arranging the equipment.

They looked up when she joined them, gave her a nod, and continued with their task.

"How do you control the curtains?" she asked quietly.

One of them pulled a small remote from his pocket. "With this. We're almost set up here. Do you need anything else? Big fan, by the way. My girlfriend is absolutely obsessed with you."

She laughed awkwardly, too full of anxiety and panic to channel Theodore's grace and acting skills the way she had been doing lately. "Thanks ... ah ... c-could I borrow the remote as well?"

"Sure thing." He tossed it to her, and she dropped it. Of course.

"You know how to use this thing?" the other man asked.

She nodded. "I just press the pedal once to record and then press it again to loop the sound back?"

"That's it!" He grinned at her. "Everything is hooked

up and ready to go. We thought you were going to dance tonight. Otherwise, we would have set this up for you before you got here."

They began to leave, but she stopped them at the last moment. "Uh, sorry, if you have a moment … is there a way for me to contact the stage manager? It would be great to clear everything with them directly before my next performance. I'd love to see what I can do regarding lighting and sound, and there's no need for me to waste Cooper's time when I can go straight to the manager."

"We don't have a stage manager," the one who had given her the remote said. "I'm the bar manager. My name is Ethan—usually, I deal with this sort of thing. Here's my number." He dug out his wallet, extracted a card, and held it out before realising she was wearing basically nothing and didn't have any pockets. He blushed slightly, flipping the card back into his palm. "I'll just give it to your friend. Reed, that is."

They left, and her chest loosened for a single breath before she walked up to the microphone and closed her eyes, listening to the low, muted chatter and laughter on the other side of the curtains.

Kalen, Elijah, Gabriel, Kilian, and Cian must have sensed through the bond that she was trying to concentrate and gather herself because they stayed out of her head. Or maybe they were busy.

Kalen certainly seemed busy.

She couldn't think about that right now.

She screwed her eyes closed even tighter and turned on the microphone.

"Good evening, Dahlia Room." Her voice was husky, but it wasn't deliberate. She was just terrified. She prayed it wouldn't crackle or break on her.

The chatter quietened, and she waited until she heard the thread of a whisper pass through the room before she began to sing without any explanation or introduction. She chose "Ilomilo" by Billie Eilish since it was the first song she had worked on with Mikel.

She kept her voice deliberately soft, trying to create an ethereal atmosphere. She projected each note with the breathy intensity she had worked on for so many months while keeping the sound full-bodied.

You need to create a subtle, vulnerable, emotional landscape. Mikel's words were hammered into her head as she drew on a practised, haunting tone. Despite the tiny stage, the room had incredible acoustics.

Mikel had emphasised not simply mimicking, but appropriating sounds for her own voice, so she did that now, inserting her own inflections, rich and subtle, blending them seamlessly into the melody. The song became hers, and her version was slow and yearning, delicate and confessional, transitioning between airiness and a deeper resonance. It was complex, but it sounded simple and effortless. The song was short—another reason she had chosen it—and she took advantage of the brief refrain to swell her voice into an elongated, two-word crescendo before dropping back to a lower, slower, exposed sound. With the curtains enclosing her in a warm, private space, she felt like the atmosphere itself was thick with her presence, entirely under her control.

She had never felt like that while singing before.

She finished on a whisper, turned off the microphone, and slid the equipment up to the curtain, out of the way, before hitting the button to open the curtains and dropping the remote. She turned her eyes up to the roof as the thick velvet parted, focusing on the little lights embedded into the natural stone ceiling. As the curtains revealed her, she felt exposed and naked, her little bubble of atmosphere popped. She wanted to pretend for just a moment more that her audience didn't exist before she tapped the pedal with her toe.

Her own voice began to play back, reverberating through the room, and she took a deep breath, letting her body fill with the sound and adjust to the slower tempo she had set before she began to dance. With the small stage and the slow, soft lyrics, she adjusted her usual style into a fusion of ballet and rhythmic gymnastics, doing her best to make the small stage seem to last forever and choosing to lean on artistry instead of strength—though, of course, it still demanded a similar cost from her body.

Each of her gestures was fluid and deliberate, pushed past their natural points. She needed that extra push, that extra little moment of astonishment with each position she held to match one of her raspy breaths over the speaker. She needed it to make up for the fact that she couldn't do anything that required running or leaping, but she already knew that she was going to pay the price for her effort.

She should have stretched in the bathroom— especially with this dance style, which required hyperextension and flexibility. That was a significant oversight, and very unprofessional. She was doing ballet moves she absolutely should not have been attempting without the proper shoes to protect her from injury. Mikel was going to *flay* her.

It was while she was balancing on the toes of her right foot with her legs split, her hands reaching behind her head to hold her other leg up into the straight, severe needle position, that she felt the little crack in her toe.

A dislocation, most likely.

Balancing on your toes wasn't something that should ever be done without shoes—and for most dancers, it wasn't even something they *could* do.

But that was what she needed to show them.

The impossible. The extreme. Proof that she didn't need to be micromanaged or handled, and that they could trust her to take complete control of both herself and the audience.

It *looked* impressive, but it was stupid. Professor Lye would have lectured her and banned her from class until she demonstrated that she could dance safely, but she wasn't there to impress Professor Lye. She was there to impress a crowd of people who saw her as nothing more than a product on a shelf. They were all there watching and waiting for her to prove that she worked the way they intended. That she would bend and twist and spin and sing the way they wanted. They wanted to push her to her absolute limits, and if she snapped, they would just toss her out and find a replacement.

Don't wince, don't wince, don't wince.

She shoved the pain to the back of her mind, staying on her searing toe for a series of spinning pirouettes en pointe. She kept her toes on the floor as light as a whisper, turning with one arm curved above her head and the other outstretched to the side, maintaining clean and graceful lines. Her core burned as she spun, her body strictly aligned, her balance perfect, each rotation precise. She spun again and again, seamless and fluid, hair rippling out in a golden cloud, pain ripping up her calf from her toe.

Holy fuck. She could feel every twitch of her muscles, every brush of the silky coverall that slipped and slid over her skin like water, the sound of her own voice beginning that elongated swell into the crescendo she had ad-libbed. With each spin, her speed increased, her focus unwavering, feet transitioning from one exacting pirouette to another and another, articulating through each position with a sharp elegance that gave away nothing of the pain tearing through her foot and calf. It felt like she was being branded or like her muscles were being torn from her skin, but it looked light as a gentle breeze, as though she weighed nothing at all and might float right off the stage.

With the final pirouette, she finished, holding her balance en pointe, still balancing on her damaged toe— because it wasn't over until it was over, and she wasn't a fucking quitter.

She could hear people gasping, but she didn't pay them any mind. This was still her time. This was still *her* dance, her moment of control, and nothing short of perfection was permitted when she was in control.

As the song finished and she lowered to stand on two feet, she finally cast her eyes around the room, taking in her audience and acknowledging them for the first time. Human men and women of all nationalities, wrapped in silk and sparkle, stitched into the finest suits money could buy. Old and young, but all of them draped in so much luxury. They were all clapping for her. Impressed by her. Under *her* control ... until they weren't. It was only a borrowed moment of power, heady but fleeting, a flame quickly snuffed out.

They shifted and stretched and turned to their companions, going about their business and returning to their crystal glasses and flutes, and dainty plates of expensive food. The bar staff stopped clapping and turned back to their tasks. The servers stopped watching and dispersed to the tables. It all felt like another choreographed dance, the servers gliding, twisting, murmuring, and demurring.

She noticed Cian and Kilian at separate tables, each with a woman, each of those women at least ten years older than them and sitting too close for comfort. The blonde with Kilian was pouring him champagne, but his pale eyes were fixed to Isobel. His guest looked up at him, trying to hand him the glass, but he didn't notice. There was heat simmering in his eyes. And discomfort. The woman touched his arm, his bicep making her hand appear tiny. She sometimes forgot that gentle, soft Kilian was still larger than other non-Alphas. His jaw tightened, his eyes narrowing, slipping down Isobel's legs before turning to the woman at his table.

He gave the woman a fake smile, shifting a few inches away, and seemed to ask her a polite question. She answered enthusiastically, her hands flapping around excitedly as she gestured to Isobel and the stage.

The brunette with Cian was accepting a platter of oysters from a server, but Cian wasn't even pretending to pay her attention. His eyes were fixed unflinchingly on Isobel, sapphire fire licking over her face and chest, surveying the dusting of sweat on her skin. He flinched when he glanced at her foot, probably feeling her pain through the bond, but he seemed ... *proud* of her. It was tucked into his eyes, swimming between the heat and the worry.

It made her feel warm inside, and even though she

had injured herself, it was the tiniest flash of *awe* in the eyes of her mates that had tears threatening to fall down her cheeks. She quickly bowed and shifted, finding Elijah at a table with four men who looked absurdly like secret service agents with their deep black suits, stony expressions, and domineering posture. Their entire table was still watching her, so she didn't linger on Elijah, who seemed relaxed and bored, fitting in perfectly with his tablemates. His Alpha size made him just a little taller than them, and his naturally muscled form screamed of a subtle, deadly strength. He didn't look intimidated by them even though the servers were giving their table a wide berth, and she could easily see why.

She continued her scan to where Gabriel sat, a couple on either side of him. The human men were talking to each other while their wives—who were young enough to be their daughters—fawned over Gabriel, fussing with his cheap suit. They seemed to be making nonsensical, tittering sounds like it was so sad that their precious doll for the night couldn't even afford a three-piece, designer suit. Isobel watched as one of the women slipped what looked like money into Gabriel's jacket pocket, her diamond ring obnoxiously large, her nails a metallic grey.

Gabriel didn't move—not so much as a sigh. He may not have even been breathing. He didn't even seem to be able to see Isobel, even though he was staring right at her.

She turned again, bowing to the audience. Pain radiated from her foot, ripping and tearing up her calf as she tried to subtly shift her weight. She found herself facing Kalen. His eyes were on her feet, but they dragged up to her face, darkening to a smoky gold. He knew she was hurt, but he looked so fiercely proud of her that she was able to ignore the little niggle of darkness and disapproval in his eyes.

His chest expanded, and the crystal champagne flute in his hand snapped, spilling champagne all over the tablecloth. Josette gasped, jumping up before any of it could get on her dress, but Kalen only tossed the crystal pieces to the table and snatched up one of the napkins, wrapping it around his bleeding palm without ever taking his eyes off Isobel.

Isobel swallowed and turned again, delivering her final bow before catching sight of Cooper and Yulia— Yulia was standing in the shadows along the very edges of the room, and as her eyes met Isobel's, she gave her a slow, veiled smile.

Isobel knew right then that she hadn't just done *well*; she had exceeded the woman's expectations. Yulia gave her a sharp nod before pushing off the wall and walking away.

That's right, Cooper. You *never* fuck with a professional dancer.

The devil himself was sitting at a table close to the stage with a few men in suits. He motioned Isobel to join them, and she swallowed a groan of frustration before she limped to the stairs and made her slow way to their table.

"Carter, darling!" Cooper stood up, taking her by the shoulders and dragging her into one of the plush seats. "Some of our board members came to watch your first performance, and they wanted to congratulate you in person."

She swallowed a scream as his manhandling caused her to kick her toe before she was plopped into the seat. Despite her best efforts, her voice still broke with a fissure of pain as she said, "Nice to meet you."

She glanced at each of them, pausing when she got to Ed Jones and Jack Ransom. She wasn't sure why she was surprised.

"We've met," Ed told her, chuckling. "You did very well, Carter. We're looking forward to more performances."

"Though maybe you could wear something a little ..." One of the men tilted his head side to side, audibly thinking as he waved his hand in time with his swivelling head. "Something a little more exciting?" he ventured, in an accented, questioning tone. He was in his fifties and chuckled heartily, encouraged, as the man to his right snickered.

"I'll keep that in mind," she said. "Please let me know if you have any other thoughts on how I can improve."

She had only forced the polite words out because she

was too afraid that she might accidentally tell them to strangle themselves with whatever *exciting* costume they were envisaging her in, but to her surprise, they did exactly as she said.

They waffled on about how she could dance better, even though they clearly knew nothing about dance. They gave their opinion on her song choice and her vocal style, though they didn't seem to know anything about those things either. Ed Jones and Jack Ransom didn't contribute. Jack even sent her a commiserating look as she nodded and numbly repeated that she would consider their advice for the dozenth time. Half an hour later, Ed saved her entirely, asking her to fetch a server for them. She did so and made her escape, gritting her teeth and refusing to cry from the pain as she limped back to the bathroom. She got changed and then just sat on the toilet with the lid down, holding her shoes in her hands, wondering how she was going to walk out of the Stone Dahlia at all, let alone in *heels*.

Her phone vibrated and she pulled it out, checking the new message.

Theodore: We finished our fights. How's she doing?

Kilian: I think you spelled "everyone" wrong.

Theodore: Yeah, sure. How's everyone, but more specifically Isobel, doing?

Cian: She killed it.

Elijah: They're going to offer her more money. She might even make more than the fights.

Oscar: Once a little rich girl, always a little rich girl.
Oscar: Did anyone record it?
Elijah: I did. I'll send it later. Saying goodbyes.

That meant they were leaving their tables. She quickly slipped on the heels, steadying herself against the wall as her leg and stomach clenched in tandem. Painkillers. She needed painkillers ... and possibly the hospital.

She didn't want to force the guys to prolong their encounters while they waited for her, so she grabbed her bag and wobbled her way out of the bathroom, heading to Kalen's table, where the others had gathered. No matter how hard she tried, she couldn't pull the same focus and hard-headedness as she could while she had been dancing to ignore the pain. It wasn't the first time she had fractured a toe, but the longer she continued to abuse it, the worse it pained her. It was beginning to feel like her entire right leg was on fire.

Yulia approached them, and Isobel fought off a small shudder. She didn't like how the woman appeared and disappeared like she was always just a whisper away, ready to strike at the most opportune times. There were no cameras in the public rooms and halls of the Stone Dahlia, of course. Their clientele paid for luxury and secrecy above all. Still, Isobel was unable to shake the feeling that Yulia had eyes everywhere.

"Did you enjoy the show?" Yulia crooned, planting

manicured hands on the table and leaning over it, fixing her attention to Josette.

Elijah and Gabriel moved either side of Isobel, tugging her hands through their arms. She immediately gripped them, trying to transfer her weight to them as they all hung back and waited for whatever game Yulia was playing to end.

"It was *amazing*," Josette breathily answered. "I knew the Sigma could dance, but she's like a proper professional now; it's just ... so impressive what you guys can do here."

"It really is," Yulia agreed, smirking, before turning her cool, icy blue eyes to Kalen. "Time to dump the Omega, Professor."

Kalen might have stiffened, but he was already like a statue. "What?" he asked calmly.

"Dump her," Yulia ordered, cold blue gaze unwavering, pink lips turning down the edges of her smile until it was a cruel, yet still unnervingly sensuous, line. "Now."

"For what purpose?" Kalen asked calmly.

"Because it would *please* me," Yulia purred, bending further, hovering close to him, her eyes crawling down Kalen's chest and back up to his face.

For all the reaction he gave, she might have just told him the weather was nice outside. He shifted in his seat, his big shoulders turning so that he faced Josette, who was looking between Kalen and Yulia with shock in her eyes, plus a little shimmer of fear.

"N-no, it's ... oh my god." Josette's laugh was too high-pitched. "It's *so* fine." She was waving her hands about, shifting away on the seat. Away from Kalen. "It wasn't that serious! I didn't mean to intrude. I would *never* ..." She wasn't pleading with Kalen. She was appealing to Yulia. "I'll never speak to him again if that's what you want!"

"Good girl." Yulia smirked, straightening and giving Kalen one last, loaded look. "Then let's get you back on the plane and back to your little home, shall we? Would you still like that picture with the Ironside hosts? Ed and Jack are right over here ..." She ushered Josette away without another word, though the brunette looked over her shoulder at Kalen, giving him a loaded look full of wide eyes, shock, and apology. It didn't so much say "Goodbye," as it did "What the hell?"

Yulia was ... going to be a problem.

8

SAFE

It only took the human nurse at the medical centre two hours to ascertain that Isobel's big toe was fractured. She fixed it to the toe beside it, using her second toe as a splint, and pumped Isobel full of painkillers. She gave her a list of all the activities Isobel needed to avoid in the following weeks as she healed, and she nodded along with all the instructions as though she had some intention of following them, even though she didn't.

She didn't have time for a fracture, or a break, or anything else that might go wrong. She couldn't afford a single day off, let alone six to eight weeks. Oscar was waiting for her when she got out, loitering by one of the hedges, his face bruised and a scowl on his lips.

Elijah had driven her to the restricted, official area in one of the golf carts after they escaped the Stone Dahlia, but he hadn't been allowed to accompany her into the medical centre.

"Do you need the nurse?" She eyed Oscar carefully, wondering why he was there. She had told Elijah she would text him once she was released, so she hadn't expected anyone to be waiting.

"Just you," Oscar said, so low she almost didn't catch it. He began walking toward the line of golf carts, and she fell into step beside him. His silence was heavier than usual. It felt like he wanted to say something but couldn't quite find the words.

They still hadn't spoken about ... the incident. The mating tie. The cock lock. The ferality. There was ... a lot to unpack. Oscar didn't seem like he was an easy person to traumatise—not when chaos shadowed his every step —but turning feral inside his mate while all nine of his best friends witnessed his lack of self-control might just do the trick.

"Are you cold?" he asked. He didn't wait for her answer; he just took her hand and slid it into his jacket pocket. He pushed his fingers between hers, locking their palms together, but he did it slowly, like he was scared of hurting her.

She was dosed up on medication and enjoying the quiet, empty campus. It was a Friday night, almost three in the morning. There were no staff, no professors, no officials, no students.

But they weren't alone.

The whole world was watching. The moment felt private, but it was anything but. The darkness and silence attempted to cloy them into opening up, spilling their secrets and exposing their vulnerabilities.

How nice it would have been, if it hadn't been a trick.

The weight of exhaustion suddenly crashed into her, descending over her mind like a dark, thick fog. She swayed into Oscar, and he stopped immediately, pulling her hand out of his pocket and scooping her into his arms. He held her like she was made of porcelain—something she wasn't quite used to from him. He carried her to one of the golf carts and carefully deposited her into the passenger seat.

He didn't say a word as he drove them home. Things between them weren't exactly awkward, and the silence wasn't truly silent, either. The space between them vibrated with unspoken words so loud it was almost overwhelming. It made it difficult to decide how to start or when to start speaking.

Tonight likely wasn't the night. It was temping to dive into her issues with each of the Alphas the second she had a spare, almost-private moment with them, but sometimes she needed to just let it go, even if only temporarily. Sometimes, she had to let go of the urgency of her existence and just let things *be*. They would still be just as urgent tomorrow, or the day after. It was okay for him to hold her hand so carefully and for her to know why, and for them to sit peacefully in their vibrating silence, because she knew they had each other, and the safety of that knowledge eased the edge of urgency that nipped at her heels all the time.

"I'm starving," she muttered just as they reached the dorm.

"You and everyone else." His voice was so gravelled she would have believed he hadn't spoken in weeks.

He plucked her out of the cart and carried her up to the dorm, setting her down before the front door. He knew she would want to walk in there and show the others she was okay, if any of them were still up. Elijah would be, at least.

She gave Oscar a small smile, which seemed to pull the focus of his dark eyes. His face was so frighteningly blank. She squeezed his hand, a silent "We can talk about it later" passing between them, and something eased in his expression. An infinitesimal softening.

Warmth trickled through her at the non-verbal communication. She hadn't ever been close enough to another person to talk to them without actually *talking*. Not even her mother. And yet she could now do it with several of the Alphas. Gabriel and Elijah, certainly. Theodore, Kilian, and Cian, to varying degrees. And surprisingly, even Moses, though his non-verbal cues were usually little challenges or moments of amusement to rile her up.

The others were more difficult, but she didn't know

why. Kalen, Mikel, and Niko had their reasons to be more guarded, she supposed.

Oscar held open the door for her and they walked into the kitchen where the others were still awake and hanging around the small kitchen. They must have also been hungry because the counter was overflowing with snacks. They should have all been in bed, snatching every extra minute of sleep they could get, but tonight had been hard.

For all of them, by the looks of it.

She had thought Oscar was bruised up, but it was nothing on Theodore and Moses, who were sporting black eyes, busted lips, and cuts and scrapes over every inch of skin she could see.

Isobel halted in her steps, her heart lurching into her throat. There was no way Ironside would air this footage —or at least they would cut it to hide all the injuries because they didn't want anyone asking questions about the Stone Dahila, but it was still absolutely forbidden to mention the secret club on camera, so she didn't comment on it out loud, speaking through the bond instead.

What exactly do these fights entail?

To her surprise, Mikel actually answered her instead of brushing off the question for another time when they weren't so obviously exhausted.

There are three levels, he explained. *Both in terms of the architecture, and in terms of the fighting style. The first level is open to all spectators and all entrants, Gifted or human. Some assholes just like to beat up Gifted, so that's what they pay money for on this level.*

Sounds awful, she said, sighing softly.

Kilian slid off his stool and gripped her gently about the waist, sitting her in his vacated spot. He wordlessly slipped off her shoe and surveyed her foot as the others watched. The skin around her toe was swollen and mottled with bruising. He lowered her foot again gently, and then circled her to press his chest against her back, giving her something warm and hard to lean against.

She sent a wave of gratitude to him through the bond, and he wound his warm, muscled arms around her waist, squeezing softly in answer.

She reached for a bag of pretzels. "Where did all this come from?" And then she added in her head, *What happens on the second level?*

She had been hoping that Mikel and Kalen would put off their lecturing about her foot until she'd had time to sleep, and was grateful that they seemed to be holding their tongues.

"We all hide food in our room where we can eat crap behind Mikki's back," Moses said, stormy eyes fixed on her tongue as she licked the salt on a pretzel. He watched until she crunched down on it, and then he shook his head like he was dislodging an errant thought.

Mikel ignored his statement, sitting on the kitchen

counter and drinking a beer. He was the one who answered her more private question.

The second level is one storey down. There's a private elevator. It's where the more serious fights happen. Gifted and humans both compete, but this time, the humans can actually lose. People bet a lot of money on these fights.

And the third level? she asked.

The same deal, but with knives, Mikel answered. *And double the money.*

She winced and quickly stuffed another pretzel into her mouth. *Which level do you guys fight on?*

Take a guess. Mikel fixed her with a slightly amused expression, his heavily scarred face taunting her.

She didn't want to answer, so she hunted through the snack cornucopia for a packet of Red Vines. Then, finally, she feigned ignorance of the fact that someone was clearly taking regular swipes at Mikel's face with a sharp object and said, *Level two?*

He grinned at her, taking a long pull of his beer. She watched his throat working, mildly hypnotised.

Mikel fights on the third level. Theodore took pity on her. *Oscar moves between the second and third level. Today, Moses, Niko, and I all fought on the second level. The men down there are all professionals, and they all want to fight an Alpha because even though we aren't allowed to use our abilities on them, we're still innately stronger, faster, and usually bigger.*

She chewed on her lip and abandoned the red vines,

ripping open a chocolate bar instead. She wanted to demand to know why it looked like he and Moses had been run over, but it wasn't like she had any other suggestions for how to wear out their aggression. With the bond damaged enough that they were *all* under threat of suddenly devolving into crazed, violent monsters, she had to admit that the need to mitigate aggression was severe. Kalen and Mikel had managed things so far without anyone getting caught or seriously injured; she just needed to trust that they had more experience with ferality than she did.

She let the conversation in her head drop.

They ate and lazily joked for the cameras, clinking their glasses in celebration of Isobel's successful first performance, Elijah's quick thinking, and Niko's success —he was the only new fighter to leave the ring uninjured —only acknowledging their Stone Dahlia successes in their heads and keeping things light-hearted until they couldn't keep their eyes open anymore, and then they all dragged themselves to bed.

But Isobel didn't go to bed.

She showered and then paced around her room, her painkillers wearing off until she was limping again. The pain was grounding for a while, but then it just became annoying, and she flopped down onto her bed, her foot throbbing and burning.

She huffed, got back up again, popped two more pills, and opened the Eleven app on her phone, clicking the button to loop the cameras for a few minutes. She left her room and crept downstairs, slipping into Kalen's office. There was just enough moonlight filtering through the almost transparent curtains for her to see by as she moved to the door to his living quarters. She knocked, but he didn't answer. She waited, shifting her weight to ease the discomfort in her foot, before finally trying the handle. It was unlocked. She opened the door and stepped inside, closing it behind her and leaning up against the heavy wood as she waited for her eyes to adjust to the dark room.

Her heart pounded out of her chest.

She should have just texted him, but she didn't actually want to *talk* about it: the sexy, bitchy, terrifying elephant in the room. She wanted to relegate Yulia Novikov to a future problem for future Isobel, but the bond wouldn't allow her to rest. The *urge* to be near him was so overwhelming, she almost suspected it was a side effect. She had felt like she was crawling out of her skin ever since she got back from the medical centre, the sensation only easing when he was nearby, when she could see him and scent him and know that he was with her and not *Yulia*.

Not that he would be with Yulia.

But her bond didn't seem to care.

She crept toward the big bed, the soles of her feet brushing over the rugs scattered across the marble floors. From the shadowed outlines of the furniture, it seemed his room was almost identical to the bedrooms upstairs.

She wished she could just *stop*, but her body kept moving without her permission until she was perched gingerly on the edge of his bed, and then suddenly, the desperate itching and scratching disappeared, leaving her with only the sound of her hammering heart and Kalen's deep, even breathing.

She winced, laying back, still three feet away from his body on the massive mattress. She carefully laid her head back. They weren't even sharing a pillow.

This was okay, right?

Maybe she could just close her eyes for a little bit.

"Why are you sneaking into my bed, Carter?" His voice was a deep rumble, only slightly husky and not at all sleep roughened. He had been awake the whole time.

"I'm sneaking *onto* it," she whispered, staring straight at the ceiling. "Not into it." She dared to pat the covers she was lying on top of.

KALEN HAD NEVER BELIEVED IN THE GIFTED GODS—NOT UNTIL he had been roped into an eleven-way bond centring around a Sigma so tiny, it was a miracle she could handle *one* of them, let alone ten of them.

And now he was sure the gods were sadistic fucking assholes, because things between him and Isobel were complicated. But what he felt for her was distressingly simple, and never more simple than when she delicately, almost fearfully laid herself out on his bed.

He had sensed her coming. Had prayed for her to choose someone else. But there she was, breathing shallowly, almost like she was trying to hide from him, her scent needy and fretful, her voice a husky whisper that travelled straight to his gut. He was probably going to do something he should regret, and he probably wasn't going to regret it even for a second.

He just hoped there wasn't a Gifted hell, because he was heading straight there.

ONE SECOND, ISOBEL WAS STARING AT THE CEILING, AND THE next, Kalen's shadowed face was blocking everything out. He had rolled on top of her, but he was holding his body off hers. He just wanted to examine her. His eyes— one amber-gold, the other multi-hued—crawled over her features.

"What's wrong?" he demanded in a deep, reverberating voice.

"Yulia told you to break up with Josette, and you did it without question." The words tumbled out of her before she had the chance to examine them. "Well, you were about to do it anyway."

"Mmhm," he confirmed in a rumble that she almost felt against her chest.

She wished his face didn't look so stern, even in the

dark, in the privacy of his own bedroom ... despite that privacy being momentarily violated. His fierce eyes were narrowed, his squared jaw flexing, his firm lips tugged down. As usual, their bond was shut down from his side. She was sure he could feel her, but she sensed nothing from him at all.

"So what if she tells you to date her instead?" Isobel demanded, though her voice sounded small and vulnerable. She quickly added, in a harder tone, "What if she orders you to fuck her?"

"She'll be in for a rude shock," Kalen murmured, settling some of his weight over her. "I'm willing to play the game, but nobody gets to tell me what to do with my body—or my cock."

"You'll tell her no?" she asked, her hard tone wobbling.

"I'll tell her she'll have better luck with a nail-studded bat."

"Gruesome." She made a strangled sound as he lowered further, nudging her legs apart with one muscular thigh. "Graphic. P-positively a-apocalyptic."

"Is that why you're in my bed, princess?" His nose ran up the curve of her neck, his hips settling between her thighs, a deeper rumble vibrating from his chest and all the way through hers.

"Wait, this is your bed?" She gasped, her hands flying to his sides to grip his shirt involuntarily. Except he wasn't *wearing* one. Her fingertips brushed his bare skin, finding tightly wrapped muscles and burning heat. She curled her hands into shaking fists, unsure what to do with them.

He chuckled, suddenly rolling to his back, bundling her onto his chest. "I'll let it slide this time. But if you do it again without permission, you'll be punished."

She settled against him, sinking into him as though he was a cloud of feathers instead of a granite slab. "Just let me stay for a minute," she mumbled as his rich, heady vanilla scent sank into her pores. "Kalen?"

"Isobel."

"I miss flying."

If she thought his body was hard before, it was nothing on how it felt now. He tightened like a bowstring, and she thought she felt him poking into her hip. She shifted in the pretence of getting more comfortable, centring her body on top of his. He definitely had an erection. It pushed up against her stomach, digging into her softness. As she settled back down again, she felt it throb.

And pretended she didn't.

"What do you miss about it?" he demanded roughly. "Tell me."

"I just liked that for an hour, I didn't have to worry about anything. It was all up to you. Whether I got hurt, whether I felt nice, whether I even remembered the day I'd had, or the week. I liked how it made my body come alive—like dancing, but someone else was doing all the effort, and it was such a relief to cry after. It just made me feel better. Is that horrible?"

"No, baby," he purred, his hands landing on her hips, large and strong and sure, though it seemed there was the slightest tremor of wavering control in his fingertips. "Do you want to fly again?"

Her body melted at his purring tone and the pet name he had called her. "So badly."

"Okay. I'll think about it." His grip tightened on her hips, pulling her an inch up his body and pressing her back down. It rubbed her over his erection and wrung a full-body shiver out of her.

"It doesn't have to be s-sexual," she said, her breath misting over his warm skin. "It can be just like it was in the club."

"That was a performance." He pulled in a deep, rattling breath. "If you come to me of your own volition and ask me to tie you up in the privacy of my own room, it won't be the same; you know that."

She felt something wet against the silk of her pyjamas. His swollen head was leaking.

"Kalen?"

"Isobel," he groaned in frustration.

"Are you wearing pyjamas?"

"No."

"Boxers?"

"The only thing I'm wearing is you."

She swallowed. "Oh."

"Oh," he affirmed, though it wasn't mocking, just a quiet acknowledgement.

"The only reason I'm not fucking you through the mattress right now is because your alarm will go off before I'm done, and you really need to get at least two hours of fucking sleep."

She squirmed, liquid heat rushing through her body. He was leaking against her silk-covered stomach, and her panties were soaked. He was so hard that she was probably going to have a bruise tomorrow from where he was pressing into her. There was absolutely no way she was going to sleep anytime soon, despite her exhaustion.

He must have felt her discomfort and frustration through the bond because he suddenly switched his grip, sitting her upright over his hips. "Let me move you," he murmured, shifting her over his thick length, the sensation shooting a bolt of desire all the way through her. Her hands landed on his flexing stomach as he grounded her in the movement, guiding her hips in a slow drag of pressure, back and forth. She could see the shadowed head of his cock peeking out from her shorts whenever he shifted her back. It was swollen and flushed with colour, twitching in need.

"Hands behind you," he growled. "Fold them behind your back."

She did, and he suddenly sat up, dragging up her pyjama top. He reached behind her, using it to tie her wrists together as his lips skimmed along her neck. "Just trust me," he whispered, his teeth scraping below her ear. "Just focus on me. Let go of everything else for now."

She closed her eyes, and he tightened his improvised knot. With her eyes closed, that subtle pull in her shoulders felt so familiar. The strong hands now dragging down her front, over her breasts, barely grazing her nipples ... those hands were like a dream. She wasn't flying, but it was *close*.

"Thank you," she whispered.

"Fuck," he groaned, his lips pressing against hers in a hard kiss, a possessive stamp. "You're so perfect."

He fell back, his hands returning to her hips, and he began to guide her again, sending wave after wave of delicious sensation through her, building the tension inside her body with every drag and shift and throb of the flesh straining up between her thighs. It was almost like a dance, this slow, controlled sway, and she sank into the rhythm, loving that she didn't have to be in control. She didn't even have to think. Kalen had meticulously studied, worshipped, and manipulated her body night after night until he knew it like the back of his hand. It was so natural for her to put herself into his hands and trust that he would only give her pleasure, even when it hurt or ached.

He knew when she was getting close, even though this wasn't a usual part of their performance. He changed his grip again, filling his hands with her ass and squeezing tightly, wringing her out over his length until she was crying out and he was forced to flip them, his hand covering her mouth as he rocked against her, drawing out the aftershocks of her orgasm. He pulled back, ripped off her pyjama shorts and panties, and then leaned over her, tugging at the hard flesh that had been tormenting her.

"Don't move," he growled, even though her arms were stuck behind her back, and he was wedged between her legs.

"Cover me," she begged ... because her absolute insanity was already established.

He swore, and she felt ropes of liquid land over her breasts and stomach before there was a slight pressure at her entrance, her soaked sex trying to grip him as he pressed forward, anchoring her hips to the bed with his big hands to restrict her movement as she felt the splash of heat inside her, without him even entering her. She froze, fear bolting through her, because apparently she wasn't over the whole Oscar incident yet, but he didn't press in. He trembled there, on the point of spearing her open, his come already inside her.

"Fucking hell, Isobel." There was a hint of disbelief in his voice. He pulled back, sliding off the bed and stalking away, disappearing into his bathroom. When he returned, it was with a soft, warm cloth, and after untying her, he gently cleaned her without uttering a word, the dampness of the water and the care of his movements sending goosebumps racing across her skin.

225

When he returned to the bed, he dragged her under the covers and tucked her into his body, his nose brushing over her neck and nuzzling into her hair, his vanilla scent so rich it almost tasted like chocolate melting on her tongue.

"You were scared?" he whispered, hand spreading over her stomach, holding her tightly to his body.

"Only for a second," she admitted.

"We'll work on it," he promised.

She sighed contentedly, lulled to sleep almost immediately, but the sleep was painfully short-lived.

Kalen was pulling her into a sitting position in no time, dragging an oversized shirt over her head as she tried to turn herself boneless in the hope he would give up and leave her to sleep. He carried her back to her room and tucked her into bed, planting a quick kiss against her lips that she guessed was supposed to be a brief parting.

Except he lingered.

She sighed against his lips, and he groaned, his tongue meeting hers. He was breathing heavily when he jerked away from her, his hand dropping over her stomach. He just stood there, and she pouted but didn't bother opening her eyes. She was happy in this blissful, vanilla-soaked space of half-sleep.

His fingers danced lower, and her eyelids began to flutter.

"No," he whispered. "Keep them closed. I never want to forget how you look right now."

She thought she heard him snatch up her phone from the bedside table, and then his fingers were on her stomach again, slipping down to the hem of the shirt he had dressed her in. He pulled it up. *Slowly*. He bunched it up above her breasts, and then over her face, blinding her even though she had kept her eyes closed.

"For privacy," he whispered, the bed dipping with his weight as he planted a knee either side of her thighs.

Holy shit. He was taking pictures of her.

Her heart raced, goosebumps pebbling over her skin. He gently circled his thumb over one of her nipples and then the other, teasing them to tight points, and then he gripped one of her breasts aggressively, squeezing tightly.

He released her, pushing the shirt further up over her face until she felt her chin slip out from the collar, air hitting her lips.

"This mouth..." He groaned, his lips hovering over hers. He kissed her like he was trying not to. Like he couldn't help himself. Like kissing her was all he thought about. She moaned and lazily writhed against him, but didn't dare try to free her arms from the tangle of his shirt or try to lower them. He moaned in heavy approval, pulling away from her mouth and tugging the shirt back down over her chin again.

And then he was shifting down the bed, roughly

shoving her thighs apart and tunnelling two of his fingers into her gripping channel. She huffed in surprise, but then her breath hitched as he slipped his fingers free and used her own moisture to smoothly glide his touch over her clit, teasing her in soft, slow circles that had her hips shifting toward him.

"Can you come like this, princess?" He pulled the shirt up to free her mouth again without pausing in his slow, torturous touches.

"I t-think so," she whispered.

He grunted, and she felt something hot and hard press against her entrance. He pushed forward and she felt the stretch of his cock—his *oversized*—cock trying to part her lips.

"Just breathe," he whispered. He must have set the phone aside, because both of his hands were suddenly smoothing along her hips, massaging her thighs.

They were ...

He was ...

Kalen West was about to fuck her. She could *feel* the snap of his control, the vibrating tension that shivered through the room, jolting her sleepy body into sudden alertness. Her arms began to move, but his sharp voice stopped her.

"No. If you look, you'll panic."

Her mouth was still exposed, but it made her ragged and choppy breaths sound far too loud. She tried to wiggle away from him, but his hands gripped her hips, thumbs digging into her hipbones, and he pushed himself an inch inside her.

"Use your words, Isobel," he demanded, voice a gravelled snarl.

She knew which words he was talking about. Green for go, yellow for pause, and red for stop. She was too scared to say green, but she didn't want him to stop. She didn't even want him to pause. But still, she was scared.

"I know, baby." He grunted, forcing his way in another inch. He seemed to be responding to the fear he could feel radiating through the bond. "But you're going to take my cock like a good girl, aren't you?"

She was *insane*. She was unhinged.

She nodded.

He slapped her thigh. "Words."

"Y-yes," she hiccupped.

"Sir," he growled, even though they weren't in his room in the Stone Dahlia anymore.

"Yes, Sir," she breathed out.

"Fuck." He sounded like he was in pain. "I can't go any further." *He was barely inside. What the fuck?* "You're stretching so tight around me. I need you wetter."

His fingers returned to her clit, and his other hand released her hip. She wondered if he had picked up the phone again.

"Are you—"

"Yes," he growled before she could even ask the question. He pulled out of her, his dick slipping up along her clit as he lowered himself over her. He tugged at the shirt blinding her until he could whisper into her ear. "I've got a little bit of a fucking problem, Carter. I *need* to be the one who takes this fear away. I can't explain why. I just know it needs to be me. I'm the one who makes you feel safe again. It's fucking me." He slid against her, making her body bow back, a low whine catching in her throat.

"But if I take you ..." His voice grew deeper, more gravelled, his cock twitching as he began to grind into her. "The possessive bastard inside me will grow unbearable. I need a way to remind myself that you're mine."

This is a one-time deal, she realised with a sinking feeling.

Kalen continued, distracting her. "I need to be able to pull up my phone and *see* it. See that I was here. That you were soaked for me, that your body curved for me like it's doing now. That your perfect little pussy got all red and swollen and sensitive from *my* fingers and *my* cock."

His rough, hungry words and the hard scrape of his penis giving her just the right amount of forceful friction was enough to send her spiralling toward an orgasm. He pulled up, the shirt covering her face now a little askew, though he didn't try to fix it. He notched himself back at her entrance and pinched her clit, like he was demanding she suddenly focus. She was so soaked that he somehow managed to press halfway into her, but before she could panic, he ground down on her clit with his palm, his other hand flashing up to twist her nipple. It was sharp and painful, and it somehow eased her from the edge of alarm and sent her tunnelling into a blissful wave of pleasure instead.

She knew she was being loud, but she didn't care. She bowed, and he caught the curve of her spine, falling over her and forcing himself deep, to the hilt, in one brutal thrust.

Holy ...

Holy shit.

Her release spiralled deeper, stealing the breath from her body. He tore the shirt from her head, pulling it up higher, but left it tangled around her wrists.

He kissed her hard, releasing deep groans into her mouth as her orgasm seemed to go on forever, clenching around his painful size, over and over again.

"I can't hold it," he groaned, pulling most of the way out and ducking his head to sink his teeth into her neck.

He bit her hard enough to leave a mark and then snatched up her phone again, leaning back as his chest rumbled, his thickness pulsing, growing bigger and harder. She tried to breathe through it, staring up at him wide-eyed and trying to convince herself it wasn't happening again.

"You're—fuck ..." His jaw clenched tightly, his pupils dilated, his eyes dark and greedy. "You're safe. You're safe with me."

She nodded, nervously licking her lips, and he gripped her hip with one hand, hard enough to bruise, as he released inside her.

He pulled out, wetness spilling across her stomach, and then tossed her phone aside, catching her chin as he pulled her lips to his. "Say you're mine," he demanded.

"I'm yours," she whispered.

He cupped her pussy. "Say this is fucking mine."

Her entire body throbbed. "It's yours."

"Don't forget." He kissed her again, his mouth dominating hers completely. "When you're ready, if you're ever ready, I'll prove it. Until then ... send me those pictures."

If Kalen finding a way to come inside her twice in one night wasn't enough of a claiming for him, then ... maybe he was right. Maybe she wasn't ready for a relationship with him yet.

He tugged up his black exercise pants—he hadn't even gotten undressed at any point—and strode from the room, his broad back full of tension.

She quickly untangled her hands, wincing at the gentle twinge of pain that immediately travelled through her body as she grabbed her phone.

There were so many photos. A close-up of her lips, with the shirt pulled up to her nose. Her breasts, her stomach, his dick notched against her. His huge length seated halfway inside her. Her face—wide-eyed, staring up at him, fearful and trusting. Ropes of white splashed across her lower stomach. She looked down, realising he had spilled some of it when he pulled out of her— probably deliberately.

Her fingers were shaking, her body squirming. Somehow, she wasn't sated. It was almost like he had awakened something inside her that just wanted *more*.

Harder and rougher.

Her phone vibrated with a message.

Kalen: Now.

She quickly sent the photos before flopping back down, her mind reeling. She really should try to get some sleep, but she didn't know how that was possible.

So she just sprawled there and stared at the ceiling in shock. She could barely even call what they had done *sex*. It had been a claiming, a healing, an instinct.

A *taste*.

Her stupid alarm went off ten minutes later.

9

CUPCAKES AND CASUALTIES

As soon as they arrived at the Icon Cafe for their shift on Saturday morning, Isobel knew it was going to end in disaster. Yulia was there again, and she handed them each a uniform, directing them immediately to the bathrooms to get changed. The cafe itself was brighter than the other rooms in the Stone Dahlia, with a lighter gold and sapphire colour scheme and a warm, welcoming glow. Individual seating areas were arranged along the edges of the room, each of them enclosed into large but cosy rooms with wood-panelled walls and exposed beam ceilings with light fabric softly draping between each beam to form a canopy. The entrance to each room was a huge, curved arch with fluttering white curtains that matched the canopy. Inside were velvet lounge chairs and curved sofas positioned around marble tables with warm, polished wood bases.

There seemed to be personal touches scattered throughout, like plush cushions, crystal vases overflowing with fresh flowers, bright oil paintings, and glass or polished wood sculptures. At the heart of the cafe was a serving area with polished wood and glass panels reflecting light everywhere. The space was haloed by ivy and designer plants that hung from the ceiling, hovering over the bar that circled the entire central cafe.

The bathrooms weren't quite as luxurious as those belonging to the Dahlia Room, but they were still slathered in marble and soft with gold mood lighting.

The uniform seemed like a death knell for their first shift, and Isobel groaned after disappearing into the bathroom to switch out her clothes. She had been given a baby-blue dress that hugged her figure tightly and ended at her thighs with small cap sleeves. The fabric had a little bit of stretch, which made it easier to move in, but that also meant that it formed over the natural contours of her body with an almost elastic grip.

Things got worse when she pushed out of the stall and came face-to-face with Mei Ito, who was wearing an identical dress.

"Oh," Mei said, her eyes sweeping over Isobel. "You're here too."

"I guess I am."

Mei sniffed, shaking out her long black hair. "Try not to get in my way, Sigma. I'm here to cultivate important business contacts."

"Okay?" Isobel said, because *what did she care?* But Mei was already out of the bathroom, the door falling closed behind her.

And then it got worse.

The Alphas had been dressed in matching midnight blue suits, several shades darker than her dress. Bellamy was hovering nearby, also suited up. He gave her a look, his eyebrows briefly jumping up, surprised to see her, before he returned his attention to Yulia.

Her stomach sank.

What had they done to recruit him?

What information did they have on him?

Did they force him to do something?

The entire human group was there, as well as several fifth-year students and a couple of fourth-year students.

"This is Ethan, our bar manager," Yulia said, once all the students had gathered, ready to start their shift. "He's here for our morning shift in the cafe." She indicated a man with messy black hair and smiling brown eyes, a dish towel slung over his broad shoulders. It was the same man who had offered his business card and helped her set up her stage the night before. "For those of you just starting today, you'll report to him at the start of your shifts. You'll work at the bar or in the kitchen until you're requested as a guest. As a guest, you will be the personal attendant to that table and that customer or group until they leave. You will wait on them, pour their drinks, serve their food, and engage them in conversation. You are to be pleasant and charming at all times. You are to make them feel special, above all. Make them feel that they're your favourite person in the world so that they come back again next week and request to see you again. Photos and hugs are allowed, but nothing else. You're allowed to touch them, but they're not allowed to touch you. They're well aware of this rule. Are we all understood?"

They all chimed in with an answer, and Ethan jumped into action without a preamble, directing everyone to stand in two lines by the entrance, where they could greet the guests as the doors to the cafe opened. Isobel did her best to smile, and was fairly sure it was warm and welcoming ... or at least it was polite and not a grimace, which was exactly what Oscar was wearing.

He didn't greet anyone.

Neither did Mikel or Kalen.

Niko may have released a few grunts. Moses didn't even lift his head to look at them.

This was *not* going to go well.

Isobel was so worried about them that she didn't even notice anyone who walked through the door, but as soon as they reported back to the bar, Ethan pointed out one of the private rooms.

"Table eight, Carter. You've been requested."

He moved on quickly, telling the Alphas they had also been requested. He skipped Oscar and Mikel and then moved on to the human group, assigning them all table numbers.

"Menus are on the bar there," he said, noticing that Isobel hadn't moved. "You just hand them a menu, be friendly, and take their orders. There's really nothing to it." He gave her a grin. "You'll do great."

She wasn't the one he should be worrying about.

Moses snatched up a menu like he was about to use it to whack someone across the face.

Gabriel refused to touch the leather-bound, gold-edged menus at all, giving them a distasteful look, even though they were likely impeccably clean. He also gave the towel slung over Ethan's shoulder a narrow-eyed glare as though personally offended by it before he strode off empty-handed.

Niko approached his table and tossed the menus onto it carelessly, sinking into one of the sofas with a frown. His room was full of teenage girls. Isobel hurried to catch up with Ethan, who was already back behind the bar.

"H-how did they get in here?" she asked quietly, nodding toward Niko's room.

"The Icon Cafe doesn't have an age limit," he told her. "Tickets are five hundred euros for a day pass, not including food and drinks. As long as you can pay up, you can come in." He handed her two menus. "We don't serve alcohol in the cafe."

She took the not-so-subtle hint as he pressed the

menus into her hands and approached the room he had indicated earlier. The curtains were closed, showing only vague outlines through the thin, fluttery white material. She slipped inside, deliberately leaving the curtain open so that she could keep an eye on the others—or what she could see of them, anyway. She didn't recognise the occupants of her own room until she was standing before the first man, offering him a menu.

Ed Jones and Jack Ransom were sitting on sofas, grinning at her.

Ed took both menus from her, passing the other to Jack. "Good to see you again, Carter." He indicated one of the sofas, and she perched on the edge of it. Her dress was too short to sit any other way.

Jack immediately handed her a fringed cushion, and she gratefully arranged it over her lap, sitting back a little more comfortably. "Nice to see you again," she said, eyeing them curiously.

"Shall we order first?" Ed perused his menu quickly before handing it to Isobel. "Does anything interest you?"

It offered a selection of gourmet snacks, some of them so fancy she didn't even recognise half the ingredients or even the names of the desserts—and she was no stranger to luxury. The Stone Dahlia was just on a whole other level. She swallowed as she scanned the lists of pastries, savoury bites, sweets, and artisanal chocolates. There were no prices listed, but she doubted they were cheap.

It felt impolite to refuse, but she was too distracted by what she could see from her periphery to formulate any kind of response. Across the cafe, Kilian was alone in his room with a man who would have been at least three hundred pounds and who had shaken out a napkin to lay over Kilian's lap. It really looked like he had used the napkin to pat down Kilian's crotch. Kilian barely reacted, but he was leaning as far away from the man as he possibly could.

"That's Jimmy." Ed followed her gaze. "James Justice? The producer for *Legendary*."

"The teenage sitcom?"

"That's the one."

"That seems wise," she grumbled. *Putting a man like that in charge of children*. She didn't say it out loud, forcing her attention back to the menu. "Can I take your orders?"

"Let's just order the high tea service, shall we?" Ed asked. "It's my wife's favourite. You'll enjoy it."

"Sounds great." She stood, collecting their menus, before remembering what Yulia had said. "Uh ... great ... choice." She attempted the compliment with a wince, but Ed and Jack only chuckled, waving her off.

After placing their order with Ethan at the bar, she took a moment to walk around the cafe and glance into each room, seeking out the Alphas. Theodore sat with a pretty woman in her thirties. She was talking to him excitedly and animatedly, her face glowing. He seemed relaxed, his charming smile fixed in place, but he sensed when Isobel drew near, and his eyes followed her until she was out of sight. Moses had another table of girls, this time in their twenties. He was refusing to sit down, probably because they had only left narrow spaces where he would have to sit close to one of them. He still hadn't given them the single menu he had brought over and was using it as more of a shield than anything else.

Elijah sat with a very nervous girl, maybe around Isobel's age. She was blushing and biting her lip, too scared to talk to him. He pulled out his phone with a sigh, completely ignoring her.

Kalen looked like he wanted to kill himself.

He was pouring coffee for a group of three young women who kept finding excuses to touch him despite the rules. Like accidentally brushing past him to switch seats or accidentally touching his fingers as they reached for the drinks he was serving them.

Oscar had been requested as Isobel was doing her rounds, and he was now stalking over to a table with a deep scowl and a menu. Cian was with two girls who looked like they had just gotten into a fight over who would pour his tea, even though he was supposed to be serving them. Gabriel looked like he was about to have a meltdown, stuck in a room with five girls. Just like with

Kalen, they kept accidentally touching him as they showed him videos on their phones.

Mikel still hadn't been requested.

By the time she finished her lap of the room, one girl was running toward the bathroom, her face red and tear-streaked, her shaking hands clutching a napkin. Isobel peered back to the room she had come from, finding Oscar sitting back with a peaceful half-smile, legs stretched out to notch against the table, arms folded behind his head.

"Oh boy," she mumbled, returning to her own table.

"What did she expect?" Jack asked, tittering and shaking his head. He seemed to be talking about the crying girl.

Isobel didn't answer, setting the cushion back over her lap as she watched the two hosts of the *Ironside Show*. She felt like they wanted something or wanted to say something. It wasn't that they weren't the types to enjoy the luxuries of the Stone Dahlia, and as she had found out, they were also official board members ... but they didn't seem the types to have celebrity crushes or to pay for the company of Icons-in-training.

Still, they didn't speak about anything of consequence until one of the servers came over with their food and drinks, setting up a tiered crystal stand stacked with tiny sandwiches, pastries, cakes, scones, and chocolates. Isobel poured tea for each of them—and then herself, at their insistence.

"So—" Jack cleared his throat, some of the joviality slipping from his expression. "How are things going, Carter? How are you finding the new group rules?"

"Fine?" she ventured, unsure. Even though she knew there weren't any cameras in the room, she still felt like she had to perform and watch every word that passed her lips. "Things are going well."

"Ironside isn't for the faint of heart," Ed added, loading up a plate with sandwiches and mini cakes before placing it in front of her. "It's gruelling, punishing, demanding. Some might say it demands the impossible and then asks for more."

What on earth was he getting at?

She busied herself with her cup of tea as she reached out to them both with her Sigma power. Slowly and subtly, like smoke slipping beneath a closed door, she felt around for their negative emotions.

Concern. Worry. Fatigue.

"Are you concerned about anything in particular, sir?" she asked, addressing him as they were expected to address all officials. "I'd love to reassure you."

Ed narrowed his eyes on her, perhaps a little frustrated with her formalities. "Believe it or not," he said, "we've been rooting for you from the start of your rise to popularity. We want to see Eleven win this show."

She arched a brow at him. "Really?"

"Really." Jack grinned at her over his teacup. "You've overcome quite a lot. Frankly, we're blown away. It would be a shame if Hero won after all you've done. Hundreds of talented settlement kids wasting five years of their lives only for *none* of them to win?" He sucked in air between his teeth, shaking his head. "It isn't right."

Isobel didn't answer. She didn't feel like she could. She wasn't human like them; she couldn't just say whatever she wanted.

There was a commotion outside their room, and she quickly jumped up, her eyes searching out where the noise was coming from.

Gabriel was standing, breathing heavily, his arm wet, and the entire contents of his table scattered and smashed across the floor as though he had suddenly swiped it all off the table in a fit of rage. Food was splattered over some of the girls at his table, and they were now making a very loud fuss.

Ethan was swearing at the bar, directing servers over to the table in a hurry.

"Oh dear," Ed muttered. "Looks like we chose a very eventful day to visit, eh, Jack?"

NIKO EXTRACTED HIMSELF FROM HIS TABLE WITHOUT A WORD, following as Gabriel stormed into the bathroom. He locked the door behind them, checking to ensure the stalls were all empty. Gabriel washed his hands, pouring more and more soap into his palms and scrubbing them together ferociously. Usually, when he was indulging in a cleaning routine, it was best to leave him alone and not interfere, but this was not a cleaning routine.

Niko slipped his hands beneath the water, managing to catch Gabriel's soapy hands.

"Squeeze," he said.

Gabriel squeezed his hands hard enough that if he hadn't been an Alpha, he might have cracked something.

"Breathe," Niko muttered.

Gabriel sucked in air, his eyes wild and unfocussed. Niko didn't try to pull their hands out from under the water, keeping them there until Gabriel seemed to return to himself, and then he released the other Alpha. Gabriel finished washing his hands calmly as though nothing had happened.

What's going on? Isobel's soft voice floated through the bond, threaded with concern.

He's had to endure a lot of people touching him the past two days, Elijah answered for Gabriel. *It was bound to end like this.*

"I'm fine," Gabriel said. He didn't seem to realise he had said it out loud instead of through the bond. He walked to the bathroom door, pausing to dry his hands before pushing out. He didn't thank or even acknowledge Niko, but that was only because his head was a mess. Niko knew he would find him later after he had finished processing the incident.

Unfortunately, this meant Niko had to return to his own table. He did so slowly, trying to see into Isobel's room as he passed. She was frowning after Gabriel, holding a cushion over her lap because the ridiculous dress Yulia had given her was so short she couldn't sit comfortably. All the other female Icons-in-training in the room were wearing the exact same dress, but for some reason, on Isobel, it was obscene. It hugged every line and curve of her body and showed off the entire length of her stunning legs, clinging to her chest in a way that had him contemplating violence because he couldn't imagine anyone holding a conversation with her and *not* looking.

He needed to stop thinking about it.

Ed Jones and Jack Ransom were also looking after Gabriel, gossiping quietly with each other. At least they weren't laughing. Niko didn't think he would be able to tolerate that.

He reached his table, which was full of giggles. The girls peered around him to catch sight of Gabriel returning to his table to apologise.

"What's wrong with him?" one of them whispered. "Is he, like, autistic or something?"

"Are you, like, unable to mind your own fucking business?" Niko shot back with a snarl, causing them to jump in their seats.

"I thought you guys were supposed to be nice to us," another one of them muttered petulantly. They had given their names; he just couldn't remember them. "Can we change our server, please?"

"My fucking pleasure," Niko snapped. "Who do you want?"

"Theodore Kane!" one of them whisper-yelled while the others dissolved into a fresh puddle of laughs.

"I'll add you to his waitlist." Niko turned on his heel and strode off. Gabriel fell into step beside him.

"They requested Kilian," Gabriel said. "Who did yours request?"

"Theo," Niko answered.

"Those two are going to be busy." Gabriel sighed. "And ... Cian," he noted, coming to a stop. Two security guards were dragging two women toward the exit. They had been sitting with Cian earlier, but now they were red-faced and dishevelled, the previously perfect waves of their hair now mussed and tangled, red scratches and welts covering their arms.

"You ruined everything, Madison," one of them hissed at the other, trying to break out of the security guard's hold. "He said he would give *me* his number if he met me at a bar."

"The number to a plastic surgeon maybe," the other girl hissed back, also trying to break out of her guard's hold.

Ethan followed behind them, looking harassed.

Niko bit back a smirk. Cian had done that deliberately.

The Alpha in question was now enjoying the food and drink they had ordered all by himself, sipping on a coffee and nibbling a cupcake, looking mightily pleased with himself. Mikel walked over to collect the plates and used cups, casually knocking the cupcake out of Cian's hand. Cian picked up another one, and Mikel knocked that out of his hand, too, saying something sharply. Cian gave him a defiant look, reaching for another treat. Mikel pretended to accidentally bump the entire platter of cakes to the floor.

Ethan was on his way back to the bar when he noticed, and his heavy sigh was comical. "We've got it," Gabriel said to Ethan. "My table wants Kilian Gray, and Niko Hart's table wants Theodore Kane, by the way."

"I'll add them to the waitlist." Ethan rubbed his brow, looking stressed, before stalking back to the bar. "Do your best to hurry with Cian Ashford's table, please. He also has a waitlist."

"I knew they had waitlists," Niko said as they stepped into Cian's room to help Mikel clean everything up.

"Stop that," Mikel snapped as Cian started licking frosting from his fingers. "You already earned yourself an extra thirty minutes on the treadmill."

"But I have to be so sickly sweet to make up for you lot," Cian drawled, sighing dramatically.

Isobel watched as Cian, Gabriel, Niko, and Mikel cleaned up the mess they had made at Cian's table, jiggling her leg nervously and making the cushion in her lap tremble.

"What were we saying?" Ed asked with a laugh, checking his watch. "It's quite eventful in here today. Like an episode of the show. Those Alphas really know how to inject energy into a room."

"I was saying that you seem concerned with my performance," Isobel said, dragging her attention back to them. "I was wondering if there was anything I could be doing differently."

"Our concern isn't with your performance." Jack was shaking his head, also glancing at his watch. "Call it more of a safety concern."

She froze, her teacup clattering back to her plate.

"He meant for your mental health," Ed interjected with a laugh, but it sounded a little forced. "The show can take a toll, especially on our top performers, and now with the new group rules, we just wanted to check in because we'd love to see your group win the game. We'd love to see *any* Gifted win the game, to be honest, but we think Eleven has the best chance."

"As for what you can do—" Jack nodded to Ed, and they both stood, buttoning their suit jackets. "—just try to follow the rules and save the drama for the cameras, you know? If the producers can trust that you'll always follow the rules, we'll be much less concerned about you."

"Thanks for your time, Carter." Ed was holding out

his hand, waiting for her, already shutting down the conversation before she had a chance to respond.

She slipped her hand into his, and he shook it firmly, Jack doing the same before they strode for the exit. Isobel watched them go, her stomach turning over nervously.

The entire interaction had been light and friendly, strictly surface-level and almost casual, but now that they were out of her sight, their words replaying in her mind, it felt like a warning.

Maybe they knew that the officials had planned to kill them all off and champion Theodore as their Icon, and they were cautioning her to stay on this path and stay within the confines of the roles the officials had sketched out for them.

She extracted her phone from where she had tucked it into the tight pocket at her hip, peering over to the bar to make sure Ethan was busy before she drew the curtains closed, hoping she could steal a few minutes before someone put her back to work. She pulled up Bellamy's contact and sent him a message, hoping he was free to answer.

Isobel: What are you doing here?

She didn't have to wait long for a reply.

Bellamy: Washing dishes because I'm not a human or an Alpha.

Isobel: I meant the Stone Dahlia.

Bellamy: ... my answer remains the same.

Isobel: What did they do to you?

Bellamy: What did they do to you?

She glared at her screen.

Isobel: Are you safe?

Bellamy: Ugh, fine. I'll go first. They said they had proof I was the one who supplied Crowe with guns last year. They said they had proof that I bullied and ostracised him and pushed him to do what he did. The proof is fake, but it looks real as shit.

Isobel: Jesus. I'm sorry.

Bellamy: Where's the quid pro quo, Carter?

Isobel: They said they had proof that one of the Alphas was hiding an illegal ability. A lie, obviously.

Bellamy: They didn't even blackmail you personally? You should have refused. This place is creepy.

He had no idea.

Isobel: It doesn't matter. We're here now. Just ... don't resist them too much. If they think they can't control you, they'll gather more collateral. That's what the others told me.

Bellamy: Appreciate the heads-up.

Bellamy: Moses saw your name on my screen.

Bellamy: He's threatening to brain me with a sauté pan.

Bellamy: I told him you were asking for nudes.

Isobel: Felt like dying today, did you?

Isobel: Bellamy?

She jumped up, rushing to the cafe in the centre of the room and stopping at the bar, where she had a clear line of sight into the kitchen.

Moses was leaning against the cold storage, his leg

bent up, foot planted on the heavy door. One arm was crossed casually over his chest and he was *whistling* as he examined the nails of his other hand.

"Where did Bellamy go?" Ethan asked, drying his hands as he darted through the kitchen. "He was just requested."

"He's in the cold room," Isobel said.

Moses scowled at her.

10

THE SCREAMING DIDN'T GIVE IT AWAY?

"TABLE TEN," ETHAN SAID, BARELY SPARING HER A GLANCE AS he rushed around, looking like someone—or specifically the five bickering Alphas in his kitchen—had ruined not just his day but quite possibly his life.

Theodore, Kilian, Cian, Elijah, and Kalen had officially picked up all the slack, but it seemed like Elijah's girl was just too afraid to make the first move and leave. She had six empty iced-coffee glasses spread out before her, and her hands were visibly shaking as she sucked on a seventh drink, eyes wide and full of terrified tears. Elijah had graduated from his phone and pulled out a tablet at some point—from where, Isobel had no idea. He was tapping away, absorbed in his work, oblivious to the girl and her overcaffeinated terror. She seemed to dredge up the courage to ask him a question, and in answer, he pulled headphones out of his pocket and inserted them into his ears.

Isobel wasn't doing as well as Theodore, who had his entire table eating out of the palm of his hand and somehow still respecting his boundaries, or Mei Ito, who seemed to have cultivated an actual, adoring fan club at her table ... but she took comfort in the fact that at least she wasn't as bad as Elijah.

She grabbed a menu and headed for table ten, reading the little gold plaques above the arched entrances to each room until she found the right one. Except, there was nobody there.

"They're probably late," Ethan said when she returned to the bar. "I think that one was an online booking. We put up your pictures last night for people to pre-book."

Behind him, Moses was glaring at a girl who had approached the bar. "We'd like to request Kane, please— uh, I mean ... the other Kane."

Rude.

"Where's the—" Moses started to ask, but Ethan was already pulling a list from his pocket.

"Kane's waitlist," he said, slapping the list down. "Might as well leave it on the bar."

Isobel slipped away and sat at her assigned table, because if she had to stand behind the bar while people told Moses to his face that they preferred his brother, she might just turn into Gabriel and swipe everything onto the floor in a rage. While she waited, she pulled out her phone, opening up a private chat with Elijah.

Isobel: Hey.

His response was immediate, but when she poked her head out of the curtain, he was still tapping away at his tablet.

Elijah: Hey.

Isobel: Your date is terrified.

Elijah: Sounds like she knows what's good for her.

Isobel: Theo, Kili, Kalen, and Cian are fighting for their lives out there and you're ...

Isobel: What are you doing?

Elijah: Playing Solitaire.

Isobel: Liar.

Elijah: I'm updating my blog.

Isobel: Liar.

Elijah: I was making a bingo sheet of everything that could possibly go wrong before our shift was over. Since then, I've just been ticking things off and writing notes on exactly how it happened.

Isobel: I wish that was a lie.

Isobel: Will we get into trouble for this?

Elijah: We are who we are. That's why people like us. It's in the officials' best interests not to shape, mould, and beat us into just another set of cookie-cutter Icons. We turned up. We'll continue to turn up. They may give us a lecture, but I promise you, this is all part of the package they're selling.

Isobel: You mean they expected this to happen?

Elijah: Of course.

Elijah: Theodore and Kilian will attract people who want to be charmed, who genuinely want their celebrity crushes to look at them and really see them, even if it's an act. Cian will attract people who ... are horny. Oscar will attract people who mistakenly think they can change someone as psychotic and unhinged as he is. If someone books me, it's for the challenge of getting someone like me to acknowledge them. This girl? I won't say a word to her, and she'll be back next week.

Isobel: That's messed up. I wouldn't come back if you ignored me.

Elijah: You would force me to pay attention.

Isobel: Yeah, that's me. Forcing Alphas to bend to my will. Been doing it my whole life.

Elijah: You would sit there with those big eyes and those perfect legs and that sweet fucking smell and I'd have to pay attention.

Isobel: What does she smell like?

Elijah: Coffee. And yes, that was before the seventeen coffees she ordered.

Isobel: Do you at least know her name?

Elijah: I think it was Erica.

Elijah: No, Ellen.

Elijah: Elizabeth.

Elijah: Edith.

Elijah: Ethel?

Isobel: I guarantee it wasn't Ethel. Nobody is called Ethel.

Elijah: I asked her. She spilled coffee all over herself and then apologised to me for it? She's a mess. Her name is Collins. Now she smells like a double-shot because she's also wearing it.

Isobel: I can see where you got all the E-names from Collins.

Elijah: Or was it Celene?

Isobel: You can't possibly have forgotten already. Your brain is like a vault.

Elijah: I was distracted.

Isobel: By your bingo chart?

Elijah: By that fucking dress.

Isobel: Which dress? We're all wearing the same one.

Elijah: On them, it's a dress. On you, it's wet tissue. It's putting all sorts of thoughts in my head.

Isobel: Thoughts about wet tissues?

Elijah: I have the most intense urge to grab one of these butter knives and see if it rips like wet tissue. So ... yes.

Isobel flushed bright red and quickly dragged a cushion onto her lap, as though it could shield her from the tightening of her own body. Her phone vibrated with another message.

Elijah: When did you text your father?

She blinked at the screen, taken aback.

Isobel: A few hours after my session with Teak, why? He ignored my message.

Elijah: I think he wanted to respond in person.

Elijah: Let us know if you need us.

Braun Carter suddenly filled the doorway, his

familiar, gold-flecked eyes taking her in with a stern, stony expression. Isobel's body locked up in fear, her phone clattering out of her hand. She worked to get her instinctual reaction under control, but it took a moment. Her body didn't seem to understand that she wasn't a little girl under her father's thumb anymore. She didn't have to listen out for his heavy footfalls in the hallway outside her bedroom. She didn't have to fear his wrath, his summons, or his heavy, dark emotion.

She had cut him off and proved to him that he couldn't control her anymore.

"Daughter," he greeted, still hovering by the curtain. "I thought we should have this conversation in person."

"Father," she responded, applauding her even tone. She calmly picked up her phone. "Take a seat."

Normally, he would have snapped something in response. *I'm not a dog. Do not direct me.*

Instead, he sat, still eyeing her. "Your message said that you wanted surrogate pills and you wanted to make a deal."

"That's right."

"I thought the pills didn't work for you?"

"I'm offering a deal, not an explanation."

He frowned, his heavy frustration battering up against her chest. It wasn't the only thing emanating from him. There was also guilt, sorrow, and a humiliation that felt dark and dangerous.

"What are you offering in exchange for the pills?" he demanded.

"What do you want?" she countered because, in truth, she wasn't sure *what* she could offer him.

"I want things to go back to normal," he said immediately. "I want regular, weekly updates. By email or phone is fine. I want a copy of the contract you signed with the Ironside recording label—"

"You won't like it," she snorted. Maybe she was testing him.

Temper briefly flashed in his eyes, but he sucked in a deep, tempering breath. "I might have been able to negotiate something better for you."

"You don't know my situation," she countered. "You don't know *me*. How could you possibly think you're in a position to negotiate for my best interests?"

"I'm not fucking stupid, Isobel." He sucked in another deep breath. "I've pieced it together. I know why you're doing this—this whole group thing, and I know you better than you think. You're half me and half your mother, following the exact same path in life that I took. I know what you're experiencing. At Ironside. In *here*." He waved around the room. "I understand you better than you think."

"Maybe you do." She sighed, her attention drifting to the curtain. It was open just enough for her to lock eyes with Mikel, who was hovering nearby, pretending to wipe down the bar, mismatched eyes trained on her with unwavering intensity. "Or maybe you don't. So, what else? You want weekly updates?"

"I want you to run major marketing decisions by me," he said, once again without thought. He had decided all his demands ahead of time. "I'm not asking for full control, but I want to know what you're planning, and I want open discourse so that I can help."

"Help, how?"

He rolled his eyes. "I know you hate me right now ... you've probably hated me since your mother died. But don't let what you think of me cloud the reality of *who* I am. I'm Braun Carter. I know the entertainment industry inside and out. I have *contacts*. I have *information*. I know how things work, and I know how to make things happen. I know when something is a bad idea and what the consequences will be. I know how to move forward when it looks like you're out of options. I'm the guy you want on your side."

"I wonder how many guys have said that to stupid little girls like me," she said, levelling her gaze on his and refusing to look away.

He didn't bother to argue with her or to correct her statement because he had said it himself: he knew the industry inside and out. He knew the "guys" she was talking about, and he knew that they saw most women as "stupid little girls." Her father wasn't a *sexual* predator, but that didn't make him less of a predator. It didn't make him less of a misogynist or a privileged asshole.

It didn't make him less of a problem.

Still, he didn't argue. She had to give him that. He didn't get defensive; he just watched her and absorbed her statement.

"I ..." He suddenly swallowed, looking uncomfortable. "I thought maybe that wouldn't happen to you because you're a Sigma."

She scoffed, not deigning to even respond to that comment.

"As an Alpha," he continued, looking uncomfortable, "I was somewhat of a commodity. Everyone wanted a piece of me because I was so rare—I was the only Alpha at Ironside the entire time I was here. I had Dorm A to myself and all the attention of the clients in here. There was always someone wanting to pay for my time or attention or someone trying to manipulate me, and it was all because I was an Alpha. I just ... I thought they might leave you alone because now they have ten Alphas to choose from." Before she could even digest his words, he was holding up a hand, warding off her response. "I'm wrong. I see that now. I watched your performance last night, by the way. People want you just as much as the Alphas, maybe even more. I just don't want what happened to me to happen to you. Despite everything, you're still my daughter. I always wondered if it was worth it and sometimes I even thought it was ... but

realising you might go through those same things has
changed my mind. Some things aren't worth winning
the game."

Some things aren't worth winning the game.

She never could have guessed those words would
ever come out of her father's mouth, and it made her
stomach curdle, thinking of what might have happened.

"What are you talking about?" she asked, brow
furrowing. "You're just confusing me."

"I'm talking about *this*." He lightly slapped the table.
"The Stone Dahlia. The way they use their top students
as prizes, as lures, as fringe benefits. Nothing is
forbidden. Nothing is off-limits. They might *pretend* it is,
but the more in demand you are, the more in danger you
become."

"I see." She folded her hands in her lap.

He seemed to shrug off his own words like he didn't
want to think about them anymore. "That's my deal.
Take it or leave it. I'll give you a steady supply of
surrogate pills ..." He pulled up the gift bag he had
walked in with, sliding it across the table. "And in return,
I want weekly updates, and I want to be kept in the loop
about all contracts you sign, all major marketing
decisions ... and I want to know the moment things
change with your role in here."

"Change how?" Isobel ignored the gift bag.

"If they start arranging private meetings with clients.
Outside of these public spaces, I mean." He gestured to

the cafe. "If they book you one-on-one time with a client in a private room."

"I need to clear it with the others," she said, picking up her phone again. "Since this affects the group."

He watched her wordlessly, offering no opinion where previously he would have raged over the fact that she had tied herself so tightly to the Alphas.

Isobel: My father wants weekly updates in exchange for the pills. Over email or phone. And he wants to be consulted before I sign any more contracts.

Elijah: Is that all?

Isobel: More or less. I can fill you in later.

Elijah: I suppose this is acceptable since you can email him updates. Kalen?

Mikel (admin): He's busy dodging hands, but this is okay. As long as it's okay with you, Isobel.

"You've got yourself a deal," she said, reaching for the gift bag.

"That supply should last you a few months," he said, nodding toward the bag. "Call me if you need more."

SHE DEBATED HOW SHE WOULD SLIP TEAK THE PILLS WHEN HER sessions were being recorded. She didn't want to hide them inside a gift because she wasn't sure if the officials would try to search anything she gave the bond specialist. Instead, she dumped all the pills into a Ziplock bag and covered it in several layers of tape to make it watertight. She tucked the little package up the sleeve of her jacket and stopped by the dining hall before her session, preparing two takeaway coffees. She surreptitiously dropped the pills into one of the cups before filling it with coffee. The top of the package still poked out of the liquid, but at least it wouldn't make a rattling sound in the cup. She squeezed a lid onto it, tucked it atop her other coffee, and made her way to the appointment.

Teak looked even worse than last time.

Isobel was seriously worried that she might not last.

"You're still sick?" she managed to sound surprised before quickly handing over one of the cups. "I picked you up a coffee."

"Oh, you didn't need to do that." Teak's voice was completely devoid of emotion. The table beside her chair was overflowing with tissues, and she hadn't bothered to turn on the light again. Her hair was unwashed and unbrushed, her fingers trembling around the cup.

"Tell me more about the bond," she said, jumping straight into the questions. "I'd love to know what makes an eleven-person bond unique compared to the traditional bonded pair."

And so their dance started again.

Isobel answered each of her questions, only sometimes truthfully, always twisting the answer to make herself and the Alphas sound as uninteresting as possible, trying to make their bond as boring and uneventful as possible. She framed each of her statements to make it obvious that her only priority was succeeding and making money—and that the Alphas were in the same mindset. She ignored when Teak randomly started crying and kept speaking when Teak frowned at her coffee, lifting the lid to look inside. Teak replaced the lid without reacting, shifting to rest the cup on the table.

By the time the session ended, Isobel's nerves were fried, her head aching from having to put so much effort and care into every single word she uttered. She performed sluggishly in the rest of her classes, fumbling at the piano with Elijah and making several mistakes during her vocal lesson with Mikel in the evening. After wrapping up her pre-dinner practice sessions, she dragged herself back to the dorm and put herself through a shower.

She blamed her exhaustion on the fact that she zoned out while brushing her teeth, her eyes riveted to the golden roses in the crystal vases fixed to the wall on either side of her bathroom mirror. She often found herself vacantly staring at the pretty soul artefacts, wondering if she should touch them, but it felt like such a risk. The chain had crawled up her chest and embedded into her skin. What would the roses do?

At first, it just didn't seem wise to tempt their luck with everything hanging in the balance and so many eyes on them. They didn't have the time or resources to mitigate another disaster. But now? Now that they were safe?

She found herself staring at them more often.

Touching them.

She would pluck one of them out of the vase just to hold the stem in her hand, wary of the sharp thorns that seemed to beg for her to bleed on them.

She blamed her exhaustion for how long she stared at them that night, only snapping out of her trance when Cian snuck into her room an hour later. She glanced down, noticing she had dropped her toothbrush into the sink at some point. With a frown, she quickly finished up in the bathroom as Cian stretched out on her bed. He wore a pair of light-grey sweats that had her immediately forgetting her exhaustion. They were slung low on his hips, his shirt wrinkled up to show a few inches of tantalising golden skin.

"Not so fast," he warned, catching the look in her eye, his own eyes sparkling with a heart-thumping mix of humour and adoration. "Oscar will be here any moment."

"Huh?" She turned off the bathroom light and dropped onto the bed beside him, reaching over him to grab the remote for the TV. She had a few *Ironside* episodes to catch up on and needed to stay on top of things. He smelled *amazing* fresh out of the shower. Like salt and sun and warmth. As her chest brushed his arm and she pulled back with the remote, his scent warmed further, and both of their breaths seemed to shorten.

Cian smirked. "He said, and I quote, 'I need someone in there to kill the sexual tension.'"

"And he chose ... you?" Isobel laughed.

"He's so dumb. Come here." He grabbed her, rolling her beneath him, and she bit back another chuckle.

"I have to catch up on *Ironside*. I'm falling so far behind."

"I'll give you a recap." His lips skimmed her throat, his cock already hardening against her thigh. "They're desperately trying to make the fifth-years interesting, but nobody cares. They think Ellis and James are fake bitches for moving on from Gabe and Elijah so quickly, but let's be honest, they're getting attention so they're probably happy." His hot mouth dragged over her collarbone, making her moan. He nipped her skin in response, his voice turning husky. "Also, people think the officials came up with the group rule to deal with the backlash they got for introducing humans into the game. People are saying they formed the human group so that they only have one chance to take the winning spot from a Gifted contestant instead of six chances." He slid down, pushing up her pyjama top, breath misting the skin of her stomach. "They're obsessed with Niko's new look. His whole moody grump thing is somehow cultivating a weird little cult following." He pushed her top up higher, revealing her piercing, which he began to pepper with

kisses. He had almost reached the top of the chain and
bared her breasts when the door opened and Oscar
stalked inside, already looking pissed off.

He slammed the door and Cian smirked against her
skin.

"The fuck?" Oscar snarled. "This is the exact opposite
of what I asked you to do."

"You just asked me to be here." Cian climbed up her
body, nuzzling into her neck and making her giggle. "It's
your fault for assuming it would kill the vibe. I *create* the
vibe."

"I can't have sex with her again, Cian." Oscar all but
snarled the words.

Cian didn't so much as flinch, scraping his teeth over
her jaw. "So? Watch. I don't care. You need to get over it.
Isobel is over it, aren't you, doll?"

"Totally over it." She gripped his broad shoulders,
laughing again as he switched to the other side of her
neck. As he sucked on her skin, the laugh tapered off into
a moan. "Kalen cured me."

Cian picked up his head, arching a brow at her. "Oh,
we're *talking* about the night you tried to scream down
Dorm A, are we?"

She bit her lip, her face flushing red. "No. Go back to
what you were doing."

Cian chuckled, suddenly rearing back. He roughly
spun her around, his palm landing heavily across her ass.
"Don't tell me what to do."

She hid her face against her pillow, trying to muffle another laugh even as heat curled in her stomach. She arched her back a little, pressing back against his hand as he lowered it to rest against the swell of her ass. He fiddled with the lacy hem of her pyjama pants.

"I've never seen these before," he noted, voice deep and hungry.

"I can feel your need from here," Oscar spoke lowly.

She could feel him as well. A heavy emotion thumped up against her. It felt like ... *torture*. Maybe they shouldn't be teasing Oscar like this. Not that she was doing it deliberately; Cian was just very good at distracting her.

As if sensing her change of emotion, Cian eased from the backs of her thighs, and he flopped onto the bed beside her again, bundling her into his side as he reached for the remote without a word.

Oscar blew out a hard breath, cautiously approaching the other side of her bed. He sat. He lowered to his back, staring at the ceiling, his arms limp by his sides.

"This is pathetic," Cian grumbled, his eyes trained on the TV screen across the room. It was above the fireplace, but they could still mostly see it.

She hit his stomach, but he only caught her hand, holding it in his lap. Right over where he was still hard.

Oscar didn't respond to Cian's dig. He didn't even seem to be *breathing*. She cast him a quick, worried look, and then dared to nudge him with her foot.

He ignored her.

Cian smirked, still pretending to watch the show, and Isobel poked Oscar again, using her toe to prod his thigh. His head suddenly fell to the side, dark eyes narrowing on her face.

"What?" he asked roughly.

"I'm not made of glass, you know."

OSCAR FELT THE BOLT OF LUST THAT TIGHTENED HIS BODY AT those words from her pretty pink lips—lips he remembered kissing over and over in the shower as he fully wrapped himself in her delectable pussy for the first time. But that was *before*.

Before he looked up and saw the horror in her eyes as he lost control.

Isobel had never been *truly* terrified of him until that moment. She often told him he was scaring her, but her scent always gave her away. It remained sweet, even when she trembled in his hands.

Until that night.

That night, her scent shrivelled and soured. It was chipped wood and butchered fruit. His chest tightened as he recalled it, and the lust inside him died. He had always gotten off on fear, on hurting people. Fucked up as it was, that was just him. But ... Isobel wasn't just *anyone*.

She was the little Sigma who had stitched herself

into his soul and *habitually* threatened to tear herself from him in permanent ways. He had faced the possible loss of her too many times to treat this casually. It wasn't casual. It was high fucking stakes. If someone else hurt her, he would kill them.

Plain and simple.

If she wanted him to tear out another eye, or kick in a kneecap, or rip off an arm, or remove a few fingers, he would do it, no questions asked.

But sex?

After the *incident?*

That might be asking for too much.

Because what could he possibly do if *he* was the one hurting her?

"Why is this not a problem for you?" He found the words slipping out of him in a sudden snarl, his eyes on the side of Cian's smug, smirking, punchable face.

"Every night when I go to bed, I pray for a magical cock lock," he drawled in return. "I'd trade everything I own for the ability to trap Isobel on my dick until I'm ready to release her."

Oscar barely suppressed an eye roll. "You're a fucking idiot."

Isobel was biting her lip, her pretty eyes still on Oscar, her cheeks flooded with colour. He could feel her every emotion through the bond, so he knew she was morbidly excited by what Cian had said.

His breathing picked up. He *loved* that deviant side to

her. But no. He fought down his reaction again. Her little foot flicked out, poking him in the thigh again. This time, he caught her ankle, deciding to keep her leg prisoner.

"You won't break me," she whispered.

"Are you actually asking me to fuck you right now?" he drawled back, hoping his crass question would dissuade her.

Her eyes traced his features. "This isn't about sex. This is about you acting like you can't even look at me or touch me. You said I was yours."

His dick filled with blood so fast it made his head spin. He sucked in a breath.

It should have bothered him that she was curled up with another man, her head resting on his arm, his hand resting on her hip, while reminding Oscar that she was his. But it didn't.

Hearing her next door with Cian or Kilian or Theodore made him feel homicidal with rage, but right now, in just this one moment, he was grateful that Cian was there. He was anchoring Isobel. Calming her. Keeping her safe and happy, her scent soft and sweet, while Oscar worked on his shit.

"You are mine," he rumbled.

Cian cleared his throat, unable to help himself. Isobel's lips curled up at the sides.

"I just want the old Oscar back," she said quietly.

Cian interjected again. "Said nobody, ever."

She began to turn, already raising her hand to hit his

stomach again, but Cian caught her wrist. She flopped onto her back, raising her other hand. Oscar caught it, instinct kicking in before he could stop it.

She glanced between them. "I can only be one person's prisoner."

"Liar." Cian grinned down at her. "You've been my and Kilian's prisoner. Kilian and Theo's prisoner. My and Theo—"

"We get the goddam picture," Oscar interrupted.

"Don't judge me." Isobel pouted at him. "Apparently, I have a high sex drive."

"How high?" Oscar demanded, even though his rage was threatening to surface at the idea of her with anyone else. "How are you able to take so much Alpha cock in your little Sigma pussy, hm? Night after night? Hour after hour? Doesn't it hurt, baby?"

Cian groaned, his head dropping to the pillow. "You did not just say that," he whined, words muffled. He still hadn't released Isobel's wrist. "You are such a sick fuck."

Oscar ignored him, watching the way Isobel's teeth dug into her full lower lip.

"It's painful, but I like it," she admitted.

"Great, I'm hard again," Cian complained, face still mashed into the pillow. He lifted up, edging closer to the Sigma trapped between them, whose smile was threatening to appear again at his antics. "Are you going to do something about this? Because I'm not feeling particularly patient."

"I don't know how to share," Oscar said honestly.

"Don't overthink it," Cian said, rolling over Isobel and releasing her wrist.

ISOBEL FELT THE FIRST FLUTTER OF NERVES AS CIAN SHOVED HER legs apart, sitting back on his heels to drink her in. He was the least gentle of her three men. Him and Oscar at the same time might be biting off more than she could chew. She wasn't left to dwell on the thought for long as Cian gripped her thighs, his thumbs brushing dangerously close to her centre.

"Are you already wet, baby?" he asked like he didn't know the answer.

It was his superpower, knowing the moment she got excited.

She nodded, her body trembling as he backed away, and got off the bed, standing there with his sweatpants tented obscenely.

"Prove it," he purred. "Show him."

She found Oscar's free hand, his dark eyes fixed on her face as she moved his hand to her stomach. He twitched but didn't pull away. She could see him warring with his control, but Cian knew her.

He knew that breaking their control was her *favourite* game.

God, she loved that man.

Liked him.

What the fuck?

Shoving away the errant thoughts, she encouraged Oscar's rough hand to slide down over the silk of her pyjama top, toward the waistband of her shorts.

"I haven't seen this before either." Oscar's voice was a low, tortured rasp as he eyed her pyjama set.

"You can ruin it if you like," she said. "I have more."

His hand fisted, halting her progress. "Carter," he warned.

Cian gripped the top canopy of her bed, leaning in, eyes intense. "Didn't I tell you to do something, doll?"

She pressed against Oscar's hand, and with a grunt, he gave up his resistance, allowing her to push his fingers past her silk waistband and into her panties. They both groaned as their fingers hit the warm, wet mess Cian had created with all his teasing.

"Go ahead and press one of his fingers into your greedy little pussy," Cian said. "Show him what he's missing."

Oscar didn't react to Cian's dirty words at all, his eyes searching for secrets in her face as he still wrestled with the control she attempted to tease away from him, his fingers following hers as she forced one inside her. Oscar groaned, his head ducking to her neck, roughly biting her tattoo, releasing it only to suck her flesh just as roughly.

But he didn't move his finger. He refused to participate past what she directed with her own hands.

"Feel good, doll?" Cian rasped, watching as she arched up in pleasure.

"Yes," she panted as Oscar licked over the marks he had made on her neck before shifting down an inch and doing it again.

It wasn't the same as when she was with her other guys at the same time. When she was with them, the focus was still on her, but they were a little more collaborative, helping each other to hold her down or tease her. It was an unspoken rule that they were allowed to cross certain boundaries—like touching her at the same time or pushing into her seconds after one of them had just pulled out of her.

With Cian and Oscar, it was very different. It was almost like they didn't exist to each other. Like they couldn't see or hear each other, even though they obviously could. They were hyper-focussed on her, locked into a scene with her alone, unable to help but give her the pleasure she so badly wanted.

It felt very intense.

"Did that not work, baby?" Cian asked with false sympathy. "Are you still not being fucked? Maybe you should try adding another finger."

As soon as she applied the slightest bit of pressure to Oscar's finger, trying to push it into her slippery entrance, he growled and ripped away her shorts and panties.

"You want to get fucked, Carter?" he snarled, flipping

her around and tugging up her hips, pushing her face down into the mattress. "You want me to fucking lose control? You better thank me before you pass out, little girl."

When Oscar lost control, he *really* lost control. He didn't hesitate or prolong this moment of uncertainty while he teased and taunted her the way she had him. He just shoved into her, right to the hilt, hitting her too deep on the first thrust and making her hiccup a sound of shock and pain as she quickly gripped the covers. She wanted to yell one of her words and claim it was too much, but the adrenaline rush from the shock and pain made her immediately dizzy with lust.

Cian appeared in front of her as Oscar pushed into her again just as violently, making her almost scream— almost, because Cian had slapped a hand over her mouth just in time.

"*Tsk*," he chastised, smoothing the messy hair back from her temples as Oscar delivered another punishing thrust, holding too deep inside her and squeezing her ass into a punishing grip, flexing his fingers like touching her there was his new favourite thing.

"We should keep it quiet in here," Cian said. "Don't want a repeat of the other night. Open up, sweetheart."

She parted her lips, and as soon as she did, Oscar picked up his pace, almost as though he was deliberately trying to make the sound slip out of her throat. Cian freed his erection, the tip already damp and swollen, looking desperate for her tongue to soothe it as he slid into her mouth with a soft moan. His piercing was cold while his flesh was hot, the slow glide of him in and out of her mouth a direct contrast to the brutality of Oscar's pounding.

"Fuck," Cian groaned, his palms on her cheeks. "You're crying, and it's not from me. I'm being gentle here, aren't I, baby?"

She felt Oscar twitch inside her and heard him groan behind her, one of his hands releasing her ass to reach between them, giving her pulsing clit all the attention she needed to spiral toward an orgasm. She tried to cry out, but Cian's cock gagged her. Oscar's nails dug into the skin of her ass, and fear shot through her for a moment as he thickened and stilled, grinding so deep into her that it was almost painful as he came, spilling heat inside her.

"It's okay," Cian whispered, still slowly dragging his cock across her tongue, his hands gently stroking her face. "It's all right. I'm here ... you're safe. Shit ... baby ... you suck harder when you're coming."

Oscar pulled halfway out of her. Just enough to ease up on the pressure, but still holding himself inside as she finished clenching around him, savouring the lingering effects of her orgasm. He released her ass cheek, delivering her a sharp, stinging slap, the sound echoing around the room.

Cian's breath hissed through his teeth, his

uncharacteristically gentle stroking inside her mouth bringing him close, his fingers tunnelling into her hair as he began to lose control, pulling her faster onto his length, pressing deeper until he was properly fucking her mouth. He hit the back of her throat and traced his fingers down her neck, just lightly massaging it as he grunted, pulsing with his own orgasm. He didn't let up until he was done. When he finally pulled out, she coughed and gasped for breath. Oscar shifted off the bed, and she heard him in the bathroom.

"Sorry, Illy." Cian pouted with false sympathy, kneeling beside the bed as she collapsed. "I forgot to be gentle." He kissed each of her cheeks, where her tears still stained her skin.

"You're not sorry." She groaned, flicking out a weak arm to hit him.

"Neither are you," he whispered against her ear. "Maybe my girl wants it rough more often, hm?"

She yawned, wriggling her body a little like she could shake off the bolt of heat that shot through her at his whispered threat.

"Okay, give me a year to recover," she joked.

Except, she wasn't joking.

Oscar returned with a damp cloth, his silky boxers tugged haphazardly back over his hips, his dark eyes serious as he surveyed her and Cian before settling on her ass, which was currently presented to him as she lay curled on her side facing Cian.

"I hurt you," he said lowly.

She glanced down at herself, noticing that bruises were already forming, and there were small, red, half-crescent marks from his nails.

This felt like a defining moment for them, and she wasn't entirely sure how to handle it.

"My screaming didn't give it away?" she asked, deciding to choose humour.

His attention flickered back to her face, taking in her sleepy, sated expression and the small, teasing smile on her swollen lips. He hovered there, perhaps also feeling what she had felt, that they were on the cusp of a defining moment ... and then he decided.

He got onto the bed and gently turned her to her back, leaning over to kiss her as he pressed the cloth between her legs. "I won't hold back next time," he promised darkly.

II

I AM NOT FOR SALE

ISOBEL KNOCKED ON THE DOOR BEFORE SLIPPING INTO MIKEL'S office. It was close to midnight, but it was the first moment of free time they were able to line up in each of their schedules. Mikel, Kalen, and Elijah were already waiting. Mikel was dressed for a run, the grey material of his shirt tight and a little damp as it clung to the ridges of his abdominals, his black shorts wrinkled up around powerful thighs as he sat with one sneaker notched against the coffee table between the couches. He raised dark brows at her in greeting as he pulled deeply from a water bottle dotted with damp condensation. Just like Oscar, Mikel liked to escape for a run whenever he felt tense. She sometimes found it surprising how alike the two Alphas were, but she shouldn't. Mikel had obviously been a very heavy influence on Oscar.

"Thanks for the meeting," she said, flicking her

attention to Kalen, who was still in a suit. He had just finished up a training session with one of the humans.

She didn't want to know *which* human on the off chance it was one of the females and they had been alone. The knowledge might force the bond to act up again. She and Kalen hadn't said a word to each other about her sneaking into his room to appease the bond ... or what had happened after, but there was something different in the way Kalen looked at her now. Whenever they were performing for the cameras, he surveyed her the same way he did the Alphas: with a razor-sharp focus, and an intimidating analysis of her every move churning behind his expression.

It dropped the moment they were out of view of the cameras.

His eyes wandered, just like they were doing now. That strong, amber gaze caressed the hem of her cropped sports top as though he was thinking of slipping his hand beneath the material to cup her breasts. His attention slid down, over her bared ribcage, fixing there like he was imagining his tanned hand spanning across her pale skin. Or *remembering* it.

When he looked at her like that, it was easy to imagine that he was seconds away from ordering everyone out of the room, bending her over Mikel's desk, and demanding she tell him she was his again. But he didn't. He only sat back and nodded at her as though his eyes hadn't just stripped her bare.

Elijah's icy stare was easier to meet, because even though he swept his eyes over her, she could tell that his brain had kicked into gear. He had already figured out why she had called a meeting with them, and he was probably already mentally an hour into the discussion after predicting what everyone was going to say. He hadn't had a chance to shower yet, because he was still in the same clothes he had worn to their evening dance practice, his pale hair drifted across his forehead, a little wavy from a full day of training, his muscled arms crossed over his broad chest.

"You've decided what you want to do in the Dahlia Room?" he asked, without preamble.

"Yeah." She moved to the seat beside him, facing Mikel and Kalen across the coffee table, but he surprised her by catching her wrist and tugging her into his lap instead.

"What do you need?" he asked, settling her sideways over his strong thighs so that she could still see all of them. Elijah and Gabriel both touched her and sought to settle their side of the bond less in group settings, and she wasn't sure if it was because they were more reserved, or if it was just hard for them to shift their focus from caring and worrying about the others to doing whatever they needed to do for themselves.

She tried to focus on his question instead of the warm and spicy, smoky clove scent that clung to his skin, smouldering warmer as soon as her thighs hit his, his big hand settling high on her leg, right where her shorts ended, his thumb stroking back and forth absently, raising goosebumps over her skin.

"I'll need a rig," she said, clearing her throat. "An anchor point in the ceiling. And I'll need them to pull down those curtains; they'll only get in the way."

Kalen's brows twitched up, but Elijah was already nodding.

"Aerial silks," he concluded, not even a question. "You're right, that fits the space perfectly with the circular stage, and I think they'll accommodate any ideas you have after your last dance. Do you have any experience?"

"I did some training as part of the gymnastics phase my father put me through. Enough to cover the basics and learn one routine, but I'll obviously need a lot more," she answered. "I can't go in there and do a basic routine."

"Let me organise it with Cooper," Kalen said. "I'll tell him Mikel and I are working on your performances together, so he doesn't question it."

She dipped her chin in an eager nod. Anything to escape Cooper. "Do you have time?"

"I'll figure it out." Kalen waved off her concern. "That's my job. But you'll need to put in extra hours. Do *you* have time for this?"

"I'll figure it out." She copied his hand movement, and his lips lifted into a small smirk, eyes dropping to

Elijah's hand on her thigh for a moment, heat flaring to life before he blinked it away.

She stiffened slightly, because it wasn't the kind of *heat* she was used to—not from her other Alphas. For the barest second, it had looked as though he might rip her out of Elijah's grip and start a brawl right there in Mikel's office, but he shook it off *so* fast.

"Well then." Kalen stood, shrugging off his jacket and stretching out his massive arms. "I've got a few things to look at before bed. Let's get started tomorrow."

IT WAS ALMOST 10:00 P.M. THE NEXT NIGHT WHEN SHE walked into the private room Kalen had booked out in the fitness complex. It was a medium-sized gym that seemed to be fit out for different types of gymnastics—a room she had never visited before, though that was hardly surprising with how large the fitness complex was.

"How'd you get that set up so fast?" she asked, spotting Kalen in the middle of the room, fiddling with aerial silks hanging from the ceiling.

She jumped when Mikel pushed off from the wall and fell into step beside her.

"It was already here," he said. "You get both of us tonight, by the way."

She bit on her lip, because none of the responses that

popped into her head seemed appropriate, though she managed to drudge one up by the time they reached Kalen.

"Are you guys worried I'm going to hurt myself?"

Kalen gave her that *look* again. "It's cold outside." His eyes skirted her bared stomach, inching up over her crop top.

"I ran here." She tried to stop her brows from popping up. "I've got a sweater." She waved her bag at him before dropping it on the floor. She bent, tugging it open and extracting Kilian's shirt, which she had swiped on her way out of the dorm. It wasn't even a clean shirt. She had picked it up after he tossed it on his bed on his way to the shower. It was *drenched* in his scent and maybe she was sick for stealing used shirts, but she had the convenient excuse of needing a bit of extra cover for this particular hour of training.

She tugged it on, the soft material falling to her thighs, and Kalen's brows dipped for a moment, before he nodded to the silks. "Show us what you've got."

She stepped up and gripped the fabric, and even though there was a falling mat beneath her, they both hovered close.

"How long has it been?" Mikel asked, as she did a basic climb, the silks sliding between her fingers as she lifted herself.

"My father got me started when I was ... thirteen, I think," she answered, directing most of her attention to the climb. "I only did it for a couple of years sporadically. My upper body strength wasn't the best back then."

It was better now. She could feel the difference, even though the silks felt a little unfamiliar and stiff. Still, it was instinctual for her legs to wrap around the soft material, her feet finding the familiar positions. She paused halfway up, enjoying the weightless feeling, the demand on her muscles, her breath easing as a slight weight lifted from her chest.

She moved through a few easier positions, stretching out her body before extending into a simple split. There was an initial spark of panic as she glanced below, but she forced her eyes back up and her body to loosen into the position. Trust in herself was essential when doing complicated or dangerous manoeuvres. It was the same on the ground as it was up in the air, and something Lye had been hammering into them in her Acro Duo classes with Gabriel and Elijah. The moment she doubted herself or her partner, her chances of injury skyrocketed.

She waited for all vestiges of panic to trickle out of her before moving to a new position. Her movements weren't as fluid as they had been when she had first learnt the basics of aerial silks, but she was still able to move with a certain amount of grace. Her body was simply trained that way: to move to a rhythm, to be as fluid as water no matter the impossible ways she twisted and positioned it.

The tension in her arms was both challenging and

oddly comforting. The ability to make herself weightless, to make herself fly, was something she had grasped at with all her strength. When the officials had dragged Kalen into the Stone Dahlia, he had turned their exploitation on its head and handed himself back control while exploiting their guests instead. And it sounded like Gabriel and Elijah had done a similar thing, though she had never seen what their performances entailed.

Now, it was her turn, and she had figured out what she wanted.

She wanted to fly above them.

She wanted to look down on them.

She wanted to be *untouchable*.

Even if it was all a fantasy, as easily crushed as a bed of fresh, soft snow beneath their designer heels and Italian leather shoes.

She felt a little spark of pride as her body began to move with better fluidity, falling into the routine her mind was slower to remember. Each twist and pose was simple and basic, but she completed them without a wobble of uncertainty or panic, and that was more important. Her finishing pose wasn't complex, but it was strong and sure, and she was grinning when she dropped back to her feet, her body tingling with adrenaline.

"I think this could work," she said, bouncing on the balls of her feet as she looked between the professors.

Their expressions were carefully guarded, which made her want to shake them and force them to *show* her something, especially since she was sure they could read everything she felt through the bond.

"I see significant potential for injury," Kalen finally admitted, sucking air between his teeth. "But you were beautiful. I just know you're going to push this as far as you can, and I'm worried about the strain it's going to put on you with all your other obligations."

She glanced to Mikel, but he seemed to agree.

He said, "It's up to you."

"I'm doing it," she declared stubbornly.

Mikel shrugged, like he did his best to talk her out of it, and Kalen's hard lips lifted slightly at the corners, like he had expected nothing less.

"Then I guess I've got some research to do." Mikel's blue-black eyes roamed over Kilian's shirt like he found it distracting. "Wear a full-length leotard that covers your arms and legs, so you don't get rope burn. We can practise two hours a night until I'm confident you won't hurt yourself, and *then* you can perform. Until then, you'll have to keep dancing—preferably without dislocating anything. Understood?"

"Understood, Professor," she answered quickly. It was easy to see when Kalen and Mikel switched from her mates to her managers. The change of tone wasn't even subtle.

They both grew still, eyes fixed to her face. It took her a minute to realise she had called Mikel "professor." In *private*. The lines between them had become so blurred, but she had stopped deferring to them a while ago, considering them partners and friends more than anything.

She wasn't entirely sure why it had slipped out in that moment.

"Oh." She laughed awkwardly. "I mean—"

"Let's get back," Mikel said, his grin a little sharp. "It's late."

"Right." She pulled her sweater over Kilian's shirt and trailed them out of the gym, enjoying the heat and mingling scents of them as they walked either side of her.

Strong, heady vanilla and storm-soaked condensation was a combination she wasn't going to easily forget. Not after Mikel had spanked her after one of her and Kalen's performances. Not after Kalen had pushed his cock down her throat. Not after they had shattered her into a thousand pieces without reaching for their own releases, muddying the boundaries of their relationship. Even after what Kalen had done a few days ago, she knew nothing had changed ... and she hated it, but understood it at the same time.

There was just something about the way Kalen looked at her, something about the stillness that sometimes overcame Mikel when their eyes met, and she accidentally said something that stirred a thought in his head.

She was already juggling a lot with Theodore, Kilian,

Cian ... and now Oscar. Mikel felt like a storm that might sweep through and leave only devastation in its wake, and Kalen felt like a dragon who might jealously hoard her away, tearing the limbs from anyone who dared come too close. It seemed like Kalen knew that about himself, too, and was just as wary of becoming involved with her as she was of becoming involved with him.

Curiously, there was no hint of that dragon in his interactions with Josette.

How much do you feel through the bond? she asked, pulling them both into her head. It was so quiet outside, most of the students asleep at this time. She could smell the pine trees lining the pathway, the scent muted compared to the drenching rain and vanilla of her mates. Their steps were deliberately short, keeping pace with her, the cold breeze forcing her hands to retreat into the sleeves of her sweater.

Mostly big emotions, Kalen answered. *If we concentrate, we can sense every little feeling that flits through you but big emotions barge right through. They're hard to miss.*

We could tell how the silks made you feel, Mikel elaborated, sensing that she needed more to understand. *But I felt nothing through the bond a minute ago when your scent changed, so it's not like mind reading.*

When my scent changed? she asked.

Sweet, Kalen answered. *Wet.*

She wasn't sure if he was talking about her *scent* being wet or *her* being wet, but she admittedly had been thinking about his dick in her mouth while Mikel spanked her a few minutes ago. She awkwardly cleared her throat, deciding to drop the conversation as they walked on.

"How's the toe?" Mikel asked, once they neared the dorm.

"Great!" she lied enthusiastically. In reality, she was popping painkillers between most of her classes and white-knuckling the pain and discomfort while she danced and practised.

Mikel let out a small growl beneath his breath. "Ice it tonight," he demanded.

"Yes, Professor."

His exhale was harsh, and he pulled open the door to the dorm, standing back to let her in first. "Good girl."

Teak began to subtly improve, and by the time fall break rolled around, she was managing to get through a session without crying.

Still, Isobel was grateful for the reprieve from their sessions and her usual classes. Since the break was only for a week, Kalen decided they would make the best of the time and spend every day in their brand-new training room, workshopping concepts for their first album. They all welcomed the change.

Their new training room was huge, with an attached

bathroom and a small kitchenette, which was restocked with energy drinks, water, tea, and coffee every night. There was even an empty office tucked behind the practice room. Mikel filled it with first aid supplies and a massage table. With the increase in their training hours and intensity, there always seemed to be something wrong with at least one of them. Isobel spent more time in there than anyone, especially while she was recovering from her fracture. The Alphas all seemed to heal from their injuries within a matter of hours or days, but hers lasted for weeks.

The back wall of the training room featured a huge neon sign of their group name, while the right side wall housed long, carved wooden benches. The left side wall featured towering, arched windows and long, transparent white drapes, and the front wall was covered by floor-to-ceiling mirrors. There were two iron chandeliers, which created beautiful patterns on the floor after the sun went down.

The officials hadn't just tossed them any old training room. They had gutted one of the performance halls and properly redecorated it. With *care*. It was simply stunning.

The first night, Isobel refused to leave. She sat on one of the benches and scrolled through her playlist until something caught her attention. The song was called "Palm Reader," and she forced Cian to come back after his shower so that she could choreograph a partner dance with him. It was upbeat and fun, the emphasis on sharp movement and perfect synchronicity, but Cian decided to do their final take without his shirt, his tattoo-covered muscles on full display, and suddenly she was sweating for a different reason. He'd touched her constantly as they ran through it for the last time, playing up their chemistry for the recording. She couldn't stop smiling because he was totally messing up the choreography, always stepping too close to brush his body against hers, shifting in the wrong direction so that she was forced to bump into him, or grabbing her hand and refusing to let go. They were both breathing heavily by the end, and she was smiling so hard it hurt.

The next day, Gabriel posted their dance. It immediately went viral, giving them a huge boost in popularity points, and the comments section exploded with pleas for her to choreograph a dance for each of the Alphas. They thanked her for giving them a dance so soon and heaped praise on Kalen and Mikel for making her the dance leader. Even the comments claiming that her and Cian were obviously sleeping together were quickly shut down by other fans, who said they were just acting and doing their jobs, and that Isobel always danced to a theme.

Things were going ... a little too well.

Kalen brought a selection of songs he had been working on into the training room the next day, and they spent two days workshopping them and narrowing down their choices for the debut album. The entire time, Isobel tried to fight back the feeling that their good luck was about to topple and crash all around them.

On the third day of fall break, she hung back again, pulling her tablet from her bag. It was Gabriel's birthday, but he had left to work on his rap sections for the album and wasn't interested in celebrating.

Kilian sat on the floor, scrubbing through Cian's recordings of Isobel workshopping dance ideas. He was pausing the video and taking notes, humming softly beneath his breath. Theodore copied the dances in the video, frowning at his reflection in the mirror. He was executing the moves perfectly but didn't seem happy with perfect. The others had already returned to the dorm, hoping to catch an extra few hours of sleep, since Gabriel wasn't interested in doing anything.

Isobel set her tablet against her knees and plucked up her electronic pencil, tapping into her sketching app.

"You're still doing those?" Theodore asked, glancing at her screen as she began to draw.

"It's not like he's getting any other presents," she said, frowning at him.

Theodore smirked. "You want me to get him a present? What do you think he'd like?"

"Hand sanitiser," Kilian commented without looking up.

Isobel ignored them, outlining a bunch of cotton blooms, her brushstrokes soft and calm. She added more and more of them until they were taking up most of the screen. She could imagine grabbing handfuls of their softness and rubbing it over her cheeks. Gabriel's clean linen scent made her feel like that sometimes. She just wanted to rub her cheek against his chest and breathe him in, but he would likely hate that.

In between the pretty little tufts, she drew hesitant, delicate ferns, their edges curling in on themselves. She coloured in the sketch and sent it while she waited for Theodore and Kilian to finish up.

Gabriel's response came half an hour later.

Gabriel: I love it.

Gabriel: Thank you.

Isobel: Did anyone else get you a present?

Gabriel: Elijah got me a pen.

Isobel: What kind of pen?

Gabriel: The one I left in his room last week.

Isobel: Are you trying to make me feel sorry for you?

Gabriel: Is it working?

Isobel: It's not NOT working.

Gabriel: You know what isn't working?

Isobel: Please tell me it isn't the pen.

Gabriel: It's the pen. That's why I left it in his room.

Isobel: I'm getting you cake from the dining hall.

She packed up her things, said goodbye to the others, and rushed to the dining hall, but it was too late to get any desserts from the dinner service. There were only snacks, drinks, and fruit available. She groaned and snatched up a packet of cookies from the coffee bar, rushing back to the dorm. She knocked on Gabriel's door, but there was no answer, so he was probably still at the studio. She let herself in, planning to leave the cookies on his bedside table, but once she was inside, she was too curious to leave. She hadn't been inside Gabriel's room, and it seemed he hadn't put up all his sticky notes from the previous Dorm A. There was still no blanket on the bed, which housed a single pillow, the sheets tucked so tightly there wasn't a wrinkle or crease in sight. His desk still housed stacks of notebooks, ordered by the colour of the cover, but there were no notes.

She was just returning to the door to see if there was a message on the back of it when Gabriel filled the doorway. He stepped inside, closing the door behind him, revealing smooth, polished wood. There were no notes.

"You feel even worse now, don't you?" He stalked over to his desk and began emptying his bag, arranging everything meticulously over his desk or into drawers. "You promised cake and didn't realise the dining hall had stopped serving for the night." He hung up his bag and then came around his desk, leaning on it and crossing his arms.

There wasn't a hint of amusement on his face, but she knew, somehow, that he was laughing at her on the inside. She wanted to crack that demeanour. It was *too* perfect. His blond hair was tamed, a few darker gold streaks daring to rebel against the rest of the uniform colour. There was no curl in the strands but a persistent, adorable flop in the locks he always tried to tuck into place by his ear. He reminded her of a leading man in an '80s movie, with that little hair flop. All he needed was a tight shirt and a cigarette to wedge between his hard lips, and the image would be complete, but of course, he would sooner use that cigarette on the forehead of someone invading his personal space than smoke it. His features were masculine but not broad and so symmetrical it made his blank stare even more emotionless and chilling.

"I brought cookies." She pointed to his bedside table.

"My favourite," he said, without even looking.

She blew out a short breath, eyeing him. He looked tired. "Sorry for sneaking into your room."

"No, you're not."

"Okay, fine. What happened to your notes?"

"They're in the dressing room."

She glanced at the closed door and then back to Gabriel. He lifted a brow.

She took a step toward the closet.

He didn't stop her.

She took another step.

He rolled his eyes.

She skipped over to the door and stepped inside, her gaze widening immediately.

His problem hadn't gotten better. It had gotten *worse*.

Notes covered the back of the door, the walls, the shelves, and the drawers. She could even see them peeking out from behind the racks of clothes.

You are not for sale seemed to be scrawled on the notes often, along with other phrases.

You are not dirty.

There is nothing crawling beneath your skin.

You do not need to wash your hands.

You are in control.

She swallowed, her throat almost too tight to draw in air. "That private dance ..." The words tasted like acid in her throat. "The one you traded in exchange for the location of the bond pieces?"

He had followed her into the dressing room. She could feel him behind her.

"What about it?" he asked.

She couldn't look at him. "Did you do it?"

"Yes."

"Who was it?"

"The wife of an official. She overheard him on the phone talking about the hair braids. He knew where they were, but he didn't know what they were, just that they had to be a secret."

"Do you still see her?"

"She's requested me at the Icon Cafe a few times. She was at your first dance performance in the Dahlia Room."

Isobel found it even harder to breathe, and her mind

raced back, trying to dredge up a face. There was a dark-haired woman who had been at Gabriel's table the last few weeks. Isobel remembered her because she was young—almost as young as Isobel, but she wore a gigantic diamond ring.

Gabriel saw her *often*.

She spun around, trying to read his impassive face. "What did the dance entail?"

"I had to take most of my clothes off. She didn't touch me. She just watched."

Her cheeks were wet. She was crying. *Fuck.* She refused to let her expression crumble, even though tears were escaping. "It was just the once?"

He nodded, his attention diverted by the tear that wobbled on the edge of her jaw. "I didn't touch her. She didn't touch me." He sounded confused, like he couldn't understand the look of pain on her face.

It wasn't pain from the bond. She hurt *for* him.

"But she *paid* for you," she said, stabbing a finger at one of the notes.

"Not with money." He shrugged.

"Is that where you draw the line?" Suddenly, she was furious. And terrified. It suddenly seemed so *easy*, so *simple* to manipulate Gabriel into that kind of situation.

He closed the distance between them and brushed his thumb along the line of her jaw, collecting her tear. "I need you to explain this reaction." His expression finally collapsed, showing her a glimpse of confusion and shame, his russet eyes glimmering. "I don't understand. If something like that can cause a minor infraction, I need to know—"

"This isn't about *me*." She pushed against his chest, frustrated. He didn't seem to notice. "I pushed you," she growled, even more frustrated.

"I'll stumble later," he promised, wiping another tear. "And I'll never make that deal again."

"You better not," she threatened, but her stupid voice wobbled. "If you're going to make a trade or a deal, it better have nothing to do with your body."

His eyes suddenly dropped to her lips, and all the air was sucked from the room.

"You care about me." He was saying it like he had *only just noticed*.

"No," she lied, ineffectually shoving him again. "I pushed you."

He stepped back calmly. She would have preferred a stumble, but beggars couldn't be choosers. He was staring at her like he couldn't understand her at all, but she had caught sight of something on the shelf behind him and was no longer paying attention.

"Is that my sweatshirt?" she asked, confused. "I lost that last year."

He didn't answer, and she stepped past him, shock freezing her into place. The shelf was full of *her* things.

The bodysuit she had worn during one of her shibari performances with Kalen. One of the dresses she had worn while dancing. A crop top, a jumper, a handful of silk hair ties, Kilian's faded yellow T-shirt that she used to love wearing to bed. And ... panties. Multiple pairs of them. They looked clean and were neatly folded.

"You washed and folded them," she said numbly.

"That's the part that surprises you?" he asked calmly, moving behind her again, his heat skittering across her back. "What am I going to do with them dirty, Isobel?"

"Should I be insulted? That you didn't want my dirty panties?"

He planted his hands on the shelves either side of her, leaning closer, boxing her in. "I only wash your clothes when they stop smelling like you."

"Everything in here looks washed."

"Then it's time I steal something new."

His hands dropped from the shelf, brushing up over her tights until he reached the waistband. There was something about his hands spanning the bare skin of her waist, the bulk of them just visible beneath her shirt, that had liquid heat immediately pooling low in her stomach, her entire body tensing in anticipation.

He paused there, both of them breathing too loudly. She wasn't sure how to proceed, but she wanted to. *Badly*.

"I ... c-can take them off myself," she whispered, her face flaming red.

He growled, his hips suddenly pushing into her, pressing her against the shelves, the movement so sudden she had to grasp the shelf to steady herself. His erection curved into her spine.

"That's not the problem," he said lowly.

"I can shower?"

"No." He tensed. "I like it when you smell like you." And then, after a pause: "I just don't know if I can be what you need."

Her stomach clenched. "You don't have a single unwashed thing here. That has to be driving you crazy. What kind of system is that?"

He chuckled, his breath stirring her hair. "Are you trying to *goad* me into fucking you, Sigma? Is that what you like to do?"

"Just stating facts. There's a flaw in your system. A production and supply issue. I thought you were better than that."

He laughed softly against the top of her head before gripping her waist and spinning her around. And then he stepped back, his hands falling out from beneath her shirt. "I know you love to test our control, but control isn't something I can give up."

This wasn't him flirting; this was him being deadly serious.

She nodded, worrying her lip. "You shouldn't do anything you're not ready for."

His smile was slight but sharp. "I don't feel completely in control, and you drive me insane. I don't think I should push things while I feel so ... rattled. I could end up like Oscar, or I could push myself past my comfort levels without realising it. I forget about those things when I'm with you."

"You don't have to explain." She wished she could reach out and touch him, and thankfully, he closed the distance between them again, large palms brushing down her arms, warming her skin, until he reached her fingers, which he twisted between his own.

"Will you sleep here tonight?" he asked. "I put a blanket in the cupboard for you."

She bit back a smile. "Are you trying to get me to rub myself all over your bed so you won't have to steal another pair of panties?"

He jerked her forward, spun behind her, and spanked her. *Hard*. "Get ready for bed, puppy."

She hurried back to her room and put herself through a shower almost numbly. As surprised as Gabriel had been that she cared so much about him, she had to admit she had been just as shocked to find out the same thing about him. After her shower, she began to reach for the shirt she had worn to bed last night, but paused, her fingers brushing the sleeve. It was Cian's.

I like it when you smell like you.

There was an odd flutter in her belly as she pulled on a cotton tank with cute, matching little booty shorts instead, texting the group to check that the coast was clear before she looped the cameras, since she wasn't sure if Theodore and Kilian were back yet and didn't

want to start a loop when they were in any of the
common rooms.

She made her way back to Gabriel's room, closing the
door and leaning back against it as she took in the sight
before her. Gabriel was sitting up in his bed, fresh out of
a shower with only black sweatpants on, his laptop
resting on his thighs as he tapped away, the muscles in
his arms twitching with the movement. Beside him was
a second pillow, and a fluffy, cream-coloured blanket.

"I plugged in a phone charger for you," he said,
without looking up from his screen.

There was also a fresh bottle of water on her side of
the bed, and a steaming cup of peppermint tea, which he
had apparently noticed she liked to drink at night. She
was a little too shocked to make a joke about it, so she
just curled up on the bed, plugged in her phone, and
cradled the tea, edging into the warmth of his side to see
what he was doing.

Scheduling their social media accounts, of course.

"You should take a break," she said.

He scoffed and continued typing.

"Seriously." She nudged him ever so slightly with her
shoulder.

"Like you do?" he asked, finally looking away from
his screen.

"What if my feet get cold?" she asked, switching tack
to tease him a little about the bedtime preparations he
had made.

"Socks are in the drawer."

She pulled away from him, rolling to her stomach and setting her tea on his bedside table. She tugged open the drawer, finding a folded pair of fluffy socks, an eye mask, lip balm, a hairbrush, and a book. *Technical Manual and Dictionary of Classical Ballet*.

She bit down on her lip to keep from laughing. "What's the book for?"

"In case you get bored."

"How could I ever get bored with you around." She glanced at him over her shoulder.

His eyes were on her ass, his fingers curled into fists. He carefully closed his laptop and rolled off the bed, placing it on his desk. His walk back to the bed was more purposeful, more of a prowl, and she felt stuck, unable to so much as twitch. It seemed like the smallest movement from her would force him to pounce, but instead, he only stretched back out and turned off the lights.

"Should I—" she began, but he cut her off.

"Come here."

She edged toward him, curling into his side as he held his arm open, making room for her.

"What if I get hungry?" she whispered.

He chuckled, aware that she was teasing him, and swatted her ass again. "Go to sleep."

Isobel's first session with Teak after the fall break had her hopes plummeting. The bond specialist's recovery seemed to have plateaued. She had lost weight, her bones now prominent beneath her skin, her once warm, beautiful eyes now sallow and empty. Their sessions grew shorter and shorter, because Isobel had no new information to offer up, and eventually, Teak changed them to once a month.

When Isobel needed more pills, she texted her father and he booked another session with her at the Icon Cafe. This time, he arrived with more than one gift bag. He was trailed in by a harried-looking assistant whose arms were overflowing with shopping bags.

"I had my personal shopper purchase suits for the Alphas," he said as soon as he sat down. He waved his assistant off, and the man placed all the bags on the floor before disappearing. "I saw them at your performance last night and they were wearing the same sad excuses for suits as they were at your first performance. I assume the ones who weren't there looked just as pathetic. What the fuck are they spending their Ironside stipends on?"

Isobel rubbed at her temples, fighting off an immediate headache. "Their families?" she ventured, drawing out the answer like it should have been obvious. "What do you care?"

"They're a direct reflection on you," he grumbled, smacking her hand away when she robotically moved to pour his tea, falling into the motions of her duties as she did every Saturday.

She blinked at him, staring, as *he* poured *her* a glass of tea.

Usually, her guests wanted her to wait on them hand and foot and got annoyed if her attention wavered from them for even a moment.

"They need to look as good as you do," Braun continued. "I had one of my assistants request their sizes from their Ironside records, but I accounted a little for the Alpha growth cycle, so they should fit nicely."

She was still staring at him, her mouth slightly unhinged. He nudged the tea toward her.

"Their suits aren't that bad," she finally said.

He gave her a droll, tired look. "Yes, they are. They need to be respected in here. If they look like they don't have two dollars to rub together, people will assume they're easy targets. People will start offering or demanding they do things for money. They need to look like they don't *need* anything. It will discourage some of the patrons from trying to take advantage of them. Mind you, I said *some* of the patrons. Not all of them."

"What the hell has gotten into you?" she demanded. "You don't *care* about other people."

"I care about *my* people," he snarled, his composure breaking before he shockingly reeled it under control, giving her a stern look.

This time, her mouth really did fall open. "What the hell are you talking about?"

"You're my daughter." He sighed, reaching for his own drink. "The only progeny I have. Whoever is attached to you is also attached to me."

He knew.

He knew they were her mates.

"Congratulations," she said, unable to help the sarcasm from her voice. She couldn't believe he knew. She needed to make sure. "You always wished I was an Alpha. Now you have ten of them."

He stared at the table for several long, awkward seconds before his chest filled with air. "I didn't wish you were an Alpha. I just wished I could look at you and not feel death."

A grimace tightened her features. "I was a baby. You can't blame me for what happened."

"Welcome to the world, kid." His laugh was empty. "That's what we do."

She had no idea what to do with this version of her father. If anything, he scared her more than the old version because it all felt like an act, a mask that would crack when she was least expecting it.

"I've been seeing someone," he blurted without warning.

"What?" Her head snapped up.

"A psychiatrist," he clarified, a hint of colour in his cheeks, his hands tightening into fists. "I also started reading your mother's journals. I know you're confused about how I'm acting. I can see it in your face."

"You told a human psychiatrist what you told me?" she asked, her brows inching higher. "About ... what happened back in the settlement? Mom? Your brother?"

He laughed. "Fuck no, Isobel. Jesus. I told him I had an abusive upbringing. I told him about my own father and how I started to repeat some of those patterns with you. It's not going to be an overnight fix ... but I'm trying. I just thought you should know."

She levelled him with a searching look before shrugging her shoulder lightly. "If you say so."

THAT NIGHT, SHE FOUND HERSELF UNDER THE SPELL OF HER golden roses again. Her preoccupation had grown worse, and she often found herself getting up in the middle of the night to close her bathroom door because she couldn't sleep when she could see them.

She was too tired to close the door that night, worn down into a puddle of limbs by Theodore, who had squeezed multiple orgasms from her body using his mouth before he flipped her over and filled her, making sure she would be too weak to ask for more.

She sighed, staring at the glint of moonlight shimmering off those gold petals. She could only see one of the vases, but her fingers itched to touch them again.

Theodore rolled onto his side, blocking her line of sight, his grey eyes blinking at her sleepily, surprised that she was still awake.

"Are you not exhausted enough, Illy?" He dragged her thigh over his hip, pulling her tight into the heat of his body as he lazily nuzzled into her neck.

She didn't answer, tucking her head against his chest and sighing in relief. She closed her eyes, trying to forget about the soul artefact.

But the bond wasn't willing to leave her alone. Almost as soon as she closed her eyes, she was dragged into a vision.

She jolted in shock, peering around. She was standing in a small bedroom, a filthy mattress on the floor. A man lay on the mattress with his pants undone and his belt unbuckled. He had a thick moustache and stringy black hair, blue eyes clouded as he puffed on a cigarette. His eyes were human, and there was a uniform jacket tossed to the side of the mattress.

He was a cop. A human cop.

"What—" she began, but Elijah swore so loudly that she jumped, turning to see the Alphas lined up against the wall behind her.

"Is this your memory?" she asked Elijah, who was as white as a sheet.

"No," he answered, voice strained.

Frowning, she glanced to the others.

Gabriel looked like he was about to be sick. His hands were shaking.

"We h-have to get out of here," he stuttered. She had *never* heard him sound that scared.

"Boy!" the cop called out. "Quit washing your fucking hands and get back in here."

Isobel's heart sank, and tears filled her eyes.

"I've seen him before," she said, staring at the man. "He came to me as a remnant with my mom and Crowe. He's dead."

"Yeah," Elijah said quietly. "Stick around long enough, and you'll see it happen."

A little boy, maybe around ten or twelve, walked back into the room. His hands and arms were red from scrubbing, his fingertips dripping with water. He was dressed in too-big, baggy clothes.

"I have to go home now," he said, russet eyes empty.

"Like fuck," the man replied. "I paid for two hours. I'm getting two hours. I didn't say you could put your damn clothes back on, kid. Come here." He jolted from the mattress, making a grab for the boy.

Isobel waited for him to dart out of reach. To run away. To fight, and kick, and scream. But he didn't. Because he was a child, and this had happened to him before.

As soon as his little back hit the mattress, her vision went blurry, and she clutched her stomach, trying not to vomit.

Make it stop, she pleaded, screwing her eyes closed. She couldn't watch this.

"Let's get you dirty again, boy," the man leered, and Isobel doubled over, dry retching onto the floor.

"It's gone," Theodore said quietly, fury and despair simmering in his voice. His hands were on her shoulders, pulling her up again. He was shaking.

Isobel blinked at their new setting. They were on the streets of what looked like one of the settlements. The moon was high in the sky, the streets shadowed, lacking any streetlights. There was a shuffling sound along the dirt road, and she peered at the wobbly outline, which slowly came into focus.

It was a different boy, this time, though he was dressed just like Gabriel had been, his clothes oversized, torn, and dirty. He had silver-blond hair, overlong, flopping into pale-grey eyes.

Elijah?

He was carrying something on his back, and as he shuffled closer, Isobel's heart dropped right out of her body. Elijah clutched pale arms around his neck, a dirty blond head lolling on his shoulders. The little boy was naked, blood smeared over his legs, bruises littering his back, arms, and thighs. He was unconscious.

"Hold on, Gabey," the little Elijah squeaked out. "Just hold on."

They stood there and watched, unable to help,

unable to interfere, as Elijah carried the broken body past them, his pace painfully slow.

Isobel glanced back at the real Gabriel and Elijah, tears spilling down her cheeks, words lodged into the back of her throat. She wanted to reach out to them, but they weren't even comforting each other. In fact, the Alphas seemed to have edged a few inches *away* from Gabriel, like they knew he didn't want them in his space. She watched him mournfully as she waited for the vision to end. He was so still, his eyes empty.

Fuck this. She edged closer and Elijah looked at her, shaking his head quickly. Usually, she would have listened. They knew each other best. But they didn't know her and Gabriel's relationship. It was more private than her connection with Theodore, Kilian, Cian, or Oscar.

But it was there, and she shakily placed her trust in it as she approached him. He never hesitated to reach out to her, to touch her. So she didn't hesitate now. She slipped her arms gently around his waist. He froze for only a moment before he bent down and snatched her up, lifting her feet from the ground, his arms like two steel bands around her back and the low curve of her spine.

It was *painful*. He was holding her too tight. She could barely breathe, but she didn't need to because *he* was finally breathing. He was sucking in deep gulps of her scent, dragging her higher up his body so that he could burrow his face into her neck. Hidden by the soft cloud of her wavy hair, he began to quietly cry, teardrops littering her skin and slipping down over her chest and arm.

She threaded her fingers into his hair, slowly stroking him, her fingers trembling.

Let's get you dirty again, boy.

She couldn't stop the words replaying over and over again in her mind. Gradually, Gabriel stopped silently crying, and the dampness against her neck dried. He let her down, and she glanced around.

"Why are we still here?" she whispered.

She turned, but Gabriel clutched her back to his body, his arms wrapped around her chest.

"Because it's not over," he said huskily.

She had no idea how long they stood there, but eventually, Elijah came back into sight, a boy with dark hair, honeyed skin, and hazel eyes striding beside him.

"My dad will help him," the dark-haired boy promised. *Niko.* "Don't worry, Eli."

"It's not good enough," the young Elijah said. "He has to listen to their thoughts. He has to listen to what they think. He can't do it anymore."

Isobel jolted into motion as soon as they passed by her, Gabriel's hold on her breaking apart. *They were going back.*

"Wait," she said, even though she knew they couldn't hear her.

Don't go back there.

She hurried after them but didn't have to go far. They stopped a few houses down and pushed inside. Isobel tailed them into the same small bedroom with the dirty mattress on the ground. The man was asleep, snoring loudly, a half-empty bottle of vodka wedged beneath his arm. His belt was still undone, his pants still hanging open.

"Wake up," Elijah demanded, and there was a strange shiver of power in his voice. Not Alpha voice, but something else.

"You can't," Niko whispered, staring at the man with wide eyes as he jerked awake, pitching upright and blinking dizzily.

"Eli," Niko tugged on the other boy's arm. "You can't use your powers on a human."

Elijah shook him off, refocussing on the man.

"Die," he said, the air shivering with that same power.

The man acted immediately, picking up the vodka bottle and smashing it against the floor.

Isobel sucked in a sharp breath as he picked up a broken shard of glass in each hand, his head shaking as he tried to fight against the compulsion. He began to shout, but Elijah cut him off.

"Shut up."

He began to stab his own legs, his stomach, his arms, his neck.

Isobel closed her eyes, unable to watch, but when the horrific sounds finally stopped, she opened them again and focussed on Elijah, who had watched the whole thing.

The younger Elijah collapsed and threw up all over the floor. Now that it was done, he was shaking and sobbing, his anger drained, replaced by ashen cheeks and horrified grey eyes.

Niko dragged him out of the house and back to the street, and then stumbled back in, searching the drawers in the empty kitchen until he found a packet of matches.

"It's o-okay," he stuttered, even though his only company was a dead man. "It'll be okay."

He set fire to the curtains first.

Isobel jolted awake, sick and disoriented. She was standing in her bathroom back in Dorm A, her hands stinging. She frowned, looking down.

Was this another vision?

She was clutching the golden roses, half in her left hand, the other half in her right hand, thorns digging into her skin.

"Oh shit," she whispered before raising her voice. "Theo!"

He was there in a second, hair dishevelled, bare, muscled chest rising and falling rapidly. "What is it? How did you get in here? Were you sleepwalking?" His eyes flicked down to her hands and widened. "Oh shit."

Isobel's room! he shouted through the bond.

The roses began to melt, pooling like hot metal into her bleeding palms, though it didn't burn her. It almost felt like a balm for her cuts, and she turned her hands, displaying her palms as the golden liquid covered her skin. It didn't drip onto the floor—it seemed alive, and it wanted to stay with her.

She heard the other Alphas bursting into the bedroom, but she couldn't look away. The gold liquid seemed to bubble and condense, turning into small puddles cradled by her palms. The puddles grew smaller and separated, turning hard and shiny again until she was staring down at ten tiny gems, all in different colours. Golden amber, midnight blue, stormy grey, clear grey, pale green, golden green, red-brown, sapphire, and glittering onyx.

"That's all?" Elijah was at her side, frowning down at the gems. "I was definitely expecting that many roses to turn into something much more dramatic. These are tiny, and they aren't even attached to you."

"They are," she whispered, realising what the little gems were.

She pulled down her pyjama shirt to reveal her sternum piercing. All of the gems that had appeared were now gone.

She pinched one of the tiny gems between her fingers and pressed into the empty casing in her piercing.

It didn't click or melt into place, but suddenly it was stuck there, and she couldn't pick it off.

"Maybe we should just—" Moses ventured, but she shook her head, cutting him off.

"No, this is what I need to do." She returned each of the little gems and then traced the piercing with her fingernail. Energy buzzed through her body, a smile splitting over her face.

She felt ... *powerful*.

"Whoa." Theodore grabbed her arms, spinning her to face him, his eyes wide. "I can feel that."

"It feels like you, but it also feels like me," Moses said with a frown, staring at the piercing.

She traced down to the pale green stone, pressing it inward. This time, it did shift. It clicked inward in the barest movement, lighting up slightly.

"Holy shit," Kilian laughed out. "You're invisible. And I can feel the draw on my energy."

They were all staring at her, so she shifted to the side. Moses's and Niko's gazes shifted, eyes crawling in her direction. Their noses were better than the others.

Holy shit.

She should have touched the roses months ago.

She ducked between Theodore and Kilian, who both turned, following the heat of her body and her scent as she escaped into her bedroom. They knew roughly where she was but truly couldn't see her.

"Oh my god," she laughed out. "This is incredible."

The little gem on her chest turned dull again, and they all followed her out into the bedroom.

Gabriel and Elijah stared at her piercing in apprehension, but neither of them said anything. She looked between them, feeling that ache of sorrow pulse back to life. Elijah's brows drew together, and he quickly spoke, as if he really wanted to focus on this interesting new development instead of the memory they had all just witnessed.

"When the piercing was giving you powers, it gave you ferality, but ferality isn't an ability. Shouldn't it have given you charm or aggression?"

"What happened exactly?" Gabriel asked, eyeing her piercing, his hand scraping down the side of his handsome face. "When it gave you ferality?"

"Crowe was ... he had me cornered. So I prayed. I've never prayed before, but Sophia and Maya had just introduced me to all this Gifted religion stuff, so I guess I thought *why not*. And then it happened. The gemstone glowed, and I got ferality."

"Maybe the gemstones don't give you our *abilities* so much as they give you our power," Kilian said. "I could feel you using my *power*." He tapped his chest. "Drawing it out of my body. So maybe you just pulled on the wrong power?"

"Or maybe the prayer worked," Niko suggested casually, rubbing the back of his neck like he was embarrassed to suggest it. "You were begging them for help. It looks like they helped you—well, as much as the gods help anyone, anyway. They gave you access to

Theo's or Moses' power, and that power includes ferality."

She stared down at her chest, feeling a *little* less lucky.

After forming their bond, she had stopped worrying that the second ferality gemstone would appear, but suddenly it felt like a ticking bomb again.

Except this time, there were three gemstones that could give her ferality. And if it was triggered in any of the others?

She swallowed, tugging her shirt back up over the piercing. "Maybe I won't experiment with the others. Seems like it only lasts for a minute or two, but I can cause all kinds of trouble in two minutes."

"Don't we know it," Kilian murmured, falling onto her bed. "Are we done with drama for tonight?"

Theodore frowned at him. "I was sleeping there."

Kilian dragged a pillow over his face, uncaring. Oscar wordlessly dropped onto the other side of the bed. Gabriel moved to the couch, lying down and linking his hands over his flat stomach. Elijah slumped into an armchair. Cian followed Gabriel and Elijah, holding out a hand for one of them to pass him a cushion, and then he spread out on the rug before the fireplace. Niko and Moses followed suit, stretching out on the floor. It couldn't have been comfortable, but they were all so tired they would have been able to sleep on a cold concrete slab.

Kalen strode to Isobel, catching her chin and pulling her eyes up to his. His jaw worked, and then he surprised her by bending and pressing his hard lips into the soft swell of her own.

"Night," he grunted, before striding from the room.

Mikel watched her for a few moments. "I'll be just downstairs."

Theodore picked her up as soon as the door closed behind Mikel, carrying her back to bed and placing her between Oscar and Kilian, and then he grabbed a spare cushion and joined the others on the rug.

This wasn't about her.

This was about *them*. Their group. Their family.

After what they had seen, they needed each other.

She curled into Kilian, and ever-so-gently cracked open her walls, stirring at the dark cloud of trauma that hung over the room, coaxing it into the cavern of her chest.

She drank their sorrow until her eyelids were heavy, and then she cut herself off, melting into Kilian's comforting arms.

12

TWISTED

ISOBEL STOOD BEFORE THE MIRROR, NERVES TWISTING THROUGH her body. She would allow it for this brief moment only and then the anxiety would have to go. It had been over a month of gruelling practise—with extra hours thrown in over Thanksgiving break—but Mikel had finally given her the green light to change up her Dahlia Room performance, and now it was time to prove she was every bit as confident as she had claimed.

In the other room, the curtains were gone. New lights had been installed, and she had coordinated directly with Ethan for her new stage, bypassing Cooper completely—though he had still insisted on approving her outfits each week. She sucked in a shaky breath, brushing a hand over her stomach. The black leotard had cutouts at the waist and hips and a wet look to the material that clung to her skin. She stepped back from the mirror, bringing her legs into focus. The fishnet stockings had been picked at very carefully in all the right places. When the silks tugged and rubbed against her legs, the stockings would tear. The black silks would also dig into the exposed skin of her waist and hips.

Her hair hung in a carefully curated, fretful tangle, and her make-up had been smudged *just* the right amount with Kilian's help. The longer she had planned for this day, the more her determination grew. It wasn't enough to make this show hers. It wasn't enough to fly above them and force them to watch her with awe instead of assessment and calculation.

She wanted to *say* something, even if they couldn't hear it.

She wanted them to feel dirty for clapping.

She wanted them to feel guilty for looking.

Slowly, her mismatched gaze in the mirror hardened. The nerves fluttered away, pushed down beneath a steel trap door. She shoved her bag beneath the sink and walked back into the Dahlia Room, nodding to Ethan behind the bar. Mikel, Oscar, Niko, Moses, and Theodore had all taken the night off from their fights to watch her first aerial performance, and she felt strangely invincible knowing all ten of her mates were scattered around the shadowed room. She couldn't see any of them because Ethan had pulled back the servers and dimmed the lights as she had instructed him to. They usually stopped for her performances anyway, but she wanted the addition of them all being in darkness. She would likely change it again for her next performance—there was an aerial hoop performance she had been thinking about that she was eager to create an environment for—but this one was all about her looking exposed and vulnerable—used and abused, even—while they hid in the shadows.

Ethan started her song as she stepped onto the stage, and the first notes of "Twisted" by Mia Vaile echoed eerily through the otherwise silent space. The song was slow and almost soft, more of a background sound to keep the focus on her movements. She had picked it because it shared a name with the first single on their album. It was a private little puzzle piece that people might only fit together later.

She gripped the silks in one hand, walking around the edge of the small, circular stage as the song crooned in a vast echo all around her. She could hear people whispering softly, so softly, unwilling to talk over the music. They were wondering what she would do. She kept walking slowly, kept them wondering. The whole time, she subtly twisted the silks, winding them around and around as she walked, and then she took off in several leaping strides, kicking off the stage and using the momentum to flick out her body, still only holding on with one arm as she flew in a slow circle above the closest gathered tables, the twisted silks unravelling to spin her body in tight spirals as she flew over their heads.

She didn't attempt to hide the pain or the effort from

her face. She didn't bother to make her movements look effortless. She *exaggerated* the strain.

This dance was a story of servitude. The silks were chains, the stage was her cage, and she was just a bird on show. They had paid to look upon her, but she had trapped them in their seats, leaving them to wonder if she was posturing or agitated, performing or fluttering against her bars in an attempt at freedom.

Her movement was continuous. She didn't pause to catch her breath or steady herself. Her transitions weren't moments of rest; they were seamlessly threaded with drops and spins that required every inch of strength in her body and impeccable timing. Her first drop was from twenty feet in the air, the rough rock ceiling close enough that she could clearly make out the individual little lights set into the stone to look like glittering stars. She paused at the top, her legs locked into a double split, her core like iron as she tightly controlled the tension in her body—and then, utterly without warning, she sent herself into a free-falling split drop, pulling herself back up mid-air into a controlled catch, her body arching backwards into a full suspended backbend. It was a dangerous move that required absolute precision, setting the tone for how demanding and shocking her performance would be.

This wasn't the type of routine she should be able to pull off with just over a month of practise, but defying expectations had become something that drew her from bed before the sun had even breached the sky every morning and set her teeth together in determination every evening when she stepped into the gym with Mikel. The drive to do *better* had been replaced by the absolute burning need to be the *best*. The best they had ever seen. That would be her power.

She was halfway through a sissonne, pushing herself explosively off the silks with enough force to send her body into a graceful jump-like movement in the air, when the lights glowed gently back to life beneath her, illuminating the faces below her just enough to drag them suddenly into her performance. She hadn't simply pulled off the sissonne, but had combined it with a controlled rotation, spinning herself around before landing back in the silks, so it took her a moment to focus on one of the faces below her. Oscar and Theodore sat side by side in a booth close to the stage, a woman either side of them. She recognised the women immediately. The one clutching Theodore's thigh and staring up at Isobel with wide blue eyes was a famous American actress, only a few years older than Isobel. Her hair was a long, lustrous golden tangle, her eyes like glittering gems lined by thick lashes, her lips open in a perfect little bow of surprise and excitement. The woman beside Oscar wasn't touching him, but she was sitting close and edging closer still, her white-blonde hair a slide of shining silk as she tucked it behind her ear. She was a famous American singer, her tanned skin shimmering just as much as her shimmering black dress, her dark eyes wide and smoky, her features etched with sensuality.

Isobel paused for a moment too long, her focus wavering.

Her breaths were short, and not just from the exertion. There was a horrible monster rearing up inside her, demanding she rip those painted nails from Theodore's strong thigh. She wanted to break them one by one. Wanted that girl to *scream*.

It was hard to breathe.

Focus. Mikel's voice shot through her mind, cool as a river of silver blanketing her thoughts.

He had seen her falter, and the edge of command in his tone was unwavering.

Release your foot, he ordered coldly, the ice in his voice dripping inside her head, helping her to hone and sharpen her attention back onto the silks. That was the voice of her coach, her trainer, and he was furious that she was putting herself in danger right now.

She obeyed him immediately, as he had trained her to do, just like Kalen had trained her to do. It was a power the two of them had carefully woven over her with weeks of practice under threat of injury, plucking at her guard until her trust was stitched so completely into their interactions that a single look, a single barked word was all it took for her body to snap into compliance. Luckily, it was a power they didn't hold over her. They hung it up at the door to her training room, a leash dangling from a hook, curling down to the floor in sensuous promise for next time. But Mikel had just plucked it up. He had closed that collar around her neck and forced her mind to snap to his.

Close your eyes was his whispered instruction.

So she did.

Now release, he said.

She did, and the audience gasped. She was still spinning from her sissonne, but had released one of her legs, so when she performed the drop, it was with only one foot held secure. She swung downward, her leg extended in a perfect arabesque, holding the position. She knew this routine. She had practised it to perfection, but her control had slipped, throwing her off balance. She couldn't stop thinking about Theodore and Oscar below and the hands that might wander across their thighs, their chests, their arms.

And then she was thinking of Gabriel and the dark-haired beauty who had paid to see him undress, who kept coming back for him, who might be sitting with him right now.

Why her mind had chosen this moment, this *crucial* fucking moment to splinter her wall of focus with these needling insecurities, she wasn't sure. Perhaps because for the first time, all ten of her mates were serving in the Dahlia Room together. Perhaps because this wasn't the Icon Café. This room wasn't brightly lit and stringently bound by rules. This place was more shadowed, more decadent. There was nothing casual about the meetings taking place in those booths, no giggling teenagers trying to get the Alphas to pay them some attention.

These people were some of the most important and influential in the world. They weren't to be rejected, disrespected, or insulted. They were the board members, the presidents, the politicians, directors, and superstars.

Double inversion, Mikel's voice was a frigid breeze, an icy balm, freezing her rioting thoughts into place.

She twisted into the inversion without thinking, her body as pliant as a tangle of string toying with the silks, taut and twisted in all the right ways to create a stunning pattern of black silk and pale, contorted limbs. She was spinning at high speed, the silks locked around her arms and legs, a little fly caught in a sparkling web, the intense burn in her core a welcome distraction as she held the inversion—but she didn't hold it long, shocking the audience once again when she dropped. Another dangerous manoeuvre that she should have completed with steady lungs and a focused gaze.

She released the silks from her legs, using only her arms, and she fell freely, her legs spread wide in a perfect split as she plummeted downward. Instead of calm, she was rioting inside. She caught herself at the lowest point, using both hands to pull herself back up with a burst of force. The mid-air catch had been flawless, a breath-stealing display of pure control and power, but the further she climbed, whispered praise spattering about below her like delicate raindrops, the more she cracked inside.

Use it, Mikel instructed sternly. Her mate would have caught her chin and lifted her shattering gaze to his. Her mate would have torn apart whoever had made her hurt like that. Her *friend* would have spoken to her softly and protected her. But both she and Mikel knew that she didn't need her friend or a mate right now. She needed her manager. She needed the man who held that leash to grip it tightly now and turn her in the right direction. She needed to hand over control of this performance to someone she trusted, because she could no longer trust herself, and without trust, she would fall.

So, she *used* it. She dragged out that cracking sensation from deep inside the cavern of her chest and spread it across her face and skin.

Good girl, Mikel crooned softly, that slide of silver whispering against her anguish. *Make a web.*

She spun and spun, locking the silks around her limbs in a complex, visually intricate spiral. The faster she spun, the tighter the web constricted around her.

Now, Mikel prompted, and she released her legs from the fabric, spinning even faster as she performed a flexibility drop, her torso curving backward in a deep backbend that seemed to defy gravity, her legs still suspended, fully extended, making her limbs appear that they were bent at an almost impossible angle. The bottom of the drop snapped her into a whip-like release that jerked her body back into an upright position, the fabric spiralling below with her movement.

Beautiful. Mikel's cool breath misted over her mind, that collar around her neck squeezing tighter until her audience dropped away. Her eyes drifted closed, and it was just her and him. He bent her, twisted her, dropped her, and issued cold orders for her to climb higher, spin faster, and stretch wider. She began to burn with each whispered breath of praise, her limbs trembling with more than exertion as she neared the end of her routine. She could almost feel his hands on her hips, pressing her deeper into the split she performed as he growled softly for her to stretch further, to sink deeper.

When her feet hit the stage again and applause broke out—louder than she had ever received—she finally opened her eyes, her fingers reluctantly releasing the silks, her chest heaving, her body burning.

She tried not to look at any of the other tables as she stepped from the stage, but on her last bow, she found her eyes slamming into a stormy, dark grey gaze. Moses' attention was crawling back up from her legs, his tongue sweeping across his lip as their eyes collided. He didn't seem to realise that the woman beside him was touching him, but *she* realised that his attention was elsewhere, ensnared. Her lips, painted a dark mauve to match her long, silk dress, pressed to his cheek, leaving a purplish smudge there against his tanned skin. His jaw flexed—he had noticed her; he was just trying to ignore her—and her hand slipped down over his chest. He caught her wrist before it reached his belt, flinging it back to her lap, but she only smirked, whispering something in his ear, her lips brushing his skin again.

Acid burned in Isobel's throat, and she quickly stepped from the stage, keeping her back straight and her head up as she pushed into the bathroom, retrieved her bag from under the sinks, and disappeared into a stall to switch out her clothes. The silk dress she had worn into the Stone Dahlia that evening was similar to the mauve dress Moses' *companion* was wearing. It made the acid roil even more, her skin burning impossibly hot as the silk slid down her body, settling against the floor. She stepped into her heels, ignored the disarray of her hair, and marched back into the room. Now that she was finished, so were they. Those were the rules.

She stalked toward the exit, barely waiting for them to detangle themselves from their companions and their tables before she stepped into the hallway beyond the room. They were quiet as they moved through the club, and that silence seemed to swell as they walked back to the dorm. Usually, they took the golf carts, but she needed the exercise to clear her head, even though her muscles were still tight and aching. She would have killed for Mikel's skilled hands to dig into her shoulders —or Elijah's, for that matter, but she was too hot. Still burning. Only growing hotter the longer she walked.

When she reached the dorm, she stalked straight upstairs and slammed into her bedroom, ignoring them all. Her anger was misplaced, she knew that, but she couldn't seem to stop it climbing. Her skin felt like it was on fire, a twinge of pain sparking to life deep in her belly. She began to pace, a sob inexplicably building in the back of her throat. She didn't expect her door to open so soon. Usually, they gave her at least a little space.

She definitely didn't expect *all* of them to spill into her room. They were carrying pillows and blankets and must have looped the cameras. They didn't have any snacks, so apparently, they could tell that her body was too tightly wound to eat.

"Who do you want in your bed?" Elijah asked, almost clinically, his eyes dropping over the front of her dress, his throat bobbing.

She glanced down, realising she had forgotten her bra. Her breasts were perfectly outlined by the silk dress, nipples pressed tightly to the fabric. He tore eyes that weren't as cold as they usually were back up to hers, pupils expanded as he raised a perfect brow in question.

"T-Theo and Oscar." She spoke without thinking, her voice thready, wavering and fragile, her breaths becoming laboured.

Elijah's eyes narrowed on her, sweeping over her again, but this time in an assessing way. "Maybe we shouldn't all be in here."

"Don't," she gasped, sudden pain shooting through

her abdomen, her hand reaching out as he began to turn. "I need you all here."

She sought out Moses. She needed to see him. He had already begun to stride from the room, possibly scenting her desperation and realising what would happen when she got Theodore and Oscar into her bed. He paused, examining her face, a little spark of realisation flaring in his before he tucked it away behind impassive features. He stalked the rest of the way to the door, but instead of walking through it, he leaned back against it, crossing his muscled arms and notching a boot up against the back of the door.

Guarding it.

Indulging her insanity.

Her bond purred in a brief satisfaction that they must have all felt, because it seemed to spur them into action. They moved differently, eyeing her carefully, a deliberateness to their movements as they set themselves up along the couches and the floor, spreading out in feigned relaxation. It wasn't until Oscar and Theodore were sprawled onto her bed and she had finished reassuring herself that the others weren't going anywhere, her eyes resting on Gabriel, that she realised what was happening.

She had felt this burning before. She had felt this pang of pain before.

In the shower, with Gabriel on the phone, whispering silky orders into her ear. He knew it as well.

His eyes were hooded and wary, dipping into the heat of his memory while teetering along the precariousness of their present moment.

The pain intensified, forcing a small gasp past her lips as her skin tingled in awareness.

"Someone get the lights," Niko barked. "I don't want to watch this."

"No," she croaked, her eyes flickering to Moses against the door.

She needed to see him.

He was *hers*.

She could still see the lipstick mark against his cheek, and it made everything inside her boil over, but she forced it all down, forced a lid onto the bubbling eagerness to reclaim her mates as she dragged her attention to Niko. He was sitting against the base of the couch Kalen had claimed, eyes digging hotly into her. Despite his words, he was making no effort to turn away. Kalen faced the roof, arm thrown over his eyes, body unnaturally still. Mikel had angled his armchair just slightly away, turning his eyes to the wall. The others were all watching.

She tried to will her voice to speak, but her throat was too tight, a whimper threatening at her lips instead.

Colour? She managed to burst into his head.

"In that dress?" His eyes dropped to her nipples, a low growling sound grating up from his throat. He didn't bother to speak through the bond, or maybe he didn't realise she had asked through the bond. "Keep it on, and I'll stay green."

The lid over her feelings shook, the pot threatening to bubble over. She needed one of them inside her body and she needed it *now*, but she held it off a moment longer, forcing her voice into all their heads.

Everyone else?

After a moment of silence, Kalen answered, "Do what you need to do." His voice was strained and deep, a low warning riding the words that she had the impression he had tried to smother. She waited a moment longer for someone else to object and then spun to the bed. Theodore watched her with burning eyes, like he could feel the side effect as much as she could. Oscar was tightly coiled, veins pulsing in his arms as he clenched his fists, nostrils flaring. She didn't know what her scent was doing to them, but she approved. She gathered the silk of her dress up to her thighs, and quickly straddled Oscar, facing away from him, her eyes snapping back to Moses like a magnet.

Moses swallowed, darkening gaze dropping to Oscar's hands as they anchored to her hips. The thick hardness between her legs was an immediate balm to the pain spidering through her midsection. It slithered away as Oscar's fingers tightened in a bruising grip, dragging her over his length, a throaty moan vibrating out of his chest. She squirmed at the way the sound seemed to shudder right through her body from her core, her hands fluttering to his strong thighs as he moved her again, back and forth, tight and fast.

"Fuck, Carter." Oscar's growl had her eyelids fluttering, but she forced them back open, fixed to Moses, whose mouth was open slightly, his breath sawing.

This was dangerous, what she was doing.

It wasn't her usual game of testing their control. This time, she didn't *want* them to break. She wanted them to hold strong, to take part in this like prisoners while she settled the bond, so that they could go back to normal tomorrow as though nothing had happened and no lines had been blurred.

She desperately needed them to maintain control.

Theodore's hand slid around her waist, dragging dark silk through his fingers, and she could feel that line of danger trembling between them all. Theodore and Oscar generally didn't play well together. She sucked in a breath as Theodore's big hand brushed up along the bottom swell of her breasts, Oscar swearing behind her as a rush of desire spilled from her body, dampening her panties and his pants. She didn't like the barrier between them but didn't have time to do anything about it because Oscar was already pushing up her hips, dragging down his zipper, shoving at his pants. His rough fingers tore at her panties, tossing them from the bed.

Distantly, she realised someone had tipped forward and caught them, and she managed to tear her gaze from

Moses long enough to see Gabriel twisting the abused lace between his fingers, brows dipped low in contemplation. His eyes flicked up to her as Oscar dragged her hips back down, both of them moaning as his cock brushed up along her slippery heat. There was something in Gabriel's expression that would have given her pause if the fire inside her body wasn't already pushing her to find the delicious friction she needed.

It wasn't just Gabriel, she realised, taking in the others. Niko and Elijah had the same look. A warning, almost. Or a darkly whispered promise sent down the connection they had to her soul. Kilian and Cian watched her with pure, liquid heat, managing to wrangle their Alpha instincts back behind memories of them digging their claim into her body and her lips crying out their names. She wasn't sure how long it would tide them over. They would be claiming her in the next few nights, forcing her to say their names over and over and painting her in their claim until the ragged edges of their possessiveness had been appeased.

With Niko, Gabriel, and Elijah, it was different. They were adding something to a tally, silently counting all the ways they would make her atone for this.

Mikel and Kalen were still refusing to watch, their bodies tight and stiff as stone.

She flicked her attention back to Moses, who had been watching the way the silk bunched around her hips with Oscar's tightening grip, threatening to show him a peek with every shift of her hips, but his eyes settled back on hers when he felt her attention return to him. He seemed to understand why he was there, the centre of her attention, and he even seemed to understand why he wasn't the one in her bed.

They all seemed to understand. Perhaps they had seen her staring at Oscar, Theodore, and Moses while she performed. Perhaps they had felt it through the bond. Whatever the reason, she hoped that understanding would extend to forgiveness as she tipped her head back, arched her back in pleasure, and moaned. Oscar was running out of patience, his grip flexing on her hips as she slipped over him, control wavering in the tight grasp. He usually would have turned them by now, spilling her to the mattress as he shoved her legs wide and stabbed into her.

Theodore seemed to be growing impatient, too, his fingers dancing around her curves, dragging the silk against her skin as she rocked on top of Oscar. He was sitting upright beside them, looming over her, his eyes a dark storm, burning and roiling as he tried to wait his turn. When Theodore's hand finally closed over one breast, his mouth falling to her other, licking a nipple through the silk of her dress and causing a strangled sound to rip from her throat, Oscar's patience finally snapped. He yanked up her hips and tilted his swollen head to her entrance, his girth a threatening stretch before he slammed her hips down in one motion. He growled low. Her channel was soaked enough to allow the movement, even though the shock of the sudden invasion had her shuddering and bracing her hands on his thighs.

Anyone else would have waited for her to adjust, but Oscar liked to make her hiccup in shock or wriggle with uneasiness as she wondered how far he would push her. He liked to dance along that line, and maybe that was why he was shoving himself into her with a slight edge to his movements. Because they were *already* in danger. They were already experimenting with explosives, having sex in a room full of territorial, unsettled Alphas. He liked it. She could tell, even though she couldn't see his face. His noises were guttural, the song of slight fear and anxiety in her blood urging him on. He lifted her body and slammed it down to meet the sharp tilt of his hips like she weighed nothing at all, taking full control as she clung to his flexing thighs for balance, whimpering at the drag of his cock inside her, feeling like it was rubbing and stoking the fire that burned her from the inside out. It was strangely erotic to have the slide of her silk dress still covering her body and the material of Oscar's pants still wrapping his strong legs.

"Fucker is getting off on this." That had come from Moses, of course. Still ready with a sarcastic quip even now, with burning eyes drifting over her rosy face, heaving chest, rocking hips, and exposed thighs. There was something slightly pained in his eyes, something that rioted across his features until his eyes met hers again and he managed to tuck it away.

She wondered at that look and what it was supposed to mean, but then Theodore's hand slipped over her taut stomach and gripped her breast again, squeezing tightly, teeth worrying his lower lip.

"Your tits are fucking divine, bouncing in this dress," he explained, voice rough as she turned to him.

She strained toward him and his hand flashed up to capture her jaw, his lips crashing down on hers. His tongue slipped into her mouth, both of them breathing raggedly. Oscar gathered her hair into his hand, tugging her head back and forcing her to arch, her hands flying to her stomach and pressing against where she could feel him holding himself too deep inside her.

"None of that," Oscar whispered menacingly. "He'll get his turn. They can fucking watch."

One of the other Alphas swore. She wasn't sure who. It sounded a little concerned, but her bond *preened* at the rough claiming, her own hands cupping her heavy breasts through the dress as she ground down against Oscar. Her orgasm was *right there*, just out of reach, but then Oscar's touch slid around to her clit, cruelly pinching where she was most desperate for attention, and she exploded with a broken moan, writhing on top of him and clasping herself helplessly.

Another Alpha swore, this time the sound more breathless and less cautious. She wasn't sure how she

knew, but Mikel was watching now. She knew it as
surely as she knew that Kalen wasn't watching. A dark,
selfish little beast inside her insisted that she wanted
all their attention, even if it pained them or caused
them trouble. Even if it sent the entire dorm into chaos.
Even if it snapped someone's control. Oscar let her ride
out the rest of her orgasm by grinding down on him
and then suddenly, he was tipping her forward, sending
her tumbling to her elbows as he rose up behind her.
He flipped up her dress, the silk spilling over her spine,
and gripped her ass tightly, his solid, twitching length
never leaving her. Someone hissed—someone on the
other side of the room, and Oscar thrust into her in
earnest.

She wasn't sure what drew Moses forward—some
sort of silent invitation from Oscar over her head, or her
own begging eyes as she looked up at him, but suddenly
he was there, and her hand was gliding over the stiffness
straining against the material of his pants. He groaned,
his hands slipping into her tousled hair as she palmed
him. She could feel Theodore's eyes on her ass as he
leaned back, almost like he was trying to block out
Moses.

"Say thank you before I change my mind," Oscar
snarled, his hand coming down hard on her ass.

Her head jerked back on instinct, looking over her
shoulder, her fingers trying to close around Moses' cock
through his pants as she clenched around Oscar. His eyes

were a glittering black, his thrusts slowing slightly as their eyes met.

"Thank you," she whispered.

His jaw clenched and he throbbed inside her. Her mate was such a contradiction, getting off on punishing her just as much as he got off on pleasing her. She smiled at him, and he breathed deeply, swelling inside her.

"Suck your fucking present before I come, Carter." The words were expelled harshly from his chest, but she only let out a breathless laugh, high on the power she had over him, that her smile alone was enough to almost send him over the edge.

Moses flexed beneath her hand, demanding her attention, and she turned around again, her forehead pressing against his thigh as Oscar did his best to distract her from the "present" he had given her. He distracted her so well that she found herself fumbling to free Moses' erection in a desperation, embarrassed about the breathless whimpers and moans tumbling from her lips and thickening the air in the room. Moses growled, taking over from her shaking fingers, freeing his cock and feeding it into her eager, waiting mouth. She groaned in relief, her noises quietened.

"Greedy girl." The dark whisper slipped through the room like a slither of dark smoke, peeling into her ears and making her squirm.

It had been Mikel's voice. Deep, velvety, and full of

menace. She closed her lips around Moses as he slid to the back of her throat before pulling halfway out again to drag the tip of his cock across her tongue, back and forth, back and forth, his dark eyes fixed to her face, his grip tight in her hair. Neither of them allowed her control over her own movements, no matter how much she wiggled and squirmed. Moses was somehow keeping up a slow and deliberate pace as he fucked her mouth while Oscar's pace quickened, even though he should have been jolting her against the other Alpha. They were both oddly in sync with their different rhythms.

When one of her hands slipped between her thighs, both Alphas seemed to vibrate with approval. Sweat dusted her skin and the fire inside her burned hotter. All memories of pain had faded away, replaced by the delicious bruising pressure of Oscar's grip and the tightness in her chest when Moses buried himself deep in her throat, his hand drifting down to cup her neck as he held himself there and blocked off her airway. Her fingers turned slippery with arousal as she touched herself, her body beginning to bow with pleasure. She was crying when she finally came again, both of them growing jerky in their movements, Moses tugging on her hair until her watery eyes flitted up to him, his growl a feral rattle in his chest as he thickened and stilled, pushing as deep as he could and pulsing there, sending his release down her throat. As soon as he was done,

Oscar released that final thread of his control, yanking her back by the hair until she was curved against his chest, her dress falling back to cover her ass.

"Lift it," someone snarled—Elijah, she thought. She quickly pulled her dress back up, and there were several gravelled hums of sound that bounced through the room.

It wasn't that they wanted to see Oscar pounding into her, chasing his release, she thought. It was because they didn't want Oscar seeing something they couldn't —not when all they could do was watch. Their possession pressed in on her from all sides, a heavy wall of it that she sensed with her Sigma power, which meant that it was twisting into a negative thing, growing too vast and ugly for them to swallow back. Oscar's fingers found her clit, pressing and rubbing until she was gasping and clenching around him again, and then he followed her over, his teeth sinking into her neck as he grunted, cock twitching, emptying into her.

Mine, he claimed, having the good sense to say it in her head.

She writhed on him, loving the claiming, and he gave her a light slap. "Do enough of that and your golden boy will never get a turn."

She eyed Theodore as Oscar laid back down, his hands caressing her ass as her dress fluttered down to cover where they were joined. He was still hard inside her, and she knew from the occasions where he had slipped into her bed over the last few weeks that if she stayed there any longer, he would turn three orgasms into six ... *especially* if he was touching her ass, which he seemed to have a particular fondness for.

Theodore was laying back, one arm stretched behind his head, his eyes carefully masked, and a small, tight smirk on his face. She quickly lifted herself from Oscar's lap, twisting to kneel on the bed between them. Almost as soon as her pussy was unoccupied, the pain returned, stronger than before. She groaned, doubling over, her arm wrapped around her stomach, the burn inside her turning feverish.

"Shit, are you okay?" Theodore asked, both he and Oscar straightening and reaching for her.

"One of you better do something about that," Gabriel snarled. "Fucking now."

Isobel was already moving, already reaching for Theodore, her hands gripping his shirt, tearing the buttons as she tried to pull him on top of her.

"Fuck me," she gasped. "Hurry, please."

He moved so fast, she didn't even see him unzip his fly. He was on top of her in a blink, pressing one of her legs out, anchoring her bent leg to the mattress as he thrust into her. The pressure was perfect, the length of him scorching her insides, long and thick and familiar.

"You okay?" he asked, even as he pulled out and

pressed himself deep again, drawing a strangled moan from her throat.

"Just don't stop," she begged, clutching his torn shirt.

"Fuck, Illy." His eyes darkened, his lips tightening, his hips stuttering. He pulled back just enough to flip her over, and then he was driving into her hard and fast, sensing how she needed it.

She mewled and thrashed against the bed, gripping the tangled sheet in one fist and a soft blanket in the other, neither helping to anchor her as Theodore twisted another climax from her body, and then another, until she was limp, and he was pulsing inside her, yanking her hips up to hold himself deep, warmth washing her core.

When he pulled out of her exhausted body, it was cautiously, as though waiting for her yelp of pain, but it didn't come. She was boneless. Exhausted—not just from the sex, but from her taxing performance, the pain of the bond side effect, and the weight of her emotions. It all crashed down on her in that moment, and she felt a *real* sob bubbling up her throat.

She knew one of the three Alphas she had just been with was about to scoop her up and into the shower, but she lifted her eyes to the one she needed in that moment. Kilian was already standing, already striding for her.

"Come on, baby." He held out his arms and she weakly clamoured into them, wrapping her arms and legs around him. "The bond was mean to you tonight, hm?"

She shook with a silent sob and could feel the pain pinging at her from every direction, aching and sharp.

"It's n-not that," she quickly hiccupped. "Just overwhelmed."

The needling of pain eased as they sensed the truth of her words through the bond. She picked at the heaviest thread, finding her eyes drawn to Moses, leaning back up against the door as though he'd never moved from it. She wasn't sure where they stood, now. He gave her a tight smile. "It was just a side effect, Carter. I understand."

She frowned, trying to figure out if there was some kind of hidden meaning in his words, but Kilian was already stealing her into the bathroom.

He stripped both of them, carrying her into the shower and sitting her on the bench inside as he fiddled with the faucet. He was half hard, his beautiful dick curving out from his thigh.

"Ignore it," he said, following the direction of her gaze. "It's having a hard time going down after that ... performance."

"Which one?" She grinned at him, obviously joking, but his eyes only flared.

"Both," he rasped, before sucking in a deep breath. "Don't worry about the others. Nobody surged. Nobody went feral. Nobody's been castrated. Yet."

She rolled her eyes. "I feel so much better."

"We're in this together," he said sternly, catching her

349

chin, his thumb stroking softly along her jaw. "We'll settle the bond however we have to—it's *our* bond. We share the responsibility. I promise nobody is going to hold this against you, and everything will go back to normal tomorrow."

13

YES, SIR

"MORE PRESENTS?" ISOBEL ASKED DRYLY AS HER FATHER
sauntered into the Icon Cafe—this time with three
assistants, all of them weighed down by heavy shopping
bags. Isobel glanced at some of the labels with a frown.
Gucci, Saint Laurent, Hermes, Armani.

"This is getting out of hand," she said.

Braun ignored her, dismissing his assistants. He sat
down with a heavy sigh, like he had carried all the bags
himself.

"How are my boys doing?" he asked, resting for only
a moment before he tipped forward and began to pour
them coffee.

He meant the Alphas.

He kept referring to them as *his boys*.

Isobel barely managed to contain an eyeroll.

It all started with the suits, but then her father began

to book in time with her at the Icon Cafe once a month. He tested her boundaries with small presents at first. A bracelet, a pair of earrings, a Birkin bag, another bracelet. She refused all of them. Four months later, he turned up the weekend after *her* birthday with nine designer scarves, one for each of the Alphas, minus Mikel, who he was pretending wasn't part of the group. Their closets were abysmally empty, so this time, she accepted. Besides, she had been spoiled enough for her birthday and she really didn't need anything else, especially not from Braun. The Alphas had all piled into her room for a movie night earlier in the week, and each of them had brought her an actual bouquet of flowers—not a drawing of one. She had kept up the tradition of drawing flowers with Oscar and Mikel's birthdays. They had all been too busy to celebrate Oscar's birthday—not that he was interested in any sort of event—but since her birthday was shared with Mikel, they all decided that it was as good a time as any to force the whole group to take a break.

It had been one of those rare nights she treasured, where everyone was relaxed and close, casually leaning on each other and touching each other for comfort while she soaked up their combined scents. They had gorged on snacks, laughed at the movies she wanted to watch the most, and eventually fell asleep splayed out in her bedroom. Even Mikel and Kalen stayed—the first time they had slept in her room since their voyeuristic night after Thanksgiving break.

Still, it annoyed her that her father was so busy trying to win her affection with gifts that he forgot her actual birthday, which was the *one* day she might have allowed him to give her one.

After accepting the scarves on behalf of the Alphas, Braun tried pushing his luck even more. In the three months after that, he came back with more and more presents, all of them for her mates, working his way up to his current display of excess.

She frowned over at him—he was currently leaning toward the curtain, trying to see what the Alphas were doing in their private rooms.

"Why don't you just book time with them instead of me?" she asked cooly.

BRAUN CARTER KNEW HIS DAUGHTER WAS EXASPERATED WITH him. He also knew he wasn't being subtle with his interest in her mates, but that was exactly his intention. His psychiatrist had told him to show interest in the things Isobel was interested in. The doctor had promised that this was his route to reconnecting with his daughter. He could have chosen dance, admittedly. But he didn't care about dance. He could have chosen singing, but he himself had declared she had no talent in that particular department, and he *really* didn't like being wrong.

What he did like was the fact that *his* daughter—his small, weak *Sigma* daughter—was bonded to ten Alphas.

Ten of them.

Alphas.

Tall, powerful, popular, charming, skilled, hardworking—and Mikel.

They were as good as his sons.

The eleven of them would win this game, and then they could be a family.

An entire family of Alphas.

But no ... he wasn't allowed to say that she was weak.

Sigmas were strong.

Caran Carter had been strong—the strongest person he had ever known. It always confused him, the concept of a strong Sigma. It was hard to admit it, but once he finished reading her journals, he finally realised it.

Caran Carter was a fucking *fighter*.

And now there was Isobel, and she ... *she* was even stronger.

He wished Caran was still alive, still writing in those damn journals so that he could read her perspective on how Isobel had turned out. She always phrased things in ways Braun never would. Always saw things from a completely different perspective. It was like opening a whole other side of his brain that he couldn't seem to reach on his own. And still couldn't.

Braun had always believed they were hurting each other ... but according to Caran, he was the only one causing pain.

His psychiatrist had said that just because he was feeling *hurt* didn't necessarily mean that anyone was causing him pain. There was a distinction to be made. Frustratingly, without Caran's journal spelling that distinction out for him, he couldn't seem to see it on his own. He wanted to promise Isobel that he would be different, but the truth was, without that perspective, his brain closed back up again.

He was trying. He often wondered if he was doomed to fail, but he was trying.

"Father?" Isobel prompted, arching a brow at him.

"I'd rather see you," he said honestly, waving off her question.

She was finally starting to articulate the word "father" without spitting it out like it was something filthy.

"But how are they?" he prompted, because even though annoyance raced across her expression, within five minutes, she was smiling.

She loved talking about the Alphas, even though after seven months and seven visits, she still didn't trust him enough to say anything personal. She only talked about their work and training.

"So the album is pretty much finished," she surmised, after babbling on about Theodore Kane's singing and Niko Hart's dancing and Elijah Reed's rapping and *blah blah blah*. It wasn't that he wasn't interested; it was just that he already knew.

While his daughter and sons-to-be were preparing their album, he was making moves of his own. He had wormed his way onto the board of directors for Orion Entertainment.

He couldn't make any policy changes, but he knew everything. He knew that Kalen West and Mikel Easton —who he was a little less enthused about, as far as sons-in-law were concerned—had created magic with the human group. Hero's album was going to be a success, but so was Eleven's.

They were neck and neck.

Hero stole the show at Ironside Row every Friday night, but Eleven created their own content in their private training room and had a fiercely loyal following.

"So, there's something we need to discuss." Isobel suddenly switched topics, her hands folded nervously in her lap. "It's about the album tour Hero is planning over summer break."

He sat back, waiting for her to elaborate. He had informed her last month about the planned tour, which would be devastating for Eleven's race to the finish line. A summer album tour out in the real world while the Alphas were stuck at home in the settlements? It would ruin them.

She cringed, wringing her fingers—an old habit he

thought she had broken out of. "We can't compete with that. You know we can't." Her eyes were strained, stress tightening her shoulders. "Kalen has been exploring our options—there's absolutely no way the officials will let them leave the settlements, but a settlement tour may be an option."

"They're going to fund that?" Braun asked, faking the doubt in his tone.

He already knew about their little plan, of course. And he had a feeling he knew what she was about to ask him.

He tried not to preen, deepening the politely confused frown on his face.

This felt good.

He liked this—her needing his help.

"They'll allow us to organise a settlement tour. They said we can organise fan meets and visit each of the Alpha's settlements only. No concerts. And if we want Kalen and Mikel to join us, we have to agree to also take Cooper and Teak. But they won't fund it," she spat out. "And they won't let us take commercial flights."

Braun let out a low whistle. "You didn't want the bracelet, but you want the private plane?"

Her expression flattened.

He whistled again, shaking his head in fake shock, trying to draw it out for as long as he could. "This is no small favour."

"It won't be a favour," she said tightly. "I'm offering

to make another deal with you. What do you want in return?"

He rubbed his fingers back and forth over his chin. "All right, I'll fund the tour, but in exchange, I want full control. I'll organise it myself."

"You mean your team?" she quickly countered, her tone challenging.

She was becoming more like him every day. He used to despise it when she challenged him, because she only ever did it with her eyes.

Like a fucking Sigma coward.

No, he wasn't allowed to say that.

Like a ... pussy? No, that was sexist.

Like a ... weak little gir—

No, that was worse.

Sometimes, it felt like the list of things he needed to fix was endless. But he wasn't a fucking quitter.

He wasn't *whatever* Isobel used to be.

She used to cower in the face of a challenge. Now, she squared her shoulders and dared him to disagree with her, doing it with all the confidence in the world.

"Yes, my team—under my direction—will organise everything," he said. "And I'll accompany you. And Mikel Easton will behave himself," he tacked on, unable to help himself. "None of those presents are for him, by the way."

He was proud of his other sons-to-be, but Easton still got under his skin.

"They never are." Isobel sipped her coffee, considering his offer. She was taking too long, and he dared a glance past the curtains, seeing several of the Alphas glance her way. She did this sometimes. Using their bond to communicate across the room, he assumed. The officials were under the impression that they didn't have that particular ability, but the officials didn't understand bonds the way the Gifted did. The darkness inside him swelled up, madness threatening to pull him under at the thought that *he could have had this*, but he laboured to push it down.

Sometimes, he had to drink himself into a stupor to push it down.

Sometimes, he found himself out on that balcony, contemplating the fall, just like his wife used to do because it was so hard to push down, to swallow, to choke on.

"I'll make no promises for Mikel," Isobel finally said, her attention sharpening on him again. "But I'll agree to everything else."

He glanced to the curtain again. Easton was standing at the bar, as usual. Nobody ever requested the ugly fucker, other than his ex-girlfriend, and that was only because Tilda was batshit crazy. Mikel was staring at Braun now, brows narrowed.

Braun felt a little spark of pleasure as he surveyed the younger man. If he were to raise his own Alpha, the boy would turn out just like Easton, he knew it. Hard and angry and ready to throw fists at the slightest disrespect.

He was still annoying, and Braun itched to wipe the arrogance from his face, but there was no denying that he was an admirable example of an Alpha. Braun could practically feel his dominance from across the room.

Yes, he was annoying, but he would do.

And besides, Braun didn't need him to be perfect.

Not when he had Theodore Kane. The others could be whatever they wanted, just as long as Kane stayed as brilliantly sparkling and talented as he was. Still, it was nice to have spares.

"Fine," he agreed, looking back to Isobel. "You've got yourself a deal."

ISOBEL QUICKLY DOWNED ANOTHER COFFEE AT THE TABLE AFTER her father left. She still had her second booking for the day to get through, but they didn't always allow her to order, and she was going to need the extra kick after seeing Braun.

Mikel came to clear her table, and she stood up to help him.

"He looks at you guys like the sons he never had," she breathed, annoyed.

"Not me," Mikel returned, looking amused. "He looks at me like he has nightmares about the time he asked if I was trying to be your new daddy."

Isobel winced, straightening away from the table to regather the high ponytail she had slung her hair into. It had grown longer, the heavy mass of waves always weighing down whatever style she tried to pull it into.

"You know," she ventured, dropping her arms, her eyes on his broad back as he bent over the table, "if I was a customer, I would request you." She had said the words without thinking, but now she was cursing herself internally.

The last thing he probably wanted was for her to point out that he was the least popular of the Alphas— even less popular than Oscar, who had made more girls cry at this point than she could even count. Tilda Anderson—the creative director—had booked Mikel a handful of times, but nobody else.

His lips twitched, pulling at his scarred skin. "Really."

It wasn't a question.

"I have a booking in a few minutes," he added, stacking the plates.

Isobel's stomach sank. The Alphas—just like every other Icon-in-training in the cafe—had cultivated a few regulars. She *hated* the ones who came back. It wasn't that she couldn't stand to see them forming friendships, whether they were real or not—it was that she knew some of their regulars fantasised about more.

The shy girl who had sat with Elijah on their first day came back once a month, just like he said she would, and she didn't even live in Paris. She begged her father to fly her down with her friends every month, spending five hundred euros just for Elijah to ignore her.

"Tilda again?" Isobel guessed, watching as Mikel straightened, stretching his arms behind his back and cracking his neck to the side. His splotchy eyes settled on her, drifting briefly down her dress. Seven months of wearing it and they still couldn't stop trailing their eyes over her body whenever she pulled it on.

"Tilda," he confirmed, a sigh slipping out.

Usually, they didn't talk about it. Their regulars. The Alphas weren't affectionate with their guests, and they didn't flirt—not in the way she knew they did in private with her. Some of them weren't even polite, and some— like Oscar, Moses, and Niko—were downright nasty.

It was an awkward dance, especially since her relationships with some of them were undefined. Technically, her relationships with *all* of them were undefined, but she had sex with Theodore, Kilian, Cian, and Oscar regularly. She felt justified in claiming them as her own and would completely freak out if they ever stepped over a line with their guests.

The others were more of a grey area. She hated seeing Kalen requested. She hated when Tilda returned for Mikel. She hated the dark-haired woman with the pretty green eyes who kept returning for Moses. She hated the constant, revolving door of girls who swarmed inside for Niko and the petite, married woman who returned for Gabriel often enough to make Isobel's stomach turn.

She hated it.

And yet ...

Every Saturday night, after enduring hours of anxiety, she always had the best sex of her life with the four Alphas she *was* involved with, and it almost made the pain worth it.

She had begun to look forward to that awful, skin-crawling sensation of having to watch her mates entertain other men and women because she knew that as soon as they stumbled back to the dorm, she would be tossed to her bed, her clothes ripped away, her body marked and filled until the itching in her skin eased and her ragged soul was appeased.

Mikel flicked the curtains closed without warning, catching her chin and lifting her eyes to his. "Everything okay?" His voice was too stern to be soft, but his eyes were concerned as they dipped over her features.

He was so handsome with his dark hair, the barest wave sweeping his forehead, the strands shot through with a blend of blackened rust. He had sharp features, a strong nose, thin lips, and angular brows. His appearance had definitely frightened her in her first year, but now all of those scars were basically invisible to her, and the severity of his expression always eased when he looked at her.

"I'm just annoyed at myself," she said when he pinched her chin a little tighter, silently demanding an answer. "I wish people would show you more appreciation, but if they did, I would hate them."

His thumb stroked along the line of her chin softly, his head tilting to the side. "This is about Tilda."

"No," she lied. "Tilda who?"

"Are you not being claimed enough, Sigma?" was whispered tightly against her lips, though he didn't kiss her. He just held her chin, tilting her face up to his, his eyes staring all the way through her. "I've been checking on the stone—it hasn't changed colour. The bond is still as happy as we can make it."

"This isn't about the bond." She was turning red. Mikel didn't automatically become *hers* just because they had formed the bond. They did it to save her life, not because they loved her.

He wasn't hers unless he decided he was, just like she wasn't his unless she decided she was.

"Then what is it about?" he asked, taking a step back, his hand dropping from her face. "You're still worried about what your father said?"

"I'm never *not* worried about it. I don't know what happened to him, but what if people—what if *Tilda* starts asking to meet you alone? What if Yulia asks to meet Kalen alone? What if one of those girls out there spending their daddy's money tries to arrange something with Theo, or Cian, or Kilian, Niko, or Moses? And that quiet girl who never talks to Elijah? She freaks me out. And that woman who is always coming back for

Gabe? She *already* got him alone. And got his clothes off."

Mikel shook his head, expression flattening in fury. "That's never happening again."

"I think it happened with my father. I think something *worse* happened with my father. If it can happen to Braun Carter, it can happen to you guys."

"Braun didn't have me and Kalen. Our boys have us. We won't let anything happen."

Again. The unspoken passed between them. Because, of course, it had already happened to Gabriel and Elijah.

"What if it happens to *you*," she spat, working to keep her tone low.

"Carter?" Ethan popped his head through the curtain. "Oh, good. Thought I heard you in there. Your next guest is waiting. Table number seven."

Isobel gave him a stiff nod and he disappeared. She began to move past Mikel, but he caught her wrist when she reached for the curtain. He pulled her back around to face him, his grip light.

"I wish we could change the world," he spoke lowly, "but the world doesn't listen just because you want them to. You think a human woman can just decide one day that all violences against her will stop? You think she can just say so? That it's over now, because she said so? No. She has to play the game. She has to wait for her moment and choose her words, or she will be laughed at, disregarded, or attacked. That's our world." He gently squeezed her wrist. "If they won't even afford half of their *own* population the courtesy of demanding that acts of violence against them should stop, then you know we have no chance."

"So if it happens, you're just going to take it?" she asked, her heart falling into her stomach.

His hand drifted up her arm, fingers suddenly circling her neck. It wasn't a tight hold, but it halted her breath all the same. He stood slightly back from her, bearing witness to the sudden hitch of her chest, the colour in her cheeks, the way her fingers twitched like she might suddenly try to grab his wrist. He carefully evaluated every single aspect of her response before speaking again.

"I never said we should just *take* it. I said we can't control *them*. But if someone comes for my body, my Sigma, or my Alphas, they *will* regret it."

He squeezed her neck lightly before releasing her and stepping through the curtain. She pulled in a deep breath and followed him out, her fingers playing across her neckline as she grabbed a menu and walked to her next table. Niko was stepping out of one of the rooms when she passed. He smelled like somebody else's perfume.

She frowned, almost tripping over her own feet.

"Movie night?" he asked, eyes tracing her downturned lips.

It was something they did, occasionally. After their particularly difficult weekends. They all gathered in

Isobel's room, dragging in the cushions from all their chaise lounges and spreading them across her floor.

"Sounds good," she said, some of the tension easing from her shoulders as she stepped into her next room.

"Carter," a man greeted, his Swedish accent subtle. "It's nice to put a face to the name."

What? She smiled at him politely, holding out the menu to him with both hands, bowing slightly. Yulia had stopped by a few times to lecture them on proper cafe etiquette, and that included how to hand over a menu.

"Lovely to meet you, sir."

He took the menu from her. "Sit."

She perched on the edge of one of the armchairs as he also reseated himself, flicking out his jacket. He was a large man with light hair, the strands peppered with silver streaks.

"Do you not watch the show, sir?" she ventured, a little confused at his "putting a face to the name" comment.

He snorted, his accent thickening. "Reality television isn't within my umbrella of interests, pet."

Pet. Only Mikel called her that, and only on special occasions. She didn't like it out of this man's mouth. Oddly, he seemed to notice, his dark blue eyes sharpening, his moustache twitching in amusement.

"What brings you here today, then?" she asked, trying to wrestle her expression back into polite interest.

He tossed the menu to the table. "I'll have an Americano. What do you drink, lovely girl?"

"I'll have whatever you're having," she said with forced sweetness, snatching up the menu and standing.

His moustache twitched again, like he knew it was all for show.

"And something sweet," he said. "I'm in the mood for it."

"As you wish, sir."

She stalked out of the room and could have sworn she heard him utter something like *brat* beneath his breath, his low chuckle following her all the way to the bar.

She placed his order and returned, perching on her chair again.

"I came because I was interested," he said, answering her earlier question. "It is rare for Kalen and Mikki to show an extended interest in anyone, let alone the *same* someone."

She blinked at him, forgetting her politeness. "Who are you?"

"A friend." He smiled, and there was something sharp in the edges of it. "I've known the boys a long time."

"How?" she pressed, all pretences dropped.

He chuckled, delighted. "They always did like the rebellious ones. I organised a ... club ... of sorts in the

Mojave Settlement. It was the first of its kind in a Gifted space, bringing a little *spice* to an otherwise bleak and oppressive nightlife."

Her mind raced, trying to put all the pieces together. "You mean you taught them the … like the … s-shibari and stuff?" She almost choked over the words.

What was happening?

"Yes." He smirked. "Shibari and stuff. I have a private club in Los Angeles. The settlement club was actually Kalen's idea—he somehow found my contact details and reached out to me by email, saying he had a business proposition. He wanted a safe place to practise kink but was worried about it being used for trafficking if it were to be managed by the settlement officials. That's where I came in."

"So you … own it?" she asked, her forehead creasing. "A privately owned business? Inside a Gifted settlement?"

"Money talks, my dear." He paused as Kalen flicked open the curtain, standing aside for one of the servers to place a tray on the table.

Everyone was silent until the server left, and then Kalen let the curtain fall again.

"Ivan," he greeted, his lips twitching slightly. "I thought I heard your voice. What the fuck are you doing?"

Ivan stood, and they shook hands. Isobel watched

them with her brows inching up. They had been strictly instructed not to interrupt each other's bookings after Niko stormed into a room and threatened a girl for touching Gabriel.

Kalen moved to stand by Isobel's chair, a possessive hand falling onto her shoulder.

"Just satisfying my curiosity." Ivan watched him with a glitter of amusement. "I was telling Miss Carter about our shared business venture."

"It's not shared anymore," Kalen responded tightly.

"Yes, yes." Ivan waved him off, uncaring. "Nasty business, losing that delectable girlfriend of yours. She was the only thing keeping your name clean back in Mojave. Of course, I understand you can't be mixed up with me now. She misses you, by the way. I've seen her in the club both of the times I visited. The last time, she begged me to use her."

"And did you?" Kalen asked blandly.

"What do you think?" He sighed, shaking his head. "She's far too meek for me, but I put her in contact with an associate of mine. He promised to visit."

"Good for her." Kalen was like a stone wall, his hand heavy on her shoulder. He wasn't moving.

"Well." Ivan chuckled, eyeing them. "So, she's yours, then?"

"Yes," Kalen snipped tightly. "Is your curiosity satisfied?"

Ivan held up both hands. "You can't blame me. I saw one of your shows." He switched his attention to Isobel. "You did beautifully."

"Don't thank him," Kalen growled. "Just look at your lap."

Isobel blinked down at her thighs in shock.

Ivan laughed even harder. "I've been nothing but polite, Kalen."

The big fingers gripping her shoulder loosened slightly. "Of course," Kalen said, deliberately casual. "I just don't want you to get the wrong idea. Isobel is owned. Privately. She is not to be shared."

"But she *is* being shared," Ivan shot back. "I watched her dance last night. Mikel also watched her. He looked at her like she was his."

Kalen made a rough noise in the back of his throat. "She's off limits."

"For the right price, nothing is off limits." Ivan smiled at them both. "Of course, consent comes first, and I can see that she is happy with her arrangement." He lifted his hips, digging out his wallet. After extracting a business card, he dropped it onto the table. "Give me a call if your situation changes, hm?" He stood. "A pleasure, as always, Kalen."

Kalen didn't respond. He snatched up the other man's card as soon as Ivan left, shoving the piece of cardboard into his pocket.

"What was that all about?" she asked.

"He watched you perform and thought we would let you fuck him." Kalen fell into the seat opposite her, taking Ivan's spot ... and then stealing his coffee.

"*Let* me?" she asked, because he looked comfortable and not at all like he was about to get up and punish her for challenging him.

He smiled behind the rim of the coffee cup, a sharp, cutting sort of smile. He seemed more relaxed now that Ivan was gone, but Isobel could feel the shiver of his influence in the air. He wasn't relaxed at all. He was just hiding it ... and he hadn't left the room yet because he was trying to get control of himself.

"I seem to remember forcing you to take my cock, Isobel," he rumbled so low, she almost didn't catch the words. "From that moment, you were mine."

"I don't remember that." She wiped all the emotion from her face and tucked her hands beneath her thighs. "Do you have any proof?"

His golden-brown eyes dipped to her thighs, his tongue running across his lower lip as he digested her reaction. It was like he was tasting her nervousness, and maybe he was. She could only scent herself when she was really close to one of them, and their scents were tangled together.

"Do you *need* proof?" Kalen asked, almost a whisper.

She wished she was brave enough to tilt up her chin and dare him to claim her, to do whatever he wanted with her. She wished she was brave enough to push the others, too, because she knew that was what they were waiting for—except Gabriel. They were waiting for her to push, because they didn't think she could handle them.

But she couldn't push, because sometimes, she wondered if they were right.

She had major trust issues, and even if she didn't, trying to manage sleeping with more than four people at once just didn't seem like something she could pull off without one of those people ending up in the medical centre and the other one in serious trouble for trying to kill one of their best friends.

She had *no* idea how she was currently pulling off the four of them with no violence.

Well, minimal violence.

Oscar had punched Theodore the other week when they both came to her door at the same time.

"It's not your problem." Kalen set down his coffee, responding to something in her expression or something he was feeling through the bond. "We made an agreement, didn't we? Your body, your choice."

"What if I choose Ivan?" She bit down on her lip, pulling her hands free from where they were trapped beneath her thighs. She crossed her legs, and Kalen's eyes immediately dipped to the short hem of her dress, a grunt releasing from his throat.

This was their game.

It had been since he took those pictures of her.

He pressed forward, and she quickly danced away. Out of respect for her, he backed off. And she teased him. Pushed him. Wondered if she could break him.

It was fucked up.

She couldn't help it.

"I can see your panties, princess."

Her body tingled. She kicked her leg in the air lightly, carelessly. "Can you?"

His breathing turned rough, and he opened his mouth to speak, before seeming to change his mind. He cast a quick look at the curtains and then returned his stare to her, heavy with command.

Take them off, he snapped through the bond. *Now. Then walk over to me and stand between my legs like a good girl.*

She uncrossed her legs, unable to hide the tremble in them as she, too, glanced at the curtain. She slipped her hands beneath the hem of her dress, her thumbs hooking into the waistband of her panties. She slid them down her legs and quickly bunched them into her fist, moving to stand between his strong thighs.

He held out his palm and she dropped them into his hand.

He stood, his body brushing along her front, and then he bent, putting his lips by her ear.

"Next time you tease me, I'll make you turn around and bend over while you're taking them off, and then ... if they're as soaked as they are right now, I'll make you jack me off with them until they're fucking ruined.

Understood?"

"Y-yes," she squeaked out.

"Sir," he corrected.

"Yes, Sir."

14

INJURED OR FUCKED

Consolidation Day wasn't anything like what Isobel had come to expect. Usually, it was a day of celebration with performances from the fifth-year students before the Icon was announced in front of all the other students and academy staff.

Today was different.

It was hardly surprising, after what Crowe had done the year before, but Isobel still felt strange leaving the academy without any sort of ceremony to signal the start of summer break. It would be broadcast later that night from an undisclosed location, and the winning Icon would be the only Gifted in attendance, which meant it was off campus.

They all piled onto her father's private plane, where Teak and Cooper were already waiting for them, along with her father's team. Teak looked rough. Her eyes were flat, dark bruises marring the skin beneath. Her skin had a sickly pallor, and she barely managed a smile when she saw Isobel before her attention drifted back to the window.

Her father followed Isobel's stare over to Teak, giving her a brief, knowing look. Like he knew exactly why she had been requesting surrogate pills all these months and knew exactly where they were going.

It was unnerving how much her father seemed to know.

He forced a smile and spread out his large arms—the charm he usually reserved for awards shows and press appearances on full display. "Isobel!" he boomed. "My boys!" And then, in a more reserved tone, "Easton."

Every single one of the Alphas stared at him.

They were having a more challenging time adjusting to his attempted reformation than Isobel was, and they knew exactly why he was so enthusiastic about them.

They had been dealing with Alpha worship their entire lives.

Niko shook his head, stalking off to claim a seat without a word. Moses and Oscar followed him, Moses cutting a look over his shoulder at Braun that clearly said, *What the fuck?*

"Thanks for the plane," Theodore muttered, giving Braun a confused look before stalking off.

Kilian stayed by her side, his arm curving around her shoulders, holding her tightly against his body.

"Braun," Kalen greeted him stiffly. "We really need a copy of the schedule. I tried contacting your team—"

"Of course, of course." Braun snapped his fingers at one of his assistants. "Have a schedule sent to everyone." He turned back to Isobel, an anticipatory glint in his eye. "They're only allowing the Alpha or Alphas whose home we're visiting to stay overnight in the settlement. The rest of us need to stay in the hotels they approved. If anything happens while we're there, it's entirely on my head, so you all need to be on your absolute best behaviour."

"Got it," she said. "No drugs and no hookers."

He acted like he couldn't even hear her sarcasm. "I've managed to secure several interconnected rooms to keep you all together—in the hotels where those rooms were available. Otherwise, I've tried to arrange lodges with enough bedrooms so you can all stay separately from everyone else."

She rocked back on her heels, a little taken aback. "Thank you."

"The stylist team has each of your outfits planned for the eight meet-and-greets and then another outfit change for the afterparties at each of the settlements. The afterparties are being funded by the official-run settlement committees—they will be ticketed events."

"People can't afford that," Mikel interjected. "Not in the settlements."

"You don't even know what the ticket charge is," Braun snapped.

"And still, they can't afford it."

Isobel waited for her father to explode. To blackmail them into compliance by threatening to pull the plug on the tour. He was quiet for a long time, staring at Mikel. Finally, his head jerked to the side, glaring at one of his assistants.

"What can we do, then?" he ordered. "The afterparties were their idea. We can't tell them no."

The group of assistants immediately put their heads together, trying to sort out a solution.

Elijah spoke up, his tone impatient, like he was already sick of waiting for the humans to figure it out, even though they had only just started talking. "Set up an online promotion. Call it Eleven Ways to Build a Bridge. Allow humans to purchase buddy passes. Purchasing a pass will donate one ticket to a lottery for the Gifted. A pass will grant them an invite to an exclusive live that we'll do from the hotel as we're getting ready for the afterparty and some sort of merchandise item signed by all of us."

"A polaroid," Gabriel added. "The merch should be a signed Polaroid—and not signed by all of us. One picture, one signature. Luck of the draw. That way, there's a lottery for the humans as well."

Braun's gold-flecked gaze was slowly flicking between Gabriel and Elijah.

"Do that," he said to his assistants, pointing at Elijah. "Mr Reed, you should sit next to me. We should discuss the rest of the tour and see if you have any other ideas."

Elijah's lips parted, a short sigh slipping out. He was tired—they all were, after putting in everything they had to get their album finished and approved by Orion before the end of the year. He was probably hoping to get some sleep on the flight since none of them knew what their schedule would be.

After a moment of consideration, he gave a short nod.

"Will you join us, Mr West?" Braun asked, shrugging off his jacket and heading to his seat.

Isobel rocked back on her heels as her father walked away, clucking her tongue. "It's giving desperation."

Cian scoffed. "I'm here under protest. Let it be known."

"Come on," Kilian grumbled, steering her to seats at the back of the plane.

She brought up her email as soon as they were in the air, loading the document her father had sent to everyone. In eleven hours, they would land in Albany, and from there, they would be driving straight to the first meet-and-greet at Moses and Theodore's settlement. Her father's team went straight to work organising the promotion Elijah had suggested, and everyone settled in for the flight.

Isobel had a straight line of sight across the plane to Teak, who still hadn't looked away from the window or tried to speak to anyone. Cooper had attempted to talk to her for a few minutes before relocating somewhere else.

"She wouldn't be recording on the plane, right?" Isobel whispered.

Kilian leaned over her, glancing over at Teak before falling back to his seat again. He slipped his hand to her thigh, the heat of his palm seeping through the denim of her jeans. He squeezed her gently.

"I highly doubt it, but I wouldn't try to bring up Charlie. You might do more harm than good. Let her come to you. She knows where you are. If it's safe to talk —if she even wants to talk—she'll say something."

Isobel huffed out a sigh and shifted closer to Kilian. And then closer. She was as close as she could possibly get when he snatched her up and sat her in his lap, his arms wrapping her waist.

"Better?" he whispered as she sank into his body.

"How very un-gay of you," Moses commented, immediately stealing her seat. "How will you explain your boner to the humans?"

"Maybe I'll find somewhere to hide it before they notice," Kilian rumbled back, fully engrossed in scenting her, his nose running along her hairline. "Somewhere warm. Somewhere wet." He suddenly lifted Isobel, razing his teeth along her neck and making her bite back a laugh that quickly turned into a whimper. "Have any idea where I might find somewhere like that, Illy?"

"You make me sick," Moses said blandly, though his eyes were fixed to the teeth Isobel had sunk into her lower lip. "The humans can see you."

Kilian let out the softest, quietest groan before lowering her back to his lap, where he was already hard and insistent. She could feel the long length of him against the backs of her thighs, but she pretended not to as she faced Moses.

"Which stop is after the Hudson Settlement?" Kilian asked, trying to change the topic.

"Ozark—Oscar's settlement," Moses answered, digging out his phone and pulling up the schedule again. "And then Green Mountain for you, Redwood for Niko, Piney Woods for Eli and Gabe, Rock River Valley for Cian, San Bernadino for Mikki, then Mojave for Kalen. Looks like Braun managed to convince the officials we needed extra time at each stop. We aren't just there for a day. He's scheduled in maintenance days, down days, and training days—I guess so that we don't lose fitness. This trip is going to last the entire summer break. What the hell is a maintenance day?"

Isobel snorted. "Laser, surgery, hair, Botox, body sculpting, liposuction, fake tanning, manicures, pedicures, and any other cosmetic treatment he can talk me into—although now I guess he also needs Orion's approval. This torture extends to you guys by the way. *His boys*."

"Since when do you get surgery?" Moses growled.

She kicked out her leg, gently brushing his thigh. "I refused surgeries and injections, but he still tries—or tried, to schedule them in. Maybe his team slotted it into the schedule automatically, assuming it was what he wanted. Or maybe the 'improvements' aren't as intense as they have been in the past. I guess we'll find out."

"You're not getting Botox," Moses snarled. "And neither am I."

"You're not getting Botox?" Cian asked, falling into the chair opposite her and Kilian—he had disappeared into the bedroom at the back of the plane to get changed and was now in a pair of stretchy sweatpants and a loose T-shirt, an eye mask slung around his neck. He was smirking at Moses. "You might want to rethink that. Your frown lines are hideous."

MIKEL WAITED FOR BRAUN TO SLIP OFF TO THE PRIVATE bedroom to sleep before he got changed in the bathroom. The rest of the humans had rehomed themselves in the conference room at the front of the jet, separated from the rest of the space, and he deliberately lingered by the lacquered walnut-toned door, trying to hear some of their conversation.

It seemed the jet wasn't Braun's usual. It was on loan from one of his business contacts—that much, he had picked up on before the group relocated. Unfortunately, he couldn't hear them anymore. He passed through the small section of the plane that housed a bar for food, a bar for drinks, and the bathrooms, stepping back into the seating area. Cooper had turned his seat into a bed and was already fast asleep.

Was it dark enough for Mikel to hold a pillow over his face without anyone noticing?

Possibly.

The seat beside him was empty, and Teak sat on the opposite side of the plane. She hadn't lowered her bed. She had barely moved at all since they took off. She was still staring out the window. She sighed, rubbing her arms, and then let her hands flop uselessly back to her sides.

Fucking hell.

He wished there was some way to help her.

Kalen and Mikel's seats were in a grouping with Elijah and Gabriel. The three of them were still up quietly discussing the tour. On the other side were Oscar and Niko, both of them spilling out of the transformed beds that would have been plenty wide and long enough for a human man. They had pillows over their faces even though the lights were turned off.

Cian and Theodore were asleep in the next row of seats, and Kilian, Moses, and Isobel were cuddled up in the back, mostly hidden from view. Isobel was curled into Kilian's lap—his chair still upright so that people didn't question why she wasn't in her own bed. Her legs were slung over the padded leather arms of the chairs, dropping into Moses's lap. His chair was also still upright, his head tipped back, eyes closed, arm draped over Isobel's legs.

Mikel hit the button to send Moses' chair into a recline and then grabbed a blanket, tossing it over him. Isobel's legs had retreated but crept out again once Moses was settled, her little toes inching beneath his blanket to brush his stomach. Moses absently gripped her ankle over the blanket and then went straight back to sleep. Mikel made sure the others all had pillows and blankets before returning to his own seat.

"Get some rest," he ordered Elijah and Gabriel. "You're going to need it."

They both sighed and stood, stretching out their tired muscles before converting their beds. Kalen moved to the bathroom to change, and Mikel made up his own bed.

But he didn't sleep. He was suspicious by nature, and even though he was sure nothing would happen to his group while they were sleeping, he just couldn't shake off the urge to keep watch.

When Theodore woke up several hours later, dragging out his tablet to entertain himself, Mikel finally closed his eyes.

ISOBEL COULDN'T STOP YAWNING AS THEY LANDED AND WERE herded into separate vans. They were driven to a hotel near the airport. It wasn't the fanciest place—especially not compared to the leathered and lacquered interior of the private jet.

Two policemen were waiting in the lobby with a nervous-looking receptionist. They shook hands with her father and did a quick sweep of their group. "Twelve Gifted, seven humans, and yourself," one of them said to Braun, ticking off something in his notebook. "We'll be back to check on you guys again before you leave. Our Gifted guests—yourself and your daughter excluded, of course, Mr Carter—are not to leave the hotel except for the sanctioned visits, and they are not to have outside guests. One of us will be stationed outside at all times."

Isobel exchanged a look with Cian, both of their brows jumping up. This was not how it was on her last settlement tour.

The nervous receptionist dispersed them across the three levels of the hotel, giving the six rooms on the middle floor to Isobel and the Alphas. Each of the rooms could be connected with one of the neighbouring rooms, and they each had two double beds per room. After they were left on the second floor with their luggage, Mikel began assigning rooms.

"Oscar and Moses, first room. Kalen and myself will

take the second. Niko and Cian, third room. Elijah and Gabriel, fourth room. Kilian and Theo—"

"I don't need my own room," Isobel quickly interrupted. "If someone else wants their own space, I'll happily share."

"It's not up for discussion." Mikel's stare swept over her, pausing on her comfortable white slides before darting back up to her messy bun. He was *Manager Mikel* right now—no-nonsense, domineering, and bossy.

"You'll have half an hour to get settled and then I want you all back downstairs. We'll be turning the lobby into a practice room today."

"What about the conference room?" Gabriel asked, looking at his phone.

Isobel leaned over to glimpse his screen, seeing that he had pulled up the hotel's website.

"Hair and make-up and crew are going to set up in there," Kalen answered. "Braun has hired a team to film us daily, even when we're not in the settlements."

Moses clicked his fingers. "*That's* what I've been missing. Cameras."

Kalen's mouth quirked up in the corner, his eyes glimmering in amusement. "The crew will cut the footage together, edit it, and upload it every night. It'll be in the format of a daily vlog, but a little more professional. Everyone on board?"

"Is this something you guys came up with on the plane?" Theodore asked, covering up a large yawn.

Kalen clucked his tongue. "That, and a few other things we think will help to boost your viewership over the break. It may not measure up to Hero's album tour, but we're going to try."

After a quick shower and change of clothes, Isobel skipped back down to the lobby, and an assistant grabbed her, steering her into a conference room, which had been set up with dressing screens and make-up tables.

They wrangled her into a chair and began to dry her hair.

"Aren't we just setting up the lobby?" she called over the sound of the hairdryer.

"Looking like this?" The woman tutted, shaking her head. "We've got cameras out there. They'll be filming you setting up—it's part of the holiday."

"What holiday?" she asked, genuinely confused.

"The ... summer holiday?" the woman replied, squinting. She turned off the hair dryer. "You're filming your summer holiday, right?"

Isobel's mouth opened and closed.

She didn't know how to respond.

Was this a holiday?

She had never been on one, before.

"Get the fuck off me," Niko's rough voice dragged her attention to the door, where one of the assistants was trying to cajole him into the room. "I don't need my

388

fucking hair and make-up done. The fans already know what I look like."

"It's just a little concealer to cover up those dark eye bags," the assistant pleaded with him. "And maybe a little texturing for the hair—"

Niko cut her off with a snarl. "Or you can get out of my personal space before I—"

"Ah." Isobel launched out of her chair, quickly inserting her body between Niko's and the assistant's. "I'll do it."

Niko's hands shaped immediately to her hips, drawing her back against him, tight enough that she could feel the sharp swell of his breath against her back as his chest expanded.

"You?" The assistant frowned.

"Just get in the seat," Isobel ordered, shoving Niko to one of the make-up chairs. "Where's the concealer?"

He sat, elbows notched onto the feeble wooden arms, hazel eyes pissed as he still glared at the assistant.

"Here." One of the make-up artists handed her a small tube. She seemed like a no-nonsense sort of person, waving off the assistant. "You know how to do this?"

"I've had my make-up done more times than I can count," Isobel assured her. "I'll just add a little." This part, she said to Niko.

He didn't care, she realised. He wasn't even paying

attention to her. He was too busy trying to eviscerate anyone who came too close to him with his stare.

Moses came in next and shrugged off the make-up artist who approached his face. He did it absently, but when the woman tried to reach up to his face again, he jerked back, snarling at her.

She tossed up her arms in defeat, looking over at Isobel. "Will you—"

"I'll do him too. Actually, I'll do all of them. Just tell me what you need. It's a ..." She struggled to explain their behaviour. "An Alpha thing. They hate ... things ... touching their skin," she settled on lamely.

What did they know, anyway? Humans didn't care about the Gifted.

She brushed the smallest amount of concealer beneath Niko's eyes, blending it out so much that she may as well not have bothered at all. And then she rubbed it off gently with her knuckle.

"This isn't going to work," she mumbled.

"Sounds good to me." He jumped up, catching Theodore in the doorway. "Carter said don't bother." He spun the other Alpha around and they marched out.

"Awesome." Moses jumped up, stalking after them.

Everyone in the room turned to glare at Isobel.

"Uh ..." She flailed. "Um, it's just that ... we're on camera all day. The fans will see us all made up and know that this feels different. It'll make the whole 'holiday special' thing feel too staged ..."

Everyone continued to stare at her.

"Too fucking early for this." One of the make-up artists huffed, yanking out her phone. She dialled a number and stuck it to her ear. "Mr Cooper? Yes, hi. We've got a bit of a problem—"

Isobel slipped out of the room, catching Kilian in the hallway. "Don't go in." She bared her teeth in a semblance of a grin. "Not unless you want to be touched."

"By you?"

"No."

"Oh. Fuck that." He hooked his arm around her neck, striding beside her—fast enough that she had to kick up her pace. "We're not going in there," he called out to the other Alphas, who were coming down the stairs.

"Where?" Gabriel asked with a frown.

"The conference room," Isobel explained nervously. Kalen and Mikel were bringing up the rear of the group, and she didn't want to get in trouble for changing everyone's plans. "The whole hair and make-up thing isn't going to work. Because ... I ... told them Alphas hate things touching their skin."

Elijah smirked, slipping past Cian and walking into the lobby without a word. Mikel shrugged, uncaring, following Elijah.

Kalen seemed amused. "Did you make a mess and then run away from it?" he asked, indicating Kilian and Isobel.

Kilian stuck his hands up, walking backwards toward the lobby. "I had *nothing* to do with this."

"Traitor," Isobel grumbled before scratching the back of her neck and peeking up at Kalen. "I think so?"

"Your hair is only half dried," he noted.

"Oh." She quickly pulled it up into a messy bun. "Problem solved."

"Brat," he mumbled, striding off to deal with the angry make-up artists and assistants.

THE HOTEL GYM WAS SMALL, SO MIKEL TRAINED THEM IN TWO separate groups that night, working them to the point of collapse. It had been a busy day of learning the choreography Isobel had created for their new songs, so the gym session seemed a little unnecessary, but Isobel had the distinct impression that Mikel was making sure they were too exhausted to get into any trouble during the night.

And ... it worked.

Kilian snuck into her bed and yanked her clothes off —but only because that's what he always did. He preferred her skin against his. As soon as she was draped over his body with only her panties to separate them, he was asleep, and she drifted off only a few minutes later.

She woke up with Theodore pressed in on her other

side and Oscar stepping out of her bathroom in nothing but a towel.

"Where did you sleep?" she asked groggily, pulling her head up from Kilian's chest.

He pointed to the spot on Kilian's other side and strode up to the end of the bed. He grabbed her ankle and yanked her down Kilian's body until she almost tumbled from the mattress, and then he leaned over her, gripping her chin as his mouth pressed to hers in a rough kiss.

The shock quickly melted into need, and she whimpered, tangling her fingers in the top of his towel.

"Nope," Kilian grumbled, sounding half-asleep. "Unless you're going to do it on the floor, there's no room for that."

Oscar pulled away from her, likely about to deliver a cutting response, when there was a knock at the door.

"Isobel?" It was Mikel. "Time to get up."

"It's like he's in trainer mode all day now," Theodore complained, dragging a pillow over his head.

None of them moved.

Mikel knocked again, louder this time.

They didn't so much as breathe.

He tried the handle.

"It's locked, right?" Kilian whispered.

The handle jiggled. It was locked.

"I can smell you lot in there," Mikel snapped.

"Damn." Theodore's grumble was muffled by the

pillow. "I bet he can't tell which of us are in here, though. Only Moses is that good."

"No, but I can hear you," Mikel returned. "Idiot."

"Oops." Theodore lifted the pillow a little, his eyes wandering to Isobel, touching on her sprawled legs, lacy yellow panties, arched back, peaked nipples, and the mess of her hair fisted by Oscar's hand. He licked his lips slowly, before groaning and dragging the pillow back over his eyes. "Someone open the door before he barges in here."

Isobel squeaked, swatting at Oscar's wrist until he released her, his lips almost twitching into a smile. She crawled over the bed, trying to find the shirt she had been wearing the night before. None of them moved to help her.

"The person who opens this door is the only person escaping punishment," Mikel growled.

She was actually starting to sweat. She finally found the shirt, tugged it over her head, and tumbled to the door, yanking it wide. She was breathing heavily, her hair in her eyes. Mikel blew out a short breath, his gaze raking over her.

"Morning, Carter." His eyes stopped at the hem of her shirt, which hadn't fallen properly to cover her underwear.

She quickly fixed it. "We were just—"

"About to fuck," Oscar inserted. "Thanks for the interruption."

"All four of you?" Mikel shot back dryly.

"He was going to use us as a mattress," Kilian sighed out. "And try to scar us from ever coming to her room again."

"We may yet still achieve that goal," Mikel drawled, his words ominous, his stormy scent slowly soaking the air. "I want everyone downstairs in ten minutes. Braun has agreed that you lot can skip the glam squad, but Isobel, he asked that I request you reconsider—"

"It's fine," she reassured him. "They'll do it faster than I can."

"All right then." He stepped into her space, hooking his finger into the collar of her shirt and dragging her a step forward until her stiff nipples were brushing against his front.

She assumed they remained stiff out of fright, but what did she know?

"Did I not exhaust you enough last night?" he murmured, his voice suddenly soft. Her brain short-circuited, and then she realised he meant his training session in the gym.

"Last night was ages ago," she replied, her face flaming red.

Why was he trying to stop her from having sex?

"Hmm." He released her shirt. "Tomorrow, I want you up an hour earlier. I'll do some stretching with you so that you don't injure yourself with training and dancing every day. Usually, you break it up with classes and singing lessons. You're our lead dancer. We can't have you injured."

"Injured or fucked, apparently," Oscar snapped.

Mikel ignored him, spinning and stalking from the room. She blew a tangle of hair from her face, the need inside her flaring back to life as soon as she spun and consulted Kilian, Theodore, and Oscar. Kilian smirked at her, and she huffed out a sound of frustration, grabbing a change of clothes and pushing into the bathroom.

15

THE COCKROACH

THEIR FIRST MEET-AND-GREET WENT AS SMOOTHLY AS COULD BE expected. They were all seated at a long table in the settlement meeting hall, and people were invited to line up and go down the table, spending a few moments with each of them.

Gabriel's Polaroid idea had taken on a life of its own, and they now had a box of printed Polaroids beside each of their chairs and a stamp at the table. One of them would randomly decide to hand out a signed Polaroid and would stamp the fan's hand to signal to the others that they had received one. In this way, the photos became collectables. People would be able to trade them and sell them to try and make complete sets.

Moses and Oscar had been seated on either side of Isobel, and by the end of the day, her elbows were sore from trying to nudge them into polite responses. Not even friendly, just *polite*. Since Niko was at the other end of the table, he was a completely lost cause.

"Carter, it's good to see you again!"

She quickly pulled her elbow out of Oscar's side, not that he seemed to notice it was there, and blinked at Moses and Theodore's father, who had just taken a seat at the table across from her.

"H-hello," she stuttered.

Moses leaned into her space, giving his father an exasperated sigh, his hand slipping to her thigh beneath the table in a seemingly unconscious gesture.

"I told you we'd see you tonight," he said. "You shouldn't be lining up like a fan, Dad."

"But I *am* a fan. Benjamin Kane," he added, holding out his hand for Isobel to shake. "We've met, but you might not remember."

"Of course I remember." She shook his hand as Moses rolled his eyes.

"Can I have one of those photo things?" Benjamin asked, as Cooper tapped Moses' shoulder, directing his attention back to the poor girl sitting opposite him.

"Oh, sure." Isobel dug into the box.

"Can I have two?" Benjamin amended. "One of each of my boys?"

"Sure." She grinned, plucking out one featuring Moses and hunting through the stack for Theodore.

Benjamin leaned over the table, peering into the box. "Actually, could I—"

"Just give him one of each," Moses grumbled beneath his breath. "He wants to put them on the fridge."

"Oh, can we have one of each?" the girl across from him chirped.

"No," he snapped.

Isobel elbowed him.

He didn't react.

"I—"

"You elbowed me," he finished. "Yes, I saw it."

"Saw it or felt it?" she asked, aware that Benjamin's eyes were darting between them.

Moses smirked, choosing to ignore her. She finished picking out each of their photos and handed the stack over to Benjamin, who slipped them all into his pocket.

"Kane," a voice boomed over her head. "Nice to see you again."

Benjamin stood, reaching out to shake her father's hand, and Isobel propped her elbow onto Moses' part of the table, resting her chin in her hand. He was just *staring* at the poor girl still opposite him, waiting for her to speak.

"Are you coming to the afterparty later?" Isobel asked, forcing a soft smile.

"Yes!" the girl squeaked. "I'm going with my friend. We got sponsored!"

A *ding* rang out, the bell hit by Niko at the far end of the table. However long he took is how long they all took. He had already been lectured several times for hitting it too early, and now he was on a timer. Cooper tapped the back of his chair when it was time to hit the bell.

"I'll see you there!" the girl gushed, moving to the next seat.

Benjamin shifted to sit before Moses, and a woman moved from Oscar to Isobel, spilling a number of objects onto the table for Isobel to sign.

When they finished up, it was with a lot of stretching, groaning, and cracking of knuckles.

"Back to the cars," one of the assistants called out, clapping her hands. "You've got a few hours to shower, change, do a quick live, and then we need to be back for the party."

"Why would we change?" Theodore asked, stretching his arms behind his head, his shirt riding up enough to distract Isobel from his question.

She wondered how he would react if she stepped into his space and teased her fingers along the sliver of golden, muscled skin.

"You've been touching those people all day," the assistant mumbled back thoughtlessly, flicking through her tablet.

Theodore's jaw almost cracked, and Oscar cocked his head at the woman, looking at her very intently. It was like he was memorising her face. Adding her to a mental list of some kind.

"Let's go," Braun slapped Cian's and Kilian's backs,

brushing past the assistant like her comments meant nothing to him. "Cars are waiting."

ISOBEL WAS TIPSY.

She had stuck to her two-drink limit like a good girl, but it didn't seem to matter. The two glasses of champagne hit her empty stomach with all the subtlety of an entire bottle.

"I want to thank everyone who participated in Eleven's first stop on their settlement tour." Cooper was speaking into a microphone at the front of the meeting hall. "I wanted this tour to be about more than just their first album, which Orion will be releasing to the public after the break. I wanted it to be about building meaningful relationships within the Gifted communities. So thank you, Gifted, for your energy, your presence, and your positive words on social media. Let's keep this momentum going as we move forward. Thank you all!"

He raised his glass, but Isobel didn't raise hers. She stared at her father, who was, in turn, staring at Cooper. Kalen had come up with the whole idea, and Braun had organised and funded the tour, but Cooper had basically just taken credit for all of it.

Kalen was used to that sort of thing—he showed no reaction whatsoever—but Braun was *not* used to people taking credit for his ideas. He was in a sour mood as the party dragged on and chose to leave in the car Isobel had slipped into instead of the car with his team and Cooper.

"Surprised?" Isobel asked him as he stared stoically out of the window.

They were travelling in black vans, large enough for a few of them to transport their entire group. Elijah, Gabriel, and Kilian sat up the front, Oscar and Niko in the back. Cian was beside her. They were able to fit everyone except Kalen and Mikel since Theodore and Moses were spending the night with their father.

Braun sat by the door, Teak beside him, her head lolling against the seat. She had followed Braun almost mindlessly, and Isobel had a bad feeling that she had started taking more than just the surrogate pills. Her father turned his head to look at her.

"What are you talking about?" he asked.

"Cooper." She folded her arms stiffly. *You're the one who hired him.* Even after all these months, she was still pushing and prodding him, secretly hoping he would explode. It didn't make sense, but it did. It was safer to believe he would never change. Then, she couldn't ever be let down.

"Bet you're surprised he turned out to be this much of a cockroach," she pressed.

Braun's heavy brows scrunched in. "You're not?"

Her laugh was humourless. "No, I was very surprised. But I'm not the one who hired him."

"I hired a drunk who knew how to manipulate people into doing what I wanted and didn't need micromanaging. He got the job done."

"He was—*is*—an abusive asshole. You can't get rid of him, and he isn't done climbing."

Braun nodded thoughtfully, that deep slash of a frown still etched into his features. "For now."

Teak murmured something, her head slipping down and landing against Braun's shoulder with an audible thump. Braun turned that same frown on her, but Isobel slipped forward in her seat, reaching out a hand.

"Could you ... just let her sleep?" she whispered.

"She's high as a fucking kite," Braun growled, causing Cian to stiffen beside her, ready to intervene. "Are you supplying more than just the pills?" He turned his head just enough to glare at Isobel.

"No." She was too worried to be angry.

He let out a heavy sigh, turning back to face the front.

"Please don't tell anyone," she added, her whisper so low she almost thought he didn't catch it, but he did, because he jerked his head in a short, sharp nod.

"She had a mate," he said, lowering his voice to a whisper to match hers. "What happened?"

"The officials happened." Cian was the one to answer, his words a quiet snap.

One of Braun's assistants was driving the van, so nobody of consequence was there to overhear them ... but assistants could be bribed or threatened. It was better to guard their secrets as though everyone would betray them.

"The pills might not be enough on their own," Cian murmured. "She might need a surrogate."

"She needs a detox." Braun's top lip lifted in the semblance of a snarl.

"She needs support," Isobel argued. "And a surrogate, like Cian said. It's just ... I don't know how to approach her. I thought she would come to me when it was safe to speak, but she isn't."

BRAUN HAULED THE BOND SPECIALIST INTO HIS ARMS WHEN they arrived, stepping out of the van as Isobel hovered around him like an annoying, concerned little bee.

"I've got it," he said, frustrated. "We can't call a doctor or any other guest to the hotel, but this isn't my first rodeo with an addict."

"She's not an addict," Isobel hissed from between her teeth.

The Alphas began to crowd around her, Niko stepping in front of her, Oscar hovering a few steps away and glaring at him.

"Calm down, you lot. I'm not going to hurt her." He smirked, pushing into the hotel, the assistants fussing around him and running ahead to open doors for him. He barked out orders for them to fetch what he needed, and then he strode up the stairs to her room, the bond specialist like a small ragdoll in his arms. She seemed to have lost her handbag, so he took her to his own room instead, laying her out on the bed.

Once done, he stalked back to the door, closing it in Isobel's face. She slapped her hand to the door, cursing loud enough for the sound to carry through to him, but he could also hear the Alphas cajoling her away.

"He was telling the truth," Niko's muted voice reached his ears. "He's not going to hurt her."

Interesting.

He returned to the bed, dragging both hands down his face. The summer break had been his only free time between movie projects. And *this* was how he had chosen to spend it.

The little bastards weren't even grateful, but that was okay. He had some atoning to do; he knew that. He checked Teak's pulse and listened to make sure she was breathing before turning her onto her side. And then he got into bed, stretching out along the other side.

Surrogating wasn't an exact science, but everyone seemed to agree on one thing at least—*someone* was better than nobody, and an Alpha was the best you could get. He reached out, plucking at her limp arm until it flopped behind her to the bed, and then he covered her cold hand with his.

Her memories were fuzzy, and it took him a few minutes of concentration to get into her head—which was normal for him. What wasn't normal was that even once he was inside, things were still blurry. He closed his eyes, letting image after image assault his senses.

Her head was full of a woman with dark eyes ringed by silver. A big smile. Straight, white teeth. That smile took over her whole face. She was littered with silver piercings and dripping with dry humour. She loved loose fabrics and how they rippled around her as she danced in the kitchen. She always danced when she cooked.

She made everywhere feel like home.

She never stopped laughing.

Until the day they took her away.

Her name was Charlie.

"CARTER?" AN ASSISTANT POKED HER HEAD INTO ISOBEL'S room just as she was about to step into the bathroom to change for her gym session with Kalen. It wasn't for another hour yet since she was in the second training group, but she didn't feel like wearing her dress anymore.

"Yes?" She backtracked to the door.

"Do you mind coming down to the conference room for a minute? We're trying to plan out the rest of your outfits for the meet-and-greets."

"Oh, sure." She dropped her gym clothes and followed the other woman back down to the first floor.

Cooper was waiting at one of the make-up tables, flicking through photos on a tablet.

"Ah, there you are, Carter. Sit, sit. We have a few options to choose from—all the outfits are on the way. We figured it would be easier to have them shipped to Hudson and then taken by courier to the hotel."

Isobel jumped as the assistant backed out of the room, the door closing heavily behind her. She debated making up an excuse, but the sharp, impatient look in Cooper's eyes warned her not to try and shirk his presence, so she squared her shoulders and moved to sit beside him at the table, shifting her chair back to gain some distance.

Guys? she called through the bond.

No answer.

They were too far away.

Cooper slid her the tablet and a bottle of water. "There are quite a few options, but we only need seven more dresses, so narrow it down for me." He stood, rolling back his narrow shoulders. "I'm going to get a drink, you want one?"

"I'm fine with water," she answered, quickly snatching up the bottle.

He shrugged, leaving the room, and she immediately deflated. This wasn't a trap. This was just work. She began to sort through the pictures, unable to help the spark of happiness that this decision had been left to her. The dresses all came with designer tags and, in some cases, notes from the designer on how they created the dress with Isobel in mind. She wasn't sure how long it took her, but she was drained by the time Cooper returned.

"Finished?" he asked, a strange smile on his blurry face.

She pressed against her eyelids, wishing she could rub her eyes, but she was still wearing her make-up and dress from the afterparty. When she opened her eyes again, it was even worse.

The whole room was spinning.

"I ..." Her voice didn't sound right; her tongue was too thick and clumsy.

She reached for the water bottle he had given her, but it was empty. She didn't even remember drinking it.

"Here's what we're going to do," Cooper said, sitting against the desk in front of her, flicking the tablet out of his way. "In another thirty seconds or so, you'll pass out. Not all the way, but just enough." He picked up the empty water bottle, shaking it tauntingly in her face. "A lovely mix of Rohypnol and ecstasy."

He stood, tossing the bottle to the floor, and then he grabbed her by the arms and tossed her over the desk. Tears were falling down her face and she couldn't find her voice, but he didn't immediately touch her. He seemed to step back.

"I'm going to take photos of you, Isobel."

She tried to shout, but her throat refused to cooperate.

"And then," he continued, and she heard his belt

being unbuckled, "you're going to do everything I say from here on out, or I'm going to release those photos."

She had to do something, but she could barely move. She couldn't shout. The Alphas couldn't hear her through the bond.

Her hand was stuck beneath her chest, and she was able to slowly shift her fingers against the stones of her sternum piercing, laboriously counting down the line as Cooper's belt hit the floor and he began to fumble with her dress, shoving it up past her hips.

She tried to press against the stone with all her might and was rewarded when her head cleared, her body falling back into a chair.

Cooper was gone.

Kalen's stone had worked. She has rewound time.

She picked up the bottle on the table, her hands shaking.

It was empty.

Fuck.

She pounced for the door, falling through into the corridor. Her legs were weak, and she was growing tired. It was only a matter of time before her vision would get blurry again. She took the stairs two at a time, accidentally smacking into the wall at the top of the staircase when she was unable to slow down. She jerked open the door to the first room and fell inside.

"The fuck?" Oscar glanced up from his phone and pulled out his headphones. "I'll call you back, Squirt." He tossed his phone to the bed and was at Isobel's side in a second, helping her to her feet. "What happened? Why can't I feel you through the bond?"

She opened her mouth to tell him but realised she couldn't.

He would kill Cooper.

He wouldn't even think twice about it.

They had gotten away with a lot, but there was no way they were getting away with killing their Orion representative. So she said the first stupid, idiotic thing she could think of.

"I took too much ... emotion." She weakly thumped her chest. "You know." She swallowed, feeling sick. "Gonna pass out."

Gabriel? She tried to reach him through the bond, desperation crawling up the back of her neck.

I'm here, he answered. *Why can't I feel you through the bond?*

Cooper drugged me. I'm in Oscar's room. Rohypnol and ecstasy. You can't tell anyone. Promise me. I'm going to pass out.

FOR A MOMENT, GABRIEL COULDN'T MOVE. THERE WAS TOO much rage, too much violence, too much *urgency* flooding through his body.

I'm coming, he sent to her through the bond.

But he wasn't. He was *struggling*. He couldn't move.

410

He was worried that if he did, he would march straight past Oscar's room. He would hunt down that piece of shit.

Go to Isobel, he ordered his body, but his mind was focussed on Cooper and how he would tie the man to a chair and start with his fingers. He would remove them one by one. And then his arms. His ears. His eyes. He would never touch her again. He would never look at her again. He would never hear her beautiful voice again.

And then he would remove Cooper's fucking dick and shove it down his fucking throat so that he would never be able to say her name again.

Ash spilled across the back of his tongue and black spots danced over his vision.

He wanted to *destroy.*

To kill.

To taste blood.

He pulled out his phone, his fingertips darkening.

Gabriel: Help. Don't come alone. Keep Oscar and Niko away.

ELIJAH GLANCED AT HIS PHONE, ALARM TIGHTLY SEIZING HIS body. "We need to go to my room now," he barked, interrupting the gruelling gym session Mikel had been putting them through.

He took off for the stairs, passing a confused-looking Cooper in the hallway. Mikel followed without question,

Kilian and Cian right behind him. Luckily, Oscar and Niko were in the second training session with Kalen and Isobel, so he didn't need to worry about them. He burst into Gabriel's room and found him with two belts locking his ankles in place and another two wrapped around his wrists.

His eyes were pitch black, and he was trying to tear through the belts with his teeth. The first was already in tatters.

"Mate," he growled in a voice that didn't belong to him.

"Jesus fucking Christ, okay." Mikel slammed the door, and they spread out around him.

"Mateee." Gabriel snarled and snapped at the belts, his voice otherworldly and rough.

"I can't feel Isobel through the bond," Elijah said without taking his eyes off Gabriel. "On the count of three. Three—"

They all pounced. Ferality didn't make an Alpha stupid. Gabriel was pinned beneath them, and Mikel yanked a handful of zip ties from his pocket.

"The fuck do you have those for?" Cian huffed out as Gabriel began thrashing like crazy.

"In case this happened," Mikel grunted. "Careful of the claws!"

They managed to secure Gabriel's wrists using every single one of the zip ties Mikel had been carrying, but their hands and arms were scratched up and bloody, dripping onto the carpet, which was thankfully dark.

"Isobel," Elijah prompted them, urgency making his skin itch.

Mikel shook out his hand, muttering, "Sorry about this," before he punched Gabriel. Once, twice, three times. It took a few heavy blows for him to stop trying to sink his teeth into Mikel's fist with every swing.

As soon as Gabriel slumped over, Mikel shot up, tugging out his phone. "Kalen?" He stuck it to his ear. "We need to find Isobel. Gabe went feral. I'll stay here with him—"

Elijah quickly hissed, "We can't tell Oscar or Nik—"

The door opened, Niko halting in the doorway, his eyes settling on Gabriel and widening.

"Niko," Elijah finished.

"The fuck?" Niko demanded.

"Stay here," Mikel ordered him. "We've knocked him out, but I ran out of zip ties. Elijah, go and find Isobel. Make sure she's protected. Cian, go find Oscar. Make sure he's okay. We don't know what set Gabriel off. Kilian, go get your phone and call Moses and Theodore and check in with them. Just to be safe. Kalen?" he barked into the phone. "I'm on my way to you."

He managed to say it all without lying and triggering Niko's ability.

They left Niko in the room, and Kalen met them in the hallway.

Mikel put his finger to his mouth, and Kalen nodded as they walked to Oscar and Moses' room. Before they could come up with a plan, the door was yanked open, revealing a scowling Oscar.

"Took you long enough," he growled out. "You could have at least replied to my messages in the group chat."

Elijah stepped behind Kalen, yanking his phone out of his pocket to check the messages.

Oscar: Isobel passed out.

Oscar: She used her Sigma power too much.

Oscar: Did she try to make Teak better without any of us noticing?

Oscar: Why the fuck is nobody replying?

Elijah winced. Moses and Theodore hadn't seen the messages yet, but they would freak out when they did, so he quickly tapped out a response.

Elijah: Everything is under control.

But everything was not under control because Isobel wasn't unconscious due to her Sigma power. From what he could tell, she had lied to Oscar and told the truth to Gabriel—and the truth had been bad enough to trigger Gabriel's ferality.

Niko and Oscar couldn't know—and neither could Theodore and Moses.

Luckily, Mikel caught on quickly.

"Gabriel went feral when he read your messages," Mikel lied through his teeth. "You're one of our best fighters. I need you in there in case he wakes up. He's knocked out right now and Niko is watching him."

Oscar ground his jaw, looking like he was seconds from refusing, though he finally noticed their torn-up, bloody arms.

Mikel didn't give him a chance to argue. He barked, "Now," in Alpha voice.

As soon as Oscar left the room, Elijah kicked the door shut and locked it.

Kalen had moved to the bed without anyone noticing. He straightened away from Isobel as they all gathered. "She's breathing, but her heartbeat is too slow for my liking. What's going on?" He directed the question to Elijah, his expression tight.

Kalen was their leader, the highest in the ranking that naturally formed between them all, so Elijah could feel his domination spilling out like a physical force through the room, a rough wall of concrete that grated against his bones. He may have appeared calm and collected, but he was anything but.

Elijah quickly took stock of the others: Mikel wore his tension on the outside, unlike Kalen. Cian had shoved up the sleeves of his sweatshirt and tied his hair back, streaks of blood in the strands, revealing that he had done it after the fight with Gabriel. He looked ready to go another round. Kilian had his arms crossed and didn't seem to realise he was bleeding onto his shirt. His eyes were fixed on Isobel like he could somehow figure out what was wrong with her if he just looked hard enough.

"It wasn't her Sigma power," Elijah said carefully, testing their reactions. Other than snapping their eyes to him, they didn't react at all. "Gabe sent me a message asking for help. He told me not to come alone and not to bring Oscar or Niko."

There was a muscle ticking in Mikel's cheek. "So Gabriel knows what happened to her."

"And whatever it was, it fucking unhinged him," Kilian finished.

Elijah gave a short nod, and they all turned back to the bed. Isobel moaned, her finger twitching.

Kalen crouched by the bed, gripping her hand. "Can you hear me, Illy?" He deliberately made his voice a soft, deep croon.

Isobel's hand visibly twitched in his.

"Can you squeeze my hand, sweetheart?" Kalen asked.

Her fingers jumped, but it was the smallest movement.

Elijah fell beside Kalen, peeling back her eyelid. Her pupils were blown wide.

He snarled, jerking back from the bed. "I'm going to—"

Kill him.

He managed to cut himself off just in time.

Isobel had been drugged, and there was only one

culprit—the one who had been skulking around downstairs like he was looking for someone. Fucking Cesar Cooper.

There was a reason Isobel had only told Gabriel.

"What?" Mikel demanded, sharp gaze narrowing on Elijah, a demand swelling in the back of his throat.

"It's a bond side effect," Elijah lied. *Fuck fuck fuck.* "I read about it once. The person turns unresponsive, but they're still technically conscious. It should wear off by morning. I'll stay with her and monitor her to make sure it doesn't turn into anything else."

He cut a quick look to Kilian, hoping the other Alpha would be able to understand his unspoken demand.

"I'll stay too," Kilian said.

The others didn't look like they were about to budge, but Kilian had picked up that something else was going on, and he forced out a grim smile. "She'll be embarrassed if we all just stand around and watch her like this. We'll turn out the lights and go to bed like normal, but we won't fall asleep."

They knew he had a point, but Kilian could sense he hadn't swayed them, so he added, "We have to protect Gabe too. And clean up the blood."

"Fuck," Mikel growled, pointing to the bed. "Look after her." He spun for the door, jerking his head at Cian. "Let's go."

Kalen didn't move, his attention bouncing between

them. "You're lying," he said quietly. "This isn't a bond side effect."

"It's not." Elijah sighed, levelling Kalen with a look that he hoped spoke volumes. "But if I tell you what happened, you'll blow our whole operation."

Kalen looked at Kilian pointedly.

Elijah shook his head. "Kilian isn't leaving her side until she opens her eyes again. And when she does, she'll convince him not to react. Your anger will get the better of you. Trust me, Kalen."

Kalen winced, turning his eyes to the ceiling, already fighting for control over himself. "Someone hurt her."

"Nobody hurt her," Elijah said. He was fairly sure of it. Isobel could use all their abilities for a few minutes, and Cooper had looked confused as hell. She could have read his mind, read his intentions, or subtly used Elijah's own power to persuade him to leave the room. She could have rewound time or turned invisible while he wasn't looking.

He didn't know how, but she had gotten away and was in the process of running away—that was why she had run into Oscar's room even though Gabriel was the only one she wanted to speak to. Oscar and Moses' room was the first in the hallway. Still, he wasn't always right about everything, which was why he was waiting for Kalen to leave the room so that he could check and make sure.

"Nobody hurt her," he bluffed again, threading his

tone with iron because Kalen still seemed to be wavering. "You *have* to trust me," he insisted. "She's safe. She's okay."

A snarl ripped from Kalen's throat as he stalked from the room without a word, slamming the door behind him.

"Help me," Elijah demanded of Kilian, returning to the bed again.

"What do you need?"

"I need you to check that she hasn't been assaulted. I'll let you do it—I think she'd be more comfortable with you."

Kilian's pale eyes dug into his. "What?" he finally croaked.

Elijah felt his hands trembling now that he had *partly* dealt with the situation. He shoved them into his pockets. "Help me or get out," he growled. "I need you to keep it together, keep your shit under control, and do not fucking leave this room."

"AS IF I WOULD LEAVE HER SIDE," he shouted, veins thickening near his temple.

"That's the opposite of keeping your shit under control," Elijah hissed.

Kilian backed away, hands up, shaking his head. "Fuck you. Fuck. Fine. *Fuck.*"

"Where are you going?" Elijah demanded.

"To wash my *fucking* hands," Kilian spat, spinning and throwing open the door to the en suite.

As soon as he was alone with Isobel, Elijah realised it was becoming difficult to breathe. His air passage was constricting, growing narrower and narrower until he could barely sip in air. He collapsed against the side of the bed and tried to gently place his forehead against her chest.

Breathe, he pleaded with himself. *Just breathe*.

The scent of sweet cherries rushed over him. Much sweeter than usual. He shuddered, the sensation like cool, sticky juice licking over his fingers. She smelled sweet enough to drink, and he closed his eyes, lost to the sensation of this languid scent as he finally pulled air back into his lungs.

"Are you okay?" Kilian asked, a touch landing gently between his shoulder blades and rubbing back and forth.

Silently, he shook his head.

He was *far* from okay.

Gabriel had trusted him with this, and she had trusted Gabriel with it.

If she had wanted to throw away their careers and endanger all their families, she would have pressed Theodore's or Moses' stone instead and ripped Cooper apart herself. He had to at least hold on long enough to speak with her.

"Just tell me what to do," Kilian said. "I'm not bleeding anymore."

Elijah didn't lift his head or open his eyes. He couldn't. He needed to keep breathing.

"Take off her panties and check for any signs of blood or fluid. Check for redness, swelling, or bruising."

Kilian didn't move to obey, his hand still on Elijah's back. He was frozen.

"And if I find any of those things?" he demanded, losing the softer tone he had momentarily laboured over.

"Then someone dies tonight. I'll do it myself."

"Good." He lifted his hand away.

Elijah felt Isobel's body shift beneath him as Kilian got onto the bed.

"I'm not watching," he said into her skin, hoping she could hear him.

She had probably been given a combination of ecstasy and something else if her euphoric, drowsy scent was anything to go off, so if she were aware enough to hear him, she wouldn't care. But that was now. In the morning, she would very much care, if she remembered.

Kilian made a small, soft sound in the back of his throat. "She's a little wet, but otherwise no."

"That would be the ecstasy," Elijah said. "Let me know when I can look again."

"You're fine. Ecstasy?"

Elijah pulled up his head slowly. His chest immediately tightened, but his throat didn't close up again.

"Do you mind?" he asked, slipping his hands beneath Isobel's body.

"I think I might." Kilian winced. "I need her too."

"Okay, move for a moment."

Kilian shifted off the bed and Elijah gently placed Isobel onto the middle of the mattress. "Her shoes," he pointed out.

Kilian immediately began removing her heels. Elijah pulled her upright, holding her up as he worked to tug her dress out from beneath her butt and over her head.

"Shirt," he demanded next.

Kilian pulled his off while Elijah still held her up with one arm, flicking her dress over the side of the bed. He tugged Kilian's shirt over her head and then tucked her beneath the covers, turning her to her side and pulling her body back into his. Kilian hit the switch to send the room into darkness before he slipped beneath the covers with them, tugging her limp leg over his waist, his head nudging beneath hers.

"I hate this," he whispered. "Even when she's asleep, she still wriggles and squirms all over the place."

"I know," Elijah breathed, his throat threatening to close again. He quickly ducked his head to her hair, sucking in her scent again.

Sweet, unharmed cherries.

She was okay.

But she wasn't *right*. His Isobel was a wriggler. He watched her when they had their movie nights. He was always on the floor or the chaise or the sofa, but he watched her shift and sigh and seek heat from the bodies either side of her.

Usually, he hated watching it. He hated that none of those bodies were him.

Tonight, he would give anything to watch it on repeat.

"Cooper drugged her, didn't he?" Kilian whispered roughly, finally figuring it out.

"You said you wouldn't leave her side," Elijah warned.

"You really think I'm stupid enough to kill him without a plan and fuck up all our goddamn lives?" Kilian shot back, still in a whisper. He would never shout so close to Isobel, not with her skin a breath from his mouth.

"You would have if I had told you immediately before you'd had time to think," Elijah countered.

He was silent.

Elijah was right.

Isobel was smart enough to keep this from everyone who would react based on their emotion alone.

He inhaled her again, his hand settling into the dip of her waist. She was so tiny. So fragile. So soft. So *his*.

And Cooper was *so* dead.

16
HER CHOICE

WHEN ISOBEL WOKE UP, SHE HAD A POUNDING HEADACHE, AND her limbs felt like they weighed a hundred pounds. She peeled her eyes open with a pained sound, blinking several times in confusion.

The Alphas were all in her room. *All of them.* They were fully dressed, standing around her bed like they were gathering for a funeral. She squinted and then did a double take as her vision cleared properly. Gabriel's face was covered in bruises. He had two black eyes. Mikel, Elijah, Cian, and Kilian had red marks crisscrossing up their arms and lacerating their fingers. They appeared half-healed.

She swallowed, her sluggish mind working overtime.

"How are you feeling?" Kilian asked, sitting on the bed beside her.

He tilted her head up, brushing strands of hair from her face.

"I feel like shit," she answered honestly, trying to remember what had happened the night before. "Did we get drunk or something?"

"No." Gabriel rocked back on his heels. "Something else happened. I'm the only one you told."

"What?" She screwed up her face.

None of the Alphas looked surprised.

"I made them wait and said you would tell them yourself when you woke up," Gabriel continued. "We aren't allowing anyone to leave this room until we have a plan in place to deal with what happened."

"Wait." She sat up straighter, trying to concentrate despite the migraine forming. Theodore and Moses were there when they should have still been at the Hudson Settlement. "You're back already?" she asked, eyes darting between them. "You barely stayed ..." She glanced around helplessly. "What time is it?"

"Afternoon," Mikel answered stiffly. "You slept the whole day. Braun sent an assistant out to buy half a pharmacy. What do you need?"

"Painkillers." She winced. "A shower. A toothbrush. What the hell is going on?"

"We were hoping you would tell us," Kilian said, still in his soft voice, his hands moving to smooth over her throbbing temples. But then he stood, moving beside Elijah.

Elijah, Gabriel, Kilian, and Kalen were deliberately blocking the door.

"I have no idea what you're talking about," Isobel said honestly.

"What's the last thing you remember?" Gabriel asked, brow furrowing.

"Uh ... I ... from last night? We went to the afterparty. Teak was passed out. My father carried her into his room. Is she—"

"After that?" Mikel demanded, waylaying her concern over Teak.

"After that, we decided the two training groups for the night. I had some dinner in the lobby with Cian and Kilian, and then I went to change for the gym ..." She pressed the heels of her palms over her eyes, fighting through the fog of her memory. "I was ... with Cooper in the conference room picking out dresses for—"

"I fucking knew it," Theodore suddenly exploded. "I told you that fuck did something to her."

"Let her finish," Elijah ordered.

"I ... I don't know what else," she said lamely, panic digging claws into her chest. "I don't remember anything. I was just sitting there on my own, picking dresses. Cooper left the room. I don't know if he came back or not. I don't remember a thing after that."

"Because he drugged you," Gabriel said. "You ran to Oscar and Moses' room but spoke to me through the bond. I went feral and messaged Elijah. He figured it out and managed to stop anyone else from losing their shit, but now we have a situation."

"Because we aren't stupid," Moses snarled.

"O-Okay." Her vision swam into a blur of colours, the panic digging in deeper and deeper.

"Isobel." Kalen commanded her attention. "Come here."

On autopilot, she stumbled from the bed and moved to stand before him. He spun her around to face the others, pulling her back against his body, his hand flattening to her chest, right where she could feel the panic threatened to rip her apart.

"Breathe," he commanded.

She sucked in a shaky breath, obeying without thought because she always seemed to do what he told her to.

To the others, he said, "No going rogue. We decide what to do about Cooper right here, right now."

"I want blood," Oscar said calmly. A little too calmly.

None of them seemed shocked by Elijah's revelation, so they must have figured out some or most of the story on their own. There had been plenty of time for them to make it look like they were in control, but she knew it was fake, because they were blocking her Sigma ability, and they only did *that* when they had something to hide.

"I'm sorry, Isobel." Mikel shifted until he could see

her face. "The buddy system is back in place, but only for you."

She nodded, barely listening.

Cooper had drugged her, and she didn't even remember how she escaped him.

"You're to have one of us with you *at all times*," Mikel specified. "And I don't want you sleeping in your room anymore. Pick one of us to bunk with every night."

"And Cooper?" Niko asked, his voice just as deadly calm as Oscar's, his hazel eyes dim, devoid of emotion. It was terrifying.

"Getting him fired isn't enough," Moses said before anyone could suggest otherwise. "He needs to die. He's a predator. Who knows what he would have done?"

Kalen made a severe, disapproving sound in his throat. "This is the real world, not a fucking fantasy. A group of immigrant-adjacents in their twenties can't just *get* away with murder."

"You mean we can't get away with it *again*," Niko scoffed.

"Eli, Gabe, and Niko got away with it," Theodore added. "And Isobel got away with it."

"And what?" Kalen challenged. "Niko is going to burn down a third building with a body mysteriously found inside? You don't think anybody is going to connect those dots?"

Isobel looked down at the big hand spanning her chest, pressing her back against a body that vibrated with barely controlled rage. If it weren't for the proximity of his body, she never would have known that he was feeling anything so violently.

She wasn't surprised to hear Oscar calling for blood. He was a psychopath. And Niko ... was damaged. And Moses? He was still learning to rein in and control his aggression the way Oscar controlled his chaos.

But the others?

She was surprised that Kalen was the only person speaking out against planning a *murder*. She was the one who had been drugged and even she couldn't think in those terms. She wanted Cooper punished. She would throw a party if he was fired and his life was ruined, but murder wasn't a normal option to just throw about.

It told her everything she needed to know about their state of mind—everything they were blocking from her. Their possessive, Alpha aggression had been pushed too far.

"Nobody is killing him." She breathed deeply, trying to centre and settle herself. Her chest pushed up against Kalen's warm grip, and he shifted his hand so that his arm wound across her front, his hand now gripping her opposite shoulder.

"I need you all to look past the bond for a moment," she begged them. "I know it's telling you all that you own me, that I'm yours, and that someone tried to hurt me or take me away—I'm familiar with how the bond twists things sometimes. But I'm *not* yours. I belong to me. This was something that happened to *me*, and it's my decision what we do about it."

"Usually, yes," Mikel agreed, gripping the back of his neck, his bicep flexing as he winced. "But this isn't something that happened in your free time. This is work and group related, too. Cooper is our manager. This is something we need to discuss as a group."

"Discuss, but not decide." She crossed her arms beneath her breasts, staring at Mikel's chest because she couldn't bring herself to disagree with him while looking him in the eyes.

It wasn't that she was afraid of him. He was just so *dominating*. If she was afraid of anything, it was that she would look up and see that she had disappointed him in some way.

"Fuck," he snapped.

"This should be Isobel's decision," Kalen declared, apparently agreeing with her despite the vibration of fury that still shivered along her back.

"I want to ruin his life," she said. "Like how you punished Wallis for sneaking into Oscar's room, but worse, because Cooper isn't a Gifted student. If we don't crush him properly, he'll just come back."

"Give me a few days to come up with a plan," Oscar said before anyone else could argue with what she had decided. "I want to make sure it's something he won't recover from."

"Thank you," she whispered, eyeing him. He was the last person she had expected support from.

He nodded, brushing his hands through his dark curls. "We should act like nothing happened—including you. Try to casually mention that the alcohol must have hit you hard last night because you blacked out and overslept. This will be easier if he doesn't suspect we're onto him."

She nodded, watching as he approached. He paused before the wall of Alphas, eyeing them. "You can move. I'm not going to dictate how she gets her revenge. That's not me."

Well, when he put it that way, she believed him.

Elijah stepped out of the way, but Kalen spoke up before Oscar reached the door. "We're going to have to work late tonight to make up for today. Everyone has half an hour to organise themselves, and then I want you all down in the lobby."

"Come on," Theodore murmured after Kalen released her and stalked from the room. His hand covered hers, strong fingers pushing between her slender ones as he tugged her back to her own room.

She rushed through getting ready and then met up with everyone downstairs. After a few minutes, she was mobbed by her father's assistants, who all pushed bottles of water and bottles of pills at her, mumbling about her "stomach bug" and how far behind schedule they were.

She frowned, tipping out a few pills and uncapping the water bottle. She raised it to her lips, but a sudden dizziness assaulted her.

She reached for the bottle. The room was spinning.

The bottle was empty.

Shaking her head, she tried to shove away the blurry memory and the sticky feeling of horror that began to coat her skin. Out of the corner of her eye, she spotted Cooper waltzing into the room like he didn't have a care in the world. He barked something to one of the assistants as his eyes flitted about, searching for someone. He paused when he found her standing there, clutching the bottle and pills, and the feeling of horror increased, spreading through her body and sizzling like acid in her blood. She suddenly wanted to throw up, but instead, she locked the feelings away and gave him a polite nod. If she wanted revenge—and she fucking *did* —then she needed to be smart about this, and she needed to pray to all of the Gifted gods that her Alphas were able to control themselves long enough for her to take her pound of flesh.

She drew on the professional inside her, allowing the shift to fall over her, kicking her brain into gear.

There was work to be done.

Cooper narrowed his eyes on her, confused, searching, before seeming to fail to find anything in her face that might indicate she knew what he had done. A showy smile slid across his features, and he continued with the instructions he had been barking. Kalen was staring between them, waiting to see if Cooper would try to approach her. They weren't going to kill him, but that didn't mean they were going to allow him anywhere near her.

She swallowed the pills dry, unable to bring the bottle to her lips, and met with Kalen to receive his notes on the choreography she had been working on the day before. She could feel the murderous rage of each of the Alphas pressing down on her, too heavy and urgent for them to hold back, but they were doing a remarkable job of pretending everything was normal. Still, as soon as she reached Kalen, he stepped between her and Cooper, blocking her from his eyes. Not quite fast enough to see the way Cian casually shoulder-checked the manager before apologising with a fake smile as the man slammed into a camera, almost knocking it down.

"The problem is your height difference," her father announced, appearing out of nowhere and delivering his entirely unwelcome opinion on the choreography her and Kalen were pretending to watch. Braun seemed completely oblivious to all the undercurrents of tension in the room.

Isobel bit back a sigh. "Yes. I know."

He shrugged, colouring slightly. "Just trying to help. How are you feeling? You usually don't even let the flu keep you down for long."

"*You* wouldn't let the flu keep me down for long," she

433

corrected, unable to curb her biting tone this time. She was trying to finish up the brief with Kalen so they could get through their first practice and not be up all night.

"And look at you now," her father preened, stepping away with his palms displayed in supplication and a shit-eating smirk on his face.

The damned asshole.

"The problem is the height difference," she said to Kalen—because she had been about to say it anyway.

"What was that?" Braun called. "Did you need me to come back?"

She spun, her eyes flashing with temper.

Kalen sighed. "Focus, princess."

She immediately switched her attention to his face, her skin heating for a different reason. He tilted his head, his gaze darkening briefly.

You look like you need to work out some emotion, he spoke to her softly through the bond.

She froze, desperately searching his expression for a clue. He was right, now more than ever. She had so much fury and disgust and helplessness tangled up inside her. He knew she was desperate to be tied up again—to feel that rush, that release, to hand her annoying emotions over for him to filter out of her by sending her into a space of airy euphoria, but he *still* seemed to be waiting for her to come to him.

Which was infuriating.

At first, she wasn't ready. Maybe she still wasn't, but

his obscene control and patience was starting to eat away at how much she cared about whether she was ready or not.

Still, she was too cowardly to respond to him, so she switched the topic back to work.

"I ... I have to either be right in the centre," she said, spinning to point at the screen that was currently playing back the choreography they had recorded on their first day. "Or I have to be out of view entirely. Otherwise, I pull the focus too much."

He briefly stepped up behind her, his large body brushing hers, his hand gripping her hip for the briefest moment as he stepped around her. A bolt of lust fired through her, completely flooring her. She wasn't sure how he did it—how *any* of them did it—but they seemed to be able to flick a switch in her body, drawing out a heated response from her whenever they intended it. She knew they could switch it on and off at will, because they did it for the cameras all the time.

Their control was terrifying.

"*You* are the lead dancer," Kalen rumbled, his voice deeper than usual as he stepped up beside her to survey the recording. "It makes sense for you to be in the centre. Play around with the formations so that small groups of members rotate on and off focus depending on whose turn it is to sing."

She nodded. "All right. I'll work something out."

"I have a colleague who could help." Braun appeared

435

again, like a buzzing gnat. "Jason Caufield—you probably know him. He consulted on a movie I did a few years ago. I could ask him for a consultation if you want?"

Isobel tried to play it cool, to hang on to her annoyance, but a bloom of excitement was already unfurling within her chest, and she spun excitedly. "Seriously? Jason Caulfield? He's the most talented choreographer *alive* right now."

"I'll take that as a yes," Braun drawled, pulling out his phone and walking away, somehow moving with utter smugness.

Kalen watched him go, shaking his head, before he tapped Isobel on the thigh. "Get to it."

She ignored the little jolt of heat from his hand, but gratitude unfurled within her chest like a flower slowly blooming, filling her with lightness. He was doing it deliberately, the heated look and the little touches, and the reminder of what he could do for her. He was distracting her, replacing her memory of the night before with other, more welcome thoughts.

She gathered up the others, working through the steps with them beat by beat as Kalen and Mikel watched. She began to divide them into groups to rotate the focus, and by the time they were finished, she had a pretty good idea of what she wanted to work on.

It was well after midnight when they packed up, and her body was beyond exhausted. She had pushed through, but it had been difficult. She had only a fraction of the strength and energy that she usually had.

Theodore shadowed her as she ducked into her room to shower. She had been too busy and too focussed to worry about Cooper while they worked, but now she felt … odd. Like eyes were on her, even though she was alone. Her hands began to shake as she moved to push her tights down, and nausea rolled through her. She quickly left the bathroom, her pyjamas and toiletries bundled into her arms.

"Can I shower in your room?" she asked when Theodore looked up. He had been sprawled on her bed, his phone hovering above his face.

He jumped up, moving to tower over her, his eyes narrowing in concern. "What's wrong?"

She shrugged weakly. "No idea. I just feel uncomfortable."

"I'll shower you myself," he decided, ducking behind her, his hands on her shoulders, steering her to the door. "Purely platonic, I promise. I can absolutely do this. I've been training for this day my entire life—or ever since I found out Kilian was doing it."

"You don't do anything platonically," she argued, but she was smiling, some of the tension already leaking out of her. Theodore was so good at that.

He scoffed. "Just watch me." He steered her right into his room, past Moses, who was on one of the beds with his phone hovering over his face in a position so comically similar to how she had found Theodore, that she couldn't help the small giggle from falling out.

"Did you see the message Dad sent?" he asked, dropping his phone and propping himself on his elbows, eyeing them.

"Yeah," Theodore laughed out, pausing in his march toward the bathroom and releasing Isobel. "Look." His phone appeared in front of her face. He tapped into his messages, selected the contact labelled *Dad*, and then enlarged the photo his father had sent.

Benjamin Kane had stuck all their Polaroids to his fridge.

"The positioning is ..." She chuckled, her fingers hovering over the screen.

Benjamin had put her at the top, Moses and Theodore either side of her. The others were in a line below.

"Telling," she finished, still trying not to outright laugh.

She really liked their family.

"He's obsessed with you, obviously." Theodore tossed his phone to the bed and marched her the rest of the way into the bathroom, slamming the door behind him. He unburdened her of her armful of possessions, tipping them onto the bathroom counter before leaning back against the door, his arms folded tightly across his chest.

"Now, strip."

There was an audible thud in the other room, and then the door to the room opened and slammed closed again. Theodore smirked. "Don't mind him."

"This was supposed to be platonic," Isobel said, pulling her sweaty shirt over her head.

His arms twitched, muscles bulging, like he was physically restraining himself from reaching out for her. His eyes weren't so restrained, however. They devoured her, even though her hair hung in a limp ponytail, the sweaty ends sticking to her lower back, and her sports bra was damp with sweat. He licked his lips, darkening gaze crawling back up to her face.

"I'm all the way over here, aren't I?" he rumbled.

She smirked at him, rolling her tights down her legs. He groaned. She leaned into the shower, starting the water before unhooking her bra and tossing it at him. He caught it deftly, crushing it in his fist.

"You're teasing," he warned in a gravelled voice. "You know I can't resist you."

"You promised." She pouted, stepping out of her panties. She tossed them at him, too, but he didn't catch them. He was too busy staring, a growl vibrating through him, his eyes flashing in warning.

She *loved* teasing them, especially Theodore and Kilian—they were her playful Alphas. She loved that she could trust they would always snap without hurting her.

Cian was a little rougher when he snapped, and

JANE WASHINGTON

Oscar, she barely dared to play with for long. He snapped the fastest and the most violent.

"I thought you were going to wash me," she taunted from the shower and was rewarded with one of those delicious *snaps* a few moments later when Theodore, still fully clothed, stormed into the shower and backed her into the wall, his hand on her neck, applying just enough pressure to lift her to her tiptoes so that his mouth could claim hers.

He kissed her until she was squirming and breathless, and then he dropped to his knees, marking her skin with small kisses and bites until he reached her core, gently drawing one of her legs over his shoulder.

"How can I resist you?" he demanded between rough licks and kisses that had her mind spinning in the best way, whimpers catching in her throat as she gripped his head with shaking hands.

He fucked her with his tongue until she was gasping out his name, and then he dropped her shaking leg and yanked at his workout pants to free his cock.

He spun her around. "Hold on," he growled, and it was the only warning she got before he picked her up by the hips, tilting her forward until she almost smacked into the shower screen. She quickly gripped the top of the screen as he kicked her dangling legs apart with his own, tugging them up to wind back around him. She hung on to the top of the shower—it was the frame she had gripped, thankfully, not the screen. Her hold was

440

desperate, her ankles locked behind him as he lined up with her entrance and shoved in.

"No matter what happens," he whispered against the wet skin of her neck, "I'll always bring that adorable little smile back to your face." He pulled out, and the scrape of him driving back in again had her back arching painfully.

"I'll always protect you," he continued, voice raspy, almost desperate. "You can always run to me, hide in me, use me to forget something bad or remember something fucking *good*." He was pounding into her hard, now, her hands slipping along the shower frame.

One of his hands curved around to her front, finding her clit and teasing her sensitive nerves until she was straining and crying with another orgasm, her arms shaking.

"You said you weren't mine," he growled, pausing his thrusting to seat himself fully inside her, his breath ragged as she clenched and pulsed around him.

"I lied," she whispered, riding out the final waves with him deep inside her.

"You're mine." It was a demand. He gripped her hips so tightly, it was painful, and he grunted as his cock swelled.

"I'm yours," she promised as he came inside her.

He caught her just as her grip failed, gently lowering her to her feet. He had what he wanted—his claim acknowledged—and his touches became adoring and soft, gentle as a whisper as he washed her thoroughly, even shampooing and conditioning her hair as she mostly turned into a sleepy, limp mess in his arms. He murmured things as he washed her like, "*good girl, so perfect, so beautiful,*" until she was a puddle of cosiness and small smiles.

It was in that little bathroom in a random hotel in Hudson that she finally acknowledged to herself that she was madly, deeply, frighteningly in love with Theodore Kane.

And not just him.

Those feelings were just as strong for Kilian, Cian, and Oscar.

Kilian was her comfort.

Cian made her feel alive.

And Oscar made her heart flutter.

She basked in her feelings as Theodore dried her and dressed her, treating her like a princess and refusing to allow her to so much as lift a finger. He carried her into the other room, where Kilian was now on the spare bed, waiting for the bathroom.

"Hey," she mumbled sleepily as Theodore tucked her beneath the blankets.

"Hey, baby." Kilian's eyes stalked her, pupils expanding. "Good shower?"

"The best," she mumbled as Theodore slid in beside her.

"Save room for me," Kilian demanded, standing and disappearing into the bathroom.

She must have drifted off, because his shower seemed to finish in the blink of an eye and he was already slipping in behind her, his body warm and smelling like heaven. He kissed her neck, and she wiggled between their hard bodies, loving how warm and large they were surrounding her.

She slipped off to sleep, but woke up some time later, her skin prickling. She poked her head out of the warm cocoon of her Alphas, noticing a large shadow at the end of the bed.

Niko was standing there, staring at her, eyes dark.

"Hey," she croaked, carefully disentangling herself from Theodore and Kilian. She pulled herself to sit up, frowning at him. He didn't answer, and after a moment, the image of him wavered and *disappeared*.

"What's the matter?" Kilian asked sleepily.

"Just another side effect, I think," she said, blinking at the door, where the shadow of Niko appeared again, like he was urging her to leave the room again. She leaned over Theodore, switching on the reading light and pointing it to the door. Theodore woke with a groan.

"Can you guys see him?" she asked, pointing to the door.

"No," Theodore said, sitting up and blinking just before Niko disappeared again.

Isobel didn't like this side effect. The image of Niko

wasn't quite *right*, seeming more transparent than solid, but she didn't like how similar it was to when she saw the remnants.

"I'm going to Niko's room," she said, scrambling to the end of the bed.

Kilian slipped out of bed with her, sticking his head out to watch her move to Niko's room, apparently unwilling to let her out of their sight for even a few seconds. She pushed into the dark room, waiting for her eyes to adjust after the dimly lit hallway. Gabriel was in the bed closest to the door. It had been stripped of everything but a pillow and the pristine, white top sheet, which had been pushed down to his hips, revealing a bare, muscled torso, one hand resting against his stomach, the other bent behind his head. He wasn't supposed to be in there—she was pretty sure that was Cian's bed, but perhaps they had rearranged for some reason. Maybe Elijah and Gabriel had decided that Niko needed monitoring. He didn't wake up as she snuck past, stopping by Niko's bed.

Her breath rushed out in a soft sigh of relief as she saw Niko in his bed, his bare chest rising and falling slightly, his handsome features twisted like he was having a bad dream. She hesitated beside his bed, unsure what to do now that she was there.

Should she sneak back out?

She turned to do just that, but a hand whipped out and gripped her wrist before she could step away. She turned back to Niko, whose eyes were slitted open, regarding her in the dark. He pulled, and she fell to sit against the side of his bed. He released her wrist, snaking an arm around her hips, and slid her across the mattress as he lifted the blanket. He curled his front against her back, his breath falling over her neck as he nuzzled the little heart tattoos marking her skin.

"Stay," he whispered roughly.

So she did.

17

I THINK YOU'RE GROUNDED

THEY PILED OUT OF THE RENTED VANS AND GATHERED AROUND the entrance to the lodge in Arkansas. Even though it was only their second stop on the tour, it felt like they had fallen into a rhythm already. They dragged all their luggage into the lobby, greeted the police who waited to take stock of their party, and began to set up the equipment that had arrived ahead of them. There were only ten bedrooms in the lodge, all with king beds, so Isobel offered to share with Oscar, since he would be spending the night of the meet-and-greet with Lily in the Ozark Settlement.

There was a two-bedroom groundskeeper's cottage, which Teak and Braun agreed to share, and a local hotel where the humans would be staying. By separating the Gifted from the humans, Braun wasn't forced to book out the entire hotel.

They spent the first day working and got up early the next morning to prepare for the second meet-and-greet. It was strange to see the Alphas dressed up in designer clothes, even if they were deliberately casual. Just when she thought they couldn't look any better, her father went and pulled a trick like this. Now she had to spend all day trying not to notice as all the female fans—and some of the male fans—fawned over them.

Oscar was more tense than usual. He ignored most of the people who sat before him as he peered down the line and frowned toward the front of the hall, looking for his sister. His tension seemed to affect the others, leaking through the room until they were all shifting nervously, each of them taking their turn to glance toward the door.

When the meet-and-greet finally wrapped up, Isobel pulled her father aside. "Do we have to go back to the hotel? Can we just stay here until the afterparty?"

His lips flattened into an unhappy expression. "You aren't really sanctioned to roam around the settlement. You're allowed in the hall for the meet-and-greet and you're allowed in the hall for the afterparty. Oscar is free for the night, but only after the afterparty wraps up."

"We need to check on his sister. She should have been here today."

Braun sighed, glancing over her head, presumably at Oscar, who she could already hear snarling at Cooper behind her.

"You have thirty minutes," he muttered. "I'll make

447

sure the van to pick you up is late. Just Oscar—if you go as a group, someone will notice. The rest of you wait in here. Cooper"—he raised his voice suddenly, walking away from her—"have you seen the view count on yesterday's video?"

Isobel watched as her father led Cooper away, muttering lowly, while Oscar took out his anger on one of the chairs, picking it up and slamming it down again so violently that the assistants all flocked to follow her father and Cooper out of the hall. Teak trailed after Braun, her glassy eyes on his shoes. She had been drinking all day, sneaking cans of alcohol in the storage room off to the side of the hall.

She wasn't walking straight. Braun paused in the doorway to the hall, glancing around until he caught sight of her.

Isobel frowned, watching as her father waited for Teak, slipping behind her like he was ready to catch her if she fell.

Did he know Teak was gay?

Was Teak gay? Or was she bi? Or fluid, like Kilian?

Isobel shook the thoughts away, running over to Oscar. "You've got thirty minutes," she rushed out. "My dad is delaying the van. We'll wait here for you."

He didn't hesitate, striding for the door and kicking into a jog as he threw it open.

"You called him *dad*," Elijah noted, leaning against the edge of the meet-and-greet table. He snatched up an untouched energy drink, popping the cap and sipping it, his eyes digging so far into her that she had the absurd urge to cover herself like he had stripped her naked.

"Did I?" She was embarrassed. It felt like he had caught her in a particularly vulnerable moment.

He hummed a sound of acknowledgement, not really answering, but after a few moments, he spoke again. "He knows your weak spot."

"Which one?" She smirked, her tone self-deprecating as she pulled out a chair and sank into it sideways, wrapping her arm around the top so that she could rest her chin on her bicep. She was tired and didn't want to smile anymore.

"Us," Elijah answered nonchalantly. "He knows that the way to your heart is through us."

She wanted to deny it: that *they* were a way to her heart. That would mean they were *in* her heart—which they were—but she didn't want them to know that.

She cleared her throat awkwardly. "What's your weak spot?"

His eyes dropped from her face to her chest, to her crossed legs, and back up again. "That's my business."

The other Alphas were raiding the snack station and likely wouldn't overhear, but Isobel lowered her voice anyway. "That's unfair. You know mine."

Elijah's lips curved into a small, humourless smile. "Guess, Illy."

"Carbs," she said quickly. "You refuse to eat them, so

you must be one dinner roll away from a carb binge at all times."

"You think my weakness is something I can't have?" he mused, tilting his head at her, a few locks of his silvery blond hair falling across his forehead.

"It's either carbs or us—the group," she clarified.

"And what if it's you?" he asked, utterly without tone, his expression maddeningly calm.

She gave a tired chuckle, thinking he was teasing, but he just kept watching her, silently absorbing her reaction to his words.

A special Elijah Reed test. She realised it a second too late, lifting her chin from her bicep. "Why would it be me?"

"Guess," he said again.

"Because of the bond?"

"No."

Her heart thumped loudly. "Because of the plan? The Ironside game?"

"No." This time, the answer was accompanied by a slight roll of his frosty eyes.

She continued to guess. "Because I'm hilarious and charming?"

"Occasionally."

She shot up a finger in victory but then let her hand fall with a frown. "I'm occasionally hilarious or charming, or that's occasionally your weakness?"

He shrugged.

"Is it because I'm the epitome of beauty and grace?"

One of his pale brows inched up, his cold eyes briefly glimmering in amusement. "Are you?"

"You suck." She turned in the chair so that she could slump backwards, blowing a strand of hair from her face and lazily kicking her legs out into a wide vee, too lazy to get up and stretch properly.

"So graceful." Elijah eyed her. "I can hardly contain myself."

She jumped up, stretching her arms over her head. His gaze immediately dipped to where her cropped shirt rose above the high waist of her jeans. "You're just insulting yourself," she drawled, moving to stand before him, her fingers walking lazily across his thigh. "I'm your weakness—however or whatever I am is a direct reflection of your unrefined taste."

Finally, he laughed. It was low and soft, and only lasted a moment, but it was hard won, and she smiled in victory. He caught her walking fingers, his grip light as he guided her own arm across her chest. And then he hooked the fingers of her other hand in another barely there grip, moving that arm to the other side of her neck until her arms were crossed over her chest, and then his grip changed. He seized her wrists and dragged her against his body, right between his parted thighs, her arms crossed and captured.

"If I acknowledge it out loud, I'll have to act on it." He growled the words right against her ear, but she was saved from having to formulate a response when the door to the hall burst open again, Oscar striding inside, his veins pulsing black, his eyes turning shadowed.

"Oh fuck." Elijah pushed off the table, striding toward Oscar. "Get in the storage room," he ordered over his shoulder.

She slipped toward the back of the hall, eyes wide as the other Alphas surrounded Oscar, but he seemed to crash into them, sending Theodore and Moses to the ground. She stopped walking, alarmed at his transformation. His eyes were dark marbles, glittering with malice, his veins infected with black. He tried to pounce on Moses, who was a second too late finding his feet again, but Mikel pulled him back, earning a slash of claws across his forearm.

She didn't know what she was doing, just that she was moving toward them instead of running away. Ferality should have terrified her—and it *did* scare her—but none of them had ever hurt her when they changed. Theodore had sat as still as a statue in the library, allowing her to sit next to him and draw his darkness into herself. When Oscar had turned feral while he was still inside her, he didn't even try to fight the others. He did nothing that could have hurt her.

She didn't understand why, and she didn't think it made any sense, but she was *sure*, somehow, that Oscar wouldn't hurt her.

"Isobel, get in the storage room," Mikel barked, seeing her draw closer.

She stopped but didn't retreat. "Just listen to me," she urged quietly as they all surged a step closer to Oscar, closing in around him. Mikel's arms were dripping blood, but nobody else was injured.

Yet.

"They're going to come back for us any minute," she said. "We can't let them see this and we don't have time ... Just let me—"

"You're not getting anywhere near him," Mikel growled, not taking his eyes off Oscar.

Her breathing accelerated, her heartbeat raced, a wave of sound beating against her ears. She traced her sternum piercing, counting the stones, and then pressed against Elijah's.

"Everyone step away from him. Slowly."

They fought against her compulsion, Elijah shooting her a wide-eyed look, something shattering in his expression.

She was going to have to deal with that, later.

"Now," she demanded softly.

They backed away from Oscar, who watched her calm approach, black eyes digging hungrily into hers like he might rip her open to consume her soul.

If this didn't work, she was going to pay. Her Alphas would be *beyond* furious, and she could get very seriously injured. It had to work. She cracked her wall a little, just as she had that first night with Theodore, but instead of drowning in his darkness, she allowed it to trickle in, drip by oily drip. She was right in front of him now, and he still made no move to hurt her.

He's playing dead. Kalen's warning from the last time Oscar went feral swam back to her, but she carefully put it to the side, folding it into a box with the rest of her terror. She reached up—because now she had a point to prove—and curved her hand around Oscar's tense jaw. He leaned into her, just barely a fraction of a movement, and she was reminded of when he surged in the hotel room during her last settlement tour.

"It's like a surge," she whispered quietly. "That animal side has taken over. He's running on pure instinct. Anything he perceives as a threat, he convinces himself it's prey so that he can destroy it. But because he's only operating on an instinctual level, he can't differentiate emotions and intentions. He can only feel your energy. You're all powerful Alphas. You're all threats. I'm a Sigma. I'm not a threat. Am I?" she asked him.

He didn't answer. He just kept staring at her.

"Mate." The world was expelled from him in a push of gravelled sound that was eerie. It echoed around her.

"That's right," she told him soothingly, able to stop her voice from trembling. She drew her hand down his throat, and his eyes narrowed, but when she smoothed it across his chest, the tension in him eased again. She tilted forward, cracking her walls a little wider and resting her head against his chest.

His heartbeat thundered, even though his breaths were quiet and shallow. His arms moved carefully around her, and she felt the strange pressure of his long claws against the bare skin of her arms.

The others hissed in warning, Cian swearing roughly, but Oscar seemed preoccupied with her, and gradually, she felt that horrible malevolence spilling off him begin to wane. He suddenly released her, stepping back, his arms shooting up and away from her, his palms displayed. His eyes were back to normal and were darting all over her as he nervously licked his lips, trying to find any injuries.

"I'm fine," she assured him, as the other Alphas all surrounded him.

Mikel had his arm wrapped up in his jacket, trying to hide the wounds Oscar had given him.

"It's Lily," Oscar croaked, still backing away from her. "She collapsed last night. They said she's not going to make it."

The door burst open behind him, an assistant poking her head in to let them know the second van had arrived. Oscar followed them instead of demanding to stay in the settlement, which was a miracle, but Isobel was sure it was because he was in shock. He didn't say another word, even when she tried to comfort him or when Kilian gently questioned him.

He ignored them all, facing the window like he was just as lost as Teak. It was like his purpose in the world had been yanked away. He went straight to his room after they returned to the lodge and closed the door.

Isobel got ready quickly, as did the others, all of them congregating in the lower living area outside Oscar's room as they waited anxiously for him to reappear. When he did, it was with his luggage.

"I'm staying," he said simply.

She was in shock, but she shouldn't have been. Of course he was staying.

"For good?" Moses asked the question nobody else dared to.

Oscar shook his head. "For the rest of the break. Until I figure out a solution, and I will. We've beaten this before; we'll beat it again. She's a strong girl." He was speaking without emotion, his eyes empty, but there was a stubborn line digging between his brows.

"We'll handle everything on this end. Don't worry about anything else," Kalen promised.

They left it at that because Oscar clearly didn't want to discuss it further. They piled into the vans to return to the settlement, and nobody questioned Oscar's luggage since he had been cleared to stay the night anyway.

He disappeared as soon as they arrived, and Kalen ran interference all night with Cooper while Mikel distracted every assistant who was sent in search of Oscar.

They all dropped their fake smiles as soon as they left the settlement that night, and Isobel found herself clicking into Lily's social media as she slipped into her room. Since the lodge was locked up at night and Cooper was staying at a hotel, she had been afforded a bit of privacy, and she was grateful for it as she scrolled through the videos Lily had posted. Most of them were of Isobel.

They stopped a month ago.

She must have gotten very sick and had been hiding it from Oscar, knowing how much he would worry.

Isobel brushed away her tears, clicking on Sophia's contact. The video call was answered after only a few rings, and Sophia's frazzled face appeared in the picture.

"H-hey," Sophia said before turning around and muttering, "*Shut up*, it's Isobel."

"Uh," Isobel blinked in shock, "are you naked?"

"What?" Sophia laughed, the sound forced. "Of course not."

"I can see your nipple."

"Oops." Sophia adjusted the camera. "That was a freckle."

"You should get it looked at."

Sophia rolled her eyes. "You're calling at midnight, and you expect decorum?"

Isobel tried to smile, but her expression collapsed. "Who's there?" she asked, just as Sophia's brows drew together, seconds away from asking what was wrong.

"Nobody." Sophia adjusted the camera again, her eyes darting off to the side.

"Hey, Carter," a male voice drawled from somewhere out of sight.

"Bellamy?" Isobel gaped. "You guys are from the same settlement? He's seen you *naked?*"

"He has," Bellamy said, pushing his way into the frame and sitting beside Sophia, jolting the camera to reveal that Sophia now had a blanket wrapped around her chest. "And yes, my family is from the San Bernadino Settlement, so I can visit whenever I want."

"I can see your nipple," Isobel told Bellamy.

"You're welcome." He winked at her.

"Ew." Sophia screwed her face up. "I can see why the Alphas hate your friendship. How's the settlement tour going?"

Isobel had called her the week before, letting her know that she was the second-last stop on their tour since she didn't always keep up with social media or Ironside news.

She hadn't mentioned Bellamy at all.

"It's about to be a disaster," Isobel confessed. "Oscar pulled out. His sister is sick. When did you two start ... this?" She motioned between them.

"Start of break." Bellamy smirked, answering at the same time as Sophia.

"It isn't happening."

"She's in denial," Bellamy explained.

"You're so annoying." Sophia sighed. "So what are you going to do about Oscar? Do you know exactly what's happening with his sister?"

"I don't." Isobel nibbled on her lip. "He didn't tell us anything specific. He wasn't ... in a very vocal mood."

"He dropped out of the tour without saying anything?" Bellamy asked, his brows shooting up.

"He said he's staying."

"And that's it?" Bellamy winced. "Yikes." He turned to Sophia. "Never complain about me again. Some girlfriends have it much worse."

Sophia glowered at him. "You're *not* my boyfriend."

"Agree to disagree." He turned back to her. "Why don't you just go to the settlement and see for yourself? You don't have to follow the same rules as everyone else."

"Don't I need permission or a pass or something to enter the settlement?"

Sophia scoffed, waving a hand. "Just sneak in. They're hardly worried about people sneaking *in*, are they?"

Isobel stared at them. "Why didn't I think of that?"

Sophia grinned. "You're too busy being railed by a baker's dozen of hot Alphas."

"A baker's dozen is thirteen. There's only ten of them."

"Only." Bellamy burst into laughter. "My god, you need your head examined."

"Not just her head," Sophia deadpanned.

"My head and my vagina are both fine." Isobel sniffed. "Sort of."

"Why sort of?" Bellamy planted his chin in his palm, looking incredibly entertained.

"The sort of was for my head," she snapped at him before turning her attention to Sophia. "Honestly, how do you cope?"

Bellamy smirked, knowing she was only teasing.

"I don't know." Sophia rubbed her temples. "I've got it rough."

"You definitely got it rough," Bellamy agreed, far too nonchalantly. "And you're about to get it rough again, so say bye-bye to Carter."

Sophia made a face. "Bye-bye, Carter."

Isobel bit back a laugh. "Bye-bye, you two."

She stared at her phone after ending the call, her mind spinning. She was already in trouble—she knew it by the looks Kalen, Mikel, and Elijah had all given her in the hall as she used Elijah's power and put herself in danger.

She might as well ... make it worse.

She jumped up, ran to her suitcase, and ripped off her clothes, pulling on dark tights, dark boots, and a tight crop top. She shrugged on her navy Burberry coat and hastily braided her hair. She crept out of her room, praying that the others were all still showering as she slipped downstairs and out of the lodge. She walked to the main road and called an Uber, waiting until she was already on the way before she sent a message to the group.

Isobel: I've gone back to the settlement. I'll be back before we start work tomorrow.

It was a few moments before her phone vibrated.

Theodore: I would have gone with you.

Cian: Oh boy, you're in trouble.

Moses: How did you leave?

Isobel: Uber.

Mikel (admin): If anyone tries to go after her, I will knock you the fuck out in the driveway.

Mikel (admin): Isobel is still under her father's guardianship. She's the only one who's free to leave.

Mikel (admin): And Isobel?

Isobel: I'm in trouble. I know.

Kalen (admin): Deep trouble.

A private message popped up on her screen and she clicked into it.

Niko: Call if you need backup. They won't even notice me missing.

Before she could reply, another private message came through.

Kilian: I can slip out of here without anyone seeing. If you need me, I'm there.

Her lips tugged up into a small smile and she thanked them both before tucking her phone away. The driver dropped her off by the side of the road and she walked the rest of the way to the settlement, pressing Kilian's stone on her piercing when she got close to the guardhouse. She slipped around the car boom gate and hurried far away from the guards. She pulled up the hood of her coat as she tried to remember how to get to Oscar's house. She had only been there once, a year ago, and she quickly got lost, backtracking to the hall where their afterparty had been held in.

Oscar was there, leaning against the door, hands shoved into the pockets of his jacket. He seemed to be waiting for her.

"Hey." He stepped off the wall, dark gaze drifting over her. "Come on." He snatched up her hand, shoving it into the pocket of his jacket, his fingers lacing between hers. He led her down the sleeping, narrow streets to an unfamiliar house. The first room was a cramped office or foyer, a tired-looking woman slumped over a desk, deep in sleep with her head on her arm, a pen still in her hand.

Oscar drew her into the next room, which was a wide, gutted space, the walls knocked out to open it up as much as possible. There were hospital stretchers lined up, separated by curtains. In the last one, by the window, Lily was sleeping on her side, a soft, fluffy elephant hugged by her frail-looking arms.

The rest of the beds were empty.

Oscar drew her over to the battered armchair close to Lily's bed, slumping into it with a sigh. He deftly unbuttoned Isobel's coat and then tugged her across his

thighs, laying the coat over her lap. He said nothing—
had barely said more than "hey," and "I'm staying," in
eight hours now. He pulled her head to the crook of his
neck and then rested his own atop her hair, breathing
deeply.

"I needed you to sleep," he whispered, like he had
somehow called her to him.

She looped her arms around his hard middle, not
quite able to stretch enough for her fingers to meet
behind him. "We'll figure something out," she promised
lowly.

"She needs a bone marrow transplant," he spoke the
words so quietly that she had to strain to hear them.
"Nobody here can do that."

"We'll find a way," she reasserted. *Against all odds*
was a language they were well-versed in. Her especially.

His tight hold on her didn't slacken until the sun
began to rise, filtered light softly spilling in through the
window to shine across Lily's bed. She made sure he was
sleeping before she carefully extracted her phone,
opening up a message to her father.

Isobel: Let's make another deal.

She checked the time. It was past five in the morning.
Oscar had been clinging to her for hours and Lily hadn't
so much as twitched in her sleep.

Thankfully, her father was awake—or her text had
woken him up.

Braun: I'm listening.

463

Isobel: Lily Sato needs a bone marrow transplant.

Braun: Then she's going to die.

Isobel: Not if we get her to a hospital.

She switched to another message, tapping out the words without moving so she wouldn't disturb Oscar.

Isobel: Hey.

Elijah: You're late. Wake-up call was fifteen minutes ago.

Isobel: I'm sorry, Eli.

He didn't respond, and her fingers began to tremble.

Isobel: I should have asked if you were comfortable with me using your ability when you refuse to use it yourself.

Elijah: You saw what happened the last time I used it. I made a man stab himself 113 times. Never touching it again is my penance.

Elijah: What will your penance be?

Isobel: Whatever you decide.

Elijah: Good. Now tell me why you really texted me.

Isobel: Can you forge ID documents?

Elijah: Yes. Send me all the pictures Oscar has of her. Gabriel can edit them into something suitable while I make the documents. What do you need? Passport? Birth certificate?

She switched to the other chat with her father.

Braun: How do you propose to get her to a hospital?

Isobel: I'll find a way.

Braun: And what do you want me to do?

Isobel: We're going to leave Oscar here. As soon as I've

figured out the rest, we need to detour back here to get him ... and his sister.

Braun: You want me to smuggle a fugitive.

Isobel: And bribe a hospital. To get her in for the operation before the end of summer break. And ... front the hospital bill. I fully intend to pay you back. You can have everything I've saved up from my Ironside stipends. I'll pay the rest in instalments.

Braun: I already make donations to a hospital in Los Angeles. I can probably swing the doctor and the bill.

Isobel: What about the fugitive?

Braun: You're not asking for a small favour, Daughter.

Isobel: Then don't ask for something small in return, Father.

She switched back to Elijah.

Isobel: I need documents to say she's a human to get her into a hospital in LA.

Elijah: Done.

Isobel: Thank you.

Elijah: We're a team, sweet girl. You don't need to thank me.

Isobel scoffed softly. The difference between Elijah and her father was painful. She tapped on the new message as it popped up along the top of her phone.

Braun: I have a huge movie set to start filming next summer. I want you to make an appearance in it. A fun little cameo. And when it premieres, I want you to come to the red carpet with me.

Isobel: Why would you want that?

Braun: The press got hold of the news that your mother passed. And now there are rumours that we're estranged. I thought this tour would help, but people are saying it's all for show.

Isobel: Fine.

Braun: We have a deal?

Isobel stared at her screen, a shocking realisation bumping into her. She would have agreed anyway.

Isobel: We've got a deal, Dad.

"C-Carter?" The small voice from the bed had her dropping her phone.

It clattered to the floorboards, and she froze, waiting for Oscar to wake up. He groaned in his sleep, hands tightening around her again, but didn't wake up.

"Hey, Lily," Isobel whispered.

Lily's dark eyes were blinking at her sleepily. "Is it really you?"

Isobel very carefully extracted herself from Oscar's lap when Lily winced, doubling over and letting out a small moan. "Gonna t-throw up."

There was a plastic sick bag at the end of her bed and Isobel quickly grabbed it, passing it into Lily's hands. She watched helplessly as the little girl heaved quietly. Though apparently, there was nothing in her stomach to throw up. She sat on the bed beside the little Sigma, her hands gently and very softly rubbing Lily's back as she opened her walls and welcomed in Lily's pain and nausea until she was seconds away from reaching for the sick bag herself. She cut off the flow, sagging back against the bed. Lily was staring at her wide-eyed.

"I barely felt you," she breathed out, wonder in her eyes.

"I'll teach you how to do it when you're better," Isobel promised, closing her eyes to ward off the dizziness. "Until you can control it, you shouldn't let anything in, okay?"

Lily bobbed her head, some of the colour returning to her cheeks. "Oskie said I'm not allowed," she agreed, placing her little hand on Isobel's forehead. "Other people's problems are theirs, not mine." She arranged a fierce expression onto her face, and Isobel realised she had been mimicking her brother. "Are you sick too? You're so pale."

Isobel scoffed weakly, her eyes fluttering closed again. "That's just how I look. And Oskie is right. Other people's problems aren't yours. You keep yourself locked up tight, okay?"

"Okay."

"I'll be right back." Isobel forced her eyes back open and slid from the bed, pausing for a moment to brace herself as the dizziness threatened to send her spiralling to the floor. She sucked in a soft breath, forcing herself to stand upright as she walked into the front office.

"Excuse me?" She gently tapped the shoulder of the woman still sleeping at the front desk.

"Huh?" The woman jolted upright, knocking over a steaming cup of coffee by her elbow—so not *still* asleep, then.

"Shit, sorry." Isobel quickly swept it up, but half of the coffee had still spilt out.

The woman swore, darting over to a table with a coffee station set up and grabbing a handful of napkins. "Sorry," she sighed out. "It's been a long few nights. How can I help you?"

"Do you have anyone here to help you run this place?" Isobel asked, frowning, as she bent to help the woman mop up the spilt liquid from the floor.

The woman laughed like Isobel had told a joke and then straightened, and Isobel could tell there was a smartass remark on the tip of her tongue, but it died, the woman's eyes widening on her.

"It's C-Carter," she stuttered out. "Isobel Carter is here."

Isobel winced. "Nice to meet you ..."

"Annabeth," she quickly supplied, thrusting out her sticky hand. "You must be here for Lily."

Isobel nodded, shaking her hand, before following her lead and dumping all the napkins into a bin beside her desk. Annabeth slumped back into her chair, regathering her bun before motioning weakly to the coffee station. "Help yourself. You look like you've had a hard night. I did see a girl curled up on Sato's lap earlier but didn't realise it was you. I feel stupid now. Of course it was you." At Isobel's horrified expression, she rambled further. "Sorry, I'm overtired."

Isobel quickly poured two more coffees and handed one of them over. "Are you a doctor?"

"I'm the best they've got," Annabeth admitted, sipping the coffee gratefully. "I don't have a degree, but I went to Ironside. Knew I wasn't going to win, and they never pay attention to Omegas there anyway, so I used my time to study medicine. They have some professors who will help you get trades under the table without the officials finding out."

"Wow." Isobel popped her eyebrows up. "I had no idea."

Annabeth smirked. "Chill, girl. You don't have to pretend. West and Easton clearly bent every rule in the book to get them to change the rules of the game for you lot."

When Isobel only stared at her plastic coffee cup, Annabeth graciously changed the subject. "I'm sorry about Lily. She's a sweet girl."

"Are you sure about the bone marrow transplant?" Isobel asked.

Annabeth nodded, her exhaustion showing once again. "Lily was in remission when I took over here, but she relapsed before Sato got into Ironside. It was some timing, I'm telling you—there was no way they would have been able to afford her treatments and medications without his Ironside stipend. Anyway, now that she's relapsed, she doesn't seem to be responding to her treatment anymore. She needs an allogeneic transplant, and there's no way we can do anything like that here. She needs a damn good hospital and an even better surgeon."

Isobel set the coffee aside. Her stomach was churning too violently to drink it. She sighed, resting her eyes for a moment. *Poor Lily*, having to live with this awful feeling constantly.

"Thank you for helping her. I wouldn't give up hope, yet. Miracles can happen." She blinked her eyes open, trying to focus on the other woman's face. "Do you have any food for her? Some water?"

"Is she asking for food?" Annabeth looked shocked and quickly jumped up. She returned, pushing a packaged sandwich and water bottle into Isobel's hands. "Take these into her. I've gotta finish up my notes from last night before I forget, and I'll be right in there to check up on her."

Lily was sitting up in bed, eyes bright, tapping away on her tablet. Isobel took the sandwich out of the plastic wrapping and handed it to her.

"Eat and drink while you're feeling better," Isobel urged, sitting beside her on the bed again.

Lily nodded, keeping quiet so as not to wake up Oscar, taking small bites of her sandwich. Isobel glanced at the screen as she tapped away. She was posting on social media.

Carter is here now. I feel better. She's so pretty. I wish she was my sister. Her clothes are so cool and she has the longest hair ...

Lily paused to try and stare at the trail of Isobel's braid out of the side of her eyes.

She went back to typing. *I'm going to grow my hair long too. Once I'm better.*

Isobel moved her attention to the beanie sitting lopsided around Lily's ears. It had shifted as she slept and now showed a hint of her closely cropped hair. Isobel surreptitiously flicked away a tear with her thumb as she went back to reading over Lily's shoulder, except Lily had already published her update and was now scrolling through what appeared to be her locked, private profile. Every post was liked by a single person.

Oscar Sato.

She tugged the neckline of her crop top up to dry the tears that kept threatening to spill down her cheeks, and then she just gave up and closed her eyes.

She wasn't sure when she drifted off, but she woke up in Oscar's arms again, her father's booming laugh jolting her awake.

"Of course, it's always a pleasure to meet a fan," he said from the front office before pushing into the room, Annabeth following behind him with stars in her eyes and a notepad clutched against her chest.

Isobel blinked away her disorientation, glancing up at Oscar's face. He was wide awake, cradling her in his arms, his jaw tight like he was prepared for a fight. Lily was also awake, surrounded by drawings and with a pack of coloured pencils scattered over the bed around her legs.

"Ah, right where I left you. Hello, Daughter."

Had he just ... *made a joke?*

"Hello, Father," she husked out, completely unsure.

"I'm here to take you back," he said. "After a long detour to the hair salon, where Cooper believes you've been all morning."

Oscar's hold on her relaxed slightly, a hard breath expelled from his lips.

"I don't think I've ever seen West so pissed," her father added, his tone positively jovial. "I think you're about to be grounded."

"That's not funny," she managed, stumbling from Oscar's lap.

He deadpanned. "I wasn't joking. You let me know if he gives you any trouble. I'm still your father—I can step in if you need me to."

Isobel groaned, rubbing her hands through her hair, accidentally tugging half of the strands from her braid.

It was too early for Braun's good-guy act.

She tugged on her hair tie, unravelling the braid as she turned back to Lily. "I'll see you soon, okay? Can you be strong for a little while?"

Instead of the wide-eyed head bob Isobel had been expecting, she was met with watery eyes.

472

"Will I see you again?" Lily whispered.

"Don't you dare talk like that," Oscar growled, voice low.

Most of the fully-grown adults at Ironside would have flinched at that gravelled order from Oscar, but Lily only shot him a sheepish look.

"Of course you will." Isobel forced a bright, carefree smile.

Thank god for Theodore and all the time she had spent studying his impeccable acting.

18

THE SADIST ASSHOLE

COOPER WAS IN A MOOD.

Before boarding the plane to Vermont, he had threatened to pull the plug on the whole tour unless Oscar returned, saying that it was all of them or none of them.

Braun had borne down on him, matching fury for fury. "You think I *wanted* this? *I'm* the one funding this shitshow, not you, not Orion, not Ironside. Sato hasn't gone AWOL. He's in his home settlement where you all wanted him to stay, anyway. That's why *I'm* funding the tour, remember? West had to beg the OGGB to let him *out,* remember? Let's just give him a few weeks, and then we'll swing back around and pick him up again before the end of the tour."

It was an uncomfortable plane ride ... made even worse because Mikel, Kalen, and Elijah were still mad at her. She was used to playing games with them where she danced around them, experimenting with their attraction to her and her to them, where they tested her in small ways, wondering if she could handle them, and she responded to their tests, wondering the same thing.

This felt like another game.

They were biding their time—probably because they had enough drama to deal with—and she was cautiously trying to take cues from them.

They landed in Vermont, and Cooper stepped off the plane first, his phone at his ear, his tone still pissed. Her father had rented another lodge with limited bedrooms, effectively separating the humans and the Gifted again. They went through their obligatory meeting with the police and then divided up the bedrooms. Braun and Teak were both staying with them this time. Teak marched straight into the kitchen and began hunting through the cupboards, slamming them in irritation. Isobel didn't need to ask what she was looking for. If Teak wasn't high, she was chasing down a bottle of alcohol.

Isobel hovered on the other side of the polished wooden kitchen island, shifting nervously from foot to foot. She wanted to take away Teak's pain, but she had already tried it one morning in Vermont, and Teak had snapped at her to "mind her own business," somehow sensing her—probably because Isobel assumed she was too drunk to notice and hadn't been as careful as she usually was.

"I could make some tea?" Isobel offered weakly, watching Teak ransack the cupboards in search of alcohol.

Teak plastered an empty smile across her lips. "No need. I think I'll put in an order for supplies. You want anything?"

"No ..."

Teak was already walking out of the room.

Isobel sighed, picking up her luggage again and hauling it into her assigned room.

"Ten minutes to recharge and settle in," Mikel called from the hallway. "Then meet up in the lounge. We need to move the furniture and set up the cameras."

ISOBEL FINISHED UP A ROUND OF SQUAT JUMPS, SHAKING OUT her legs to ease the burn as she eyed Mikel. He had let everyone go an hour earlier, but he was still working on her. Or torturing her. She wasn't sure which.

They were outside on the huge balcony that wrapped the front of the lodge. The mountainscape was swallowed by darkness because they were still doing their workouts at night to save the daytime for their filmed activities.

There was light spilling onto the balcony from the

inside of the lodge, but they were still half in shadow. Music played softly over the outdoor speakers, turned down so low that she could still hear her own laboured breath and the brush of Mikel's shoes pacing over the wooden deck.

"Split jumps," he demanded. "Until I say stop."

She stretched her neck to the side, narrowing her eyes on him. "I think I've jumped enough," she ventured, testing his anger. It had been simmering for days, pushed far down and slowly rising. It seemed it had finally reached the surface.

"You've had enough when I say so." He stopped before her. "Split jumps. Now."

She started the exercise, her calves and glutes on fire from the way he was stacking exercises of the same muscle groups together.

"Higher," he snapped.

She let out a grunt. It was all she could muster.

Just before she began to cramp, he told her to stop.

"Plank," he demanded, pointing to the floor.

She got into position and felt his foot against her ass, pushing her out of it so that she tumbled onto her side.

"Plank," he said again.

"Seriously?" she growled.

He ducked down, his hand loosely circling her neck, his mouth a breath from hers, his eyes drilling into her. "Plank," he whispered before releasing her and standing again.

She planked again.

He planted his shoe against her hip and toppled her over again.

This time, she swore and regained her position before he could demand it of her.

"Good girl," he crooned, his tone cruel. "We're going to keep going until you learn how to do as you're told, even if you don't like it."

She growled as he kicked her over again. "This is fucked up."

She got back into position.

He laughed, the sound hollow, and crouched beside her, one hand landing over her ass, pressing down. "Hold your position," he demanded, his free hand gripping her face and turning her eyes to his. "You want to know what's fucked up? *My* mate ignored me and stepped in front of someone who could have buried razor-sharp talons into her chest before she could fucking open her pretty little lips and squeak for help. *Hold it*."

Her arms trembled, and his grip on her ass shifted, filling his palm with her flesh as he squeezed painfully hard, still trying to press her down. She was wearing booty shorts and a loose cutoff shirt over her sports bra, so his fingers dug into the lower curve of her butt cheek. She tried to stop it, but the rough, domineering grip sent a flood of heat to pool low in her belly, and she could feel herself getting wet.

Furious, but wet.

"And then she ran away and put herself in danger again when she was under strict orders not to go anywhere without an escort," Mikel finished, his demanding fingers releasing her.

She waited for him to push her again, but instead, he stepped away from her. "Meet me in my room in ten minutes. I was going to let you off with a rough training session, but if you're going to *enjoy* it, then it's time we levelled up your punishment, pet. Say yes, Sir."

"Y-Yes, Sir." She flopped onto her butt, staring up at him in shock, trying to hide the shiver that passed through her as the words left her lips.

It didn't feel the same as when she called the officials "sir" or "ma'am," and by the way Mikel froze, it wasn't a line he had intended on crossing just yet. His breath seemed sharp, his eyes dropping down her sprawled legs. His big chest swelled as he sucked in air, and then he turned on his heel and left her there.

Ten minutes seemed unnecessary. Likely intended to punish her even more because it definitely wasn't enough time for her to distract herself with anything else. She stepped into the lounge room, finding Moses and Niko reclined in chairs with a view directly out to the deck. They were already showered and dressed in comfortable clothes, ready for bed, lazily flipping through channels. It was a farce. They didn't have *time* to laze around and watch TV. They should have been in bed, stealing every minute of sleep that they could.

"You're both evil if you enjoyed watching that," she accused, folding her arms over her chest.

"He let you off easy," Moses remarked, giving her a very similar look to the one Mikel had just given her, his eyes trailing the line of her legs.

"He's not done," Niko noted, seeing the despairing look on her face. He chuckled, shaking his head. The sound was dark. "This is why we don't piss off Mikel, mat—"

He cut himself off. *Mate*, he had been about to say. But he swallowed it instead.

"Will it work if I run crying to Kalen?" she asked, pretending not to notice. She and Niko were still sorting out what they were to each other. They were slowly getting back to where they were, just as he was slowly getting back to *who* he was.

She didn't want to push him, and she knew he was terrified that he would lose control the way Oscar had. She felt it from him in waves whenever she tried to get physically close to him.

"Kalen will tell him to double the punishment if you do that." Moses *tsked*, shaking his head.

"What should I expect?" She pouted, slipping to the couch beside Niko.

His hand landed over her thigh immediately, like he couldn't help himself, and he pulled her closer. It was instinct, but he never let it go too far.

"We're not his sub," Niko murmured close to her ear.

"Something tells me he isn't going to put you on a suicidal diet or make you run for three hours with weights strapped to your ankles."

"I'm n-not his sub," she stuttered.

Moses regarded her cooly. "She says, all subby-like," he drawled.

She glared at him. "I'll give you subby."

He smirked. "I'm waiting."

"Ugh!" She pounced up, pointing at him. "I can't believe I'm being sub-shamed by a virgin."

He gripped her finger, hauling her across his lap, his hand landing heavily over her ass—the cheek that was already sore from Mikel's squeezing. She yelped, and he flipped her over, arching a brow as she sprawled there, struck with shock.

"Let's get one thing straight," he snarled as he surveyed her ungainly, shocked posture. "Just because I didn't want my brother's sloppy man-whore seconds back in Hudson, or any of the slobbering fangirls at Ironside *doesn't* mean I'm going to be your easy target in this relationship."

This relationship. It was the first time anyone had acknowledged the possibility of them all being in a relationship of some kind, and he hadn't just mentioned it; he had said it like it was a given. Something that already existed.

"It's not my fault you're such an easy target," she

rasped, because Moses *always* seemed to draw out this side of her.

Argumentative, immature, bratty.

He grinned, his nostrils flaring.

"Keep pushing," he warned. "I'll make your first time with Oscar look like a walk in the park."

Niko scoffed from the other couch.

"And your first time with Niko," Moses added.

"Hey," Niko snapped. "Why the fuck am I catching strays?"

Moses shrugged, standing and setting Isobel on her feet. "Because you're there? Off you go, trouble. Daddy Easton is waiting."

She screwed up her face, but both he and Niko were laughing, so she only rolled her eyes and made her way to Mikel's room, knocking gently on the door. He opened it, the heat in his eyes burning as intensely as it had been on the deck as he grabbed a handful of her slouchy shirt, pulling her into the room and stepping into her body, pushing her up against it and using their momentum to snap the door closed behind her.

He flicked the lock and then backed off, giving her whiplash.

He walked over to where he had set up his luggage, silently searching through his suitcase. She realised he had changed. He was wearing a pair of low-slung, charcoal grey sweatpants and no shirt. There were scars all over his arms and chest, some of which were pinkish-white.

"Did you have the world's fastest shower?" she questioned, noticing the water droplets still clinging to his dark hair.

His lips twitched. "I thought a cold shower would help me settle down." He finally extracted what he had been searching for. A bottle of red wine.

Isobel blinked at it. "What's that for?"

"I found it before Teak could and hid it in here." He gripped the cork in his fist and yanked it out, and then he walked back to her and touched her shoulder, steering her to his bed. He pressed down, and she sat. He handed the bottle to her.

"You're going to need this," he said, dragging a chair over to face her.

"Why?" she asked nervously.

He sank into the chair, planting one leg against the side of the mattress beside her knee, his abs flexing as he reached forward, stealing the bottle from her hands and tipping it to his mouth. She was staring at him, but she couldn't help it. Mikel was *hot*. He exuded so much raw masculinity, and she wanted to squirm at the way he had almost boxed her in against the bed.

He handed the bottle back to her, wiping the back of his mouth. "Drink. We're going to discuss your limits."

"What limits?" She raised the bottle to her lips by

reflex, and he waited until she had obediently taken a sip before he answered.

"That's the question, pet. You're in need of punishment but we can't act until we know where to draw the line."

"Um ..." She tried to keep her eyes on his face. "My limit is being punished."

His lips switched. "That so?"

"Y-Yes, definitely."

"Nice try." He reached to the bed beside her, snatching up his phone and tapping into a note-taking app. "How about blood play?"

She took a much larger sip of wine. "No, thank you."

He made a note. "Knife play?"

"Wouldn't ..." She swallowed nervously, trying again. "Wouldn't that be blood play?"

"No."

"Do you put it inside?" she whispered, leaning forward, totally horrified.

He chuckled. "The blade?" He laughed harder, his hand rubbing over his abs and drawing her eyes down that way again. She yanked them forcefully back up.

He shook his head, still laughing at her. "Cutting up your pretty pussy isn't something any of us would be into, Isobel."

The breath *whooshed* out of her. "Are you going to share these notes with the others?"

"Absolutely. So, knife play?"

"Define play." She was getting drunk on the way he was staring at her and the tableau of muscles stretched out in front of her.

"Teasing, no cutting." His voice turned into a rasp and her stomach clenched, seeing the glitter in his eyes.

Holy shit, yes. Anything that brought that look to his face.

"Okay," she whispered, taking a *gulp* of wine this time.

"Good girl," he purred, quickly noting something down before he leaned back, shifting his hips up. He was getting comfortable.

This was not the punishment she had been expecting.

"Ropes are a yes," he mused, running his finger along his lower lip. "How about other restraints? Handc—"

"Yes."

"You didn't let me finish." His eyes simmered.

"I love restraints."

"Noted." His voice was deep and contemplative. "What about consent-non-consent?"

"Meaning?"

"One example is I sneak into your room at night, and you pretend not to know it's me, and we agree that I won't stop no matter how much you struggle and scream unless you say your safe words. Another example is you finish that bottle of wine and we agree that I can do whatever I want to you after you pass out."

She could feel herself getting wetter.

What the fuck was wrong with her?

Picturing what he described made her nervous and tingly with excitement, but it also terrified her because that was wrong—what he was describing was, objectively, *wrong*.

"No," she bluffed, avoiding his eyes.

"No lying," he demanded.

"Maybe," she amended, her breath stuttering out. "With ... parameters."

"Consent-non-consent is all about parameters," he assured her, tone gentling again, making her blood heat. "It should always be discussed beforehand. Somnophilia?"

"Somnowhat?"

"One of us fucking you while you're asleep. I'm also interested in how you feel about being fucked while you're drunk or on drugs."

"No," she burst out before quickly backtracking, her eyes wide. "I mean ... to being drugged."

"And the others?" he asked calmly.

She bit down on her tongue, considering her answer. "The others are a maybe. Do *you* like that?" she quickly asked before he could move on.

He tilted his head calmly but shifted his hips again.

He was *hard*. The long, thick length of him pushing up against his sweatpants.

"Yes," he said plainly. "If agreed on beforehand. But actually, it was Kalen who suggested I ask that."

For a moment, her brain short-circuited, remembering what Kalen had done to her, and she knew a flush was creeping across her chest. "Did he ... does he ... is he also into temperature play?"

Mikel looked surprised that she knew what temperature play was. She didn't, really—unless it was exactly what it sounded like.

"Because he *loves* playing it hot and cold," she grumbled, drinking deeply.

Mikel's deep laugh was a drug, but he quickly moved on.

"Spanking?" he questioned.

She nodded, pressing her thighs together.

"Flogging? Caning? Paddling? Whipping?"

Her eyes widened. "What in the corporal punishment?"

He huffed out a brief sound of amusement. "Hits and welts but no blood?" he guessed, trying to make it easier on her.

"Maybe," she agreed before realisation slammed into her. "Wait, no. Absolutely not." He had distracted her with his muscles and his disarming laugh and had somehow swindled her into agreeing to be *caned* and *whipped.* "And no to everything else!" she exploded, shaking her head in disbelief.

His grin was sly. "The intent isn't to spank you like an errant child and send you to your room without dessert, Isobel. The intent would be to break you into pretty pieces until you're crying and whimpering and quivering in desperation for my cock."

"Sounds messy." Her eyes were wide, and her body was screaming *yes, that's my kind of mess.* "It's a maybe."

He made a note. "Humiliation?"

"Like what Elijah and Gabriel used to do to people?" She felt her eyebrows jumping up.

"Not dissimilar," he responded vaguely. And then he shot forward, gripping her by the hips and hauling her into his lap, right over his swelling erection. His hand cupped the back of her neck while the other caught the wine bottle before she could drop it. His lips lowered to her ear, his words a breathy growl.

"Do you want to be put on your knees like a filthy little slut? Do you want your other mates to stand around and watch while I fuck your whore lips until you're a dirty, sobbing mess? I'll pull back right before I explode so that you have to chase my come with your desperate little tongue."

Filthy. Slut. Whore. Dirty. Desperate.

It sounded so wrong, so why did it feel so *good*?

A whimper caught in her throat, and she squirmed against him. He groaned softly at her reaction and then gripped her hips again, setting her back on the edge of the bed. He snatched the wine from her, drinking quickly before handing it back.

"That's a yes to *light* humiliation," he rasped, picking up the phone he had dropped on the ground.

"Shouldn't you have checked *before* you did that?" she asked, eyeing him cautiously.

He laughed quietly. "Just keeping you on your toes, Illy."

She blushed, liking that he used her nickname.

"Exhibitionism?" he shot off.

"I think so."

"Choking? Breath play?"

She already knew the answer, but Mikel had worked her into a state, and she was desperate for him to do something about it. "What's breath play?" she asked, hoping for another demonstration.

"You want a reward, pet? Finish the questions."

She pouted at him, and he noted down her answer because he knew what it was. "Caging? Confinement?"

"No."

"Edging?"

"You mean like this?"

He grinned. "Funny girl. Toys?"

"Yes. Unless they talk."

"Why would they talk?" he asked, amusement sparkling in his eyes, swimming with the desire that never quite receded.

"I don't know," she defended. "As long as the vibrator isn't saying it wants to f-fuck my s-slutty ..." She trailed off, because Mikel was laughing *loudly*.

"You're so cute." He sighed, and the unguarded look on his face made her heart constrict painfully. "I think that'll cover the basics for now." He put his phone aside. "Now stop breathing, Isobel."

Her breath halted out of shock, but the slight grunt of pleased sound that he made when she accidentally obeyed had her continuing to hold it.

"Take off your clothes," he commanded, voice a low, gravelled whisper.

She waited for him to say that she could breathe again. He didn't. With wide eyes and shaking hands, she set the wine bottle on the floor and then slipped off her top and shorts, standing there in her panties and sports bra.

He tutted softly. "The longer it takes you, the longer you have to hold it."

Alarmed, she quickly pulled off the bra and stepped out of her panties. He swept her panties off the floor, slipping them into the pocket of his sweats.

"Breathe," he said, and her breath rushed out of her in relief.

His burning eyes slowly trailed over her body. "So pretty," he said. "Those freckles."

She glanced down at the rogue freckles scattered in random places across her torso and breasts.

"Thank you," she whispered.

He smiled—amused by her gratitude. "Sit on my lap."

She put a hand on his shoulder, nervously eyeing him as she straddled his lap. His smile, she realised, had an edge to it. It was a little too sharp. Sadistic, almost. He reached into his sweatpants and fisted his dick, arranging it the way he wanted before both of his hands landed on her hips. He slammed her down, right over his length.

His head lowered, his rough words whispered over her ear, "Stop breathing."

This time, he used Alpha voice, and the breath was *sucked* from her throat. They never used Alpha voice on her, so the sudden shock of it frightened her, but then he dragged her along his hard erection and licked the shell of her ear, rasping out, "Still green, baby?" and she found herself nodding.

She was so insane.

"Such a good girl," he praised, a growl catching in his throat. "Don't stop moving." He released her hips, and she couldn't have stopped even if he had ordered her to. She was desperate for the friction, the softness of fabric teasing her clit, and the throb of him on the other side was driving her wild. He palmed her breasts, squeezing roughly. "Breathe."

She moaned, the sound loud, desperate, and

probably embarrassing, though he distracted her from any shame by pinching both of her nipples.

"Does it feel good, baby?" he rasped, one of his hands brushing up, over her piercing, briefly tracing the hearts tattooed into her skin before settling in a loose hold around her neck. The other dropped to her hip, forcing her to move faster, to grind down more heavily against him.

She whispered, "Yes."

He dragged her forward by the neck, bending his head to catch her lips. It was a soft brush at first, their ragged breath filling the space between their lips as he pulled back. He groaned, tightening his hands and slamming his lips against hers, his tongue demanding entry. His dick was escaping the top of his sweatpants, and he tugged her hips up until she could feel the hot hardness of him pressing directly over her entrance.

His sounds of pleasure were snarled, and hers were whimpered as he savagely claimed her lips and pulled her onto him, her back forced into an arch.

"You're so fucking wet," he said, making it sound like praise. "I could force myself into you to the hilt right now and there's nothing you could do to stop me."

She felt a rush of wetness pool between her thighs.

"Stop breathing," he ordered silkily, still in Alpha voice. He shifted her hips back and forth only a few inches so that she drenched that exposed part of him. It was causing his sweatpants to slip down further. He was grinding her clit against him again, and she was desperate to moan or scream or cry as her orgasm crept up on her, but then he suddenly stopped, yanking her hips up, severing the contact.

She wanted to demand why, or plead that he push her back down again, but he had both hands gripping her tightly, preventing her from moving, and she couldn't even *breathe*. She struggled, hitting his chest. In response, he ducked forward, drawing her up higher, and sank his teeth into the flesh of her breast. She flinched in shock, leaking in desire, and tried to hit him again, but he suddenly stood and dropped her to her knees before sinking back down, staring at her sprawled in shock between his parted thighs.

"Breathe," he allowed, before darting forward to capture her neck again so that even though she was no longer under the command of Alpha voice, she still struggled slightly. "Did you think I was going to let you come?" he demanded cruelly. "Absolutely fucking not, pet." He pulled himself fully out of his sweatpants, and she eyed him in a daze. He had a very pretty dick. Like Kilian's, but slightly thicker. Unlike the rest of his body, it was smooth and unmarked, velvety and blushing a ruby rose colour, two thick veins running down the sides.

"Your penis is stunning," she said, without thinking.

It twitched, enjoying her compliment.

"I'm glad you like it." His voice was husky and

amused again. "Because you're about to get very closely acquainted. Open your mouth, Isobel."

She did, looking up at him, completely subdued, waiting for his next words. She wasn't sure what had come over her. It was almost like when Kalen tied her up. She felt a little floaty, a little frustrated, and entirely focused on the man before her like he was about to whisper something very important to her, and she didn't want to miss it.

She couldn't explain it.

It was like a haze. He had somehow spelled her under his power.

"Stick your tongue out," he said.

She did, and he set the head of his cock against it, tapping a few times and making a wet, slapping sound.

"Now I'm going to fuck your throat," he warned her, eyes swimming with dark malevolence. "I'm going to use your mouth like a little fuck doll until I'm done, and then I'm going to send you to bed without an orgasm, because you were a bad girl, weren't you, Isobel?"

With her tongue still out and his dick a direct threat to her throat, she had no choice but to nod and lie to herself about the obscene amount of wetness between her thighs.

She was ill.

She needed help.

Right after she did this, though, because there was

no way she was leaving this room without getting exactly what he promised.

"That's my good girl," he said, showing her a flash of tenderness as he gently caressed her cheek with his thumb ... before he grabbed her neck again and forced his cock down her throat. "That's ... my girl. Shit." He used her throat roughly, and when she let a moan slip out, he slapped her cheek, holding himself so deep in her that she began to choke.

"This isn't a reward," he reminded her as tears streamed down her face. "This is what you get when you put my mate in danger."

He pulled out, stabbing down her throat with a vicious rhythm until she was a sobbing, quivering mess, and then he pulled out, his hand pumping along his glistening length.

"Will you disobey me again?" he asked, glaring at her like he already knew the answer.

"Probably," she rasped, her voice rough.

"Then you better get used to this," he said, picking her up and tossing her onto the bed. He bent up one of her legs, pressing it to her chest as his head lowered threateningly between her thighs. He attacked her pussy without warning, hungrily lapping at her desire, circling her clit in demanding licks before thrusting his tongue into her. There was no hiding how much she had enjoyed his rough treatment of her, and the evidence of it seemed to drive Mikel wild. He shoved her to the edge of release and then stopped before she could grasp it. He pulled back, wiping his mouth with the back of his hand, his eyes dark.

"Fuck," he groaned, an actual wince seizing his features as he stared down at her.

He was about to snap.

He was about to lose control of himself and the entire situation and she *loved* that. She licked her lips, waiting for it to happen, her belly clenching.

"Stop that," he demanded, eyes on hers.

"Stop what?" she whispered.

"Like you think I'm about to fuck you, and you've never wanted anything so badly."

She reached for him, trying to pull him on top of her, but he slapped her thigh sharply. "Lay still," he ordered. "Hands above your head. Display that perfect, pretty pussy for me." He gripped her knees, pushing them out and spreading them wide on the bed. "Good girl." He was stroking himself over her, devouring the way her position arched her body and pushed her breasts out in display for him.

"I'm going to come," he growled out like a warning. "And then you're going to get out of here before I fuck you—and you're not to touch yourself or ask anyone else to touch you. Understood, pet?"

"Yes," she breathed, her entire body clenching with the need to *touch* and *rub*.

"Yes what?" He delivered the order in a rough bark.

"Yes, Sir," she demurred, arching deeper like it might somehow bring him closer.

"Fuck," he groaned, squeezing himself as he exploded, shooting ropes of white across her bent thighs and stomach. It was still spilling out when he pressed the head of his pulsing cock to her entrance, shoving in just an inch and holding there with a long, drawn-out moan.

It was so similar to what Kalen had done, and she felt a flash of frustration that they wouldn't just *cross that line* when they seemed willing to cross every other line.

"Do it," she tried to goad him, even though her voice was still rough from his treatment of her throat, and a little breathy and desperate.

He smirked, stepping back off the bed and pulling up the waistband of his sweatpants again. He was still hard.

"I already told you: no orgasms."

He gently pulled her up to a sitting position and tugged her to the edge of the bed, kneeling before her, his hands on her knees as her feet fell to the floor.

"How are you doing?" he asked, gently soothing away her tangled, tear-soaked hair.

Wow, she didn't realise she was that much of a mess.

"Could be better," she grumbled, twisting her hands in her lap. He covered them with his, separating them and pushing his fingers through hers.

He pressed a soft kiss to her mouth. "You're not getting what you want, Illy. But," he tacked on, kissing her softly again, "you're also not going back to your room. You're sleeping here tonight."

She perked up, her core fluttering as she glanced up in hope.

He laughed at her because he was a sadistic asshole.

"It's still not happening," he said, delicately pulling her to her feet. "Let's get you cleaned up, and then you can go to *sleep*."

19

WHEN YOU NEED ME

ISOBEL'S EYES FLUTTERED OPEN, AND SHE STARED UP AT THE ceiling, tugging herself out of a confused, drowsy haze. She was surrounded by the calm, clear scent of rain, so potent that she hugged her arms, expecting her skin to be damp. It was windy outside—she could hear the breeze whipping the leaves of a tree a few feet from the window and see the pattern the waving greenery made in shadows against the far wall.

But it wasn't storming as she had expected.

She frowned further, the night slowly coming back to her. Her eyes widened, slipping to the side. Mikel was in bed.

With her.

More specifically, she was in *his* bed.

He was spread out on top of the blankets while she was cuddled warmly within them. He was wearing sweatpants again, but a different pair—this pair was more faded and had a ragged drawstring. He was lying on his back, one hand against his scarred, ridged stomach, the other stretched along the pillow above her head, his fingers tangled in her hair like he had fallen asleep stroking her head.

She carefully rolled to her side, glancing at the clock beside his bed. It was ten minutes to five. Ten minutes before they had to be up and suffer through their third meet-and-greet. This time, without Oscar.

She sighed, wiggling subtly closer to Mikel. He had hypnotised her the night before, using his powerful Alpha dominance and his uncharacteristically pretty cock to bow her into submission, and she found a small sigh slipping from her lips at the fact that even deeply asleep, he still looked harsh and intimidating.

She wondered if she should slip out before he woke up and decided to punish her again, but she didn't think he would. He had made his point. And it had worked, because as fun as it had been, she *still* felt achy and unfulfilled, frustrated from not being allowed to climax.

His phone alarm went off early, and she jolted in fright. He woke *quickly*, almost instantly, reaching over to turn it off before settling back down, his arm bent over his face, hiding his eyes. His nostrils flared.

"Surprised you didn't sneak out," he commented, moving his arm up to reveal his sleep-darkened eyes.

"I thought about it," she admitted.

They stared at each other.

"Why didn't you have sex with me?" *Oops.* She hadn't quite intended to ask that.

He groaned. "It's not a punishment if I let you cream all over my cock, Isobel. *That* is a reward."

"Is that the only reason?" she pressed.

He examined her quietly. "Do you want the truth?"

"Yes."

"Then, no. I don't know how to make you mine and then watch you share yourself with everyone else. I honestly don't know how Kalen did it."

"He took pictures."

"What?" Mikel stilled, his dark brows inching up in surprise.

"To remind himself," she whispered. "Pictures of him inside me. Of his ... of me ..." She trailed off, too nervous to articulate it properly, but then she pushed on because there was something she still needed to get off her chest.

"This whole ... holding back thing ... It makes me feel like we're all dancing around a ticking time bomb. Everyone thought Theodore wouldn't be able to handle it, but he does. Everyone thought Oscar wouldn't be able to handle it, but he does. You guys aren't even *trying* to handle it or to see if we can make it work, so it just makes me nervous. I'd rather try. I'd rather know."

"Even if we fail?" he asked.

She nodded.

He traced her temple, her cheek, the curve of her jaw. "Tell me how you five make it look so easy."

"Without even trying, most of the time," she answered.

"Why isn't Oscar ripping into the others? Why isn't Theo going feral? Kilian might be less ... *angry*, but he isn't less savage. And Cian? He would never share someone he had feelings for. How are they standing it?"

"We haven't discussed labels or anything, but we're in a relationship of some kind. I think that helps. We all anticipate each other's needs, not just me for them and them for me. It's a group effort. I think Oscar secretly likes that Kilian will always be there for me when he's too rough because he doesn't always know the right words to say. Theodore wants to hate it, but he can't hate anything that makes me happy no matter how hard he tries. Kilian's the same. And I think ... I think Cian knew all of this would happen right from the start. He acts like there's no point in fighting against the inevitable. And we have a ... a kind of security, with Oscar, I guess. They know he'll protect me, but it's not just me. Kilian soothes *everyone*. Theodore really does want *all* of us to be happy. Oscar doesn't just protect me; he protects *us*, and Cian is always looking out for us, always thinking about the little things that nobody notices. We have a relationship —all of us. It might only be sexual between me and them, but it's emotional between us all."

Mikel's fingers traced the planes of her face as she

spoke, listening intently to her interpretation of how the others felt.

"So if we have a relationship—" He paused, swallowing. "—not just a sexual agreement, they won't fight against it?" His voice was a low grumble, his tone disbelieving or shocked—certainly, it was the opposite of what he had thought.

She was surprised that he was taking her seriously. That he was really considering what she had said. She wasn't sure what she had expected, but a small part of her worried that he might be insulted if she tried to explain his own Alphas to him.

"That's how I see it," she confirmed.

"And you want a relationship with me?" He pinched her chin, a hint of the domineering Mikel peeking through his sleepy expression.

She licked her shaky lips. "I don't know what that would look like," she admitted. "I couldn't be your submissive all the time. When we're ... I mean ..."

"When we're fucking?" He cocked a brow.

"Uh, yes. It's fine then, I mean, more than fine. It's exciting, and I love the hazy, floating feeling I get, but I can't always do what I'm told. I know you're used to that with the others, but if you want a relationship with me, I have to be more than your responsibility."

He nodded, his eyes far away, mulling over her words. "Tell me what that would look like."

She thought about it for a moment. "I defer to you for

most things—you, Kalen, and Elijah. Your minds work differently from mine, and you've taken on the burden of organising and training us all. With training, I'll obey you. If it's about Eleven and our performances, I'll do as I'm told. If it's about my life or my relationships—even if it puts me in danger—that will be my decision."

"What else?" he asked, showing no reaction to her words. "What does a relationship look like to you?"

"When you need me, you have me. When I need you, I have you."

"What if you're busy?"

"We all *care* about each other," she emphasised quietly. "I might come with company—it just means they support you too."

"That's not a role I'm used to," he admitted, and she realised he was right.

He cared for everyone else. He didn't allow them to care for him.

Mikel's head was spinning.

He hadn't been expecting this conversation. He hadn't been expecting her serious, multi-hued eyes to be staring into his soul at five o'clock in the morning and tempting him into a world he hadn't even considered.

He couldn't stop stroking her soft skin, even though his mind was in overdrive. He was glad she had taken out her contact before stumbling into the shower the night before. Those spotty, colour-warring irises had grown on him. It grounded him when they were the same colour. At first glance, the hue was chaotic and messy, but the longer he stared, the calmer he became.

Well, sometimes.

It was either calm or savagely worked up.

But her expression was so deeply serious that even though the swirl of her desperate cherry scent had woken up his cock the minute he opened his eyes, he was able to focus entirely on the world she tempted him with. The fantasy.

Him and her.

She painted a cosy dream, but he didn't know how to believe it. He was in charge. That was his role. He organised them. He trained them. He protected them. He punished them and rewarded them and cared about them, but he didn't know how to let them in.

Kalen was the only one who knew—

The world around him shifted.

"Oh shit, not this again," Isobel whimpered, fear painting her tone.

Oh shit, indeed.

He never allowed himself to think about it, and the second it popped into his head ...

He called it into being.

He was standing in another memory, Isobel and the other Alphas huddled together as they stood inside a small, beaten-down house in the San Bernadino Settlement.

Mikel knew it was that particular settlement because this was *his* memory.

His beaten-down house.

His pounding fist on the door.

Isobel jumped, and Oscar immediately yanked her against his body, his hold tight.

"Doing all right?" Mikel asked him, because the tacit Alpha was barely answering their text messages.

Oscar gave him a nod. "This your memory?"

"Unfortunately," Mikel muttered, stepping out of the way as the door crashed in.

"Dany?" A younger version of him—by five years—rushed into the house, hair a wild mess, eyes wide in fear.

He did his best not to remember this day, and now it was here, playing out for him like a fucking movie.

"Dany?" the younger Mikel called again, darting past their entire group. "She's not here," he said to himself, tugging his phone from his pocket.

"I'm here," a female voice called from the doorway, drawing all their eyes back in that direction.

Seeing her again was a direct punch to his gut.

Short, bouncy black hair. Full lips, wide smile, a cross dangling around her neck. She had flitted between the Gifted religion and the human religion before settling on the Gifted. Still, she never got rid of the cross.

She was in tight black jeans, and her green eyes were manic.

"You can't say shit like this," the younger him declared as Dany rushed up to him and then quickly bounced back like his anger was a physical force. "If you don't think you're my mate, I'll kill myself and prove it?" he seethed, reading the message from his phone.

"I don't want you to leave," she begged him, tears filling her eyes, turning her stare into the mossy green ocean that had haunted his dreams for years.

"I *have* to go," the younger him insisted, struggling to control his anger. "We talked about this." He softened his tone, trying to reach for her. She curled into him immediately. "I promised Kalen. Those boys need all the help they can get."

"*I* need you," she countered weakly.

"We've been planning this for a long time." He tried to soothe her, falling into the practised speech he had already given her half a dozen times. "We've been planning this for so long, Dany. I can't back out now. It's just for five years."

"It's different now," she begged, her voice weak. "I'll prove it, Mikki." She was digging into her handbag, tears falling freely down her face. She pulled out a small silver handgun.

"Where the fuck did you get that?" The younger Mikel stared at it in shock, his eyes slowly widening with realisation.

He never really took her seriously.

"I paid Mr Breaker—" she began, but Mikel cut across her.

"Give it to me, Dany." His hand was held out, palm displayed, forcing a calm he hadn't felt.

"N-No, I'm going to prove it." She stumbled a few steps away, her black curls trembling, her tears spilling over.

She was terrified, but she really believed it would work.

"I'm your mate, Mikki. I'll show you—"

"Give me the gun." Mikel's Alpha voice rolled over her, his demand halting her.

She cried harder as it forced her closer to him. She began to shake violently when she raised her arms, offering the gun.

With the barrel pointed at her chest.

When the shot rang out, Mikel glanced away from the scene, his jaw tight. He heard Isobel's yelp and could feel the others moving between him and the body that had just thumped to the floor.

Only Kalen knew ... until now.

He felt fucking *exposed*. Especially when the younger version of himself began to cry. Not small, shocked sounds. Guttural cries that reeked of pain and guilt and ownership.

Because this was what happened when he didn't have control.

The people he loved got hurt.

Isobel reached out to touch him—he knew it was her even with his back turned. It was too gentle, too soft, too hesitant. That touch seemed to jerk him back to his real body, ending the vision.

"Mikel," she breathed, sorrow in her voice.

But she didn't move or say anything more, and he couldn't feel her eyes searing into him. He glanced at her, seeing that she was staring at the ceiling, her eyes welling with tears, sucking on her lower lip like it could stop her from crying. She knew not to force her grief on him or comfort on him.

She always seemed to *know* what to do—not just with him, but with the others too.

He also turned to stare at the ceiling, waiting until his ragged breathing had eased. There was a soft knock on his door, but he ignored it, and the person eventually went away. He felt a brush against the back of his hand and then Isobel's small fingers wrapped around his.

When you need me, you have me.

That *fucking* bond. Always trying to prove a point.

"You're cursing out the bond right now, aren't you?" Her voice was soft and quiet, but her tone was dry.

And despite it all, he felt a little smile tug at his lips. "It would have been better if they barged in here with ice cream and sad war movies."

"Sad war movies?"

"I'm not sure how they comfort each other."

"Face masks, backrubs, and Twinkies."

He slitted his eyes to her. The slightest smile was on her face as she stared upwards, avoiding his gaze.

"Twinkies aren't in their diet plan," he growled, feeling his dick twitch at the way she squirmed like she could feel his tone all the way through her body.

He could sense her through the bond. *Tingly pleasure*. He liked that much better than the sorrow she had been feeling earlier.

"All I'm getting is a puny hand squeeze," he said pointedly, still staring at her.

"Will you look at that." She checked her watch. "It's time to get to work."

He caught her as she tried to sit up, dragging her out of the blankets and draping her over his body. She laid her arms casually over his chest, propping her chin on top of her stacked wrists and kicking her legs behind her like this was what she wanted right from the start.

It probably was.

"If you're late to work, who punishes you?" she mused.

He slapped her ass. "Not you."

She yelped and then pouted. "I could be a good Sir. Ma'am? Madam? Mistress?"

"Pet," he growled, a little distracted by the fact that his spank had pushed up the T-shirt she had worn to bed, revealing the pale, perfect side swell of her ass.

"Hmm ..." She pretended to think about it, before

ultimately shaking her head and dismissing it like he was giving her options and she had a choice. "What if I don't call you Sir but you still call me pet?"

"What would you call me?"

"Mikki."

For being so bold, he gave her another spank. Her attempts to distract him and draw a smile from him prompted a confusing array of reactions from his body. He grew hard, and his heartbeat quickened. And he *hurt*. His chest hurt. His soul hurt.

He wanted her so badly it was painful.

She was a perfect little angel, and he was the fucked-up, damaged monster who should have existed only to protect her. But he was selfish, and he wanted more.

He wanted that dream she dared to paint for him.

When you need me, you have me.

He wasn't sure if he could be anything other than a *Sir*.

Could it really be that simple? There was no way.

He quickly flipped their positions, forcing himself between her thighs, his hand slipping around her neck. He *loved* her neck. He knew the others were obsessed with it too. He caught them always holding it, always looking at it. It was long and slender, with those hearts stepping up either side, marking her as theirs.

His.

Shit.

"What if I try?" he whispered, staring into her shocked eyes.

She knew what he was talking about. She nodded, and his lips fell over hers with a heavy groan.

Holy shit.

Maybe it could be that simple.

He drew back before he got carried away, enjoying the dazed look on her face.

"Contacts," he ordered, pointing to her eyes. "And get dressed. I want you downstairs in ten minutes."

He was an asshole to test her, but she jumped up, giving him a mock salute. "Yes, *Sir*." She bounded out of the room before he could retaliate.

"I'm Sao-Yeong," the woman before Isobel whispered like it was a cheeky secret. She had round apple cheeks and kind, shimmering eyes, her greying hair pulled into a messy bun, paint streaked over her arms.

She pushed a little square toward Isobel.

It was a small canvas the size of Isobel's hand in a thin, delicately carved wooden frame. Isobel knew what it was immediately and could barely tear her eyes from it to shoot an astounded look at the woman.

"This is a Baek painting," she whispered, stroking the delicate frame.

Her mother had collected them. Each one depicted a

miniature nature scene or an animal, the brushstrokes so small and delicate they were almost invisible. They were always charming and highly detailed, and they were worth *thousands*.

The little Baek in her hands was of a deer in the forest, sunlight dappling its coat, lush green foliage hinting beyond a warm, glowing clearing. The soft yellows and gold were beautiful, the gentle expression of the deer making her throat tighten. The traditional Baek frame wrapped the painting—hand-carved with the most intricate little patterns, polished to a soft sheen so that the natural grain still shone through.

She eagerly turned it over, looking for the title of the painting—they all had one stamped in delicate gold lettering on the back of the frame, like a secret.

To be protected.

She lifted her eyes to the woman, who could never have known how much these paintings had meant to her mother. The woman was staring back at her in shock. And ... pride?

"You know my paintings?" she asked.

"W-what?" Isobel almost dropped the little treasure. "You're Baek?"

"Baek Sao-Yeong." The woman bobbed her head, looking overjoyed. "Well, Sao-Yeong Gray, now. I'm married. My husband, Frederik, makes the frames." She pointed to the back wall, where a man was standing with a camera, taking pictures of them.

He glanced up, surprised, and gave them a large smile and a wave.

Isobel waved back, in total shock.

"My mother loved these paintings," she said, tracing the frame. "She was obsessed. She went to every art auction, always trying to find them. They're so rare—I mean—" Isobel laughed awkwardly, a little starstruck. "—obviously you know that."

Sao-Yeong was beaming, her apple cheeks stained with a blush. "I had no idea they were so popular."

"You ..." Isobel blinked at her, and then it dawned on her.

Gifted weren't allowed to run businesses that serviced the world outside the settlements. Sao-Yeong was selling her paintings illegally. That might explain why she didn't seem to realise they were selling for thousands. The officials must have been pocketing most of the money and allowing her to continue.

"You haven't tried googling yourself?" Isobel whispered, leaning forward.

Sao-Yeong also leaned forward, eyes wide. "My paintings are on the Google?"

Isobel *hated* that they were taking advantage of this beautiful, sweet, *insanely* talented woman. She nodded quickly. "You should look it up when you get home, search Baek paintings—"

"Kilian wanted to request that you kindly stop

monopolising his mother," Moses whispered, ducking his head beside hers.

She glanced down the table in surprise. All the seats past Sao-Yeong were empty, and they were all waiting on her. Kilian's lips were curved into a soft grin.

"Eomma," he complained, though he did it in an indulgent voice. "What are you doing?"

Sao-Yeong flushed brighter, quickly standing. "My son asked me not to come. He thought I'd tell you about his little crush, but I would never. Kili!" She skipped the other seats, sitting in front of Kilian and reaching over the table to cup his cheeks. "Have you been eating?"

Isobel refused to release the painting for the rest of the meet-and-greet, though Cooper kept sweeping past to collect all the gifts the fans had given them. She kept it in her lap, sneaking glances down at it often, unable to believe what had just happened.

"I protected Kilian from bullies for three years," Moses ranted as they packed up for the afternoon, "But did I get a painting? Or even a thank-you?"

"Nobody has ever tried to bully me," Kilian stated dryly, tugging his jacket over his arm and striding for the door.

"I'm literally your best friend," Theodore complained. "I didn't get a painting either."

Kilian chuckled, looking at his phone. "All the photos Dad took are of Isobel and me. Damn, baby, the parents love you."

"Enjoy it while it lasts," Elijah mumbled. "We're headed to the Redwood Settlement next."

Niko's settlement.

She mulled over that statement as the others continued to complain about not receiving a painting from Kilian's mother and all the ways in which they were deserving of one.

Isobel checked in with Oscar while they were getting ready to do their live video and somehow made it through the afterparty without stabbing Cooper as he made yet another speech about how the whole tour was his own personal triumph.

She was marginally less on edge about the possibility of them going off the rails and trying to deal with Cooper on their own now that Oscar wasn't anywhere near him, but Niko and Moses still concerned her. The Niko of seven months ago would have already done it, and without apology.

She knew she would have to decide how to deal with Cooper very soon—especially now that Oscar was preoccupied with more important things—but the only thing she knew for certain was that they couldn't sabotage him while he was on tour with them. It would be too obvious. She needed to wait until they were back at Ironside, and then they could find a way to ruin him *without* it pointing back to them. She tried to soothe her anxiety over the situation by telling herself that she still had plenty of time.

Isobel was exhausted when they arrived back at the lodge. Teak had passed out in the van during the afterparty, and Braun carried her into her room as Isobel and Theodore slumped onto couches in the small lounge, pretending to watch the TV above the fireplace when, in reality, they were waiting for Braun to come out of Teak's room.

"There's no way they're having sex," Theodore muttered under his breath, his expression quizzical as he stared at the door.

"And they're not staying up late talking," Isobel added, checking her watch. "He's been in there half an hour. She's *unconscious*. What the hell is he doing?"

"Surrogating?" Theodore sounded confused. "This is okay, right? Should we be stopping it?"

"I have no idea." Isobel checked her watch again. "Teak follows him around like a drunk puppy. So I guess she doesn't mind? Have you noticed? She tried to follow him into the bathroom the other day."

"Did you ask Sophia about it?" he questioned lowly as Moses strolled past the kitchen, giving them an odd look.

Isobel replied, "All she could suggest was a surrogate, which is exactly what everyone else has been saying anyway. Did you know Sophia and Bellamy are together?"

"Does Sophia know that?" Theodore asked, smirking.

Moses flopped down into one of the free armchairs,

glancing over at the door to Teak's bedroom, which they were still staring at. "What are we doing?"

Elijah entered the room, answering before they could as he dropped down on Isobel's other side. "Wondering what Braun is doing in there."

"I bet he's just bragging about us," Theodore said. "To the only person who isn't sick of hearing it."

"An unconscious person," Elijah agreed. "That's a likely scenario. If he calls us 'his boys' one more time, I'm changing my gender and giving up my Alpha designation."

"It's too late for you," Isobel told him. "You're his second favourite after Theo. He's never letting you go. You're too calculated and devious."

"What odd qualities to value," Elijah noted dully. "What does he see in Theo?"

"What doesn't he see?" Theodore shrugged. "I'm the full package."

"Wow." Moses stared at him. "You really believe that, don't you?"

Theodore grinned at him. "Hard not to."

Mikel strode into view and stopped in the hallway, right outside Teak's door, which they were all openly facing, having given up all pretences of watching TV. He looked behind him, and then back at them, and then cocked a brow.

"Why are you all still in formal clothes?"

Shit. They were late for training.

"Isn't the workout cancelled tonight?" Moses looked confused.

"That's what I heard?" Theodore agreed, stroking his chin. "Elijah?"

"I heard it too." Elijah relaxed back into the couch, his arm lightly draped over Isobel's thighs. "Carter?"

Isobel gulped as Mikel stared at her, waiting for her to pick a side. "Yep, cancelled," she squeaked out.

Mikel rolled his eyes up to the ceiling, but instead of snapping an order at them and promising to work them twice as hard, he expelled a sigh and nodded.

"Movie night it is."

"Really?" Isobel perked up.

He stalked into the kitchen, pulling out his phone. "You all need a break. I'll text the others."

They dragged all the cushions from the couches and all the pillows from the beds, piling them into the tiny movie room tucked into the back of the lodge. It only had four recliners, which were quickly claimed by Kalen, Mikel, Cian, and Niko. Theodore, Moses, Elijah, and Gabriel spread out on the couch cushions on the floor, dividing up the blankets between everyone. When Isobel tried to step over Moses to join Theodore, he tugged her down between his legs instead.

"They get you all the time," he defended as she glanced at him in question.

She was entirely relying on them to communicate with her when they were feeling the need to soothe their bonds, so she was grateful when they asked—wordlessly or otherwise—for attention. She didn't want to give it if they didn't want it.

She relaxed back against him, and Mikel began to flick through the available movies, settling on … a sad war movie.

She chuckled under her breath.

"What's funny?" Moses asked, his arms slipping around her waist and pulling her back flush with his chest, his lips brushing against the top of her head.

She stretched out her arms over his muscled thighs, absently picking at the fabric of the lounge pants he had changed into.

"This is Mikel's idea of a bonding session," she said. "Sad war movies."

"Why sad war movies?" Theodore asked, tilting his head back to catch sight of Mikel.

"How the fuck do I know?" Mikel grumbled. "Do you have a better idea?"

"No, no." Theodore chuckled. "Sad war movies are perfect. Proceed with the bonding."

She snuggled back against Moses, enjoying his sweet, crushed-petal scent as it slowly unfurled around her. She turned her head to the side, brushing her nose against his shirt, and his arms tightened around her.

There was a pulse between her legs and a heightened tension in the room, as if everyone could suddenly smell the spike in her arousal. She couldn't help it. Moses turned her on. He always had ... and that was the problem. He turned her on *too* much. It scared her, always making her back away. She rubbed her cheek against his shirt, trying to soothe her thoughts.

I'm not going anywhere. His voice whispered into her mind through the bond. *Just relax, Illy.*

She turned a little, just enough to hug one of her arms around his middle as she curled up. Just like the others, he knew exactly what to say. Using her nickname was like a secret code word that everything between them was good, and she could relax.

She had nothing to worry about.

20

THE BOYFRIEND EXPERIENCE

Braun: The surgeon is on board. Send me everything the settlement doctor has on Lily.

Isobel glanced up, meeting her father's eyes across the room. He nodded at her and then raised his phone to make another call. She quickly screenshotted the message and sent it to Oscar, his reply coming moments later.

Oscar: I'll email you everything now.

The little typing bubble kept popping up and disappearing as he seemed to struggle over a second message. She stood there and waited—they were having a brief break before heading back into the choreography anyway. After several minutes of typing and deleting, he finally sent another message.

Oscar: Thank you.

She had told him she was trying to sort out a way to

help Lily, but he didn't know what that entailed yet. She debated waiting until the plan was more concrete, but now that they had a doctor, it seemed inevitable, so she took a deep breath and quickly tapped out a message.

And then deleted it.

And then tried again, and deleted it again.

And then called him.

"That was painful," he murmured, picking up on the first ring. "Aren't you in the middle of work?"

"Just taking a quick break. You're missing some crucial stuff, you know. Today, we worked out that Cian has been going in the wrong direction every single time we do the turn."

"The bridge turn or the one near the end?"

"The bridge turn."

Oscar chuckled, sounding tired. "I was doing the same thing. It's harder when you aren't here. Lily's been trying to fill your shoes."

She heard a small, feminine voice squeak something in the background.

"She claims she's great at it, and I'm the one who sucks at following orders," Oscar relayed. "What else have I missed?"

"Kilian's mom is literally a world-famous artist, and his whole family didn't even realise. I told her what to google, and she's been sending Kilian articles about herself all afternoon since he came home from the settlement. She's thrilled. Even though she's being ripped off by the officials."

"How'd you find out?"

"She gave me one of her miniatures. Just me, by the way. I'm the favourite."

He snorted. "That appears to be a theme. What else have I missed?"

"Is that Oscar?" Moses asked from directly behind her. He grabbed her hips, spinning her around and pinching her phone away from her ear, hitting the speaker button. "Hey," he said.

"Hey," Oscar replied.

And then nothing.

"Oscar's on the phone?" Kilian asked, appearing at her other side.

"Can I have a painting?" Oscar asked after another few beats of silence.

"You're going to have to join the queue." Kilian shook his head in exasperation, his lips curved. "She's been telling everyone she knows that she's famous, and now they're all lining up down the street for a Baek miniature."

Oscar grunted out a sound of amusement.

"Was that Oscar?" Cian asked, stopping by Moses and notching his elbow on the other Alpha's shoulder.

They waited for Oscar to say something, but he didn't.

"I *swear* he was just chatting Isobel's ear off," Moses grumbled.

Isobel tapped the speaker button again, raising the phone back to her ear. "Everyone says hello, but actually, I called you for a reason." She lowered her voice and slipped off to a quieter corner. "That doctor isn't just a second opinion. He's agreed to do the operation. At a hospital in LA."

"There's no way I can afford that." Oscar's voice was also low. Strained.

"My father is going to front the bill. I told him he could have everything I've got saved up and I'd pay him back the rest in instalments. We can smuggle her onto the jet when we come to pick you up right before we go to Mikel's settlement. It's only a few hours' drive from the hospital. Elijah already forged her a birth certificate. That's all we need since the doctor is pulling some strings for my dad."

He was silent for a long time, and when he spoke again, his rough voice broke. "I'll pay you back. Everything I have is yours. Everything from now until I die—it's yours, okay?"

There was no way she was accepting that, but she also knew it would drive him insane to feel so indebted to anyone, so she quietly said, "Okay."

"Is this really happening?" he asked, so low it was almost inaudible.

"Don't tell her yet," Isobel begged. "I still have some

more details to work out—like how to get her back to the settlement. Elijah said he had a few ideas, but we were waiting to see if my father could get the doctor to agree before we went any further."

She caught sight of the others—they had gone back to work without her, probably sensing through the bond that she was in the middle of something important.

"I won't tell her yet," Oscar said. "I can't get her hopes up like that. I wish I had your ability." The last part rushed out of him on a low grumble. "She's barely eaten since you visited. I just want to take away everything she's feeling."

"I think that's the first time anyone's ever said that to me."

"That they want your ability?"

"Usually, it's the cool ones they want. Like invisibility, or that mind-speaking thing Bellamy pretends is just a cute party trick."

"Why are we talking about Bellamy?" he growled lowly.

She chuckled. "First example I could think of."

"Every time that fucker makes you laugh, I want to kill him."

"You could try to be funnier," she said casually.

"I'm fucking hilarious. You should come to one of my fights. I made a guy's nose explode before break."

"And it was ... funny?" she asked.

"Funniest thing I've ever seen."

She laughed, and he exhaled deeply. "Was that fake?" he demanded.

"You'll never know," she returned. "Gotta go. Mikki is contemplating how many push-ups he's going to make me do tonight from across the room."

"You're calling him Mikki now?"

Mikel's eyes narrowed.

"Only when he can't hear me," she squeaked.

"He read your lips, didn't he?" Oscar sounded amused at her expense.

"Yes," she groaned. "I'm going to be so sore tonight."

He released a frustrated, gravelled sound. "That's just mean."

She quickly hung up when Mikel crooked a finger at her. She jogged nervously back to the group.

"I think we've practised as much as we can without Oscar," Mikel announced. "Let's move on to 'Fix Me.'"

Their first song for the debut album was dance-heavy, but "Fix Me," their second song, was a ballad, and they had decided it would be their most vocally focussed option. No matter how hard they trained, there was no way they would be able to perform it while dancing. Only four of them actually sang it, and it was far too technical without having all of them rotating through the singing and dancing. They also didn't want the focus to be away from the song. Kalen had written the lyrics, Mikel had produced the track, and they had all fallen in love with it as soon as they heard the demo.

It was the first time she was ever genuinely *excited* to sing.

"I think you should just line up," Kalen said, pointing out spots on the floor. "Cian, then Theo, then Isobel, and Kilian here." The main singing group.

They lined up, and Mikel handed them all microphones. "I know you're not used to standing still, and you're used to selling emotion with your bodies, so we're going to need to work on your expressions. When we film the video for this song—and any shows we do—the cameras will be right up in your face to catch everything."

They nodded at him, and Isobel caught sight of Cooper striding back into the large sunroom where they had set up for filming. He was on the phone, talking quietly, his eyes automatically snapping to Isobel before drifting around the others, almost like an afterthought.

He still hadn't tried to speak to her since the night he drugged her. It almost seemed like he was deliberately keeping his distance, but instead of putting her at ease, it frightened her.

"Let's go," Kalen said, and the backing track began to play.

Kilian opened the song, his voice a sweet, soft whisper. His sound was vulnerable and strong, a beautiful contrast that always had her breath catching. He was able to project his voice and stretch it out while keeping the sound a gentle brush of air, and it gave her goosebumps every time. He also had a deeper tone, but he didn't use it much because several of the others had strong baritones.

"Don't look at each other," Mikel said, pointing to the cameras. "Look into the lens or to the front."

When it was Isobel's turn to sing, Kalen stopped the backing track. "You're all too self-aware. Theo, stay there. The rest of you come and watch."

He led them to the screen behind the cameras, where they could watch a close-up of Theodore's face.

"Can you just sing everyone's parts?" Kalen called out.

Theodore lifted a shoulder in a shrug. Of course he could. He sang all of their demo tracks on his own.

Kalen started the song again, and Theodore began to sing, doing a terrifyingly good imitation of Kilian's voice. The camera was zoomed up so close to his face that it took him out of his setting, and she never would have guessed from his expression that he was sitting in a random sunroom surrounded by crew and equipment.

He looked like he was centre stage, beneath a clear spotlight, with thousands of people holding their breath and hanging off his every sweet inhale and sexy rasp. The storm in his eyes was quiet, the darker tendrils of colour through the grey of his iris standing out in high definition.

"Skip Isobel's section," Kalen called.

Theodore finished with Kilian's part and then

lowered his head, his long, dark eyelashes sweeping
down as he closed his eyes, gently swaying in the
smallest of movements like he was listening to Isobel
sing, even though it was just the backing track playing.
He mouthed the words to the song as he opened his eyes,
his pupils expanding and contracting as he focussed
again, his tongue peeking out to moisten his lips as he
made the briefest eye contact with the camera. Isobel's
stomach swooped, tingles racing through her. He
gripped the top of the microphone, his lips brushing it as
he sang again, imitating Cian's raspy baritone. The way
he could copy their sounds so perfectly was astounding.
He moved through the song, sometimes singing,
sometimes swaying, sometimes closing his eyes and
sometimes mouthing the words, threading through
moments of rare eye contact with the camera until she
felt like she was holding her breath and waiting for him
to look again. When he finished the song, he dropped his
microphone back down to his side and checked his
phone, like what he had done was *nothing*.

"That's the connection you need to make," Mikel
explained. "We want people to feel like it's just you and
them—not like you're singing a song to them from a
stage, but like you're alone in a room with them only a
few feet away, staring into their soul and singing like
you're trying to communicate with them. Got it?"

"Got it," they agreed, moving back to their places.

They spent the rest of the afternoon on the song, took

a half-hour break and then split into two groups to train with Kalen and Mikel. She would have loved to end her day after that, but there was one more matter that needed to be dealt with, so after she dragged herself through a shower, she knocked on Elijah's door.

He was already in bed when she slipped in, his tablet in his lap, his hair still damp, dark circles beneath his eyes.

She halted halfway through the doorway. "I can come bac—"

"We need to talk," he said plainly.

She closed the door, perching on the end of his bed, her legs folded, bouncing her water bottle on her knee. "You said you had some ideas for how we can get Lily back to Arkansas?"

He nodded, setting his tablet onto the bedside table. He regarded her thoughtfully, his black-framed glasses making him look even more handsome. They just framed his features so perfectly.

"What about Bellamy?" he asked, shocking her. "His family is from the San Bernadino Settlement. He can come and go as he pleases, and didn't you say he's been staying there with Sophia?"

Isobel nodded, her mind turning over the possible scenario.

"I can get a passport made for Lily," Elijah continued, "and he can take her back on a commercial flight and sneak her into the Ozark Settlement. It turns out the company that smuggles out Sao-Yeong's paintings handles settlement commissary deliveries country-wide. And they aren't just exploiting Sao-Yeong. I can anonymously blackmail them into leaving one of their vans in town and forgetting about it for twenty-four hours. Bellamy can hide Lily in the back and drive it straight through and back out again."

"Wow." She blinked at him. "You're terrifying."

He didn't react at all, merely said, "I know."

"How do I get Bellamy to agree to this?" she asked. "We're friends, but we're not *that* close. And he and Oscar really don't get along."

"Rope him into the deal with Braun," Elijah said. "He might be taking a back seat for now, but he's not stupid. Now that we're competing as a group and the humans are competing as a group, he's actually third in line in terms of winning."

"So he can't back out now," Isobel mused, nodding slightly. "His father won't let him. And he's specialising in acting—so a cameo in one of my father's movies would be huge." She nodded. "You might be right. I'll call him."

She fished her phone from where she had tucked it into the waistband of her pyjama shorts. She face-timed Bellamy and pulled her phone up, resting it on her raised knee, but it was quickly pushed down again, flattened to the bed.

"Hello?" Bellamy answered, the sound muffled.

Elijah was frowning at her, his cold grey eyes dropping to the lace that bordered her soft cotton tank ... and then lower, to the way the cotton outlined the swell of her breasts. She wasn't wearing a bra, and her nipples gently protruded beneath the fabric.

"Helloooo?" Bellamy drawled.

Elijah made a soft sound of frustration before pulling off his T-shirt and tossing it to Isobel. She slipped it over her head as she grappled for the phone.

"Sorry, hi." She pulled it back up to her face. "I dropped you."

"How's the tour going?" he asked. "Did you all finally wise up to Sato being *totally* bloody inappropriate for a life in the spotlight and leave him behind?"

"Not quite." She gave him a bored look. "But actually ... that's who I'm calling about."

His brows jumped up, his face turning to the side. He tucked his wavy brown hair behind his ear. "I'm intrigued. I'm listening. You have my full—*hey*," He dropped the phone, leaving her staring at a ceiling. "That's *my* burger, you little wench."

"And yet it *looks* so much like mine," Sophia's voice carried through the phone.

Bellamy returned, picking up the phone again. "She made me drive to In-N-Out," he grumbled. "The guards are starting to get suspicious. They literally searched one of the burgers and tipped out my drink."

Isobel winced. "So ... you *don't* want to take on a professional smuggling job?"

He tucked his hair behind his ear again. "Okay, now you *really* have my full attention."

"Oscar's sister is sick. We need to sneak her into a hospital in LA—that part, we've got covered. But after her operation, we need to somehow get her back to Arkansas."

"Carter." Bellamy deadpanned. "Today, I killed a Coke. Do *not* put me in charge of a human."

"We have a plan," she promised him. "You just need to escort her on a commercial flight from LA on a fake passport, pick up a commissary van from town, and drive it into the settlement. That's all."

"What in the James Bond?" he demanded, a short laugh falling past his lips. "Do you hear yourself, you nutter?"

"In return," she pressed on, ignoring him, "we'll do a cameo in a movie my dad is doing next summer break. And go to the premiere together."

The humour dropped out of his face, replaced by serious consideration. Sophia popped into the frame, giving Isobel a narrow-eyed look, a half-eaten burger clutched in her hand.

"Oscar's sister is a little kid, right?"

Isobel nodded.

Bellamy snatched the burger off her. "Now you can be jealous *and* hungry," he said, taking a huge bite.

"You suck." She flounced off camera again. But a second later, a slipper collided with the side of Bellamy's face.

With a sigh, he held out the burger, and her hands reappeared, snatching it away.

"All right," he said. "I'll do it. I want a contract for Braun's movie. I need it in writing."

"Done."

"You know the shirt you're wearing is inside out, right?"

She glanced down, seeing the tag at her neck. "Oops."

"Just out of curiosity—what were you wearing when you called. You know, before you put the phone down to change."

"This shirt, but not inside out."

"That makes sense," Bellamy drawled. "Who's sitting there with you?"

"Nobody," she lied. "I'm allowed to make phone calls unsupervised, you know."

"I'm trying to decide which one of them would be able to control themselves from bursting into view when I asked what you were wearing a few seconds ago—I thought I had him then, for sure."

Isobel rolled her eyes.

"Gabriel," he guessed, undeterred.

"No."

"Elijah?"

"No."

"You blinked. It's Elijah. You're a terrible liar."

She scowled. "I'm a fantastic liar."

"Go on, tell me a lie," he goaded. "Tell your old buddy Bellamy a big fat lie, Carter."

"You know, Sophia messaged me last night," she said.

He leaned into the phone, darting a look to something off to his side. "What did she say?" he whispered. "She loves me, right? It's just in a way that *looks* like hate. Right?"

"Dude. That was the lie. Are you okay?"

"That was mean." He drew back, frowning. "Elijah should punish you. You're a cruel and heartless person. You know Silva throws darts at a picture of you, right?"

"Damn. I wish he had shown that kind of passion when we were dating."

Bellamy laughed. "I'd say it was the least passionate relationship I've ever witnessed, but ... I saw Elijah and Ellis." He waited for a retaliation from the Alpha sitting across from Isobel, who just kept staring at her, expressionless. When Bellamy didn't get a reaction, he huffed in disappointment.

"All right, I'll let you get back to grading papers," he said.

"Guess again."

"Solving complex equations?" He squinted at her.

"Experimenting on human subjects? I don't know what that guy does in his free time."

"I like to read," Elijah said, still emotionless.

"Thrilling." Bellamy glanced at something off-camera. "You're *sure* she's banging them all?"

"Jesus," Isobel muttered, closing her eyes. "How many people have you said that to?"

"Nobody." Sophia appeared in the frame again. "Except this idiot. He's actually very discreet, I promise."

"So how does it work, anyway?" Bellamy asked. "Is there a lotto to assign each of them a day of the week, and the others just miss out?"

"Yes." Isobel's tone was dry. "That's exactly what I do. Every Monday night, I host a lotto."

Out of the corner of her eye, she caught Elijah's half-smile.

"Okay, well, this has been enlightening." Bellamy shared a look with Sophia. "We're going to go and practise smuggling ..." He cocked a brow at Sophia, waiting.

"Tacos," she decided.

"She's just using me for fast food," Bellamy explained, turning back to the camera.

"I know," Isobel told him. "Bye."

She hung up and dropped her phone, leaning back on her hands with a deep sigh. Elijah was resting against his headboard, loosely crossing his arms over his bare chest.

"We should talk about the other thing," he said.

She quickly snatched up her water bottle, popping up the mouthpiece so she could nervously drink. "Okay," she mumbled.

"What happened to Gabe, Niko, and me is complicated," he said. "Niko feels responsible for everything because he wasn't involved with the orphanage. While we were being abused, he was protected by his parents. It took a while for Gabe to figure out how to block off his ability, but he told me that Niko used to warp the whole incident, changing it in his head so that he was responsible for more than he really was. He turned it into *his* idea that we went back there. It wasn't. It was mine. He would claim responsibility for killing that man if he could—and not just out loud. He would do it internally if he could trick himself that much. When the people he cares about get hurt, he takes ownership for it. He bottles it up inside and makes it his fault. For someone who's supposed to be a human lie detector, he lies to himself more than anyone I've ever known."

This wasn't what she had been expecting. She nodded lightly, not wanting to interrupt, and he continued.

"The officials we were sold to thought Gifted people were dirty. That was a word they used a lot. It was a word Gabe had to hear in their minds a lot—that he was dirty, like an animal. Less than human. A rare commodity but still a commodity. I know you understand that feeling. He worked hard to block out those voices and shut down his ability, but the truth is he never *fully* separated it from himself. There's a reason he's more perceptive than your average person, just as there's a reason people listen to me and obey me even though I'm low in the hierarchy of the group. It isn't just because we're smart. If Theodore cuts himself off from his ability, he'll still be charming. If Moses cuts himself off, he'll still argue with everybody and stir up trouble. To be honest, I didn't fully understand it until Maya told us the truth about those two. But now I see that it'll always be part of who we are."

"That makes sense," she said softly.

"I understand why you used my ability." He regarded her so calmly, his smoky, spicy scent a calming balm, making her feel like she was somewhere warm and safe. "You feel lost in this group sometimes, with all these strong personalities, and you don't trust that people will step back and listen to you when you tell them to. Not in a crisis situation. Not the way they listen to me, or Mikel, or Kalen."

"Can you blame me?" She chuckled hollowly. "After the whole Cooper incident?"

"No, I don't blame you." He shook his head. "You're right, unfortunately. We treat you differently than how we treat each other. We hoard you and protect you and swear to avenge you whether you want it or not."

"Like dragons guarding your last bar of gold," she agreed wryly.

"I'm sorry for that." He winced. "We try to control it."

"I know ... and I don't *hate* that I'm protected."

"That's why we've all agreed that you should use your powers"—he waved at her chest, where her piercing was currently hidden—"whenever you feel you need to. Mine and Gabriel's included. If we're being bull-headed, lost to our Alpha senses or bowed by the bond, then use our own power against us. Make us listen. Make us obey. Do what you need to do. You're powerful, too, Isobel."

She blinked away the sudden feeling of tears welling in her eyes, a warm sensation of relief flooding through her whole body.

"Did you think you were in trouble?" Elijah questioned, an elegant brow inching up, likely feeling her emotion through the bond.

She shrugged. "Maybe. Kinda. Yes?"

He chuckled, attention dropping to her folded legs for a moment. "I thought Mikki already punished you?"

"About that ..." She chewed her lip, lowering her voice. "Will that happen *every* time I do something he doesn't like?"

For some reason, Elijah laughed. *Loudly*. He tossed his head back, his broad shoulders thumping against the bed. He laughed so hard, he had tears in his eyes, and he wiped them away as he took in her shell-shocked expression.

"Sorry," he managed, still fighting back a chuckle. "Did that bastard let you walk out of there thinking you were going to get a scene every time you upset him?"

"A scene?"

"Pretend punishment."

"*Pretend?*" She shook her head. "No, that was a real punishment."

"Oh, sweetheart." He looked at her so pityingly that she tried to whack him with her stainless steel water bottle, but he deftly caught it and placed it on his bedside table before grabbing her thighs and dragging her onto his lap so that she was forced to straddle his thighs.

His face was now close as he stared down at her with an expression she didn't quite understand. It almost looked like adoration or indulgence ... but with a heavy dose of amusement. His hands were a light pressure against her thighs, fingers spread out as he eyed the tag hanging off the neckline of his shirt, which she was still wearing inside out.

"Mikel doesn't know how to have a normal relationship," he said with a sigh. "The only way a partner could get close to him was in a Dominant-submissive setting, by playing with him, proposing a casual scene, or entering into a relationship with the understanding that it would be utterly transactional and that all romance or sex would be as Dominant and submissive. Him punishing you is just him feeling out of control with how he feels about you—you're not actually being punished."

"How ... do you even know what he did?" she asked, squinting at him.

His hard lips crooked up at the corners. "He texted us, saying you were banned from orgasms for a day and what your limits were for play."

"So he was just using what I did as an excuse?" she asked.

"To get close to you, to play with you, yes."

"Hmm." She eyed him. "Do you like the whole 'Sir' thing as well?"

His smile broke free, spilling across his lips. "I'd prefer to hear you say my name, or the nickname you use when you think I can't hear you."

"Eli?"

He lowered his chin in the barest of nods before lifting it again, staring down at her with a sudden intensity. Something had softened between them. That little thread of intimidation he always seemed to inspire in her had loosened. She spent plenty of time alone with Elijah, but they were usually working.

She was tired, but she didn't want to say goodnight or end their conversation. It had always scared her, the idea of growing this close to so many of the Alphas, but she was beginning to feel that wall with Elijah crumbling. It was then that she realised it had been *her* wall.

He wasn't the only one holding things back between them. She had participated in not allowing things to deepen, to soften, to grow *more*. She understood why it was hard for him, Gabriel, and Niko to get close and fall into relationships now.

"I like this," she whispered, flicking her eyes between his, wishing he had taken his contact out. "I like talking to you. I wish we did it more."

He seemed to stop breathing, his fingers digging into the skin of her thighs. "We can do this as much as you like."

Her heart was beating fast, her palms beginning to sweat. She was more nervous for this than she was having them strip her clothes off and boss her around.

These soft, fragile moments were more challenging than anything else.

"I don't want to be claimed tonight," she said, well aware that she was going to *entirely* the wrong person for this. "I want ..."

She couldn't say it.

It was too embarrassing.

"All this yearning," he whispered, one of his hands creeping up to her chest, his fingertips just barely brushing against her through his shirt and her pyjama top. "Tell me what you want."

She sucked in a deep breath, shaking her head. "Never mind. It's dumb."

He frowned, debating whether he should force her to tell him or not. She could tell he didn't want to shatter this softness between them, but it also *killed* him not to know something.

"I don't want to feel like a mate," she blurted, forcing the words out. "Or a s-sub—I mean, I like that, I promise. I like it when—but I mean—"

"Will you be my girlfriend?" he interrupted, his eyes going wide like he was surprised at the words that fell out of him. "Be my girlfriend," he doubled down, recovering from his shock, his hands slipping up to her face, cupping her jaw with long, careful fingers. "Be the person I can be gentle with, or rough with, whatever you like. Be the person I can laugh with. Be the person I can look at and have a conversation just with our eyes. Be the girl who teases me and challenges me. Let me take care of you. Come to my room and talk to me about nothing or all the important things. Tell me how you feel about your dad or how much your feet hurt. Let's get each other real presents instead of exchanging flowers on our birthdays. Be my girlfriend."

He tugged her lips up to his, kissing her so softly. "Please don't say no."

"I won't say no." Her heart was on fire, her throat tight with emotion. She couldn't believe all of *that* had come out of Elijah.

"So it's a yes, then?" He kissed her again, a groan catching in his throat.

"Yes," she breathed.

He swooped her up suddenly, making her yelp as he stalked to the door and threw it open. He walked down the hallway of rooms, pounding on each of the doors.

"She said yes," he announced. Everyone appeared in their doorways, most of them looking like they were either getting ready for bed or already in bed.

"To what?" Kalen asked, eyeing her with concern.

Her face was bright red, and she was holding a hand over her mouth so that she wouldn't laugh, but her heart had gone from burning to *melting*.

"Figure it out yourselves," Elijah drawled, carrying her back to his room and slamming the door.

"Are you evil?" she asked him.

"Yes, but I'll be sweet to you unless you want to play."

"I want sweet Eli tonight."

He stopped walking, freezing for the second time that night, his eyes jumping between hers before he seemed to jolt back into action. "The full boyfriend experience?"

"Yes, please." She grinned as he tossed her down onto the bed. "What do I get?"

"Anything you want."

"You said you like reading."

He tilted his head to the side. "I do."

"Will you read to me?"

He sat on the bed, pulling her between his legs. He tugged off the shirt she wore over her pyjamas, tossing it to the other side of the bed before pausing, catching her jaw and forcing her lips up to his for a slow, drugging kiss that had her head spinning and her breath turning choppy before he released her.

"Get comfortable," he ordered.

"This is a bossy boyfriend experience," she said, lowering down and curling up between his legs, her head on his muscled thigh as he pulled the blankets up to her chin.

He turned off the lights, picked up his phone, and seemed to spend a moment choosing the book he wanted before he rested back against the headboard and began to read.

"In my younger and more vulnerable years my father gave me some advice that I've been turning over in my mind ever since. 'Whenever you feel like criticising anyone,' he told me, 'just remember that all the people in this world haven't had the advantages that you've had.'"

His voice was a deep and smooth glide of silk, and she closed her eyes, trying to settle into this feeling of comfort, giddiness, and breathlessness. It felt like too much to hold inside her body, but the longer he read, the more she settled, her body growing heavy, his scent seeping into her pores until she felt like she was floating.

His long, talented fingers threaded through her hair absently, and she sank into acceptance, letting go of the feeling that everything was too good to be true.

21

BRAUN'S BOYS

"I don't have a good feeling about this," Cian muttered as they headed into the hall to set up for their fourth meet-and-greet.

They had been on tour for a little over three weeks now, and with the exception of Teak ordering alcohol to their accommodations and passing out most nights, things were going well. They were performance-ready for their first and second songs, and Cian had begun cutting together a music video for their first song, "Twisted," from all the footage taken of them learning the choreography.

Thanks to his editing, it was cute and fun, cut with flashes of serious and dramatic choreography. It perfectly showcased their chemistry and relationships— Kalen and Mikel stalking the sidelines of everything, cutting in to direct and coach them. It was very kind to

Isobel, who was also shown coaching them through the dance, laughing with Theodore, and resting against Elijah, her head on his broad shoulder. The sweet moments were cut with flashes of her dancing, her expression intense and focussed. It meandered through scenes of Niko practising moves flawlessly on his own and Oscar and Moses sneaking away to try and escape being roped into extra dance practices and grumbling and groaning as they were forced back into the group. It lingered over Theodore, showing him singing *constantly*. It revealed him singing while they were dancing, stretching, and taking breaks. It zoomed in close to Kilian's face on one of their more serious practises, showing his pale, intense eyes and sweat-slicked hair, his shirt flying up as he did a high kick, revealing a stack of pale, porcelain abs. It showed Cian, Niko, Elijah, and Gabriel spinning to the front of the formation after the chorus, hair stuck to their faces, small smirks breaking free as they moved in *perfect* synchronicity. It wasn't an easy dance by any measure, but they made it look like effortless, sexy fun.

Things were going *very* well.

It almost felt like puzzle pieces falling perfectly into formation.

She hated to admit it, but a small part of her had been waiting for this moment. Cian's words and the way his face twisted with worry had her stomach sinking, but it wasn't a surprise. This was how it worked.

They took two steps forward and a giant's foot appeared out of nowhere above them, threatening to squash them and sending them scrambling to haul up defences.

"If you've got a bad feeling, it's probably because of me," Niko said quietly, glancing toward the door of the hall. This was his settlement, and unlike Theodore, Moses, Kilian, and Oscar, he didn't seem excited to be moments away from seeing his family. "I haven't been calling them as much as I should have. They just … kept demanding to know what happened to me, saying I was different. I didn't know how to answer them."

Oh, shit.

"Are they coming today?" Mikel asked as everyone sat at the table. Niko had been moved to Isobel's other side now that Oscar had been freed from her left elbow. Moses was still on her right side, still receiving her little jabs whenever he was impolite.

"Don't know," Niko grumbled, falling into his chair, big hands pushing the dark waves of his hair from his face. He was tense but deliberately keeping his body slouched and loose.

Isobel struggled to relax as the people began to file in, and it seemed the others were also on edge, waiting for the inevitable confrontation. When the final person got up from the table and Cooper stepped forward to announce the end of the meet-and-greet and thank everyone for coming, Niko seemed to deflate, sinking several inches further into his seat.

She could feel his devastation, and it made her breath wobble as she tried to think of how to comfort him. Everyone else's families had come, even though the Alphas had asked them not to—so this was a slap in the face for Niko.

As the hall began to clear, Isobel noticed a group of people huddled in the corner, staring at Isobel and the Alphas as they began to pack up their things and stretch out their sore muscles.

It looked like a large family, the grandparents still young. The two younger couples would have been around five years older than Isobel, and two little kids were sitting on the floor, playing with colouring books. Niko perked up as soon as he saw them.

"Hey," he called, jogging over to them, the rest of his words lost in the low shuffling noise of people leaving the hall.

"Uncle Niko!" the kids yelled, jumping up and hugging his legs.

"The meet-and-greet is over. Please make your way out of the hall," Cooper boomed into his microphone, clearly looking at the group Niko was speaking to.

"It's his family," Kalen snapped.

Cooper glared at him and then at Niko's family. "They have ten minutes," he declared.

Braun looked at his phone. "Ah, the first van is here

early, Cooper. Let's head off. How do you feel about steak tonight? My treat."

Her father was getting remarkably good at wrangling Cooper. Isobel was sure he didn't know about what Cooper had done, but it was painfully apparent that the entire group had become extremely hostile to Cooper. There was no missing it. The Alphas had set aside their fake respect and deference, and they now bit his head off with their snarled responses and derision. They may not have tried to kill him, but they weren't playing nice anymore. Not even close.

As Braun managed to distract Cooper and get him out of the hall, Isobel sidled up to Theodore.

"She's staring at me," she whispered, stepping partially behind him.

The older woman of the group was glaring daggers at her across the hall while she spoke to Niko. The discussion seemed heated. They had hugged briefly, but now it seemed things were taking a quick downturn.

"That's his mom," Theodore whispered back. "Maybe we should get out of here and give them some privacy."

"Let's just ignore them," Gabriel suggested, nodding toward the catering table at the back of the hall. "Give them some space, but still be here if he needs us."

They relocated to the back of the hall, pretending to be busy organising and dividing up the remaining energy drinks, water, and snacks, except for Kalen and Mikel, who shared a look and then nodded at each other, pushing off the table and striding over to Niko and his family, who had begun shouting.

"You changed when *she* moved in!" Niko's mother loudly declared, her accented voice taut with emotion.

Isobel's hand shook as she tried to uncap a water. Elijah took it out of her hands, removed the lid, and passed it back to her, his hand softly rubbing her shoulder.

Theodore settled his grip around her hip, squeezing gently. "You didn't do anything wrong, Illy."

"I know." Her voice held no conviction.

She didn't do it, but it was *because* of her.

"Shit," Kilian muttered. "He's coming back."

"Let's go," Niko snarled, grabbing Isobel's hand and making her squeak. He marched her across the hall, his grip like iron as he interlocked their fingers.

He didn't say a word as they waited by the van, but as soon as Kalen and Mikel caught up to them, he suddenly spoke, his hand tightening on Isobel's.

"Apparently, some website said I was surrogating for Isobel, and they think that's why I changed. They want me to drop out of Ironside."

"What?" Kilian looked shocked.

"They said they would disown me if I didn't drop out."

"They didn't mean that," Kalen said gently. "You know they didn't. They're just trying to protect you, and they're resorting to drastic measures."

"This is how I *am* now," Niko snarled, thumping his chest. "This *is* me. Forcing me to come home won't change that. Forcing me away from Isobel won't change that. They need to accept things for how they are. I wasn't forced into this. I made my decision that day, when I decided to bond my mate. It was my decision to make, and I don't fucking regret it. They can't force me to regret it. They might not know the details or that she's my mate, but they can't force me to rewind fucking time."

The others were silent, absorbing his outburst.

"You're right." Isobel spoke softly as she stared at the ground. "People change. You can't stop them from changing; you can't force them to go back to how they were. That's not how relationships work."

He looked at her, his eyes blazing, a little spark of gratefulness visible behind all the turmoil. "I'm not staying here tonight."

"You don't have to." Mikel gripped his shoulder, squeezing it. "You've got us, all right? We're not saying you should abandon them, but until they're ready to accept you for who you are and the choices you made—which we're *proud* of you for, by the way—then don't for a second feel like you're left alone. We're a family too."

Mikel's gaze flickered quickly to Isobel before resettling on Niko.

"All right?" he demanded.

Niko nodded, looking like he was struggling for words. "Thanks, guys."

"Of course." Theodore reached around Isobel to pat his other shoulder. "We've got your back. Always."

This was her group. Her family. She could have been bonded to anybody—or several anybodies—but she was given these incredible, talented, complex, protective, *caring* men. Yes, they were sometimes violent. Yes, there were a few skeletons in their closets. Yes, they sometimes punched each other and sometimes made other girls cry ... but they were also her role models. She didn't just think they were hot. This wasn't a crush. She respected the hell out of them.

AFTER THEIR FIFTH STOP ON THE TOUR, THEY HEADED TO ROCK River Valley. Teak was sober for the first day, but Braun seemed to walk in on her doing something in the kitchen the morning of their sixth meet-and-greet, and they got into a whispered fight that had her angrily filling a flask with the welcome wine they had received. She drank the entire drive to the settlement and parked herself in the back of the hall, snapping at anyone who came near her.

Isobel watched her nervously for a little while before raiding the catering table and bringing her some crackers and a water.

"Thanks." Teak's eyes were glassy, her pupils blown

out. She wasn't just drinking. Maybe that explained the fight in the kitchen.

"Let me know if there's anything I can do," Isobel said, but Teak just waved her off, as she always did.

Isobel helplessly returned to the table, packing away her frustration and fear for the other woman. She plopped down between Niko and Moses, mentally steeling herself for another day of trying to be half as charming as Theodore.

The doors to the hall opened and a boy a few years younger than Isobel burst inside, running straight up to the table and ignoring the assistants who rushed forward, trying to usher him into a line.

Cian grinned, pointing to where one of the assistants waited. "Line up, Logan, you idiot."

The boy rolled his bright blue eyes, jogging back to the correct place and bouncing on his feet until the assistant waved him into the first seat. He shifted around anxiously until he got to Cian, and they hugged over the table before sitting down to chat. When he got to Isobel, he leaned forward and grinned at her like he knew a secret she didn't.

"You're even prettier than you were last year," he said, winking at her.

"Oh wow." She tried to bite back her laugh. "You must be Cian's brother."

"Bet you wish you could trade." He let out a dramatic

sigh. "Don't worry, you'll still have me as a brother-in-law. I've always wanted a sister—"

"Getting a bit ahead of yourself, aren't you, Logan?" Moses leaned into Isobel's space, turning away from the woman across from him.

"Um, no?" Logan grinned at them both before quickly grabbing Isobel's hands. "You'll come visit us when you—"

Niko and Moses both gripped one of his wrists, lifting his hands away from Isobel, who slid her arms beneath the table because the last thing they needed was for Niko and Moses to beat up Cian's adorable little brother.

"No touching," Niko warned him seriously before dropping his wrist.

Logan was undeterred, still smiling brightly. "Anyway, Mom and Dad are here too." He pointed to a couple now at the front of the waiting line, who waved enthusiastically back. "They can't wait to meet you."

"What about us?" Moses groaned. "We exist too."

"Oh, yeah, of course. You guys as well." Logan grinned at Isobel. "Anyway, nice to meet you!"

A small laugh spilled out of her. "Nice to meet you."

Cian's father was more reserved, keeping things polite and paying her the same friendly attention he did the Alphas, but his mother tried to surreptitiously slip her a little gift.

"It was my mother's," she whispered nervously. "I didn't tell Cian, I—"

"Oo, what's that." Moses leaned over her and snatched up the little pouch.

"It just a ... a gift," the woman, who had introduced herself as Hannah, said. She was blushing. "Just something that's been passed down through the women of our family."

Moses shook a ring out onto his palm. It was a thin, slightly tarnished gold band with three tiny blue stones. Either this was a precious family heirloom, or those stones weren't real since surely they would have sold something that valuable to afford a few more luxuries within the settlement.

Moses ducked down, catching her eye. "Tell me straight, Carter. When did you and Cian get engaged?"

Isobel snatched the ring off him. "Last night, if you must know."

"My congratulations to the happy couple," Niko drawled sarcastically from her other side.

"Ignore them." Isobel turned back to Hannah, holding the ring like it was made of glass. "And thank you ... but are you sure you want to give this to me?"

"You didn't say that when Kili's mom gave you a four-thousand-dollar painting," Moses drawled, leaning back in his chair with his arms crossed over his chest and a smirk on his lips. "Are you playing parental favourites?"

Cian's dad—who had called himself Hanale—was

ping-ponging his eyes between Isobel and Moses from his position across the table from Moses.

"I'm not," Isobel grumbled.

"Please keep it." Hannah reached out, capturing her hand and closing her fingers around the ring. "And keep him safe, okay?"

"I will," Isobel promised, heat staining her cheeks.

She slipped the ring onto her finger, and Cian seemed to notice, leaning forward to eye their little group.

"That was weird, right?" she whispered under her breath to Moses as Cian's parents moved down the table. "Why are they acting like me and Cian are a done deal?"

"Maybe they heard you screaming down the lodge in Piney Woods," Moses whispered back.

"How do you know that was Cian making me scream?" She lowered her voice even further as a girl settled into the chair across from her.

He leaned closer, his lips brushing her ear. "You have a different scream for each of them, Sigma."

She coughed as he drew away, attempting to focus on the girl, who thankfully handed over a dozen pictures for her to sign so she had an excuse to have momentarily lost her voice. The rest of the meet-and-greet flew by without incident, and Cian pulled her chair back as soon as Cooper announced that it was over, tilting it on the back legs so that she squealed in shock and reached up to grip his arms.

"What do you have there?" he asked huskily, his

sapphire eyes glittering like the stones on the ring he stared at. "Did my stepmother propose to you?"

"Actually, it was an engagement gift," Moses said, shoving back his chair and standing to stretch. "They want to know if you guys will honeymoon here in the settlement or somewhere a little more exotic like here in the settlement, but down the road."

Niko chuckled, also standing.

Cian ignored them, lowering her chair back down. "You better watch yourselves, or you'll be uninvited from the wedding."

Nothing was going to get him down tonight. He was too happy seeing his family. It made her so warm to see the unfailing grin on his lips, but also sad to see the way Niko had eyed Cian's parents like he would do anything for that level of excitement and devotion.

She slipped her arm through Niko's on the way out to the van, sticking by his side all afternoon as they got ready for the afterparty and did their mandatory live video. That night, she dragged Kilian with her and slipped into Niko's room. This wasn't something they usually did, so it was a little awkward. They walked in just as Niko was getting into bed, and he stared at them in question, like they had come in to give him some kind of news.

"Can we sleep here?" Isobel asked.

Niko wordlessly moved to the other side of his bed, pulling the covers back. Isobel gave Kilian a relieved look, but he only smirked back at her—he had told her Niko would want this.

She quickly slipped into the middle of Niko's bed, wiggling close to him as Kilian got in the other side and flicked off the lights. Niko wasn't the type who liked to talk things over, but he flipped her around to face Kilian and dragged her into the curve of his body, his thick arm wrapping her waist. She reached out, her fingers tangling with Kilian's.

"Thanks," she whispered.

Niko tightened his grip on her, dropping a quick kiss to the line of hearts climbing up her neck. They had been so close before they bonded, but then he was torn away from her and himself, and they had been forced to rebuild everything again from the start.

She felt like they were almost back to that place after all this time, the space between them warming, simmering with heat, comfort, and familiarity. Their connection had always been based on their friendship, so it had taken time to build that up again with the new version of Niko.

Maybe one day, he would call her *mate* again.

Maybe he would kiss her again.

Maybe they could find their way back to that day by the stream, where his beautiful hazel eyes looked down at her like she was a miracle and the most beautiful woman he had ever seen.

Until then, she would just be grateful that she was getting her friend back.

AFTER A WEEK OF WORKING ON THEIR THIRD SONG IN ROCK River Valley, they boarded the plane to detour back to Arkansas. Despite how thoroughly they had combed over the plan, she was still nervous about getting Lily out. The rest of the Alphas weren't allowed to leave the plane, but Kilian turned invisible and slipped out with Isobel and Braun.

They had done what they could to minimise the chance that someone would notice him missing. Braun had offered Cooper the private bedroom to catch up on sleep, while he put his team to work in the conference room. They only needed the plan to hold for a couple of hours.

When they got to the Ozark Settlement, the guards allowed them to drive the car into the settlement along the main road, which was just wide enough. They had to park and walk the rest of the way, but since it was nearing midnight, it wasn't an issue.

The officials had instructed them to keep their visit under ten minutes and between the hours of ten and midnight to "minimise disruption," but that worked in their favour because the medical centre was empty when they arrived.

Oscar opened the door for them. "Hey." He stepped aside. "She's out cold."

He waved them through but caught Isobel's wrist, holding her back as Braun strode into the other room, Kilian turning visible again as he followed.

"Is this your secret mission outfit?" he asked, plucking at the collar of her tweed, designer coat. "Were you out of black hoodies?"

"I'm too fashionable for hoodies."

"Rabbit." He ducked his head, fixing her with a stare. "You live in tights and borrowed shirts."

She grinned.

He yanked her into his arms, lifting her up so that he could steal her lips in a hard kiss before he set her down again. "Let's do this."

Her father reappeared in the doorway, a bright, false smile on his face. "Oscar, my boy!" he declared like he had only just walked into the medical centre. "Ready to rejoin the tour?"

Oscar ground his jaw as Isobel groaned, scraping a hand down her face.

"Yes," Oscar finally forced out, because he couldn't exactly be rude to the man helping to save his sister's life.

They returned to the car, Kilian staying quiet and invisible as he carried Lily. The guards shone lights through the car and did a quick search of the boot before waving them through. Lily woke up on the drive back to the airport, but Oscar had already told her the plan, and she kept quiet as they drove onto the private airfield.

They boarded the plane again, and Braun extracted Cooper from the bedroom, explaining in a low voice that Oscar was on the verge of a breakdown and needed to be separated from everyone else. Oscar helped the narrative along by glaring at Cooper with such a menacing expression that Cooper decided to go and supervise the crew as Oscar claimed the back bedroom.

It was a nerve-wracking flight, even though the door to the bedroom was locked, and an even more nerve-wracking drive as they once again hoped nobody would notice that Kilian had suddenly disappeared. Luckily, Braun had organised another lodge to separate the humans from the rest of the group, so they were able to leave Lily hiding in the back seat of the van as they checked in with the police, who cleared out after a quick headcount.

As Braun and Teak retired to the guest cabin, Isobel, Gabriel, and Elijah stared after the two of them. Isobel couldn't help her puzzled frown.

"He doesn't strike me as the sleazy predator type," Gabriel commented as Braun and Teak disappeared into the cabin with their luggage. "Narcissistic asshole with an opportunist streak a mile long, yes, but not a sleaze."

"Some of the best predators don't look like predators," Elijah argued.

"I'm with Gabe on this one." Isobel shook her head.

"He seems *annoyed* with her more than anything. She's the one always following him around."

"Are we making bets on whether Braun and Teak are fucking again?" Cian dropped his luggage as he joined their group and stared over at the cabin. "Because my vote is no. I think he's barely tolerating her."

"That's just how he is with everyone," Elijah insisted, still playing devil's advocate.

Moses joined in the conversation, picking up on what they were talking about. "Except 'his boys.'"

Isobel groaned, striding away from them to find her bedroom.

There were eight bedrooms, so she put her luggage into Cian's room before slipping back downstairs to plant herself in the foyer, nervously waiting for her father to reappear. He did, and he strode over to the van that Lily was hiding in, getting into the driver's seat. It was a three-hour drive to the hospital, and they had all agreed he should get her there as soon as possible.

Oscar strode back outside, acting like he was checking the van for any luggage left behind just in case Teak was watching from one of the windows. He climbed into the van for a few moments, then stepped out again, closing the door. He seemed unwilling to let it go, even when Braun turned the engine over.

He moved to the passenger window as it slid down, and they exchanged a few words, and then Braun drove off.

This felt like the biggest risk she had taken with her father.

It was hard to trust him this much.

A little girl's life was at risk, and if he betrayed her in any way, it was done between them. She would never speak to him again. But if this worked, if he saved Lily, she might just think about forgiving him one day.

Maybe even "his boys" would forgive him one day.

Or maybe not.

He could save all the little girls in the world, and none of it would matter if he ever laid a hand on Isobel again.

22

THREE TWO ONE, ACTION

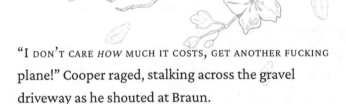

"I DON'T CARE *HOW* MUCH IT COSTS, GET ANOTHER FUCKING plane!" Cooper raged, stalking across the gravel driveway as he shouted at Braun.

It had been several weeks since they arrived in San Bernadino—they had fulfilled their tour duties at the settlement and completed weeks of training, filming, and album workshopping ... but they hadn't left. Braun had faked some emergency repair work for the jet they had been using, forcing them to postpone their last stop on the tour. Of course, there *was* no problem with the plane.

They were waiting for Lily.

They could have moved on and trusted everything to Bellamy and the doctor, but that was too much of a risk, and there was no way Oscar would ever agree to it.

Isobel winced and slowly pulled the window shut, stepping back through the lounge to the outside deck, where they were filming for the day. They had stopped because Braun and Cooper's distant shouting could be heard echoing through the mountains to the other side of the lodge.

"Might as well just take a break," Mikel decided, handing them all drinks.

Isobel plopped onto one of the deck chairs, blinking up at the sun as she sipped the electrolyte water. Her phone vibrated, but it must have been a group text because she wasn't the only one who reached for their device. It was the group chat they had made to communicate with Bellamy.

Bellamy: She's being discharged.

Bellamy: Operation Kiddie Smuggler is a go.

Isobel winced, quickly tapping out a reply.

Isobel: Do NOT call it that.

Oscar: That's it? No more news?

Lily's operation had been successful three weeks ago, but Oscar had been convinced that something would go wrong during her recovery period.

Bellamy: She can't quit her treatment, but they seem pretty happy with how she's recovered. She's responding well to meds. She was dancing yesterday. She said she's going to grow her hair all the way to the floor.

Bellamy: Bit gross if you ask me, but it's her choice.

Oscar closed his eyes, leaning against the railing opposite Isobel, his hand shaking as he pressed his fingers to his eyelids.

Isobel: Oscar says thank you.

Bellamy: I say you're welcome.

Elijah: You're clear on the plan?

Bellamy: Take the kid to the airport. Fly on the plane. Pick up the van. Put the kid in the van. Drive the kid to the settlement. Drop the van back off. Did I miss anything?

Oscar was looking at his phone again.

Oscar: Yeah, check the house over, will you? Make sure she's got everything she needs?

Bellamy: Nah, that's too much work.

Bellamy: Kidding.

Bellamy: She's asking if we can have monster pasta when we get home. What's that?

Bellamy: Am I her new brother, now?

Isobel chuckled but quickly bit it back when Oscar's dark eyes flashed up to her. She held up her hands in surrender, and he went back to texting.

Oscar: Just look after her or I'll kill you.

Bellamy: Look how close we've grown.

She giggled again. Oscar shoved his phone away. "That's it," he growled, stalking over to her. She launched from the sunlounger, trying to run away, but Moses quickly caught her, tossing her over his shoulder and delivering a sharp spank to her butt. The cameras were still rolling, so hopefully, the assistants wouldn't include that footage in the daily video they put up that night.

Braun shoved open the glass door and stepped out

onto the deck, prompting Moses to set her back on her feet.

"I just saw the email," she said to her father, causing him to pause, his brows furrowing. "About the plane?" She gave him a fake, searching look. "How they finished the work? It's ready to go again? We can leave tonight."

"Well." He blew out a relieved breath. "Thank fuck for that. Pack your bags, everyone. I'll go tell the asshole the good news."

He stepped back inside, striding off, and Moses leaned close to her ear, whispering, "I can't believe he's calling someone else 'the asshole.'"

Isobel smirked, elbowing him. "I elbowed you," she said when he didn't react.

He gripped her elbow. "My sides are well acquainted with this little chicken wing."

She gasped. "How dare you."

"Children," Elijah sighed out. "Stop fighting."

Moses ducked behind her, hauling her into his arms and hovering her over where Elijah was sitting on a sunlounger texting—likely double checking that Bellamy wasn't going to fuck up any of the steps in his plan.

"Attack," Moses ordered darkly, and Isobel tried to jab Elijah with her elbow.

He didn't react at first, but she could see him starting to break.

He sighed, putting his phone away.

Jab.

He tried to look bored.

Jab jab.

His lips curved up at the corner.

Jab jab jab.

He chuckled, catching her arms. "All right, you menace, I concede."

"Do we let him concede?" Isobel glanced over her shoulder at Moses.

"Never," he growled. "Attack!"

Before she could jab Elijah again, Moses suddenly spun her to face Mikel, who stood at the railing, looking at them like he didn't know whether to laugh or take his chances jumping over. She jabbed him.

He cocked a brow, his expression saying "do you really want to do this?"

"Get him," Moses whispered silkily into her ear. The devil on her shoulder.

She jabbed Mikel again.

His lips twitched just like Elijah's had. Two more jabs, and he was laughing.

"All right." He shook his head, pushing off the railing. "Get the fuck inside, the both of you. We've got one more stop on this little *holiday tour*."

They had more free time when they were at Ironside, and that irony was lost on none of them. Moses tossed her back over his shoulder, dumping her into Kilian's bed since she had somehow ended up keeping most of her things in his room despite bouncing between their beds.

They packed up their luggage, piled back in the vans, and boarded the jet for the last time. At the end of their stay in Mojave, they would be boarding the busses back to the airport with the rest of the Ironside students from that settlement. She checked her phone constantly during the flight, reading Bellamy's updates.

The first was a picture of Lily holding a packet of cigarettes, and the message read:

My new sister's reward for clearing customs.

Isobel peeked nervously at Oscar—who sat in the seat opposite her—but he wasn't swearing or scowling. He almost looked like he was smiling.

The second picture came after they landed. It showed Lily pursing her lips at a flyer for a strip club.

Bellamy: Just stopping for lunch before we pick up the van.

The third was a picture of Lily huddled into the back of a van with a piece of tape over her mouth, her eyes wide in exaggerated terror.

Bellamy: Operation Kiddie Smuggler underway.

They were checking into a roadside motel when they got that message, and Isobel failed to unlock the door to her room multiple times as she fought back her laughter.

The next picture came as they were rearranging the lobby of the motel to suit their filming purposes. It was a picture of Lily waving inside the door to her home, her smile huge, her eyes exhausted but still bright.

Mission success, Bellamy's message read.

Oscar quickly disappeared to video call Lily while they finished setting up. Her father cast her a questioning look, and she grinned back, mouthing, "We did it."

He seemed shocked. It took her a second to realise it wasn't about Lily, but because she was *smiling … at him.* So she stopped, awkwardly coughed, and went back to work.

An hour later, another photo came through. It was a selfie of Bellamy laying down on the couch wearing a pink headband.

Bellamy: I live here now. Lily said I sound like Harry Potter, and she loves me more than she loves Oscar.

Bellamy: But seriously, I have to go now. Everything looks good here.

She quickly tapped out a reply.

Isobel: Thanks, Bellamy.

Theodore: Thanks, dude.

Moses: Thanks.

Niko: Thanks.

Elijah: Thank you, Bellamy.

Gabriel: What they said.

Cian: You aren't so bad.

Kilian: We owe you.

Kalen: We really do.

Mikel: If you ever need anything, ask us.

Oscar: You can be friends with Isobel now.

Bellamy: And you can date her now.

Isobel snorted, tossing her phone aside, her heart light as they went back to work.

THEIR FINAL MEET-AND-GREET WAS CHAOTIC. SHE HADN'T realised the Alphas had been *behaving* during the last seven appearances, but that became quickly apparent. They couldn't hold focus, constantly talking to each other instead of the fans, forgetting to hand out the Polaroids, starting fights for fun and, in several cases, simply standing up to bounce around on their feet or stretch.

They were too excited, too anxious, too full of restless energy, because the tour was basically over, and it had been a *raging* success. Hero had done a small worldwide tour with limited appearances, and they weren't getting half the attention that Isobel and the Alphas were getting. Videos of Hero's concerts were getting hundreds of thousands of views, but the videos her father's team were putting together and uploading of their daily activities were getting *millions* of views.

People loved watching them work hard to put their album together. It fit with their theme of inviting their fans into their process every step of the way, including them as they created their music. Orion had yet to release their debut album despite releasing Hero's album before the summer break, but there was no way they would sell less than Hero. Her father predicted they could double or triple the sales of the other group.

Even Cooper was happy, encouraging them to have another drink at the final afterparty despite them having already surpassed their two-drink limit. Isobel sipped at her fourth glass of champagne, twisting through what had turned out to be a very raucous crowd compared to the other parties they had been to as she made her way to her father. Josette had sidled up to Kalen, and she didn't feel like scowling at the beautiful woman while tipsy.

She turned back to see Kalen extracting himself and stepping away, but she was still fighting off a violent need to drag Josette outside and push her pretty face into the dirt as she locked eyes with her father.

BRAUN WATCHED IN CONFUSION AS A HAND WRAPPED AROUND his daughter's mouth, someone pulling her back into the crowd. At first, he assumed it was one of her mates, but he yanked out a chair from the nearest table, standing on it and searching the room. Theodore, Elijah, Gabriel, Moses, Niko, Cian, Kalen, Mikel, Kilian, Oscar. *Shit*. They were all accounted for.

Gabriel was looking at him, brows drawn inward in confusion. Braun motioned at him urgently, jumping down from the chair and ploughing through the people to where he had last seen his daughter. Gabriel met him there.

"Which way did she go?" Braun demanded.

He could barely smell her—her scent was mixed with everyone else's, but Gabriel didn't have the same problem. He took off immediately, Braun following him. They burst through a side door.

"Do the mind communication thing," Braun demanded. "Call the others."

"Already have." Gabriel took off at a run, not even questioning that Braun knew they were bonded and could speak to each other in their minds.

After a few moments, the others caught up to them.

"She was just with me," Kalen growled. "How did she disappear so quickly?"

"They must have been waiting for us to be occupied," Gabriel said as they ran down the dark street—everyone was either at the afterparty or shut up inside their homes.

They approached a house, but Moses suddenly halted, his nostrils flaring. "Fucking *Cooper*," he hissed.

"Wait." Braun stepped in front of them, tugging out his phone. "If you barge in there without any proof, he'll just do it again. Trust me, I know how these people work."

"We don't trust you," Elijah seethed quietly.

"We need *proof*," Braun insisted gravely. "You have to

think like them. If you want to control them, you need to get information on them. You need to blackmail them." He stepped closer to the house, but instead of going inside, he circled to the window, raising his phone to record.

He heard the shuffling of the Alphas joining him, but several of them were surrounding the door, waiting to burst inside at the first signal from the others.

The window looked into a house that appeared abandoned, except for the mattress on the floor and the lamp in the corner. Braun knew houses like these. He had been inside them.

He had spent his entire life fighting to get *away* from houses like these and to ensure his family never returned.

And now here she was.

His only daughter, in one of these *fucking* houses.

His hands began to shake, the taste of ash on the back of his tongue, but he bit it back. He wanted to rage, but his girl needed him now more than she ever had before.

Cooper dragged a chair into the room, and two men dropped Isobel onto it. She was quiet, her head dipping to the side, her hair covering her face. She almost slipped off the chair, but one of the men caught her shoulder, pinning her back. He had human eyes.

The men who came to these houses always did.

The men who came for the *dirty little Gifted*.

"How long do I have to wait for her to wake up?" Cooper demanded.

"You can talk to her now," one of the men replied. "She's just drowsy. We injected enough to make her floppy." He laughed, grabbing Isobel's face and pushing it back. Her hair slipped from her cheeks, showing drowsy, hooded eyes. She blinked slowly, like it took immense effort.

Beside him, one of the Alphas let out a low, dangerous growl.

Just wait, Braun thought, feeling his own rage begin to spill over. *Just hold on*.

He needed more.

One of the men pulled a wad of cash out of his pocket. *This was what he needed*. Braun waited for it to exchange hands, but Cooper didn't seem to be interested in the money. He rounded the chair, adjusting his position to face Isobel.

"Did you think you could outsmart *me*?" he taunted, grabbing Isobel's face.

Hold on, hold on.

"I'll tell you what I'm going to do," Cooper snarled, bending over Isobel, his face drawing close to hers. "I'm going to fuck you, Isobel Carter. I'm going to break you. I'm going to rape every one of your whore holes and these men right here are going to film the whole thing before they have their turn. And then when we get back to the academy, you're going to come every time I call, and you're going to get down on your knees and service me, and if you don't, I'll release this video to the whole fucking world."

Cooper licked her face, his hand cupping his obvious erection.

Braun saw red, dropping his phone. Fuck the proof. Oscar had already kicked in the door. They stormed into the house, and he tore one of the men out of the way, snatching up his daughter from the chair and holding her against his chest as her mates lost control. It was a whirl of movement, a scream cut off by a growled Alpha voice telling them not to make a sound. Braun backed himself into the wall, watching the violence with widening eyes.

This wasn't normal.

This was ...

Several of them had black eyes, black veins, and black talons. The fuckers were *feral*. Not all of them: Elijah, Kalen, Mikel, Cian, and Kilian had backed up, like stepping away from a pack of rabid dogs tearing into carcasses, because that was what was happening. Niko, Oscar, Moses, Theodore, and Gabriel were savagely tearing into the bodies of Cooper and the two humans, tearing their skin like tissue paper. Blood sprayed out and Braun swallowed, nausea roiling in his stomach as he saw bone and muscle exposed. The men were dead, but the five Alphas didn't stop fighting over their bodies until they were nothing but scraps. And then they turned to the furniture, the walls, the doors, the kitchen cabinetry. They were spreading blood and viscera everywhere. It was the most horrific thing he had ever seen, and he was too scared to move. If he did, they might notice him and Isobel.

"This isn't going to be fucking fun," Mikel said lowly. "Five against five aren't good odds."

They weren't going to fight *them, were they?*

Sweat began to drip down his face. This wasn't how he wanted to die. And to lose her after doing all of this to win her back?

To die like this?

By ferality?

The very thing that took his mate, and his wife's mate, and started this dark, sickening void inside him that sucked away everything good and happy?

It was almost too much to bear.

The monsters began to turn on each other and Kalen swore, his expression desperate. "Fuck. Now or never—"

"Wait," Elijah said, his expression creased in pain. "Everyone, wait."

His voice was coloured with power. It filled the room like a crackle of electricity. The monsters *stopped*. They weren't attacking or tearing anymore.

They were waiting.

"Step away from each other," Elijah said softly. His eyes were watering, so much pain in his expression. "Wait," he reiterated, as Kalen dismissed them immediately, striding over to Braun. He held out his hands in silent demand, and Braun handed Isobel over, shocked into silence as Kalen draped her over his chest, his arms wrapping around her, his hand cupping the back of her head. A second power stirred the air, and slowly, Isobel began to stir.

What the fuck?

ISOBEL MOVED HER ARMS AS SOON AS SHE COULD, HER SLUGGISH brain struggling to comprehend what was happening as she clung to Kalen. She could smell his vanilla, soured by rage, wrapping around her, his power working to bring her body back from the drugged state she had been shoved under.

Again.

She peeked over his shoulder as her arms wrapped around his neck, seeing five bodies lined up, eerily still. They were covered in blood, breathing heavily. Oscar, Moses, Theodore, Gabriel ... *oh no, Niko.*

They all had pitch-black eyes and were staring at Elijah.

He had told them to wait, and they had obeyed.

He had used his power.

Grief clogged her throat, seeing the strained look of pain on his face. She wriggled, and Kalen reluctantly set her down. She ran over to Elijah, her father stepping out to try and desperately grab her.

"Don't—" he said, alarmed, but Kalen caught his wrist, pushing his hand down.

"They won't hurt her," he promised.

Isobel stopped before Elijah, who wouldn't take his eyes from the five Alphas lined up before him. His breaths were short and sharp, tears staining his cheeks, his grief and horror so overpowering it almost bowled over her. He had said he was coming to terms with the fact that his power was a part of him, but he had still been miles away from comfortably reaching for it again. This was breaking his heart.

"You're doing the right thing," she whispered, turning her back on the others, reaching up to cup Elijah's face.

She carefully wiped away his tears, sipping at his heartbreak. These feelings weren't for what had happened tonight—he was barely even standing in the room with them. These feelings were from when he was a little boy, as stark now as the last time he had used his power.

"You did the right thing," she soothed, letting the emotion pour into her. Her fingertips shook as she held his face.

Finally, his eyes dropped to hers, and he drew in a sudden, deep breath, almost like he had dropped back into his body. He grabbed her, pulling her against his chest.

"We can't cover this up with fire," he said. "We're going to need a new cover story."

"There were too many witnesses at that party." She heard her father's voice and stiffened, her face stuck against Elijah's chest.

She had completely forgotten he was there.

"They'll be able to say we all disappeared for an hour," he continued, and she could hear the thin tremor in his deep voice.

He was shaken.

She didn't blame him. They were standing in a house of horror, with three deaths to cover up and five Alphas in the throes of ferality just *staring* at them.

She was surprised her father wasn't already running for the police.

"He burst in here just like we did," Kilian said softly, probably feeling her surprise through the bond. "He's in this with us whether he likes it or not."

"I don't like it, for the record," her father growled. "But I don't regret it. I would have killed them myself."

Isobel cracked her walls, beginning to siphon away the horrible darkness that swelled in a giant wall behind her ... but there was so much of it, and she was already weak, so she cut herself off after a moment, looking up to Elijah for help. He rubbed between her shoulder blades. "Don't do any more," he answered her unspoken question. "We'll figure this out."

"I think they're starting to come back anyway," Cian noted, his tone husky with the stress of their situation.

She turned in Elijah's arms, watching as those black veins began to recede. It was a slow process. Painfully slow. With every minute that ticked by, the reality of their situation seemed to sink in with a more profound and terrifying clarity.

They were *fucked*.

As soon as the Alphas' eyes blinked back to normal, Niko hurried to Elijah, crushing Isobel between them as he pulled the other Alpha into a quick hug.

"I'm sorry, man," he mumbled.

Elijah nodded when he pulled back, and Isobel quickly caught Niko's hand, squeezing his fingers as they all glanced around.

"Well?" Gabriel asked, moving into the kitchen to wash his hands. "Who's got a fucking plan?"

"I assume we've ruled out fire?" Niko asked, his voice crackling with the weak attempt at humour.

"You assume correctly," Kilian said.

"I really wish you would all stop mentioning fire." Braun was rubbing his temples. "I'm learning far too much about everyone tonight."

"This would have been much easier if there were bodies left to manipulate," Gabriel mused, stepping away from the sink.

"Oh, I'm sorry," Oscar drawled. "My bad."

Moses rolled his eyes.

Braun flicked his attention between them like he was seeing them for the first time. "No wonder," he said, finally.

At Isobel's questioning look, he elaborated.

"No wonder you changed so much."

"Okay," Kalen clapped his hands to get their attention, ignoring her father. "I have an idea. And it's insane."

"More insane or less insane than fire?" Niko asked.

"Exactly as insane as fire," Kalen answered.

"We *can't* do fire again," Mikel insisted.

"Of course, we can," Kalen insisted. "Fires happen all the time. We just need a solid alibi, and we're going to have one because we aren't going to be here when the fire starts. Cian, any matches in the kitchen?"

Cian began searching the torn-apart kitchen cabinet. "Bingo," he said, pulling out some candles and incense sticks. He reached behind them, extracting a box of matches. He tossed them to Kalen.

"All right, everyone. Get the blood off your hands and button your jackets. You're fucking splattered with it," Kalen ordered. They moved to obey, Elijah standing still with Isobel.

He hadn't moved or spoken much.

Once they were cleaned up, Kalen stepped up to the oven. He pulled out a match and struck it, watching it burn down to his fingertips before he narrowed his eyes. It burned in reverse, the fire eating its way back up the match until it was perfectly new again. He stabbed that same match into the matchbox, facing up, and set it on top of the oven.

And then he turned on the stovetop without igniting the burners, turning all of the knobs.

"We need to leave," he advised, nodding to the front door. "Straight to the vans. Teak is passed out in one of them, right? I saw her leave the party early."

"Let's fucking hope so," Moses mumbled as they moved to the door. "How long do we have before that match starts burning again?"

"An hour," Kalen answered. "And we need to be live at that time. All ten of us, with Braun stepping in at some point to wave to the camera."

They hurried back to the vans, finding Teak passed out in the first one. Isobel watched her phone the entire way home, watching the minutes tick by, everyone else struck silent.

"I can't believe we used fire again," Niko said, as they exploded out of the van at the motel.

"Five-minute shower," Kalen ordered quietly—the rest of her father's crew was staying at the motel, though they would have been asleep at that time. "I want you all *clean*, and back in the lobby in *exactly* seven minutes."

He strode off as Braun ducked back into the van,

picking up a sleeping Teak. The others quickly dispersed to their rooms, and all Isobel could think about was whether the police would choose that moment to do one of their random drive-bys as she raced through a shower.

It wasn't like she even had blood on her, but she was in complete shock, and the cold water helped. She dressed in comfortable loungewear, tossed her hair into a messy bun and raced back to the lobby, meeting up with everyone else.

"Game faces on the count of three," Kalen demanded, setting up his phone as they gathered in the small waiting area. Braun slipped into the room, also fresh from a shower, watching them with shock still painted over his face.

"Three," Kalen said, and they deliberately relaxed their poses.

"Two," he counted, and Isobel quietened her thoughts. *Just another performance. You can do this.*

"One," he mouthed, starting the live video.

"Did you miss us?" Theodore drawled, his eyes heavy-lidded, his smile lazy. "Because we missed you guys. I know we did a live this afternoon but … we're not ready to end the tour, yet." He sighed dramatically, his head falling back against the couch. "Ahh, it's been so fun."

Braun stood in the shadows behind the camera and Isobel raised her eyes to his briefly.

He nodded to her, his expression now schooled into calm.

"So we just wanted to drop back in before we sleep and say thank you." Kilian's eyes sparkled softly as he looked into the camera. "This has been ... the time of our lives."

"We want to end it on the right note," Cian agreed, looking like he was already halfway asleep. "And we wanted to thank the man who made all of this happen for us—*the* Braun Carter."

Her father stepped up behind the couch, ducking to wave and smile at the camera.

"It was a pleasure," he boomed, his personality switched up to a hundred per cent. "I'm honoured to have been involved in something so special." He let out a smooth, easy laugh. "I won't bore you with a speech. You aren't here to see me." He winked, moving back behind the camera again, that smooth mask falling away as he watched them.

"We should go," Kilian covered a wide yawn. "Or we're going to fall asleep in front of the camera. Goodnight, everyone." He waved. "Thanks for everything." Theodore slipped forward, ending the live and handed the phone back to Kalen, who turned to Braun.

"What happened dies right now, in this room," Kalen said. "Everything you just saw."

"How many fires have you set?" her father returned.

"As many as we need to," Kalen held onto his calm, "to make sure she's never hurt again."

Braun considered them all before his eyes rested on her. "All right," he said, nodding like he was talking to himself. "It dies here. We never talk about it again."

BONUS SCENE
CHANGE THE ENDING

Braun stepped onto the jet for the last time that summer with a strange feeling in his heart. For a long time, he had only cared about himself.

He had taken so much *care* to lock away all fear and weakness, and the second he truly allowed himself to worry about Isobel—that strong, terrifying, troublesome, *damned* Sigma of his—the fear came rushing back in.

The break was over, the tour a success—though, of course, the tragic death of Cesar Cooper was something they would all keenly feel—and the album was going to far exceed Orion's expectations.

But he was still terrified.

Isobel was going back to Ironside. She was more popular than ever, and he could no longer justify all the things they would do to her as they turned her into …

well, *him*. He wanted to go back to only caring about himself, but it was too late. The bell was rung and he couldn't seem to un-ring it. He was starting to see that second perspective that had always been closed off to him. He started to see it the second she called him *dad*.

He settled back in his chair, staring up at the ceiling. He had sent his team home and was finally alone.

It felt ... strange.

Empty, almost.

A door slid open behind him, and he frowned, leaning out of his chair, his mouth dropping open. "What the fuck are you doing here?"

Annalise Teak was sober, for once. She held up her hands. "Hear me out."

"What else was I going to do?" he shot back, confused. "What are you doing here, Anna?"

She cringed, and he dragged his hands through his hair. "Sorry—your memories, that's what she called you."

"It's okay." Annalise sat across from him, levelling him with a serious expression. "I can't go back there. I can't go back to my settlement. Either option, I die. They'll kill me."

"So naturally, you snuck onto my jet," he said.

"I've heard it's not even yours."

He frowned. "I have my own. I needed a bigger one."

She leaned forward, reaching forward to grab his hands. They had gotten comfortable holding each other's hands, sleeping beside each other, and confiding in each other. He had seen most of her memories, and she had listened to him talking about all the things he would never have said to anyone. Luckily, she didn't remember any of it.

"Take me with you," she begged. "Hire me as an assistant—I'll wear contacts. Or hire me as a fucking maid, a cook, a cleaner. I don't care. Just take me with you. When I'm with you, it isn't so painful."

His hands felt cold in hers. "I've done this before," he said quietly. "It didn't end well."

"So, change the ending," she whispered.

He frowned at her, a strange sensation rising in his chest. It seemed he hadn't just rung the bell for Isobel.

"All right," he gritted out. "We can figure something out."

Isobel dropped her bag in the entrance foyer, her eyes tracing up the familiar marble staircase as the others spilled into Dorm A behind her.

"Year four," she said, turning to face her Alphas. "We ready?"

"Please." Theodore tucked her beneath his arm. "I'm always ready."

She picked up her bag again, but Theodore wrestled it off her, slinging it over his shoulder as he took the stairs two at a time. She watched the others go up, separating to the bedrooms, until it was just her, Mikel, and Kalen left.

Will you stay with me tonight? Mikel's voice swept into her mind. His tone sounded like he was delivering an order, but he had definitely attempted to phrase it as a question. She bit back a laugh.

Just to sleep? she asked, because he was taking their budding "relationship" slowly—testing the more emotional aspects to make sure he could provide what she had told him she needed before he moved onto the physical parts. Which she appreciated ... but it also made her so attracted to him that she *desperately* wished he would just skip to the physical parts.

God, you're a brat. His response rumbled through her mind. *Yes, just to sleep. But keep teasing me, and I will absolutely spank you first.*

She bit back her smirk, running after the others up the stairs. She found her bag in her room, waiting on her bed, but she ignored it, heading to her desk.

She had to start this year off on the right foot. With a clear goal in mind.

She grabbed a pad of sticky notes from her desk and scrawled a message onto one of them, ripping it from the stack and walking back to her door. She closed it, sticking the note in the centre.

The Gifted are not for sale.

I HOPE YOU ENJOYED GLISSER!

If you want to chat about this book or catch all the teasers for my next book, scan the code below to check out my reader's group!

If you enjoyed this book, please consider leaving a review. Indie authors rely on the support of our incredible readers, and without you guys, we wouldn't be able to continue publishing. Thank you for everything you do for the indie community!

Thank you!!
Jane xx

CONNECT WITH JANE WASHINGTON

Scan the code to view Jane's website, social media, release announcements and giveaways.

Made in the USA
Las Vegas, NV
14 February 2025

18169280R00353